VALERIUS AND
THE BASTARD SON
The Valerian Chronicles – Volume 4

T. R. Rankin

VALERIUS AND
THE BASTARD SON
The Valerian Chronicles – Volume 4

DOUBLE DRAGON

DEDICATION

To Lauren,
Who insisted on asking the question

Cast of Characters

Alair - Infant daughter of Valerius and Eomer, named after V's mother

Bokmar - Prime Minister of Cartho

Boltar - Mate of Valerius' flagship, *Valadator*

Brenda - Nurse to Valerian and Alair

Celia -- Old friend and correspondent of Vahla's in Palmeria

Chad - Servant of Vahla

Condor - Bastard son of Fantar

Coram - Condor's stepfather

Darios - Squadron commander at Palemia

Eldred - Cousin of Vahla, newly anointed king of Palemia

Emmet -- Chief Mortician in Dulcai

Enid - Condor's mother

Eomer - Wife of Valerius, High Queen of Valeria

Fantar (deceased) - Former tyrant/emperor

Fargo - Newly anointed king of Falkan

Gainor -- Commander of Palemian forces whom Condor replaces

Grumwald - Commodore of Valerius' fleet

Hagreb -- Renegade Captain of the *Recluse*

Illana - Niece of Reuters, King of Dulcai

Karghan - Leader of Scythians

Koltar - King of Kantar

Malecium - Original Captain of the *Steiger*

Quamous - Leading merchant, Head of Council in Cartho

Ragnar - Newly anointed king of Zagorbia

Reuters - King of Dulcai, Eomer's father

Rondo - Dulcaian Ambassador to the court of the High King

Sardin - Steward to Malecium and then to Condor

Scarf -- Assistant to Chief Mortician in Dulcai

Shadowy Figure - shadowy figure

Thorngere - Atheling of Thuringia, old companion-in-arms of Valerius

Vahla - Enchantress of Valeria, Valerius' half-sister and wife of Thorngere

Valerian - Son and heir of Valerius

Valerius - High King

Volkmir (deceased) - Former Mage of Valeria

Zimlait - Ruler of Cobanos

Prologue

In the months following the fall of Fantar in the hills east of Palmeria, the remnants of his brutal host-and the regime they supported-dissipated like a foul mist before the rays of a new day's sun. They scattered and secreted themselves in hidden corners of the Empire like damp settling into the timbers of a great ship, and there began to fester and rot.

As the ancient Imperial order reasserted itself under the High King, Valerius, the worst of this element were flushed out and dealt with. Some were summarily put to the sword or cross. Some were sent to the benches of galleys at sea, others to various dank and dismal gaols. But many-the lower echelons of non-commissioned officers, men at arms, and the like-were taken at their oath and left to shift for themselves. Some lucky few of these returned to find home and family, others drifted to settle here or there, wherever circumstance or the urge to move on left them. Before Fantar's rise and conquest of the Inland Sea, many of these men had been brigands and petty outlaws of one sort or another. Now, some fell afoul of the law yet again. Some fell victim to their own companions.

But one night,on the road north of the tiny town of Koth, just across from the port city of Palemia on the River Sule, two in particular fell victim to something worse.

They were not the most pleasing companions, nor the most sterling of characters. Twenty-year veterans of Fantar's scourge, they had marched the entire circuit of the Inland Sea and back under his black flacon banner. They had fought together in all the major engagements of that time and had seen and done things even they would not own. Sergeant and NCO, they had belonged at the last to a regiment of Fantar's Imperial Guard and had marched eastward with him from Valeria to meet his fate in the dry hills beyond Palmeria. Not remotely interested in joining their more fanatical comrades in a fight to the death, these two switched sides early in the final melee, and afterwards, made good pickings off the corpses of their former fellows before slinking off in the night and making their way westward.

Now they sat late in a small, mud-walled tavern, their chins sunk low over their cups, and groused rather too loudly about the fate of their former leader. There were few customers in the place at this hour-the tavern catered mostly to local farmers, early risers who had long since stumbled home to their beds-and those few still scattered about swayed groggily or slumped over their tables. Even the bartender dozed on his stool, and as the discussion of the two veterans grew heated, no one seemed to notice their rising volume-no one, that is, except for the one other upright figure in the room, a hulking youth who sat listening to every word at a table in the corner behind them.

The sergeant had declaimed on the madness which had seized Fantar near the end and which had driven him-and his faithful Guard with him-eastward to the barren hills beyond Palmeria, a full eight hundred miles from the capital of Valeria. There, under a blistering desert sun, and at the very start of a battle with the resurgent High King, Valerius-a battle which the sergeant still claimed they could have won-Fantar had fulfilled the prophecy by dying at the hand of his Halfling servant, one who, according to the Oracle, he could only "half see."

"Aye" said the sergeant of the Halfling, "A scrawny little runt he was, not high enough to kiss your arse... Stuck ole Fantar like a pig, he did."

"You lie!" snarled the youth, suddenly rushing forward and looming over their table. He was a rough country lad dressed in a farmer's smock too small for his huge frame. His fisted hands were like hams waving in the sergeant's face, and while there was as yet but the lightest fringe of down upon his cheeks, his eyes burned fierce, and anger bristled around him. "Fantar would not die so."

But the veteran was not to be perturbed by such a raw youth, imposing though he was. "Would not die so? As if his corpse isn't rotting this very moment and himself wailing away in perdition! And what would you know about it, laddie boy? You were there, I suppose?"

"No, but I know."

"You know!" the sergeant scoffed, rising to face the youth who still towered over him. Several other patrons had awakened by now and moved quickly aside. "You don't know my arse from your mother's dug. Now go sit down before I... "

The youth lunged over the table, his fingers closing on the veteran sergeant's throat. The two fell clattering to the floor, thrashing about and upending furniture. In an instant, the other veteran thrust the broken table aside and flung himself onto the pair, a dagger glinting dully in his upraised fist. But before he could drive the blade home, the barman caught his upraised arm. He yanked the man aside and kicked the other pair apart, then stood over the three brandishing a large wood axe.

"Here!" he commanded, "There'll be none of that in here. You, Condor, hie yourself home where you belong. And you two, get your kits and clear out of here. I'll not have the likes of you wrecking the peace of my establishment!"

The youth, Condor, abruptly fled into the night, the door swinging wide behind him. But the other pair protested. "What do you mean?" the sergeant whined. "We were minding our own business here!"

"I heard your talk and I don't like your business," said the barman, brandishing his axe. "We had enough of 'your business' around here long before Fantar One-Eye got his due. Now clear off I tell you!"

"We paid you for lodging, we did!" claimed the sergeant, thrusting out his chin.

"And I'll lodge this axe in your skull if you push me," growled the barman. By now, several other patrons, suddenly very sober, had lined up behind the barman. Some brandished weapons of their own, while others held stools by the legs.

The veterans decided against confronting such odds. Grabbing their packs from the wall by the door, they marched sullenly out into the night. Nor was this the first time since Fantar's fall they had been so driven from the prospect of a comfortable bed.

The half-moon was past its meridian and cast a pale light along the road as the two trudged north between newly sown fields. They were headed towards a stretch of woods, which promised fuel for a fire and security for the night. Neither spoke, but both replayed the scene at the tavern with a growing sense of indignation. So seldom were they the victims that this incident seemed to justify a host of past sins.

"He was a big-un," said the NCO as the trees began to close around them.

"Aye, but barely a whisker on his chin."

"Suppose he's still lurking about?"

"Nah, home to his mama, more like it. That type has no stick to 'em. Just keep an eye open anyway."

But the sergeant was wrong. In fact, it was already too late. Behind them, the youth, Condor, stepped quietly out onto the road, and as the words left the sergeant's mouth, he smashed a large rock down onto the NCO's head, spattering blood and brains, and killing the man instantly.

"Hey!" shouted the sergeant flinching away from the spray and spinning to face their assailant. In an instant he drew sword and dagger and stood crouched at the ready. "Oh, now you've done it, laddie-boy," he snarled, glancing quickly at his fallen comrade. "Now you've done it!" And he lunged, sword whistling in the night air.

But the big youth was quicker. As the sergeant advanced, he hurled the rock. It struck the sergeant flush in the chest, knocking him back and driving the wind from his lungs. Then the youth was on him. Grasping both of the man's wrists, he drove him to the ground and landed on top of him. The sergeant tried to roll and wrestle himself free, but the youth was too big, too strong for him. Then he lay still, his arms firmly pinned to the ground by the youth's massive fists, and glared up into the face of his antagonist. He saw, momentarily, a look of uncertainty there.

"Hah! What are you going to do now, you bastard!" he spat. "Move one hand and I'll drive steel into your gizzard so fast you won't have a chance to blink."

Instant fury contorted the youth's face. His mouth twisted open and he drove his head down, clamping his jaws onto the sergeant's throat.

"Arrgh... !" the man tried to scream, but the sound was cut short as Condor twisted and bit and ripped at his throat, growling like a dog. Then he reared his head in the pale moonlight, his eyes raving wild, his mouth foaming with blood, and the sergeant's dripping larynx clenched between his teeth. With a strangled cry, he spat the gristle away, lurched to his feet and ran off into the woods.

He ran until the fury left him, then fell sobbing among the dead and rotting leaves. After a time, he quieted and lay still until a sound, or something like a sound-it could have been a rustling in the leaves-trip-hammered his heart and he leapt to his feet, crouched, tense and ready.

He had run far into a dark, primordial section of the forest. Around him, immense and ancient trunks mingled with the surrounding shadow, and the late moon cast only the slightest shimmer through the thick foliage overhead. He could see nothing. Or could he?

There, off to his right, a bit of shadow seemed to resolve itself against the trunk of a large tree. Then it moved and he could see the distinct outline of a hooded shape. It approached silently and Condor looked around quickly for a rock or a branch, something to use as a weapon. But the figure made no hostile moves. It stopped about a body's length away and stood there, as tall as himself, slender, yet still wholly indistinct, a bit of black shadow, shaped from the darkness of the night.

"Who are you?" Condor demanded.

"The question, my friend, is who are you?" The thing spoke in an unearthly voice, a soft, sibilant whisper, like a distant wind. "Are you proud of yourself for this night's performance?"

"They had no right to speak of him thus!"

"No right to speak the truth? Ah Condor," the figure used Condor's name with an easy familiarity and laughed softly, the sound like scales scraping along a rock, "you would be a tyrant indeed if you could suppress Truth! But what will you do now?

Go home as if nothing happened? They will soon find the bodies, you know. You left a rather untidy scene."

Condor opened his mouth but said nothing. He had not thought of anything beyond the urgency of his rage. Now he pictured the small sod hut that was his home, the old barn and attached shed, leaning together for support, the figure of his mother, bent and withered now where once had been a lithe beauty, and the hard, embittered visage of his step-father, his curses, the beatings. No, if he went back there now, he would kill him, too.

"I can help, you know," said the figure, as if reading his thoughts.

"How? Who are you?"

"Let's just say I am one who knows who you are... And what you can become. That is what you want, isn't it? To become like him? You who are twice cursed, the bastard son of a bastard son?"

"How can you do that?" Condor tried to sound derisive, but his voice came out plaintive.

"Ah, there's a secret, isn't there?" crooned the figure, moving swiftly closer. "The Truth here, Condor my lad, is that I can make you better than him." And he leaned towards Condor, the shadow of his hood seeming to envelop his head. Condor started to pull away, then stopped for just an instant, as something of the shadow seemed to pass into him. Then the figure was gone and Condor dropped to the ground like a sack.

He was awakened by a shaft of bright sunlight, which slipped through the leaves and seared his eyes. Instantly alert, he leapt up and looked around. But the wood was quiet and peaceful. He had slept late and the sun was well up, dappling the ground with a golden shimmer. Condor stretched, pulling the muscles tight across his shoulders and feeling the hardness where they bunched on his arms. Slowly, he clenched his fingers before his face, curling them into fists. He could feel power there, and he smiled, a hard, knowing light glinting in his eyes.

He made his way westward, sticking to the forest and moving swiftly but carefully. At a stream, he drank deep, spitting and rinsing the foul blood from his mouth, then scrubbed himself clean. Following the course of the stream, he waded in the bed as it meandered towards the river. Where it crossed the road, he crouched between its banks looking each way and listening carefully before slipping across the narrow ford. He was well to the north of where the bodies lay and he saw and heard nothing.

West of the road, the stream deepened as several other rills joined it and the land tilted towards the river. The stream tumbled into a larger brook, which cut a deep gully as it neared the river. When the brook became too deep to wade comfortably, Condor scrambled along its banks, clambering over large rocks and forcing his way through tangled flood debris, undergrowth and brambles. Finally, the stream shot out from its banks, tumbled down a steep fifty-foot rock face and poured into the River Sule.

Condor squatted at the top of the face to catch his breath. He ignored the hollow ache of hunger in his belly and stared out over the river. The sun was high now, pushing westward, and the river was broad and deep, nearly a mile across and still swollen from spring rain in the mountains to the north. The current was swift and sinewy, flexing like the muscles of a great serpent, too strong to swim. Directly opposite, the head of an island split the current and beyond, hazy in the glare of the far shore, was the port city of Palemia.

The island, he knew, stretched several miles to the south, past the town of Koth and almost to the Inland Sea. Between here and the town, the riverbank was high and the water deep right up to the shore. No one lived along here until the land subsided, just north of the town. But that was where the tavern was.

Something upstream caught his eye. It was a large bush, uprooted somewhere in the north and drifting along towards the sea. As it neared, Condor sprang out like a great ape, and plunged down fifty feet into the water. Coming up under the base of the bush, he caught hold of its lower branches and pushed it ahead of him as he kicked towards the island.

Several days later, in the port city of Palemia, the mate of His Imperial Majesty's war galley, *Steiger*, looked up to see a large, hulking youth amble up the gangway. He was dressed in rough breeches and a loose smock-farmer's clothes-and looked like he had been sleeping in the woods. But he had an air of confidence about him, and acted like he owned the boat.

"What do you want?" the mate growled, barring the way at the entry port.

"A berth," said the youth.

"A berth? The war is over these three months past, lad! Everybody else is trying to get out!" But the youth just stood there, implacable.

"Well you look rugged enough, though a tad young... And it's not like we don't need hands. What do ye know of seamanship?"

The youth stood at the rail and surveyed the ship from stem to stern, casually taking in her beaked prow and high forecastle; the long, double-row of benches-empty now with the crew ashore-and the sweeps neatly lashed; the tall mast and taut rigging; the square sail tightly furled against the yard; the high poop deck aft with its tiny cabin tucked below. And he nodded.

"I know," he said, looking the mate straight in the eye. His eyes were hard and black, yet somehow compelling. They were the eyes of a much older man, the mate thought.

"Well," he said, "let's see what you do know. What do you call that?" he asked, and pointed to a peg set in the bulwark by one of the benches.

Condor looked at it, the words forming in his mind. "Thole pin," he said.

"And this?" the mate asked, pointing to a similar pin in the rail surrounding the base of the mast.

"Belaying pin."

19

"And attached to it?"

"Halyard."

"All right, then. Let's see you cast off the main gaskets."

Without hesitation, Condor leaped for the shrouds, hauled himself up the mast hand over hand and began to loosen the sail. "All right!" yelled the mate. "Belay that. You may look like a farmer, but there's a right seaman in you, I'll warrant that."

Chapter 1

The morning sun danced bright off the deep blue of the ocean and bleached white the occasional foaming crest. Valerius stood at the lee rail of the Imperial trireme *Valadator* and drank it all in, never tiring of the vast, restful majesty of the gently sparkling sea. Overhead, the great main and fore sails strained and billowed, stretching the sheets that held them and heeling the massive ship so that its lower ports had to be closed against the surge. Before him, the deck and catwalks stretched clean and orderly from the high poop where he stood, over the waist decks with their massed crew and triple banks of oars, past the main and fore masts and away forward to the peaked prow with its stumpy bow mast and carved figurehead of Trices, goddess of truth. To his left, off the port bow and hazy in the morning distance, he could see that the great gray cliffs that had guarded the shore for most of their journey south had flattened and shrunk during the night and had turned to light brown sand as they approached the narrow isthmus that girded the mouth of the bay. Even now, in the far distance ahead, he could just begin to make out the lighter blue of the bay waters above the dividing strip of sand. In little more than an hour now, they would make their turn into the narrow entrance and head up the bay towards the city of Dulcai.

He was almost sorry the journey would end. Eomer, he knew, was eager to see her father and her home, and to show off the grandchildren. But for him, stepping ashore meant stepping back into his mantle as High King. Oh, it was not that he wasn't catered to royally here on *Valadator*, and not that he had anything particularly royal to do in Dulcai-after all, this trip was planned as a much needed vacation after two hard years of work stitching the empire back together after Fantar's fall-but still, there would be the inevitable round of processions and ceremonies, audiences and receptions. A world at peace, he had found, had nearly as many demands as one at war, and he knew he would face long hours of receiving lines with chamberlains whispering names in his ear, while he mouthed platitudes and smiled blandly, always mindful of what he said. He was not just anyone, after all, but Valerius Everreigning, High King of Valeria and all the Inland and Outer Seas, and his lightest word would be passed down the generations.

While out here, standing on the rolling decks under the clear infinity of sky, he just felt like a man.

Ahead, the blue of the bay was plainly visible now, the brown strip of the isthmus clearly etched between, like a fence crossing a flooded pasture. What was the state of the tide in the entrance, he wondered? Would they need to row, or would the great sails push them through? He could probably tell from the masthead. But before he could move to act on this thought, a curt order from Grumwald, his captain, sent a young sailor scampering off on that very errand. Valerius subsided back into his place, his hand having never left the rail, and watched the lithe youngster scramble up the ratlines. It would not have been seemly anyway, he thought, for the High King to go swarming up the rigging like a carefree young tar-especially a High King who had lately come into possession of so much girth.

A hand touched his arm and he turned to see the face of his wife, Queen Eomer, smiling up at him. Her hair was swept up and tied at the back and her deep blue eyes were radiant with excitement.

"Good morning, my dear," said Valerius, a broad smile breaking out on his face in response to hers. "Have you got your shore-going clothes on this morning? It won't be but a few hours now."

"Oh, my lord, you know we'll be going ashore in state. You'll have to come below and put your robes on, too."

"Aye, I know. I know. When I used to come here-when you were just a girl-I'd just vault over the rail with a dock line in my hands, and that would be it."

"Well, you can still do that if you like. We'll just have to tie your crown on with a scarf."

"Ha!" Valerius laughed aloud. "Wouldn't that be a sight? We could probably charge for a show like that and reduce taxes! But I'm afraid it wouldn't show proper respect for the dignity of your father's realm. No, we'll dispense with scarf and dock line and don our purple instead. Are the children up yet?"

At that moment, in answer to his question, the nurse emerged from the companionway, bearing the infant, Alair, and leading two-year old Valerian by the hand. As his feet hit the deck, the boy broke free of the nurse and ran to his father who scooped him up like a toy. "Ah, there's my little prince!" he said. "Are you ready to help steer the ship into the channel?"

The boy looked at his father, his black eyes wide, then strained his little body around to see the two men at work holding the great arm of the tiller. "See," said Valerius to the boy's mother, "he knows how the ship is steered-don't you, my lad? He'll make a right sailor before he's ten! He can take old Grumwald's job," he added loud enough for his voice to carry across the deck.

"Is he ready for that, then, Your Majesty?" returned the captain, hobbling down the tilt of the deck and dipping his head twice or thrice in an informal obeisance. He was a grizzled veteran, with ragged gray hair and a short beard that appeared to have been trimmed with a knife's edge (which it was). A long scar, white now with age, ran the length of his face and his stocky frame was settling into odd angles like the timbers of an old cottage. But his eyes were still a lively blue, and as he stooped to peer into young Valerian's face, they sparkled as bright as the sea. "Are ye ready to skipper a great ship such as this, little Highness?"

The boy nodded with deep solemnity and held his arms out for Grumwald to take him.

"Well, come to your uncle Grumwald, then, little man, and we'll show you how to make these buggers dance... Beggin' your pardon, ma'am."

"What's the tide, Grumwald?" Valerius wanted to know.

"Just starting to ebb, Your Majesty. We'll have to buck it up the channel, unless you'd rather sit off and wait it out."

"What think you: will she make it under sail, or will we have to row?"

"I don't know. Wind seems to be freshening a bit. We can bear off some and make a good run at it. But I'll want to have oars ready in case: we don't want to get caught abeam and driven up on the beach."

"Surely, there's no risk of that!" Eomer exclaimed, her hand flying to her throat.

"Not with this young prince here in charge, Ma'am." Grumwald replied, jouncing Valerian up and down in his arms. "But it has happened to some lesser skippers."

"Ha!" laughed Valerius. "He means me, the old pirate! I tried running this channel against the last of the ebb once in the old days, and when the current grabbed us, I yelled out 'starboard oars' instead of port. Put us up on the spit for half a day before the flood pushed us off."

"Well, you're not the only one to sit out a tide here-abouts, I warrant. Fortunately, it's all sand, and unless you're driven up on the outside with a running sea, there's little harm done. So we'll try it under sail, if you like, and see how this great girl carries on. But I wouldn't worry ma'am, she answers well to the oars and with my young Prince here to point the way, we'll slip on through in no time. Isn't that right, my man?"

"Ba ta," said the boy, pointing off at the figure of the mate across the deck.

"Right you are, my lad. That's Boltar himself, sloughing off, as usual. Shall we go and give him what for? Aye, let's do. Beg pardon, ma'am, your Majesty, but the young prince here has spied out a near mutiny, and insists I put it down immediately!"

"Well carry on then, Master Grumwald," said Valerius. "Far be it from me to interfere with proper naval discipline." And the two parents watched, smiling, as the grizzled old captain bore young Valerian off to accost Boltar, the mate.

"I never thought that terrible old warrior would behave so with a babe," said Eomer. "He spends more time with Valerian than his nurse does."

"Well, his life has been hard, but his heart is still tender. I believe he had a wife and babes of his own once, before Fantar and twenty years of war. It's good to see him shine so. But look," he added, pointing off the port bow, "you can see the channel clear now. And way beyond, on the far horizon, that tiny speck of white?"

"Dulcai!" Eomer breathed. It was her first sight of her homeland in more than three years.

"Have you missed it so?"

"Oh, yes and no," she said, taking her husband's arm and hugging herself to it. "I do miss the city-I grew up there, after all-and my father. I've missed him most. But there's so much more now and I'm so happy with you and the children, with everything. I wouldn't want to go back."

"Well, good. Because we don't want you to, either. And I don't just mean the children, and me either. I mean the whole Empire!"

Eomer took little Alair from the nurse and the pair subsided into silence as the great ship swung around and steadied on course for the channel. The wind had freshened, and as the ship came directly before it, the huge linen sails billowed even tighter against their sheets and brailing lines, and the hissing of their bow wave increased perceptibly. Running with wind and waves now, the ship no longer heeled, but took on a slow, deliberate pitching motion as the waves ran up under her stern quarter, then worked their way forward. As they lifted the stern, there was a rush, a sense of sliding downhill, then of gliding along as the crest passed amidships. Then, as the speeding waves pulled away forward, the bow with its bronze-sheathed ram settled down off their backs and they slowed, like they had dropped a towline.

Valerius balanced easily against this motion and stood watching their progress like a great bear. His arm curled gently around the golden form of his wife and their tiny daughter, he let his mind drift back to another day when he had stood on a pitching deck in this very spot and watched an entirely different scene unfold before him. On that day, he had been at the head of a fleet, and opposing him across this very isthmus, was another fleet, commanded-at least to appearances-by Reuters of Dulcai, Eomer's father. Eomer had been kidnapped by Fantar's minions and Reuters had been forced to cooperate against Valerius. But then, at the last minute before the fleets were to engage, Eomer appeared, flying down the wind on a speeding pontoon boat steered by Thorngere. At the instant he saw his daughter, Reuters turned on Fantar's galleys, and the south was secured for Valerius.

"Are you thinking what I'm thinking?" Valerius said to Eomer.

"Yes. I was never so wet in my life as that sail down the coast with Thorngere!"

"Well, I never saw anything more beautiful in my life, I can tell you that! And it wasn't just because a battle with your father was averted, either." Valerius leaned down and kissed the top of his wife's head. "But you know what else? That was a major turning point for me, even aside from the battle and falling instantly in love with you."

Eomer looked up at him quizzically. "Yes," he said. "I think it was. I always knew that I would fight Fantar. Ever since I was fifteen and he overthrew Valeria and killed my father, I knew I would fight him to the very end. But I always believed the end would be mine, that at some point I would fall in battle or be taken and executed. I never really believed we could win-until that moment. When Reuters turned his ships against Fantar's galleys... "

"But you were already a crowned King then. And you had the power stone."

"Yes, I bore the title of rightful High King, but really, I was king in name only. And as for the Eye, well, I knew no more how to use it then than I do now. So, I had control of Kantar and the Hidden Valley, and had a force of maybe two thousand. But to go against Fantar's entire Empire? It was impossible. But then, at that moment, when I saw Reuters turn, I realized that the momentum was with me-just as old Volkmir always said it would happen-and that as surely as the current was bearing us into the channel, so a greater tide would bear us to victory."

"Well," said Eomer, watching as the ship began to breast the current and the relative motion of the approaching sand spit slowed, "I'm not sure the momentum is with us now."

"Aye," said Valerius and cast a nervous eye over towards Grumwald, standing by the helm. The captain was still jouncing Valerian in his arms and talking to him, but his practiced eye was moving quickly between the sails billowing overhead and either side of the approaching channel. "We've way yet," he said and tried to appear nonchalant.

The ship slowed even more until, as its bow touched the invisible line dividing sea from bay, its progress could be measured in inches. At the long tiller bar, the two helmsmen worked the great sweep back and forth, partly to offset the contrary thrusts of the current, and partly to help scull the great ship forward. At a nod from Grumwald, the mate, Boltar, stepped to the rail separating the poop from the waist decks and barked out a command. "Out oars!"

In a well-practiced movement, one hundred and twenty long sweeps shot out as if the ship had suddenly sprouted legs. "At the ready!" And Boltar looked back, awaiting the signal from Grumwald who stood watching the shore intently with his head cocked to one side and neck exposed, feeling the force of the following wind. Still, the ship made way.

"Steady," said Grumwald to the men on the tiller. He spoke quietly, and indeed, the whole ship had fallen silent, as if too much noise might disturb this delicate balance between wind and water. Only at the bow could be heard an incessant gurgle and swish where the ship's stem cut the out-rushing current. Still, she inched ahead; the bow now several yards past the midline, but her progress was nearly imperceptible.

At the rail, Eomer found she was holding her breath and clutching the baby tightly to her breast. She forced herself to relax. In truth, there was no crisis here, only a game of men against sea. The oars could pull them through in a trice, but the oarsmen sat like statues, holding their great sweeps at the ready, waiting for the command. But their leaders had to try, had to see how it would go, and they would risk grounding and humiliation, even risk the ship itself to see if it could make it through unaided.

To her eye, it appeared they had stopped, that the force of the current pushing out exactly balanced the force of the wind pushing them in. The ship was in the exact middle of the channel, exactly halfway through. On her left hand, she could see the long sand spit, stretching away to the north. On her right, the equally sandy shore curving away south and then east towards the distant white spot of Dulcai. She glanced at Valerius, and then followed his tense eye to Grumwald whose head was darting back and forth, his body leaning forward, willing the ship to move, while young Valerian perched in his arm, watching the proceedings like a hawk.

She felt a slight shudder in the hull and saw the bow begin to edge left. Instantly, the men at the tiller pushed the bar in the same direction. The bow came back, then edged right. Again the helmsmen corrected. Still the ship sat, and still Grumwald held back the command to row.

Again the bow slid left, but this time Grumwald leapt back to the tiller and let his own hand guide the bar. He let the bow fall off a bit more, then pushed the tiller. The bow came back, then went right. Again, he let it go just a bit further, and in the process, even Eomer could see the ship slide ahead. Back to the left, and this time, the movement was definite. The whole ship edged to the left and as it did, slid ever so slowly forward. Then, as they passed the focal point of the current, the ship broke its hold and shot forward into the calm waters of the bay.

At the command "Ship oars," the crew cheered and on the poop deck, officers and High King grinned like boys. Even Valerian held his stubby arms aloft in victory. "See, your Majesty," yelled Grumwald, "I told you young Valerian here would get us through!"

Eomer, tried in vain to repress her own smile, then shook her head at the old man in mock disgust. "You men!" she said. "You'll never grow up. Any of you!"

Chapter 2

It appeared that the entire population of Dulcai had turned out to watch the arrival of the High King and Queen Eomer. As *Valadator* coasted in towards the dock and the lines were heaved, crowds filled the harbor basin and pressed forward along all the converging streets, the bright colors of their holiday clothes in vivid contrast with the pure white of the buildings, the surrounding brown of the desert, and the stark blue of the sky. Soldiers had cordoned off the immediate dock area and formed a thick phalanx around the Dulcaian royal party that had followed king Reuters' curtained litter down from the palace as soon as the great trireme entered the harbor.

King Reuters was helped out and stood holding onto the arm of a young, raven-haired woman by his side. Despite the southern heat, he pulled his royal robe closer about his shoulders and peered intently along the busy decks of the ship. "Damn these eyes!" he said to the woman, his voice tremulous. "Can't see a thing anymore. Can you see her yet?"

"Not yet, your Majesty. The crew is still tying ropes to the dock."

Indeed, as the ship had entered the harbor, Reuters' royal daughter, along with the High King and the rest of his entourage had hurried below to don their ceremonial regalia. They stood now, just inside the great cabin, adjusting their finery and awaiting a signal from Boltar that the procession could proceed. Valerius stood with his head bent under the deck beams while Eomer, ever the dutiful wife, fussed with the folds of his purple robe and straightened the heavy golden chain which hung about his neck and secured the huge red gemstone that was the symbol of his authority, the Eye of Valeria. She was careful not to touch the stone itself: even in this shadowed, semi-darkness, lustrous flashes lurked within its depths as if it were alive.

"What's it doing?" she whispered. "It looks as if lunch didn't agree with it."

"I don't know," said Valerius, chuckling softly at her aversion. "It does that periodically. But it won't bite, you know."

"Nor will I give it the opportunity," she retorted, smoothing his cloak once more. Then she reached up and gave him a playful pat on the cheek. "There, you look as Imperial as any Valerius who ever reigned.

"Very witty, my dear. Very witty. And you, I think, are lovelier than any queen who ever graced the realm of Valerius Everreigning. But come, let's go and see your father."

Announced by a fanfare of trumpets and followed by their retinue, Valerius Everreigning, High King of Valeria and all the Inland and Outer Seas, and Queen Eomer emerged from the cabin and made their way between kneeling files of sailors and stopped at the entry port, posing in full view of the cheering throng. But as they stepped from the gangway onto the soil of Dulcai, the thousands of onlookers dropped to their knees in obeisance. The ranked soldiers presented arms and a deep hush fell over the scene. Only Reuters and his beautiful young attendant stood erect, the latter helping the old man totter forward to make the official greeting.

But in the sudden silence, a loud, clear voice rang out over the multitude and froze the principal actors in their steps. It wailed in a prophetic chant:

"Beware, Valerius, bewaaarrrre!

Beware the spawn of the evil seed,

Beware the power of the unseen deed.

Awake, High King, Awake!

Shake sleep from your peace-addled mind.

Your ruby Eye has left you blind!"

As the sound faded, Valerius saw a dark figure duck back behind the parapet of a nearby roof. But as a squad of soldiers rushed off in pursuit, he ignored the incident and the fearful rumblings of the crowd, and proceeded across the jetty at a regal pace and stopped to receive the homage of King Reuters.

Eomer was shocked to see her father, the man had aged so, but like Valerius, she kept her public face calm and her smile warm and fixed. She was politely delighted at how beautifully her young cousin Illana had blossomed in the three years she had been away, and it was not until the official ceremonies were over and they entered Reuters' private quarters in the palace that she was able to express her real concern.

"Oh, you needn't be concerned, my dear," said the old man, easing himself back on his couch with a heavy sigh. "I've had a lingering summer cold is all. I'm almost over it. But look at you, my dear! You look radiant. And you've brought me two lovely grandchildren to grace these poor old eyes. Even you, your majesty, are looking robust and healthy."

"Too robust, you mean," said Valerius. "I've spent too much time at my desk... " But Valerius, too, was shocked at the appearance of his old friend and one-time protector and he trailed off, leaving an awkward silence. Always a stalwart fellow, even somewhat portly, Reuters had been a strong, vigorous leader. Now he was sallow and sunken, the skin hanging from his frame, his eyes dull and listless.

"Well I'm delighted you've taken the time to visit us here in Dulcai, though I must offer my apologies for that little incident at the dock."

"Ah," Valerius waved away his concern, "if you stopped the mouth of every would-be prophet, we would have a very quiet realm. Is the fellow known?"

"If he's the one I think he is, yes," said Reuters. "He's a hermit who wanders the hills to the east and claims to be a holy man. He comes into the city begging for food every month or so. "What meant him, you think?"

"I know not," Valerius shrugged, "but it has to do with the Eye of Valeria, no doubt. That's surely the "ruby eye" which has supposedly left me blind. But what it is I don't see, I'm afraid I can't guess."

"Aye," said Rcuters, "I know what you mean. They tell me I'm going deaf, but I never hear it for myself."

Valerius laughed politely. "Well, perhaps your men can convince him there are better ways to beg alms off the High King, eh?"

"Will you talk to him if they catch him?" Eomer wanted to know. "Find out what he meant?"

"If you wish it, I will, my dear," said Valerius, wishing to change the subject. "But these fellows seldom have much meaning in them. Madmen, mostly. They say even true prophecy comes directly from the god and that the prophet is only an intermediary. But if they catch him, I will see him. So, now, Reuters... "

But the exertions of the welcoming ceremony had been too much for the old man. His head had dropped back onto his couch and he was snoring softly.

Motioning them to silence, Eomer took Illana's arm and the three of them moved to an outer chamber. She sat Illana beside her on a pillowed couch and kept hold of the girl's hand while they spoke. "How long has my father been ill?"

"It's been several weeks, your Majesty," said the girl, her large, dark eyes returning Eomer's look with an openness only a little tinged by awe. "As he said, we thought it just a cold, but it lingers so we've been very worried. Today was the first day he's been up, really. He insisted on meeting your Majesties at the dock."

"Has he been eating? He's lost so much weight I hardly knew him!"

"Not much, Ma'am. He'll take some soup if I feed him, but not much else."

Eomer's eyes searched out her husband's and spoke the fear she dared not even think. "Well," she said, patting Illana's hand. "You've been wonderful to him, and I'm sure he'll mend."

"Yes, Ma'am," said Illana and looked away.

Later that evening, after two receptions and a state dinner, Valerius joined Eomer in their bedchamber. Reuters' men had caught the prophet and he had been down to question him. Eomer lay propped against several pillows in the huge poster bed nursing little Alair, her long blond hair spread out around her like a fan. Valerian was asleep in the adjoining chamber. As Valerius entered, her eyes spoke the question. He shook his head in reply and sat down softly by her side, watching his infant daughter suckle.

"I think he's just mad," he said. "He's a dirty, pitiful creature and just ranted on and on. Most of it was incoherent. I don't even think he knows now what he said. He certainly couldn't repeat it, and when I held the Eye up in front of his face, he didn't even seem to know what it was."

"Are you sure he's the right man?"

"Well, pretty sure. But I only got a quick glimpse."

"What did you do with him?"

"We let him go. He's harmless enough."

"Do you think... ?"

"His prophecy could have been real?" Valerius shrugged and held up the great red gemstone by its golden chain. It glimmered in the candlelight and seemed to give off a light of its own. "I would think it less likely if he had been more coherent."

"Then you believe it?"

Again, Valerius shrugged. "What's to believe? Do I look asleep? Am I blind because there may be some things I cannot see? That's too much of a riddle for me. I don't know what to make of it, true or otherwise. How's your father?"

"Asleep. He took some soup and a little bread. But he's just so weak! I don't think he could have held the bowl by himself. Illana is very good with him. She's really a lovely girl."

"Well, you're not such bad tonic yourself. I'm sure he'll mend." But they both knew he didn't mean that and their eyes spoke what they would not say.

"What will we do?" she asked.

"Well, if worse comes to worst, that will be up to you, my dear. You will be Queen of Dulcai."

The next day, the men of the High King's party were given a tour of the Dulcaian mines by Reuters' former ambassador, Rondo, who had retired from diplomacy to manage the city's business enterprises. They did not speak of the king's health, but his absence did (though Eomer thought he did seem brighter and plainly wanted to come along). No one was prouder of the mines of Dulcai than Reuters, and he rarely missed an opportunity to lead visitors into the blackness of their depths.

Other than the mines, there was not much to recommend Dulcai. A flowing agricultural port in ancient times, gradual climate shift over several centuries had withered the farms upriver to barren sand and turned the surrounding country into desert. Now, instead of exporting food, Dulcai imported it, and were it not for the mines, the area would have been abandoned long ago.

But under the swirling sands and shifting hills lay vast wealth in gold, minerals and ore: enough to make Reuters-though he tried his best to hide it-the richest man in the Empire. It had been Reuters' gold that financed Valerius' fight against Fantar, and iron and bronze smelted from Reuters' ore that had made the weapons he used. And it was the product of these mines that now allowed the population of Dulcai to live in comparative opulence and made the city a veritable oasis in the desert.

Gold had been found first. As climatic conditions became yearly more arid, the holding cover of grass and brush gradually receded, exposing the bare hills around the slowly starving town to the eroding effects of wind and weather. As lighter material was blown away, there was found in the gravel shiny yellow bits of metal mixed with quartz. Gold!

In hardly more time than it takes to say the word, a mining industry sprang up, under the active direction of the king, Reuters' distant ancestor. From plucking surface ingots, eager Dulcaians soon began digging pits, then delving underground and refining their techniques for extraction. Other ores were discovered in the process: copper, tin, and within the last generation, when efforts extended further into the interior, huge fields of high grade iron ore.

Now, after a dozen generations, the industry was well established. Processing technologies had been honed to the peak of efficiency, and the extraction of ore from solid rock reduced to a science. Somewhere along the line, it had been discovered that fire would, if not soften, at least tenderize the hard, ore-bearing rock. Huge bellows assemblies had been devised, driven by trip-hammers and powered by horse-drawn turnstiles, which pushed air down into the depths where fires were set against the working faces and left to blaze for days. Doused with cold water and quickly cleared of ash, the faces were then attacked, first with tools of hardened iron, and then, as forging and tempering techniques were refined, with hard, bright steel, and large baskets of ore laden rock were hauled to the surface with blocks and tackle.

The rock was then pulverized by trip hammers, then by men with sledges until it was ready for shipment north for smelting in Kantar. The labor was brute but fortunately, the successive kings of Dulcai passed down a keen sense of management, and so paid these workers the highest wage. As a result, the hammer men of Dulcai were highly respected and admired and there was never a shortage of willing applicants. The work built these men into incredibly powerful specimens, and when need called and they stood wielding battle-axes in a fray, few could stand against them.

Valerius had seen the mines many times before, of course, and had even worked as a hammer man himself in the days before he was able to reclaim his name and patrimony-when he was known simply as Balazar. But now protocol dictated that he tour the works anew, smiling and greeting the workers in their thousands, and even descending in a rickety cage to the depths of the shafts themselves.

"The first time I ever met King Reuters was in one of these," Valerius said as he and Rondo squeezed into one of the small cages. "And he knew every shaft and tunnel down there."

"I think he still does," said Rondo as the cage lurched away from the loading platform and began its dizzying drop into darkness.

"He keeps a close eye on things, does Reuters."

"Sometimes too close," Rondo muttered, too softly to be heard above the screeching of the blocks and the echoing cacophony of clanging and banging noises that rose up from below.

"What's that?"

"I said, I worry that his Majesty wearies himself on such things," said Rondo, raising his voice this time. "He should let others worry about these matters for him."

"Reuters does as he thinks best. But I'm sure he appreciates all your efforts."

"Thank you, your Majesty." But could Valerius have seen Rondo's expression during this exchange, he might not have been so flattering.

They visited a face where the fires had just been pulled away and men with picks and hammers were viciously smashing away the crumbling rock. The place was as hot as an oven and still choked with smoke, but the men worked at a furious pace. So urgent was their task that they paid virtually no heed to the man who ruled them from far away Valeria, and after a short stay in the cramped tunnel, Valerius turned away and began making his way back along the main gallery to the entrance shaft. Flickering torches set in brackets along the walls lighted the mine, and air came in ragged, whooshing gusts from the bellows above, so that the place seemed alive.

Intersecting shafts led off on both sides of the main gallery and at one of these stood an austere, bearded figure, dressed not in tunic and miner's breeches, but in the long, flowing robes of a mage. Valerius stopped abruptly at the sight of him and held up his hand to stay the party behind him. The fellow looked familiar, but the light was so dim it was hard to see. Was it the prophet again? He seemed so, though how he would have been allowed down here Valerius couldn't imagine. And then, for another moment, he looked like someone else as well, someone he definitely could not be.

Valerius was about to speak when the figure motioned for him to follow and turned away down the intersecting shaft. Valerius began to follow, but the mate, Boltar, laid a restraining hand on his arm.

"Majesty, the main tunnel is this way."

"I know where I am," said Valerius. "Wait for me here," and he stalked off down the dark tunnel.

The way was not lit, being unused, but as it curved around and the walls blocked out the torch light from behind, a soft glow arose from some phosphorescent material in the rock itself. The tunnel was suffused with a faint, blue light that gently brightened as he made his way. It was not far and soon he could see the dim figure of the old man, standing at the entrance to a small gallery at the tunnel's end. Again, Valerius was struck by a sense of familiarity about the fellow, but just then, he turned away and stepped into the vault.

Valerius stopped at the entrance. The gallery was an irregularly shaped dome, roughly hacked from the rock and left when the vein of ore ended. It was perhaps fifteen feet across and a dozen high, diffused with watery-blue phosphorescence, and empty save for the figure of the old man standing in the center, his head bowed in shadow.

"What would you have of me?" Valerius demanded, his voice unnaturally loud and hollow in the confined space.

"Behold, High King, what your Eye doth see," said the mage and swept his arms up and out towards the walls.

Valerius felt the great Eye Stone on his chest suddenly throb and looked down to see it pulse and glow red and erupt in a rainbow of colors which fanned out and up and spiraled around the walls and ceiling, like a kaleidoscope. Colors of every hue spun and swirled about the chamber, flickering shadows of light and dark across the irregular surface and candy-striping the mage and his long white beard like a painted pole.

Valerius had seen his Eye Stone in action before, but never anything like this. Before, when excited-and how or why it became excited was a puzzle-it had shot forth red beams like arrows, or had exploded with light and power. Once, it had knocked him off his feet. Another time, it had blinded the old mage, Volkmir, for several days. And once, if the tales were true, it had burned out the right eye of his own bastard half-brother, the usurper, Fantar. In his own attempts to use the Eye (it was, after all, supposed to be a vision stone that allowed the rightful High King to see the future and into the hearts of men) he had occasionally seen murky shimerings in its depths, swirling patterns which suggested meaning, and which, on a couple of occasions, had prompted prophetic dreams. But there had never been anything like this. Then again, he had never been schooled in the use of the Eye-his father had thought the thing a mere bauble-and had no idea how to command it, if he could command it, or what it could do.

Now he was beginning to see. On the far wall, the colored patterns began to shift and resolve, and suddenly, a shadowy figure loomed. It spun slowly around the room, its dark shape filling every crack and crevice, once, twice, then met another hulking

45

form, more substantive but still compounded of refracting light. The two figures merged, the darker shadow melting into the lighter, and then the hulking figure appeared to move towards Valerius. It came closer and more and more clearly into focus, and then, for just a moment, its face loomed large on the wall. It was his own face as a beardless youth. Then it sprouted a scraggly beard of young manhood and Valerius realized it was not his face at all. It was Fantar's! Or was it?

Suddenly, the light winked out and Valerius was momentarily blinded by the comparative dark. As his eyes adjusted to the blue phosphorescence filling the chamber, he found himself alone. The old prophet was gone.

Turning, he hurried back to the main tunnel where Boltar, Rondo, and the rest of his entourage waited. "Did you see him?" he asked.

"Who, my lord?" Boltar replied.

"The old man."

"No my liege. We saw no one."

"He's gone?"

"Perhaps he slunk off down some side shaft," said Rondo.

But Valerius shook his head. "There are no side shafts off that tunnel."

Valerius was shaken. He put a good face on it, of course: it would not do for the High King to show anything but confidence and surety in public. But at the public reception and luncheon that followed, his mind was distracted by the visions he had seen, and he stumbled twice over the names of people he knew well. He ate little, and was so inattentive during the following remarks made by Reuters' head of mining, that he missed a polite joke aimed at him. When the audience laughed and looked his way, they saw his dark face clouded, his eyes distant, and their laughter trailed into an awkward silence.

Back at the palace, he was scheduled to confer with Reuters, and found the man much recovered and basking under the loving ministrations of Eomer and his grandchildren. He was still plainly not well, but sitting there with Valerian on his knee and Eomer beside him, cradling tiny Alair, there was color in his cheeks, and a brightness in his eyes that reflected the happy smile on his face.

"Ah, Reuters, my old friend!" said Valerius, "I see you are looking more like your old self."

"Old may be just the right word! But who would not feel improved in the company of three such beautiful creatures as these? I thank you from my heart for bringing them to me, Valerius."

"Well, you are entirely welcome, Reuters. They are my joy as well." But Valerius' broad smile did not quite have its usual warmth, a sign not lost on the quick eye of Eomer.

"Come, Valerian," she said, helping the boy hop down off Reuters' lap. "Daddy and Grampa Roy have business to discuss." And acknowledging her husband's concern with a quick glance, she took the children from the room.

Valerius sat opposite Reuters and for a long moment studied the tiled mosaic of a goddess on the floor. It would be better, he thought, not to break his news immediately. "So, how are you feeling?" he asked instead. "You are looking much better today."

"I feel better. But to tell you the truth, Valerius, a week ago I thought you would get here just in time to light my pyre. Now, today, I think I may have a few more months at least."

"Well, you're needed for much longer than that, my friend. You're the only grandfather Valerian has got, you know. Alair, too. You can't shirk that duty."

"May your words reach the god's ear! But how are you, my friend? How is Thorngere, and Vahla, everyone? And how goes the peace? It's been what, two years now since Fantar fell? How does it feel to be master of the world? Tell me everything. I'm very isolated down here."

Valerius' smile was very warm this time: this was more like the Reuters he knew. "It goes well, Reuters, overall, very well. Of course, as soon as there is peace, everyone wants a piece, so I often feel more like the world is the master of me. But when I look at what's been accomplished in two years, I'm really gratified. I mean, Fantar did everything he could to ruin the Empire for seventeen years, and that we could rebuild this fast is amazing.

"But it's been a lot of work. A lot of work. This little trip has been, literally, the only break I've had. And that's taken a toll. I mean, look at me Reuters!

I try to train as often as I can, but still, I look like an aging eunuch."

And indeed he had aged. His hair and beard were rapidly graying, and the great strength in his frame was beginning to settle into a noticeable paunch. But Reuters had a different perspective. "Your majesty," he said, "you're too hard on yourself. Take it from a truly old man; you haven't even begun to deteriorate yet! There's so much more to go!"

"Ah, Reuters, you are such a comfort." And the two men laughed.

"But how are Thorngere and Vahla doing? I haven't seen them since their wedding. Any news of 'impending events' from that quarter?"

"Not that I've heard. They're both in the north-you know Thorngere is Atheling of Thule now-and we haven't seen either of them for a year or more. Ragnar, we saw on the way down here: he has Zagorbia thriving. He's extended the walls, built a huge new market complex, expanded the guilds. But I think he secretly wishes there was still a war! The man is a born fighter and, like me, he chafes at all the administration. He's doing well though.

"Koltar of Kantar also, though I expect you have more to do with him than I, given the trade between you two."

"Yes, Koltar and I correspond frequently. He is an amazing fellow, full of ideas! And having his heavily timbered valley for smelting within a few days sail has been a real blessing. In fact, since Grumwald disposed of your old friend, Haradin, the whole triangle of trade between Dulcai, Kantar and the Fortunate Isles has been going very well."

"Yes, Koltar told me the Iblis have been quite docile. Kantar still has troops there, of course, but the Iblis have been working well at their farming, and some of the younger ones have even been showing some interest in learning crafts. I wish it were going as well in other spots."

"Problems?"

Valerius still could not come to the breech. "Well, more like irritations, petty squabbles. There's still some resistance to the new order. We defeated Fantar, but our new broom did not exactly sweep clean. There are still bands of former Fantar supporters causing problems all over the place, and quite a number of pirates plaguing the seas-playing the same game we did when Fantar had us on the run-and with the economy still shaky after years of pillage, the cost of chasing them down is increasingly a burden. Then there are the Baalamists in the area of Telos and Cobanos. They're quite disruptive."

"What about your new Scythian friends?"

"Very well on that front! Karghan and his people wander the plains north and east of Palmeria with their flocks and are providing a very effective buffer against other wild bands in the north. The city itself is having difficulties-it, too, was one of Fantar's main strongholds-but I'm hopeful that will settle soon. Fargo is doing very well in Falkan. Did you ever meet him? No, I thought not. He was the last remaining vestige of old king Caramon's bloodline, and after we retook the place, we found him out in the desert, tending a shaduf. He's a strange fellow, something of a mystic. But the people count him as very wise and he's taken well to the crown. Would that Eldred could do the same in Palemia."

"Eldred?"

"He's Vahla's cousin on her mother's side, the son of her younger brother. Strictly speaking, Vahla is the rightful heir to Palemia, but she decided to go north with Thorngere so Eldred was the next choice. I would that it were different."

"Is he that bad?"

"Ah, perhaps I'm being too hard on him. I confess, I just don't like the fellow. But he is still very young and very new to power-perhaps he'll come around."

"What's his problem?"

"Well, you know, Reuters, there are two kinds of rulers: those who serve the people, and those who think the people serve them. He's one of the latter-thinks that whatever pleases him must be good because he's the king. He spends his time in sport and idleness, doesn't hold court, and serves justice to the highest bidder. He's even farmed out tax collection, a sure recipe for corruption."

"Have you spoken to him?"

"I tried a few months ago. He was full of flattery-was 'so grateful' for my advice-but I knew it would make no difference. I tell you, Reuters, I wanted to grab the puling little bastard by the throat and toss him out of the palace. But a High King can't be quite so arbitrary, I'm afraid."

"Well, not unless you have sufficient grounds to depose him."

"I know, and I don't. That's what's so frustrating: I have no doubt he will give me sufficient grounds in time, but meanwhile, the people of Palemia will have to endure him. That's what seems so unfair. They've just gotten rid of one tyrant, and here I've stuck them with another."

"Well, you can only do the best you can. And it sounds like things are going fairly well overall."

"True, but there is something else."

Reuters raised an eyebrow as Valerius hesitated.

"I don't quite know how to say this, other than bluntly," he said at last, "but I fear some great evil threatens. I feel it. I hate to cut short our visit, but we must return to Valeria."

Disappointment shook Reuters like a blow, but his eye shot back sharply. "Was it that mad prophet fellow?"

Valerius hesitated, not sure what to say. He thought it better not to mention his experience in the mine. "Partly that."

Reuters lay back on his couch, suddenly very weary. He could see russets of light simmering deep in the facets of the great stone dangling from Valerius' neck. "I see," he said. "You don't know any more than that, then?"

"Not in terms of hard facts, no. But I know."

"Oh, I don't doubt you, Your Majesty. I only ask to be of assistance."

"Well, you can help, Reuters. You can do a couple things. First, stay healthy-and I don't just mean that because you're Eomer's father and the children's grandfather. I need you. The Empire needs you. You are the tower that guards the south. Second, keep the ore going to Koltar. I fear we may have need of more weapons."

"I will do my best on both scores, Your Majesty. But there is something you could do for me as well, if you would."

"Name it."

"Take my niece, Illana, back to Valeria with you as a handmaiden for Eomer."

Valerius was surprised by this request. "Certainly, Reuters, but why not keep her here by you? She is a comely lass and could ease your lonely hours," and he gave Reuters a wry look.

"Ah, would that could be!" Reuters laughed. "But alas, my friend, that flame in me has been long extinguished... or at least, this girl arouses it not. You will see when you have grown daughters of your own. Besides, I believe the girl is pure. She comes of a good family and I'm sure will do better for herself in your court than in mine. And I do believe Eomer has taken a liking to her."

"Yes, she told me as much." Valerius thought the matter over for a moment, and then came to a quick decision. "All right, so be it, then. Illana will come to Valeria."

Chapter 3

As one of the ship's boats towed *Valadator's* bow away from the dock, the great trireme spread her banks of oars like a huge water bug and inched out of the harbor. Gaining way with each stroke, she slipped around the sandy headland and went with the morning tide down the bay towards the open sea.

At the dock, King Reuters watched for as long as there was ship to see, then-with Rondo's help-climbed heavily back into his litter for the trip back to his empty palace. He had put a good face on the necessity of the High King's departure, had smiled when Eomer kissed him and when little Valerian gave him a solemn hug, but now his heart felt like a lump of ore. He was bitterly disappointed and already lonely. Would he ever see them again, he wondered? He had not even realized how much he had been looking forward to their visit, but now he feared that expectation was all that had been keeping him alive. He flopped back against the pillows with a heavy sigh and closed his eyes. Rondo closed the curtains for him, cast a last, hard look seaward, and then with a quiet smile, motioned the bearers onward.

Eomer, too, was disappointed at their early departure, though she knew Valerius would not have it so without good reason. She sat nursing Alair in the great cabin, watching through the stern windows as the city dwindled in their wake, and worried about her father. The sight of him had been such a blow, so contrary to every impression she ever had of him. He had always been so strong, so vigorous. He alone, of all the monarchs of the old Empire, had stood firm against Fantar, and Valerius, she knew, would not have won back his crown without him. But now, how he had aged! How timid were his steps, how frail his arms! It had been all he could do to hold Valerian, though he held him like a precious treasure. Would he recover, she wondered? And what would she do if he did not? In the far distance now, among the surrounding desert wastes, the tiny city shimmered white under the deep blue of the sky. Eomer hugged Alair closer to her breast as a tear rolled down her cheek.

On deck, Valerius watched as the ship approached the narrow channel that let out into the sea. The tide was with them this morning, but as the heat of the day mounted, a freshening sea breeze was already kicking up white caps where the current pushed into the sea. Valerius could feel the current's pull as the ship entered the inward end of the channel. At Boltar's command, the oarsmen held their stroke and the ship began to surge ahead in a strange silence: water, which had been gurgling over the long bronze-sheathed ram and along her sides, was now racing along with them. The helmsmen tightened their grip on the long tiller arm of the steering oar and everyone seemed to hold their breath as the great ship shot through the narrow slot and tossed up a rainbow of spray as its bow met the first sea.

"Now!" Boltar yelled and the oarsmen bent their backs as the mallet man hammered out the stroke. The ship drove against wind and sea to claw its way clear of the land. "Pull!" Boltar yelled in time with the wooden mallets knocking against the sounding board. "Pull!" He paced back and forth along the catwalk overlooking the triple banks of oarsmen, warming now to their work. At thirty strokes per minute, the ship shot ahead nearly at ramming speed, spray flying high over the bows, soaking the decks and the backs of the rowers below. At the rail, Valerius grinned.

As they cleared the shore, the water deepened and the short, steep breakers lengthened out into an even swell, and the ship's bow rose over them in more stately fashion, only to swoop down and spear the next one with her ram. Grumwald headed her off a bit towards the north to ease her motion, and when a comfortable three miles had been put between them and the land, he turned due north and gave the command to ship oars and set sail. Freed from their long sweeps, the men swarmed along the decks and up the main and foremasts to loose the large, square linen sails and trim them to the wind. *Valadator* heeled to its pressure. Running parallel to the swells now, she took on a long rolling motion, and sailed along easily on her course.

From his spot on the windward side of the poop deck, the fresh breeze tussling his hair and beard, Valerius' gazed ahead into the far distance, his mind outpacing the ship as it probed northward, seeking the threat he knew was there. Whose face was it, on that gallery wall, and what did it portend? In all the time since he had recovered the Eye-years spent fighting the forces of an entire empire-he had never been given such a warning.

Watching the activity from under the overhang of the poop deck was Reuters' young niece, Illana. This was her first time at sea on such a ship, as well as her first time away from home, and she could hardly contain her excitement. As soon as Eomer had given her leave, she had hurried to this spot and marveled at all the frenzied activity required to make the ship go. From the shore, great ships had always seemed so majestic, their motion as graceful as a dance. But now, to see all the furious effort behind it, to see the power and authority of such a man as the mate, Boltar, striding back and forth on the catwalk above her, his clear voice ringing out over the tumult like a bell, and to see the men all pulling in unison, the muscles of their shoulders and legs bunching as they hauled on their oars, was so exhilarating to her she forgot even to be afraid-which she had very much been as she left the weeping arms of her parents that morning and timidly followed the Queen aboard. Now thoughts of home and fears of the unimaginable deep were fled and as the ship settled on her northerly course and the sailors returned from setting sail, Illana ventured up the steep steps to the poop deck above, but then shrank back again quickly as she saw the figure of the High King himself standing by the rail.

But he had already seen her and smiled and beckoned to her almost as if he were relieved to be distracted from his thoughts. She stepped out onto the high deck and marveled to see the vast expanse of blue sea spreading all around and the distant shadow of the land, blue now in the morning haze. She curtsied politely, and then stumbled as the ship rolled.

"Ho, my girl!" laughed Valerius and reached out, but she caught herself just as she was about to fall. "We can dispense with the formalities of court out here at sea. The rule here is, 'one hand for the ship, one for the man'-or for the lady in your case. So how are you finding our little adventure so far-to your liking?"

"Oh, Your Majesty!" the girl breathed. "This is tremendously exciting!" She had never been this close to the High King before, certainly had never spoken to him directly, and the color rushed to her cheeks.

"You're feeling all right, then?"

She looked at him strangely, unsure what he meant. "Yes, Your Majesty, I feel fine. I mean, I miss my parents... "

"No, I mean your tummy, girl, your tummy. The motion isn't bothering it?"

"Oh! No, Your Majesty, not yet."

"Good. It does some people, you know. They step aboard a ship-even a boat sometimes-and, well, let's say it doesn't agree with them."

"Well, so far I feel fine. Wonderful, in fact! I had no idea it took so much work to make a ship go."

"Well, it'll be less work for a while now, if this wind holds. Did the Queen say she was coming up?"

"She didn't say, Your Majesty. She was feeding Princess Alair when I left."

"Ah. Perhaps I'd better go down. She's feeling a bit low, what with us having to leave so quickly and all."

"Your Majesty?" Illana asked as he turned to go. "Would it be possible for me to see more of the ship? I've never been aboard a ship before and..."

"Well, let's see what can be arranged. Commodore Grumwald!" Valerius called out as if he were on parade, though in truth, the old man was standing by the helm, not ten feet away. He shuffled over and bobbed his head.

"Yes, Your Majesty. Good morning, Princess."

"Would there be a man in your crew honest and trustworthy enough to escort young Princess Illana here about the ship?"

"I believe Master Boltar could be spared for a bit, Your Majesty."

"The very man I had in mind."

Grumwald summoned the mate with a similar quarterdeck yell, though Boltar was, in fact, at his station by the break of the poop, not six feet away. Formal introductions were made, instructions given, and the two were left alone, Grumwald returning to his station by the helm and the king ducking quickly below.

Boltar was no stranger to the fair sex. At thirty-two, he had been nearly twenty years at sea, many spent aiding the resistance with Lord Thorngere, roaming from port to port about the Inland Sea aboard the sloop Elusive. A rugged, athletic fellow with curly black hair, the deep, blue eyes of the north, and a quick, flashing smile, he had found no shortage of opportunities. Now, however, as his seniors left and he looked down into the bright, blue-green eyes of Illana-eyes that not only met, but also held his gaze-he suddenly found himself rather perplexed. This was not the kind of woman he was used to. Not the rank and definitely not the beauty. Nor had he Illana's practiced social graces, so while her verbal felicity had covered her awkwardness with the High King, he stiffened in gawky silence, his tongue feeling rather like a sausage in his mouth.

Delighted with this reaction, and pleased to have the handsome, burly mate as an escort as well, Illana let him hang for just an extra moment before dropping her gaze. "I'm sorry to be a bother, sir," she said demurely. "If you're too busy... "

"Oh, no! No, not at all," Boltar blurted. "It would be my pleasure to show you the ship, ma'am. Miss. Princess."

"Please, just Illana." And this time when she looked up at him, she added a warm smile.

They started with the tiller. While most war galleys and even large triremes had fairly pointed sterns and steering oars on the side, Boltar explained, *Valadator* was built with a broad, square stern like a cargo vessel in order to accommodate high-ranking passengers aft. So she was hung with a steering oar directly off the transom, which was controlled by a long pole called a tiller arm. In heavy weather, he said, they added purchase to it by attaching blocks and tackle secured to rings set in the deck along the rails. He was not sure how much of this she followed, but the talking relaxed him. "If we didn't do that," he said, "and we got slapped with a really big wave, that tiller could fling a man right over the side!"

Illana's eyes widened and the two men on the tiller swelled with self-importance till a sharp look from Grumwald recalled them to their duty.

"Has that ever happened when you were running the ship?" Illana asked as they moved forward to the catwalk. It was narrow and she moved close to him, feeling the strength and grace in his frame.

"Well, no," he said. "But I haven't been on *Valadator* that long."

"Were you on a bigger ship?"

Boltar laughed, thinking of the tiny scow Elusive, kept purposely seedy so as not to attract the attention of Fantar's war galleys. "No, no," he said, "much smaller. Besides, there is no ship bigger than *Valadator*."

Illana's eyes got wide again. "Really! What did you do on the other ship?"

"I was the captain."

61

"Oh, I knew you'd be a captain!" she flirted. It wasn't fair, she knew, but she was enjoying the effect she was having on him. "Why aren't you the captain here?"

They had stopped by the foot of the main mast now and Boltar looked up at the great billowing sail. He would have much rather discussed the mysteries of rigging. Below, two bo'sun's mates walked along the benches, trying in vain to keep the men from gawking up at the princess. One man started to yell something, but a quick cuff silenced him.

"Well, Princess," Boltar answered, "it's complicated, but sometimes I am. You see, Grumwald is the Commodore. When the king is not aboard, he takes the big aft cabin, and when we're sailing with other ships, he has charge of the whole fleet. Then I'm Captain of *Valadator*. But with His Majesty aboard and with no fleet, we sort of take one step down. Grumwald is captain and I'm mate."

"I think you must be a great captain," Illana said. Her eyes were shining again and Boltar found it hard to meet them.

"This is the main mast," he said. "We have two, you see, the main and the fore. That way, we can get more force from the wind and balance the load. See, most war ships are meant to be driven primarily by oars: they can go faster and maneuver better in battle that way. But *Valadator* is also built as a flagship. She's bigger and built to carry more stores for long trips like this, so we rely mostly on sail power and only use oars when we have to. Now, the main mast... "

At that moment, the ship rolled abruptly as a seventh wave, larger than the rest, surged beneath her hull. Illana, who was looking up at the time, following Boltar's pointing finger, lost her balance and toppled into him. He caught her easily in his arms, and then blushed to his toes as the crew below broke out in loud cheers. Even the bo'sun's mates, as they lay about themselves left and right to restore order, wore broad grins. Boltar quickly put Illana back at arm's length. But in that unguarded instant, while his hands still held her shoulders, their eyes met fully, and something passed between them so raw and potent that Boltar's knees buckled and he almost lost his balance.

It was over in a second, but the effect was like a blow to his mid-section, and he stood, blinking stupidly at the girl, his nautical lecture flown from his brain. Recovering, he hurried her forward to the forecastle deck where, while it was not exactly private, they were not center stage for the entire crew.

"I'm sorry, Princess," he said, "You should not have been subjected to that. Rest assured the men will be punished."

"No, please!" she said. "It was my fault. I wasn't paying attention." Again, a look passed between them, a force so compelling it was difficult to tear their eyes away.

The rest of the tour passed awkwardly. They stuck to the subject of the ship, but Boltar's descriptions were wooden and Illana's responses distracted. He showed her the great bronze-sheathed ram used to sink other ships and then took her deliberately along the lower deck, right between the benches of the oarsmen, who under his glare and with a princess in such proximity, kept their eyes lowered and looked chagrined. He pointed out the three tiers of ports and explained how the lower ones were kept closed when they were under sail. But clearly, nautical matters were not at the forefront of his mind, and just as clearly, Illana was no longer just flirting.

He left her at the door to the great cabin and climbed back up the steps to the poop deck. Grumwald was there, his gray, shaggy form swaying easily with the motion of the ship, his eyes peering intently forward at the set of the sails. But the old commodore wore a wry smile and his eyes twinkled with amusement. Boltar turned away and resumed his station by the catwalk rail. Grumwald moved up beside him.

"A fine young filly, that." Grumwald said. He spoke in a low, gravelly whisper.

Boltar felt himself flush deeply. He looked quickly at the old man, then away again. He started to speak, but the words died without sound. There were no words. Grumwald nodded to himself, the smile fading from his face.

"Watch your helm, lad," he admonished softly. "That's royal blood, you know. Way different from the likes of you and me." Then he was gone, turning back to the men at the tiller. "Hey," he yelled.

"Watch your head, there! What are you doing, driving us onto the rocks? Bring her up, bring her up, I say."

The passage from Dulcai to the Hidden Valley of Kantar was a full five days sail. And even though the *Valadator* was a very large ship, there was no way Boltar could avoid contact with Princess Illana, especially when she seemed to go out of her way to seek him out. When they did meet, he was polite and differential, but he avoided her eyes and made no attempt to engage her in conversation. Still, even though he told himself she was forbidden, he found himself waiting constantly for her to appear. His heart raced at the sight of her, and images of her flashing smile and lithe form so flooded his thoughts that on several occasions subordinates had to announce themselves two or three times before they could get his attention.

This abstraction on the part of the mate was, of course, noted by the crew. When 130 odd men are crammed into a ship approximately 100 feet long by 20 wide, there are very few secrets, and laughing conversations frequently fell silent when he passed. The old Boltar would have laughed as well and made as much sport of himself as the men did. But now, he flushed deeply and found himself unable to respond. Even Valerius noticed the attraction between the two-the eagerness with which Illana approached Boltar, his obvious discomfort in dealing with her, and his longing glances after her- and once or twice opened his mouth to make some teasing remark. He liked Boltar and they had always had a friendly, relatively casual relationship-as casual as can be when one party is High King and ruler of an empire and the other a sailor risen up from the ranks-but something in Boltar's look made him hold his tongue. There was a sensitivity there that would not deflect a jest.

Illana was both puzzled and hurt by his reaction. She knew she had acted, well, shameless was much too strong a term, but certainly a bit forward in flirting with him. But she also thought they had gotten beyond that. There had been, she was sure, a connection on a deeper level, even if only for a moment, to which the flirting had only been prelude, and she wanted to establish it again. That there was a major difference in rank between the two and that this might affect Boltar's attitude towards her, did not occur. Reuters' court in Dulcai bore none of the trappings usually associated with royalty and though he was certainly deferred to, he still walked the streets-or had when he was able-as easily as any other man, and treated his subjects as neighbors. Illana and her mother had always lived in the palace (her father, Reuters' younger brother, had died when she was an infant) and been attended by servants, but with such a familiar affection that the notion of superior rank never developed in her mind. To her, Reuters' chamberlain was Uncle Bremin; the cook, Auntie Jemma; her mother's maids, Lucy and Camile. She, of course, was always called Princess, but in such a way that it simply seemed her name.

Nor had she any real experience in matters of the heart. She was still young, of course, but even so, there were no eligible suitors for her in Dulcai-which was Reuters' main, though unspoken motive in sending her north-and as open and informal as the palace environment appeared, Illana had been kept rather cloistered. She knew several young men, of course, who treated her in a friendly-though now that she thought back on it, rather reserved-fashion, and as she blossomed into young womanhood, she had flirted experimentally with a couple of them. But they evoked no such reaction as Boltar had. That had been as much of a surprise to her as it had to him, and his subsequent coldness pained her deeply. She didn't understand it and didn't know how to deal with it.

So it was in this frame of mind, after three days at sea and after being apparently rebuffed several times by him, that she found herself alone with Eomer in the stern cabin after the evening meal. Young Valerian was on deck with the King, "helping Grumwald make sure everything was secure for the night," as he said, and the Queen was nursing Alair before the broad stern windows. Behind, their wake stretched straight and clean to the horizon and the setting sun cast a ruddy glow across the deep blue of the sea.

The nurse had retired for the night and as Illana sat on a stool beside Eomer, the talk soon turned to the subject of romance: how Eomer had met Valerius and what he was like; how they had fallen in love. He was still called Balazar then, Eomer told her, and she only fifteen. No one knew he was royal and he had treated her like a little girl. But still, even then, she knew. Then, when he returned as King, and they met on the dock, she could see him fall.

"But what did you do?" asked Illana.

"I don't know," said Eomer. "I remember once watching some boys practice at wrestling and the coach kept saying, 'use your opponent's strength against him.' And while I never thought of His Majesty as an 'opponent,' I do think I helped him fall in love with me that way. It sounds silly, but when he looked at me, it was like his spirit rushed out at me-like one of the wrestlers. And my spirit didn't try to resist or go against that rush, but went with it. Our spirits merged in that one instant, and we were one. I think we will always be one."

"But what was it that made you know, early on, when you were still too young."

Eomer thought, her eyes drifting softly back through the distance of the years. "I don't really know how to explain it," she said. "He was like a great bear, so huge and strong. Even then, though no one knew who he really was, people deferred to him. And it wasn't just because they were afraid-though he was certainly a man to fear! No, there was something compelling in him, something that made you trust him and rely on him. But when I looked at him, it was like I could see inside, beyond all the muscle and the great strength. And I could sense a great yearning in there, a great need and a caring, pain and sadness. Other men seemed to be concerned only about themselves, but Balazar was always concerned for others. I could sense that in him. He was kind. To me he was like light and warmth, and strength and need, all wrapped up in one. And I think I could just sense a place for me there, a fit, like we were two parts of something that needed to be one... Oh, I don't know Illana. I can't explain love! It's just there, and when you step into it, you'll know. It just takes you away, like this great ship!"

'I do know,' Illana thought. 'I do know.'

The next morning, early, Valerius rose just as the sun broke over the high cliffs that now lined the eastern shore, and went out onto the tiny stern gallery. It was the only private place on the ship. Eomer was still sleeping in the cabin beyond, but still he moved to the far side of the narrow platform, beyond the edge of the windows. Facing the sun, he held the Eye stone up, cupped in his hands so it just caught the light, and looked deeply into it. But after a few minutes, he shook his head in disgust and turned away, stalking back into the cabin and flopping down onto the bench behind his worktable. He shuffled a few papers absently, and then fell into a brown study, staring out at the following sea. Beneath the thick mane of his hair and beard, his face was troubled.

Chapter 4

The city of Kantar was easily the most heavily fortified in the world. Situated in a hidden valley and cut off from the sea by thousand-foot high cliffs, the only approach was through a long, pitch-black cavern that the river-and the Kantaran people-had carved beneath them. Valerius and *Valadator* sat outside this cavern entrance now, awaiting the turn of the tide and making final preparations to enter. The ship's huge main mast had been unstepped and lay fore and aft, lashed along the length of the vessel and the decks were piled with coiled rigging. The foremast, too, was coming down, and men rushed about like busy ants, dismantling their colony.

The three women, Eomer, Illana, and the nurse, Brenda, watched from a quiet corner of the poop deck. Eomer and the nurse had seen it before, but Illana marveled at how the men had levered out the huge mast with a simple tripod and how they managed to lay it so neatly along the deck without so much as a thump. But now, as she watched the foremast come down in similar fashion, she kept looking from the ship to the black hole that was the cavern mouth and wondered how they were ever going to fit.

She had not long to wait to find out. When it was clear the tide had fully turned, a pair of boats were lowered and positioned at the bow with towlines. At Boltar's command, a single tier of the ship's oars were manned, and she moved slowly towards the narrow entrance. Silence fell over the ship like a blanket so that the seethe and suck of the surf against the cliffs could clearly be heard. On the poop deck, Valerius, Grumwald and Boltar glanced anxiously from entrance to following sea, concerned lest a rogue swell disturb their course.

As the ship neared the cliffs, Illana's fears grew. The black hole grew larger and larger as they approached, and while the sensible portion of her mind repeated that, of course they would fit, that they had done this many times before, and that the King would certainly not place them in such danger, another, deeper part of her mind rebelled at that logic and urged her, somehow, to flee before they smashed against the rocks, or before that gaping black maw swallowed them whole. Since she was a tiny girl, she had had a fear of confined, dark places, and as she tried now to control her claustrophobia, her body began to tremble. And as the ship's bow passed into the dark maw of the cavern and Boltar gave the command to ship oars, she found herself involuntarily moving across the deck to stand beside him.

It was a narrow fit. The ancient Kantaran who had enlarged the cavern had no notion of a ship the size of *Valadator*, and as she folded her wings like a great bird, the boats at the bow took up their slack and she slid between the rocky walls with mere feet to spare on either side. At the bow, a lantern suddenly glowed in the enveloping blackness, and as the stern slid into the darkness, Boltar looked down to see a trembling Illana looking up at him, fear widening her eyes. Without a word, he placed a protective arm around her and drew her close.

The cavern stretched through subterranean blackness for more than a mile. Illana stood close to Boltar, drawing comfort from the strength that enveloped her. She did not speak lest the sound of her voice break whatever spell had brought them together, but snuggled close and closed her eyes. For Boltar, the spell was equally delicious. His hand lightly cupped her shoulder and he reveled in the soft feel of her flesh against him, inhaling again and again the jasmine scent of her hair. He would not let his thoughts stray beyond the instant and willed that the cavern might last forever. Finally, however, as the ship rounded a slight bend, a tiny light appeared in the distance.

"That light is the end," he whispered. "Are you all right now?" It was still too dark to see her face, but he felt her turn towards him. Still, she did not speak but he felt hr head nod. A small hand squeezed his and then she was gone. He gripped the deck railing tightly to steady himself against the surge of his emotions, and as the distant light grew, recalled himself to duty by forcing mind, step by step, through the procedures for docking ship.

As the great ship was towed clear of the tunnel, Valerius shielded his eyes against the sudden glare. Ahead, the Hidden Valley opened before him, a broad panorama of neatly tended fields and soft hillsides stretching away on either side of the river, and in the far distance, the ring of mountains that encircled the place. To his right rose the city itself, its tall, crenellated walls looking at first vague and insubstantial as his eyes adjusted to the light, then focusing in sharp, meticulously maintained delineation. His first view of Kantar and the Hidden Valley was always like this; emerging from the blackness of the tunnel, it was like something materializing from a dream.

The city had changed much in the years since he had first seen it, when he had stumbled from the cavern's track, a shipwrecked and exhausted castaway. The place was a hovel then, inhabited by the backwards Iblis under the rule of a twisted snake of a man named Chubar. Generations before, the Iblis had invaded from the north and driven the diminutive Kantaran natives into the hills. They had hunted, cannibalized and even interbred them for years until, with Valerius' help, the Kantaran had retaken the city and transported the Iblis to a series of lush, tropical islands offshore. An active race of exquisite craftsmen, the Kantaran had rebuilt their ancestral home until now, it was a shining jewel of a city, easily the most beautiful in the empire.

As at Dulcai, the entire population had turned out to welcome the High King, and there was much ceremony and a banquet to be gotten through before Valerius was able to get to the real purpose of his visit: a private chat with Koltar, the Kantaran King. A purebred, even smaller than most of his subjects, Koltar nonetheless possessed a brilliant mind and had become one of Valerius' most respected advisors and closest friends. But they made an odd pair as they left the hall, the huge, black-maned high king looking even more outsized among the Kantaran-sized throng, and the tiny Koltar, looking from behind like a five-year-old child walking beside him.

But a glance at Koltar's face belied that image: not only did he sport a full, dense beard, but his face bore the deepening lines of middle age and years of weighty responsibility. His eyes, though, black as obsidian, still sparkled with lively interest, and his mouth curved with warmth and humor.

They settled into Koltar's private study on either side of a small table stacked with scrolls and books. The room reflected his wide and varied interests. More books and scrolls lined the walls and several work tables bore evidence of his various projects: architectural drawings on one, chemical paraphernalia on another, administrative documents on a third, ancient scrolls and an in-process manuscript on a fourth.

"I see you've been keeping yourself busy," said Valerius. Koltar's experiments and inventions had been a long-running joke between them since, in their earliest encounter-before they had become allies-the former queen had ordered Koltar to poison him. It was one of the few things he had failed at.

An outsized chair had been provided for Valerius, and oil lamps placed about the room cast a warm glow. They sipped mulled wine and talked of trade, of Reuters' illness, of the voyage north, and of common acquaintances. But Koltar sensed an edginess in Valerius. He was surprised the royal party had returned so soon after their trip south to Dulcai, and knew there was something serious on Valerius' mind. Finally, the huge king heaved a sigh and got to it. Koltar had just suggested a trip inland to the New City during his visit, but Valerius shook his head.

"Nothing would please me more than to see the place again," he said. "But I fear we can only stay long enough to rest and provision."

Koltar raised an eyebrow. "There is a problem?"

"Well, yes and no. There's nothing overt, but I fear there is some mischief afoot."

"Anything I can do to help?"

"Perhaps. How much do you know about the Eye?" he asked, indicating the large red gem suspended from his neck.

Koltar shook his head. "Only what is common, I'm afraid."

"You've come across nothing about it in your ancient archives, the ones from before the Iblis?"

"Only that the high king bore a vision stone and that it was the symbol of his power. But then, I've never really looked for those references. Is there something specific?"

Valerius heaved another great sigh. Other than the mage Volkmir, from whom he had gotten the stone, Eomer, and to a lesser extent, Vahla, he had never really spoken to anyone about its powers. To admit he could not use it, he feared, would undermine his legitimacy. But how else could he ever find out? And something told him-perhaps even the Eye itself-that if he didn't find out, his legitimacy might not matter.

"Well-," he said, finally taking the plunge, "and I'm sure I can count on your complete discretion-I was hoping you could help me figure out how to use it."

Koltar did not try to mask his surprise and listened carefully while Valerius described the prophecy at Dulcai, the incident in the mines, and how he had been troubled since by "certain disruptions" whenever he tried to use the Eye. Then he said:

"Valerius, you know of course that you can count on my complete discretion, and you know I would instantly do whatever is in my power to help you, but matters of this ilk are far beyond my ken. The old Mage was of no help when you got the stone from him?"

"Well, yes, somewhat... And maybe I know all there is to know already-all that has been given to know. That's what Volkmir said. But it just seems that, well, the Eye is not a willing tool. It responds on its terms, when and if and even how it wants. Many times I look and there is nothing, other times, vague somethings I hardly know what to make of. So, as I say, maybe this is all there is supposed to be. Then again, maybe I'm doing something wrong."

"Have you consulted Vahla on this?"

"No, not yet. She has been in the north with Thorngere. I just wondered if you had ever come across any references to the Eye in your researches. You know, it's been with the High King for so long, I don't think anyone even knows where it came from or how the original Valerius got hold of it."

"Well, I will certainly search the archives here, but as you know, they deal mostly with trade and local matters."

"I would appreciate anything you could find. There are also archives in Valeria that Fantar did not destroy. I plan to search those as well. In the meantime, as I say, I sense there is some serous mischief brewing, but I have nothing specific to put my finger on."

"Whatever it is, Your Majesty, I and my people stand ready to assist you."

Valerius smiled and raised his cup in toast. "And valuable assistance it is, my friend. You have the Empire's eternal gratitude in return."

"But speaking of help," said Koltar, assuming nonchalance, "I could use some from you. Would it be possible for you to meet me at the river in the morning? There's something I'd like to show you."

"What? You've invented another new sailing rig?"

"Something like that," said Koltar, and pressed though he was, would say no more.

Next morning, the sun was just spilling over the rim of the eastern mountains when Valerius, Grumwald and Boltar made their way along the docks crowding the river to the place Koltar had indicated. The docks were already busy at this hour, and the trio breasted the throng of tiny Kantaran porters, workmen and farmers like teachers crossing a crowded playground. They were anxious to see what the little king had come up with this time. Surprises by Koltar were the kind of things that won wars. They found the dock indicated beside a small shipyard, and there, rafted against the outboard side of a Kantaran war galley, was a new ship, the like of which the three had never seen.

It was about the size and shape of the galley, but instead of being an open shell with benches and oars, it was decked over completely from bow to stern with a long cabin trunk down the center and another forward. And where a typical galley's bow swooped down and out to a protruding ram, the bow of this craft swept down and back in a graceful curve like a sword blade, shaped to slice the sea. Two masts rose from the hull, one just forward of amidships, and the other, shorter, halfway to the bow. Taut stays of braided hemp supported the masts fore and aft and tarred shrouds, criss-crossed with ratlines rose up from chainplates set in the rails. The rig was the same fore and aft, boom and gaff arrangement Koltar had experimented with several years before. It had proven marvelously effective in going to windward, but had been near fatally unstable.

The three men on the dock looked at each other with some misgivings. "Ain't this the same rig he used on that galley when you rescued me?" asked Grumwald. Some years before, he had been consigned as a galley slave after accepting an 'amnesty' offer by Fantar. It was his ship Valerius had grappled and taken after Koltar's experimental galley had been rammed and was sinking beneath them

"Yes," said Valerius, looking the ship over again. "You were with us that day, weren't you Boltar?"

"Aye, and I remember bailing till my arms nearly fell off! But maybe that's why he's decked her over, so she won't ship so much water when she heels."

"The heeling was one thing," said Valerius. "But I was sure we were going to capsize several times."

"Well, if I know Koltar," said Grumwald, "he's figured out how to fix that."

Boltar grunted. "I hope it's not by building a boat that can sail upside down!"

The arrival of Koltar and several attendants ended their speculation. His eyes were glowing with delight as he took them aboard, and the issue of stability was the first thing he brought up:

"Now, I know you sailed this rig on a galley hull once before and weren't exactly pleased with the way she behaved when sailing on the wind."

"It did go to windward very well," said Valerius, trying to be polite. And it was true: the fore and aft rig had allowed them to outpace Fantar's conventional galleys-until the wind began to blow hard. Then it began slipping sideways almost as fast as it went forward and shipping water like a bucket. Twice it nearly capsized in the gusts.

"Well, I came up with two solutions to the problem," Koltar went on. "The first is the catumaran you know about. With its two pontoons, it spread the force of the wind horizontally over the surface of the water."

"And made it sail like the blazes!" Valerius added. It was this catumaran that had brought Eomer and Thorngere down to Dulcai when Valerius had faced off against Reuters. The thing had skipped across the water like a stone, going twice the speed of a normal ship.

"Yes, it went very well. And my first thought was to simply expand on that design, but when we tried to make bigger ones, the cross members couldn't take the stress and the hulls kept breaking apart. So then I thought, well, if I can't go wide, maybe I can go deep. Look here," he said, taking a drawing from one of his attendants and spreading it on the cabin top. It was a profile drawing of the ship, showing a long deep keel. The three outlanders frowned at it, clearly confused.

"There's more under the water than on it," said Grumwald.

"Well, that's not exactly true," said Koltar, "but she does draw over eight feet."

"Eight feet! By the gods," said Valerius, "*Valadator* only draws five and she's over twice this size."

"In length and breadth, yes," said Koltar. "She's what, 130 feet overall and displaces about 30 tons?"

"About that."

"Well, this girl is 60 feet overall, but displaces nearly 40 tons."

The three men stared about in disbelief. "What did you do," said Grumwald, "build her of iron?"

"Not quite, but she does have nearly 14 tons of iron ballast along her keel. I won't take you through all the math, but the whole thing worked out beautifully. A galley is designed to be powered primarily by oars, so it's built light and shallow to skim across the top of the water. This ship is designed to be powered primarily by the wind-though we do have four sets of sweeps for auxiliary power-so I needed the ballast below to counter balance the wind's force, and the full underbody shape to resist slippage or leeway. She had to be built heavy to support that, and that in turn, meant I had to give her more sail area to drive her. Hence the two masts. And since you don't row her, she only needs a crew of eight or so. That meant I could do something else with all the space aboard. Come on, I'll show you."

He led them aft and down a companionway ladder. Far from an empty hold, the space below had been beautifully appointed as living quarters with a large saloon with cushioned settees, a galley with an iron stove, and several private cabins with bunks for sleeping. Way forward, with a separate companionway from the deck, was a smaller cabin for the crew. There was full headroom, fore and aft, even for Valerius. Exotic woods had been used throughout with exquisite joinery and all finished with clear, bright lacquer so the whole interior glowed with warmth and comfort. None of the men had ever seen the like. Indeed, the accommodations were more spacious, more plush, and much more beautiful than those aboard *Valadator*.

"But whatever will you do with her?" Valerius wanted to know.

"I'm doing it right now," said Koltar with a smirk. Then added to the three questioning faces looming over him, "I'm giving her to you, Your Majesty. She's a present to the High King from the people of Kantar. And she has no other purpose than to take you where you will. You rule an empire which spreads across the sea: this is your personal sea chariot!"

"But the King must travel in state!" blustered Grumwald.

"You don't call this 'state'?" said Valerius.

"Well, it's lovely, of course, but I mean eight crewmen: how will the King defend himself?"

"I thought of that," said Koltar, plainly enjoying himself. "First, it is probable that the King would travel in concert with other ships such as *Valadator*-which, by the way, would mean you do not have to give up your cabin, Grumwald. Second, this ship can probably out sail most anything you would run into-at least, to windward. And third, I thought of another little something that can probably make this the most dangerous ship afloat. Let's go back up on deck."

He led them forward on the outboard side to a spot just before the main shrouds where a pair of holes had been drilled in the rail. "There are sets of these all around the ship," he said, and nodded to two Kantaran workmen who set a pair of what looked like bow staves into the holes. But rather than each having a bowstring, the two were tied together with a sling arrangement at the top.

"You remember my little firebombs, of course?" he went on. And of course they did. It was Koltar's firebombs-a secret combination of chemicals that burst into flame on contact with air-that had given them the edge in breaking the siege at Zagorbia. The chemicals were carefully poured into special clay pots, and then fired from catapults. "Well, I thought catapults might be a bit problematic onboard here, so I've made some smaller pots that can be fired from this double bow-stave arrangement. Do you want to try?"

A small pot was carefully set into the sling and at Koltar's direction, Boltar hauled it back until the staves were fully bent, then let it fly. The thing arced across the river and exploded into a little ball of flame in the wet grass on the far side.

"You don't quite get the range of a good bow," said Koltar, "but I think the effect on a wooden ship will more than make up for that."

"I think so," said Grumwald, picturing those liquid flames spreading across the deck of his beloved *Valadator*.

"Well!" said Valerius. "When can we try her out?"

"She's ready to go right now. But there's one more thing I want to show you."

"More?"

"Just one thing. Well, two actually," he said and led them back to the stern. Here, an entire section of the deck had been lowered about three feet with benches set into the perimeter so there was room for a half-dozen or so people to sit comfortably. In the center, running nearly the length of the space was a sturdy table with leaves that folded down. But what struck Valerius and company was that at the after end of this, instead of a tiller to steer the ship, was a wheel arrangement set on a pedestal with a large gourd set into its top. Again they turned to a smirking Koltar for an explanation.

"This was an interesting chain of ideas," he said. "I've never liked being tossed around in a boat, so I was thinking of a way passengers could sit comfortably, down out of the wind and spray. So I thought of this well. Then, the idea of a well reminded me of the winding drum arrangement we use in the old city to haul up a water bucket, and I thought, hey! here's a way to eliminate that cumbersome tiller bar and increase the mechanical advantage of the steering system." And he stood proudly by the wheel as if they should intuitively understand how the thing worked. They didn't.

"So... ?" Valerius said.

"So, this wheel steers the ship," said Koltar. He looked hopefully from one blank face to another, then sighed. "Look, it's simple. See the way this rope winds around this drum? Well, it goes down under the deck, through a set of pulleys, then back to a yoke on the rudder head. If you turn the wheel this way, the rope winds up on the drum and turns the rudder this way. Turn it that way and the opposite happens."

"So you just turn that wheel in the direction you want the ship to go?" said Boltar.

"Yes! Simple, isn't it?"

The three men exchanged looks of wonder. "Yes, actually," said Valerius. "Now that you've explained it. But how you think of these things is beyond me."

"What's this?" asked Grumwald, inspecting the gourd on the pedestal. It had two corks stuck in its top, like ears.

"Ah, now, this is interesting," said Koltar, and climbed up on the table so he could reach the thing. "We have a stone you can find back in the mountains that attracts metal. I've fooled with the things for years, and a while ago, I had one suspended from a string and noticed that it always oriented itself the same way: one end of the stone always pointed to the north. I spun the thing around, took it different places: it always pointed north. So I thought of our ships sailing back from the Fortunate Isles: if they could always be sure of north, even in fog, they would always know where the land was!"

To three sailors who had spent many anxious times in fog and who had always feared losing sight of the land, this was indeed interesting. Koltar explained that he had mounted a stone on a little wooden disk and floated it in the gourd.

"That's what the corks are for: to keep the water from splashing out. Now, to use it-here, you try, Your Majesty-you pull the corks, look through the back hole and let light in the front."

Valerius looked and saw a neatly carved wooden disk with an oblong stone in the center and symbols all around its edge.

"Do you see the vertical line inscribed on the front of the gourd?"

"Yes."

"That corresponds to the bow of the ship. What's the letter on the disk just below it?"

"W."

"That stands for 'West.' I've put initials for each of the directions on the disk, so the letter under the line indicates the direction the ship is heading."

Valerius shook his head. "I wish Thorngere was here to see this."

"Well, you'll just have to sail up to Thuringia and show him," said Koltar. "You said you wanted to see Vahla anyway."

"That's not a bad thought. But let's see how this baby sails! You say she's ready to trial now?"

"At your pleasure, Your Majesty."

Boltar was dispatched to assemble a crew-all of his men from the Elusive were aboard *Valadator*-and within half an hour, they had cast off and were gliding down the river, rowing easily with the current into the cavern. Unlike *Valadator*, the masts of this ship cleared easily and before long, they slipped out from under the massive cliff face, and under the direction of Koltar and his Kantaran shipwrights, set sail.

The morning was pristine and as the sun burned off the early mist and a breeze filled in from the west, the ship performed beyond expectations. Feeling as solid underfoot as *Valadator*, she rode the swells like a swan, and yet, was nimble and quick. On the windward tacks she lowered her shoulder and surged along, the water creaming along her rail, and sailed within three points of the wind. Off the wind, with her booms spread wide and her sails bellying, she seemed to lift herself free of the sea and soared like a gull. There was none of the tenderness that had nearly sunk Koltar's previous experiment, and none of the crabbing off to leeward. Valerius was delighted and spent much of the day steering the ship himself. The wheel arrangement took some getting used to-it worked in the opposite direction from a tiller-but it provided a mechanical advantage which made the boat very easy to steer, and once he got used to it he found great delight in its responsiveness.

Strangely, for a man who ruled an empire, Valerius spent most of his time feeling constrained. He was bound by duty, bound by obligation, bound by tradition, so bound that he often felt himself more draft-horse than king. That's what this vacation had been about in the first place, but with the prophecy, Reuters' illness, and his worries about the Eye, that sense of release and freedom he sought had been replaced by a deep foreboding. Now, as he steered this strange, enchanting craft, it came back. He knew it was an illusion, that his cares would return, but for the moment he felt totally free, totally in control of himself and his destiny. An infinity of paths lay open before him and he had but to turn this wheel to go anywhere. It was exhilarating and as he stood on the slanting deck, at one with the ship and the wind and the sea, he grinned like a boy let out from school.

Towards midday, the wind kicked up something of a sea and the little ship flung spray high in the air as she drove her curved bows into the waves. The crew, sitting on the high side of the deck with their backs against the cabin, took the spray like fine rain and laughed in delight.

"This is like riding a thoroughbred!" Valerius yelled to Koltar as the deck reared and plunged.

"You like her then?" The tiny king was perched on the edge of one of the seats, holding on to the coaming and bracing his feet against the table.

"Oh, I do, my friend, verily I do! You've built a wonderful craft here."

"What will you call her?"

"With your permission, King Koltar, I will call her *Kantar* in honor of your people."

Koltar bowed at the waist. "My lord, it is you who honor the people of Kantar."

It was late by the time the weary, windblown crew of the *Kantar* guided their little vessel back into the cavern. Valerius was delighted and had already decided to sail his new 'sea chariot' back to Valeria. Boltar was appointed captain-much to his delight as well-and his old crew from the Elusive elected to continue aboard the new vessel. Eomer, however, decided the new ship was a bit much for two little ones, herself and her nurse. Valerius was disappointed but had to admit, finally, that *Valadator* was more suitable for his young family. But as he left the palace nursery, Illana presented herself in the hallway and begged a quick audience. She, it seemed, wanted to sail on the new ship as well.

At first, Valerius dismissed it out of hand. There was no room aboard such a vessel for a young maiden, she had no experience with this kind of sailing, she might be ill, she might fall overboard when the vessel heeled. But the girl was persistent and to all of his objections, she offered reasonable arguments. She and her maid had no more privacy aboard *Valadator* than they would aboard the *Kantar*, she loved the sailing they had done so far, had not felt a trace of illness, had gotten her sea legs after just a couple days, and was just aching to see how this new type of ship sailed.

"But you'll be all alone among a bunch of men," he protested.

"No more so than I am now," she said. "I have my maid, and, of course, you'll be there."

"Well, there's no room for idlers aboard such a vessel. We all have a job to do."

"I know how to cook, your majesty. I can help with that!"

Finally, with the girl in tow, he returned to the nursery and asked Eomer: was a vessel like that any place for a young maiden?

The queen looked up from her suckling babe and smiled softly. "You're asking someone who sailed from Kantar to Dulcai in a twenty foot open catumaran," she said, to which Valerius, High King and Emperor, had nothing to reply.

And thus it was settled. Illana would make passage in the *Kantar*.

Chapter 5

Thanks to Koltar's foresight, provisioning the *Kantar* was quickly accomplished and they left the next day in company with *Valadator*. In the light morning breeze, the larger vessel kept her crew at the oars and pulled away from *Kantar*. But as the breeze built, the other's sails filled. She put her shoulder down, and amidst much cheering from her crew, soon passed her huge consort.

By nightfall, she was just a distant white speck under the rising moon. Grumwald watched her from his quarterdeck until the darkness swallowed her, then turned to see the children's nurse standing by the taffrail, looking out over the phosphorescence of their moonlit wake. He went over to wish her good evening and hoped she was well. "Tis a beautiful night," he said.

"Indeed it is," said the woman, Brenda. "And I am very well, thank you, your lordship."

"I'm glad to hear it, ma'am, and no need to call me 'lordship,'" he said and leaned against the rail by her side. "I'm just an old sailor, after all."

"I wouldn't call being Commodore of the High King's fleet and Captain of the *Valadator* 'just an old sailor.'"

"Aye, well," said Grumwald, embarrassed by the praise. "I do my duty, but I'm still an old sailor for all that. My young prince is asleep then?"

"Yes, he finally gave in about half an hour ago," and she laughed softly. "He's afraid he'll miss something if he goes to sleep, that one."

"Aye, he's a cracker, he is. Already thinks he's Admiral of the fleet."

"And no wonder," the nurse teased, "the way he's feted and spoiled around here."

"Well, he takes to the sea, he does. You can see, even as young as he is, that he already understands the ship."

"Surely you don't mean... ?"

"That he knows every line and brace? No, no, of course not. But he has the feel of it, you can tell. He knows when she's running free, when she's laboring." Grumwald saw that she didn't follow him. "Look," he said, "most people look around a ship like this and they see lines and timbers and oars and men running all about, and they think it's just a huge brute of a thing that we can just drive when and where we will. But a ship like this-any ship, really, and especially that fancy thing his Majesty just went tearing away on-is, well, it's a delicate thing. As massive as her timbers look to us, they're nothing to the sea. And as thick as our shrouds, as heavy our sails, they are nothing to the might of the wind. The sea pushes us this way, the wind that, and we set our sails and trim our helm to make her go where we want. It's a question of balance and harmony. I'm not sure I can explain it. I'm a better sailor than I am a talker."

"No, no, go on," she said, turning towards him. "This is interesting. I've never heard a ship talked of like this before."

"Well, all right, let me take another tack and see if I can get it better. You see the mainsail there? You see how it's set? Well, look you the wind: it's right off our beam, coming straight in from the sea to the land. So we've set our sail to make the most of it, see? If we braced the yard around more and set the sail flatter to the wind, all it would do is push against the ship, drive our rail down and strain the rig. But it wouldn't push us forward, see? And if we went the other way and eased the sheets, why then the sail would lose the wind and she'd luff until she was in tatters and we wouldn't do a knot. So it's balance. You want to use the wind to drive the ship, but not strain her, you see? And some people just have a feel for when she's right. Valerius has it, King Koltar certainly has, and so has young Valerian."

"How do you 'feel it'?" Brenda leaned her elbow on the rail and was gazing up at Grumwald's face. Though it was scarred and grizzled in the moonlight, his eyes shone with warmth and animation. He, too, was standing much closer than he realized, and for now at least, was not feeling his ship at all.

"How? Why, it's everything, really. You feel it in the deck and the helm; you can see her labor when she wants trim. When there's a sea running, you can hear her complain and groan, and sometimes, when it comes on to blow, you can hear the rigging scream."

"You speak of 'her' as if she were a live woman."

"Seamen have always spoke thus, and the ship does seem alive. Though why a woman I wouldn't venture to say."

"You mean you're just too polite to say."

"Well, meaning no disrespect, ma'am, but she does have her moods." Brenda laughed at this, a full-throated, merry laugh and Grumwald smiled to see the light in her eyes, the sheen of her hair as it shook in the moonlight. It made her look young, he thought. And pretty. "Is this your first trip, then?" he asked.

"First long trip, yes. I sailed on short hops before-Dulac to Zagorbia when my husband joined his Majesty, and then, of course, with the Queen once Valerian was born."

"Is your husband in the crew, then?" he asked, a sudden alarm in his voice."

"No," she said, turning back once more to gaze out over the shining wake. "He fell at Zagorbia."

"Oh, I am sorry to hear that."

"Many have fallen," she said, straightening her back and turning away from the wake and her grief. "But Fantar is gone and that's what's important. If we can make the world better for the little ones, it will have been worth it."

"Aye, and we will. His Majesty will, to be sure. But don't give us old ones up for lost. We're not done quite yet!" And in the moonlight, he could see a smile soften her face.

"No, we're not," she said. "No, we are not."

In the morning, Valerius and his schooner were out of sight. But far to the north, cruising the waters of the Inland Sea south of Palemia, another of His Majesty's war galleys, the *Steiger*, exercised her oars. She was a medium sized craft with a double bank of 60 oars and a crew of about eighty. Her assigned duty, which she exercised faithfully, was to patrol the waters off the mouth of the river Sule and protect shipping in the area from the ravages of pirates.

It was not arduous duty. Two years after the fall of Fantar, the reconstituted empire under Valerius was still very much in its honeymoon phase. Hopes of prosperity still kept many would-be malcontents on the straight and narrow, and many of those beyond redemption, like the men whose backs propelled the *Steiger* through the quiet morning waters, had had their day and were now chained to the benches of His Majesty's fleet. And in any event, what pirates there were avoided the waters this close to Valeria.

So the *Steiger*'s duty was very much routine and an easy billet for the man standing on her tiny quarterdeck, Captain Malecium. But that was not to say he took it easy. No, a ship of war was nothing were it not ready for that eventuality, wherever and however it might appear. And *Steiger* was ready. That was why the crew exercised at the oars three times a day, why rigid discipline was maintained even in these easy times, why the formality of naval traditions was insisted upon even among the officer's mess. In Malecium's view, it was the lack of these same virtues that had made the old Empire vulnerable to Fantar in the first place, and after spending twenty years of his life trying to restore legitimate rule, and after having at last landed for himself a position of some eminence and security in the new order, he was damned if he would jeopardize it by allowing even the least laxity among his rag tag crew. Who, after all, had he been fighting against all these years if not many of these same wretches who now sat chained to his oars?

So *Steiger* shot through the quiet waters at twenty-five strokes per minute for a full turn of the half-hour glass. Afterwards, the sweeps were secured, sail set, and after a quick tour of inspection by her captain, breakfast was served to all hands. Malecium himself retired to his cramped cabin where his steward had waiting a plate of fresh eggs and ham. The crew ate watery porridge mixed with the leavings of the previous night's stew.

So life was good for Malecium. At forty-five, he had reached an age where his sense of propriety had solidified with his stoutness of his figure. He was quite confident of his feelings on most subjects and, at heart, felt a great contentment at having achieved such moral rectitude. He was, he knew, in harmony with the will of the gods themselves, and the fact that he had not yet been rewarded with the laurels of high command was, he was sure, but an accident of the times. He had but to stay his present course for a few more years and they would be his. Nor was this any particular trial, as time at sea also meant time away from his shrew of a wife.

Breakfast over and his digestive system relieved of its daily burden, Malecium turned his attention to duty and marched from his cabin. But he stopped with a single foot over the threshold and his hand on the cabin door. There, not six feet away from him and squatting with his back towards him, was his mate, Condor, once again deep in conversation with one of the galley slaves. This was preposterous and in direct contravention of his orders! A half-dozen times at least he had spoken to Condor about exactly this flagrancy. Why he would want to associate with such filth when he was otherwise such an exemplary officer was beyond Malecium. Still, it was gross insubordination and not to be born.

"Master Condor," he snapped. "I will see you in my cabin, Sirah. Now!"

The mate squeezed his huge frame through the cabin door and stood hunched over under the deck beams while his captain fumed before him. It was Malecium's way to first intimidate subordinates with wrathful silence in such situations before delivering the lightning bolts of his displeasure. But on Condor-perhaps because of his inordinate size in such a confined space, or perhaps because of the way his dark, brooding eyes seemed to bore right through one to that tiny, hidden place where fear lived, and awaken it-the tactic did not seem to have much effect. Malecium found himself coughing and clearing his throat in order to regain that deep, authoritative tone his voice had suddenly lost.

And indeed, he was at a loss. This man, Condor, was the best of his crew by far. From a raw recruit when he came aboard two years before, the man seemed to have absorbed seamanship through his very pores. It was like he had been born to it in another life and had only to see a thing to know it. And he had leadership qualities, too. Though always quiet and reserved-some might say brooding-he emanated confidence and whatever activity was underway, men seemed naturally to follow his lead. When the previous mate had unfortunately fallen overboard during heavy weather one night some few weeks back, there was no question-indeed hardly even any choice, it seemed-as to who would replace him.

So why would a man with so many qualities, a man so recently landed on the upward path and with such promise before him, risk it all by deliberate disobedience? It made no sense and perplexity further cut Malecium's anger. Still, discipline demanded action. Malecium cleared his throat again.

"I fail to see, Sir," he began, posting himself before Condor as ramrod straight and formidable as possible, "why you feel it necessary to disregard my orders-my repeated orders, Sir! -and consort with such filth as are on the benches. Explain yourself!"

But Condor did not react to the posturing either. His eyes did not so much as flicker but bored into Malecium with a dark energy that was decidedly disconcerting. It was all Malecium could do to keep himself from taking a step back.

"Well!" he said, nerving himself.

"Because they tell me things I want to know," said Condor, his voice a quiet rumble, his eyes steady and dark.

"What kinds of 'things,' Sirah. I demand to know!"

"They tell me about Fantar. One of them knew him."

"Fantar! That fish-spawn, may he rot in hell! Why would you want to know about him?"

The dark force in Condor's eyes seemed to flare into a sudden malevolence and his face, without changing expression, hardened. His body seemed suddenly to loom and Malecium felt a tinge of fear. "Because," said the dark voice, "he was my father."

Now real fear leapt into Malecium's face like sudden fire and he took a step back. It was true! He knew in that instant that the face before him-a face now beginning to seethe with a deep wrath of its own-was the very image of that other face whose hated likeness he had seen defacing public monuments and buildings for too many years. He had never made the connection before but there was no doubt: it was the face of Fantar.

He began to quail in spite of himself and backed away until the bulkhead of his sleeping quarters stopped him. Condor advanced upon him. "You should not have pushed me, little man," he said, his voice still quiet, but now with a sharp edge, like a dagger. "And you should not have said that about him."

Malecium could not have defended himself had he tried. As it was, his bowels turned to liquid and he froze like a rabbit as Condor's huge hands reached for his neck. It was over quickly: The massive muscles in Condor's forearms bunched, his fingers flexed. He gave a quick shake and Malecium's neck snapped like a chicken bone. Condor released him and he flopped to the floor like a rag doll, his eyes glassy and fixed. He made only the slightest squeak as he died, like a small animal, pitifully protesting the sudden appearance of eternity.

Condor made sure there was nothing of value on Malecium's person, and then unceremoniously dumped his corpse out the stern windows. The helmsman, standing on the deck above, never even heard the splash.

Condor sat for a time on the narrow bench behind Malecium's desk and surveyed the galley's cabin with satisfaction. It was a tiny, cramped affair, occupying the narrow space between the captain's sleeping quarters to starboard and the mate's even tinier quarters to port. In addition to the desk, there was a small wardrobe secured to the outboard bulkhead, and on the inboard side where the weight of its contents would be most nearly amidships, a large arms locker. In there, Condor knew, were sixty boarding pikes, enough naval cutlasses to arm the crew several times over, and the ship's strong box. The key, Condor also knew, was in the drawer by his left hand. He pulled it out, looked at it thoughtfully, and dropped it into the pouch at his belt.

The other key aboard the *Steiger* was an iron rod hanging from a hook by the cabin door. This was about six inches in length with the bottom inch bent over at right angles and a wooden handle secured to the top. It opened the locks that secured the galley slaves' chains. Condor palmed this as he left the cabin.

Closing the door carefully behind him, he walked nonchalantly back to the last row of benches and squatted down beside the slave with whom he had been speaking when Malecium accosted him. He spoke quietly with the man for a few moments, set something on the deck by his foot, then climbed back up to the quarterdeck and resumed his watch.

It was a pleasant, midsummer's morning with the warm sun casting a golden sparkle across the ruffling sea and a few white, fleecy clouds drifting lazily across the deep blue of the sky. The wind was still off the land at this time of the morning, and Condor stationed himself on the windward side of the quarterdeck and looked off to the north where the distant shore lay wrapped in haze. It would be just possible, he thought, for a good swimmer to cover that distance, and ordered the helmsman to alter course three points to southward.

The watch passed quietly, the galley slaves lolling about on their benches and snatching whispers of conversation behind the backs of the patrolling guards; the on-deck crew at ease at their stations along the catwalk; the off-watch crew on the raised foredeck or sleeping in their cramped quarters below; the lookout standing atop the cross-tree, leaning back comfortably against the sling which held him to the mast. The wind was fitful and the great sail filled and flapped, filled and flapped as *Steiger* glided slowly southeastward over the quiet Inland Sea.

Just before noon, the wind failed altogether, and Condor ordered oars. The steward, just then coming aft along the oar deck with the captain's lunch on a tray, had to duck and dodge the butt ends of the long sweeps as their blades were thrust out through the ports and slid into the sea. At the first stroke, the ship shot ahead, and as the crew swarmed up the mast to furl the now impeding sail, the steward balanced his tray on one hand and opened the door to the captain's cabin with the other.

He was not surprised to find it unoccupied. It was quite the usual thing for Malecium to indulge in a morning nap, especially after standing the early watch, as he had this morning. The steward set the tray down on the tiny desk and opened the door to the captain's sleeping quarters. Now he was perplexed, for this, too, was unoccupied. Had the captain already gone on deck and he not seen him? Leaving the luncheon tray where it sat, he climbed the steep steps to the quarterdeck, and when no captain was there either, cautiously approached the mate at his station by the quarterdeck rail.

"Beg'in pardon, sur," he said, knuckling his forehead and bobbing a slight bow, "but has you seen the cap'n, sur? I've his lunch ready, sur, an' you know how particular he is, sur... "

The mate turned a face of perfect perplexity to the steward. "He's not in his cabin?"

"No, sur. Nor have I seen him anywheres, sur."

"Come, come, Sardin, this ship is not that big. You can't have lost the captain!"

"Sur?" The steward took a step back now from the strange, almost gleeful expression which had come over the huge mate's face.

"Do you hear that, men?" Condor boomed out, his voice filling the ship, stopping the oars in mid-stroke and bringing the on-deck watch to their feet. "Sardin here says he has lost the captain. Has anyone seen the captain?"

Silence filled the ship fore and aft as *Steiger* glided to a halt in the empty sea, all eyes on the mate.

"Captain? Oh, Captain?" Condor sing-songed into the silence. His face held a huge joke he could barely contain. "No captain? Well, Sardin, I don't know what you've done, but if there's no captain, we'll have to elect a new one-won't we, men!"

This last was directed at the sixty slaves massed below on their benches. With a roar of assent, they leapt to their feet-feet whose fetters were somehow no longer secured to the deck-and tackled the stunned guards. In moments the ship was theirs, and Sardin, now firmly in the grip of two burly mutineers, watched in amazement as the face of Condor spread in a wide, manic grin.

"You said you had lunch for the captain?" said Condor, turning on him.

"Aye, sur... In the cabin, sur."

"Then you had better get ready to serve it, don't you think?"

Sardin was not sure yet what had transpired, why he was being held, what had happened to Malecium. But he knew how to obey orders and that was enough for him. "Aye, sur," he said, and as the mutineers released him, turned and went below.

"Chain those fools to the benches there!" Condor commanded. "And get this ship under way. Let's see how they like pulling the haft of an oar."

"What course, sir?" called the man to whom Condor had given the key and who was now directing the helm.

"What course? What course? That depends on what you will, my friends." And here Condor paused to survey the entire ship and her new crew. "What will you, my friends?" he said, meeting their eyes in turn. "Will you have freedom?" And the newly released slaves chorused assent. "Will you have riches?"

"Aye!" came the reply, louder this time.

"Will you have wine and women?"

"Aye!" came the reply, thunderous now with cheering.

"Then we head east!" yelled Condor over the tumult. "East for plunder!"

"But wait!" he yelled again and the noise subsided. "Hear this, too. You were chained for serving one they called the Bastard. Aye, Fantar the Bastard, they called him. Fantar One-Eye. Now, know you that it is the bastard son of that bastard who has set you free!"

And as the impact of this statement dawned on them, cheering began again, slowly at first like the first tiny flicker of flame under dry kindling, but then flaring quickly into a wild, roaring blaze.

Chapter 6

On their fourth day out from the Hidden Valley, just after four bells of the morning watch, the lookout atop the mainmast on the schooner *Kantar* spied the peak of the thousand foot promontory at Zagorbia-which marked the entrance to the Inland Sea-rising from the blue distance of the horizon. They had made excellent time and if the wind held, stood a good chance of reaching Valeria before nightfall. Koltar's innovative craft had proven herself a lovely vessel in all respects; fast, comfortable, easy to handle; and as they had found two days before when a series of squalls had set the wind to screaming, marvelously stiff and weatherly. Valerius was delighted with her, as was her nominal captain, Boltar. In fact, the two vied with each other for time at the helm, leaving the crew-whose normal task it was-quite put out. Since when did the High King and a senior Captain steer their own ships? It was unseemly.

But it was also exhilarating and Valerius suspected-quite rightly-that a good part of the crew's pretended umbrage lay in the fact that they enjoyed steering *Kantar* as much as he did. The ship flew along before the wind with such grace and power, balanced so adroitly between wind and water, was so responsive to the lightest touch of her helm, that her qualities transmitted themselves to the man at her wheel, imbuing him with a tremendous sense of joy and well-being. To control a thing of such power and beauty was to partake of it, and for Valerius, who had the helm that morning, the simple act of sailing this vessel gave him precisely that sense of freedom and relaxation he had sought when he left for Dulcai in the first place. Gone were the pressures of state, though he knew well that the faster this little ship sailed, the sooner he would face them again. Gone, too, were the dark shadows and that sense of impending evil that had so weighed on him in Dulcai. In the light of this fine morning, with the sun warm on his face, the wind ruffling his hair, and with his strong hands lightly guiding *Kantar*'s wheel, all seemed right with the world.

All seemed right as well with Boltar and young Illana, he noted with a quiet smile. Although Boltar had behaved with the strictest propriety toward the Queen's royal niece, it was quite clear he was helpless before her. His eye followed her every move, and whenever her eye chanced to meet his, his face lit up as from a sudden burst of the sun. They spent much time in company and as the voyage progressed, seemed to weave about themselves a cocoon of solitude that was almost magical. It seemed as if they were the only two beings aboard and the rest, King and crew, were but wraiths, enchained to order their realm. In short, they were in love.

Now the two sat at the forward end of the cockpit, he to port, she to starboard, tucked comfortably into the angle between the deckhouse and coaming boards. They did not touch-there being at least three feet between his knees and her feet, their closest proximity-yet in spirit they seemed as one. They spoke little as the morning progressed, but shared their little corner of the ship, and what they still supposed was their little secret, in consecrated silence.

Indeed, other than a single spate of heavy weather, the voyage had become such an idyll that there was very little communication among any on board. The events of the distant world and the novelty of their ship had all been talked through during the first days of the voyage and now, as the sea breeze filled in after the morning lull and *Kantar* swooped along on an easy reach, leaning into her work and soaring gracefully over the long, low swells, her crew-the King at the helm, the watch on deck lolling against the house forward, the lookout in his swaying eyrie aloft-all seemed caught up in a similar magic, and mesmerized by motion, moved as one with the ship.

It was Illana who finally broke the silence. "Is anybody hungry?" she said, uncurling her long legs from her corner and startling Valerius who was so intent on the set of the sails that he had lost track of his other surroundings.

"I am, now that you mention it," he said. "What would you like: I'll call the cook."

"No, I'll do it," said Illana climbing to her feet and starting towards the midship companionway. "If I don't do something I'll fall asleep. And besides, if the High King and his exalted captain can steer the boat, a lowly princess should be able to rummage about in the galley."

Boltar watched her make her way gracefully along the low side of the deck and climb nimbly down the companionway ladder, not removing his gaze until several long seconds after her head had disappeared. Valerius watched him, a half-smile on his face and a gentle jibe on the tip of his tongue. But he said nothing. For him to even acknowledge their relationship would be tantamount to consecrating it, a thing he was neither prepared to do, nor even sure he should.

There was much against such a liaison. For one thing, their stations in life were very different and while it was true Valerius could make of Boltar anything he wanted, such an act would have huge practical ramifications among the other officers in the fleet, not to mention robbing Reuters of a very valuable commodity. Illana was a very lovely young lady and while Valerius had grown quite fond of her very quickly, there remained the fact that as a princess, her duty in life was not to find love and raise children, but to be a willing tool of state: to cement alliances and raise heirs. It was not fair, of course, but it was the price of living royally, and while there was no potential enemy on the horizon who could be lured by her beauty, having that capability available could potentially save thousands of lives.

So it was no easy thing to allow the captain of his personal yacht to make away with a princess. Besides, a little shipboard romance was one thing (and he made quite sure it remained pure), but there was no telling what might happen once they docked in Valeria and Illana got a taste of life at the palace. Boltar might not seem such a romantic prince then.

"You want me to take a turn at the wheel?" asked Boltar, starting Valerius from his thoughts.

"Maybe in a bit," he said, rechecking the sails. But just then, the lookout called down.

"Deck there! Ship off the starboard bow."

"What do you make of her?" yelled Boltar, leaping to his feet.

"Appears to be a war galley, sir! Moving under oars."

The somnolent atmosphere aboard *Kantar* evaporated like a mist and tension filled the ship. Then, a few minutes later, the lookout yelled down again that the ship was flying a Valerian Naval Pennant and the crew relaxed. The two ships were closing at a rapid pace and soon the galley could be seen clearly from the deck. She was obviously a patrolling naval galley, but still, something did not seem right about her. As she neared they could see that while many of the oars were rowing in synch, others were not.

"Must have a bunch of raw hands aboard," said Boltar.

Valerius grunted in assent, but still something did not feel right. They both sensed it and exchanged questioning glances.

"Why doesn't she hail us?" asked Boltar as the ship drew near within voice range. The galley had angled towards their stern as it approached and now was turning with the obvious intention of coming along side.

"I don't know," said Valerius. "Hail them."

"Ahoy the galley!" Boltar yelled. "State your name and business!"

A gruff reply came from the galley's quarterdeck. "This is His majesty's galley of war, Revenge. Stand by to be boarded!"

Boltar and Valerius exchanged another glance. Neither had heard of a galley named Revenge. Across the narrowing waters, they could hear the bosun's mallets aboard the galley, picking up the tempo to overtake the sailing schooner. The ship surged closer, her clumsy oars pulling hard.

"This is His Majesty's schooner, *Kantar*," Boltar yelled back. "On official business bearing dispatches for Valeria. Stand off!"

"You are not familiar to us!" came the reply. "Stand to, I say!" The ship was close enough now for them to see the speaker, a large young man with a downy black beard.

"We'd better do as he says," Valerius said quietly. "It is his duty."

"Standing to!" yelled Boltar. Valerius turned the ship's bow up into the wind. The jib backed and her speed slackened. The galley glided closer and shipped her port oars. Hands stood at bow and stern, heaving lines and grappling hooks at the ready. It was clear she meant to board whether they would or no.

"Deck there!" came the sudden voice of the lookout again. His voice was hoarse and urgent, as if he was trying to make a whisper carry like a shout. "Her benchers are arming!"

This was definitely not normal. Even if this galley were manned by freemen, no naval ship would arm its entire crew to board and inspect an unresisting merchant vessel.

"Let go the starboard jib sheet!" Valerius yelled and spun the wheel hard to port. *Kantar*'s bow began to fall away from the encroaching galley just as her bowman heaved his grappling hook. It lodged on *Kantar*'s rail, just forward of amidships and several of the galley's crew began to haul taut the line.

Several things now happened in such quick succession that afterwards, Valerius was at a loss to explain them even though, in his memory, their separate components seemed to revolve in slow motion. *Kantar*'s sails caught the wind and filled with a pop. Her booms slammed to port and hands scrambled to trim her flogging jib sheet. She began to pull away, tightening the heaving line grappled to her rail and dragging the galley's bow closer. Other grapples soared through the narrowing space between the two hulls, lodging at various points along her starboard rail.

On the galley, armed boarders crowded the rail, shoving and yelling and waving pikes and swords in the air, while their captain, evidently the huge young man with the downy beard, thrust his way forward through them like a great bull, heading for the spot where the two hulls would meet. Valerius, Boltar, and another hand who was not trimming sail, leapt to the rail and began cutting lines and dislodging the grapples before they could be secured.

That's when Illana appeared on deck, carrying a luncheon tray.

The appearance of a beautiful young woman seemed to add frenzy to the howling mob aboard the galley, but it also distracted the men hauling the grappling lines just enough so the *Kantar*'s crew could heave all but the last of them into the sea. A crewman attacked this one, sawing away at it with his rigging knife.

It parted just as the galley's captain leapt like a great ape across the remaining eight or nine feet between the ships and landed on *Kantar*'s deck beside Illana, knocking her tray clear across the ship and into the sea. For days, the memory of that tray and its contents, spinning in the air, haunted Valerius.

Freed from the drag of the other ship, *Kantar* leapt ahead, and the galley, with no one at the oars, began quickly sliding astern before any more of its crewmen could follow their captain's lead. He, seeing the situation, tossed Illana over his shoulder like a sack of flour and began sprinting aft. Boltar leapt to stop him, dagger in hand, but Condor-for it was indeed he-lowered his shoulder, and using Illana as a battering ram, bowled Boltar out of the way. The blow slammed him back into the main mast and he settled in a heap on the pin rack at its foot. Valerius then dove for the man's legs, but missed as the huge renegade leapt, full-stride onto

113

Kantar's quarterdeck rail, and with an prodigious bound, hurled himself and his captive across the rapidly widening gap between the ships and into the arms of his screaming crewmen.

Meanwhile, with no one at her helm, *Kantar*'s bow began falling off rapidly to leeward. The ship heeled crazily in the stiff breeze, driving her port rail under water and spilling the unconscious Boltar into the scuppers. In seconds, she was at risk of gybing completely around and either breaking her rig from the sudden shock, or driving right back towards the floundering galley. Crawling along the side of the tilting deckhouse and sprawling into the cockpit, Valerius grabbed wheel and brought her back under control. *Kantar*'s rail came up and as she came onto the wind, foam began to curl about her forefoot and she shot away to windward, putting nearly a quarter mile between her and the galley before the latter was even able to get its oars back in the water and begin pursuit.

Bloody, wet and bedraggled, Boltar hauled himself to his feet by the main shrouds, and staggered back to the cockpit. He was bent over in pain, clutching the ribs on his left side.

"Break out Koltar's fire bombs!" Valerius snapped, looking over his shoulder at the galley, now pulling hard in their wake.

"But Illana... " Boltar cried before a savage look from Valerius jolted home the absurdity of his thought. He turned, calling for all hands, and hobbled off below.

Valerius ordered the sails trimmed just a bit, then turned the wheel over to Boltar's best helmsman and went below to get his own great falchion and a battle cap. When he came back on deck, Boltar and a crewman were busy setting the bow staves into the stern rail. Fresh blood was dribbling down Boltar's back from his matted hair. Along the cockpit seat on the low side, were several boxes of Koltar's firebombs. The galley was visibly closer.

"She's overhauling us."

"I know," Boltar gasped, glancing quickly astern.

"Fall off just a bit," said Valerius to the helmsman, "you're pinching her."

The man nodded and nudged the wheel to port. *Kantar*'s rail dipped a bit more and they could feel her accelerate.

But it was not enough. Valerius and Boltar studied the pursuing galley for several minutes. "She's still gaining," Boltar said.

"Aye, but how long can she keep it up?"

"I don't know, but look at her oars. They're all pulling in unison now."

"He's probably put his mutineers back on the benches. Must have been the former crew we saw rowing before."

"Well, we'll see how good they are. If they can keep the pace they should be on us in half a glass."

"Let's let him think so," said Valerius. Boltar shot him a glance and realized, from Valerius' aggressive stance and the way his jaw was thrust out towards the pursuing ship, that they were no longer just trying to get away, and his heart lifted. Perhaps Illana was not lost after all. Hobbling forward, Boltar sat down heavily on the top of the deckhouse. It was difficult for him to draw breath.

Valerius studied the pursuing galley for some minutes more, counting her oar strokes and watching the distance diminish between them, and then turned back to Boltar.

"Let's let 'em get close enough to smell our butts, then when they get really, really tired, see if we can't lead them on a merry chase."

"Where to?"

"Well, I don't know that yet. Masthead there!" he cried then. "Any sign of *Valadator*?"

"No, Your Majesty," came the reply.

"Well, we'll see," he murmured. "Maybe we'll just have to burn the son-of-a-bitch," and went back to studying the pursuing ship. Silence fell aboard *Kantar* then as the sand trickled slowly through the half-hour glass and the galley kept up its steady pace astern, drawing inexorably closer. Trying to ignore his pain, Boltar kept shifting his gaze between King and enemy and saw, when Valerius did, the first sign of their oars faltering: the line of blades on the return stroke became uneven, and the splashes ragged when they hit the water. He could imagine the men at their looms, gasping for breath. Still, the galley had drawn almost within bowshot.

"Captain Boltar," said Valerius, a smug look on his face, "what say we ease our sheets and fall off a bit."

"Aye, sir!" said Boltar, forcing a grin that was more grimace.

At full speed, or about thirty strokes per minute, a war galley could exceed twelve knots, faster than the *Kantar* by about three knots on this point of sail. But that was considered ramming speed and how long any particular galley could keep it up depended on the conditioning of her crew. *Kantar* sailed her best with the wind nearly abeam, either slightly forward on a close reach, or slightly aft on a broad reach. When she sailed close to the direction of the wind, or close hauled, as they had been, or sailed directly before the wind on a run, she was less efficient and sailed slower. Now, as Boltar ordered the helm down and the crew slacked off on the various tackles that controlled the sails, *Kantar* shot ahead.

"That will do for the moment," said Valerius. "I think we're matching her now." And as Boltar looked back, he could see the galley was no longer gaining, but maintaining her distance, and that her oar strokes were even more ragged.

"He'll have to slack off soon, Sire, or risk fouling his oars and splintering some shafts."

"Aye. And when he does, we'll fall off more southward and try to draw him back towards *Valadator*."

So that was the game. Heading south would put the wind on the beam. That meant the galley would also be able to set sail. Under sail and with fresh oars, the galley could easily overtake *Kantar*. They could still probably set her afire, but that would

117

mean certain death for Illana. But if they could keep the rowers exhausted by going to windward whenever they tried to sprint, they might just be able to lead the renegade galley back within range of *Valadator*. And if *Valadator* could close and board, there was a chance they could get Illana back unharmed. It was a slim chance-given the way the galley crew howled when they first saw her, there was a good chance she had been ravaged already-but any chance was better than none.

If their large young adversary agreed to the game. And there was also a good chance he would not. How they played it was critical. If he thought the task was hopeless, or if he thought he was being led, he would surely give up the chase; unless, of course, Illana had said the High King was aboard, which would make the quarry that much more valuable. But Boltar did not think she would. Then, they were already very far off shore-even from the masthead, the distant mountains were only a low smudge on the horizon-and few sailors were brazen enough to risk that. His renegade crew might insist he turn back. Unless they could be convinced that their quarry was equally leery of venturing too far to sea.

That was the key, the fine line they had to balance on for their ruse to work.

As expected, as soon as the galley's commander saw that *Kantar* was now matching his speed, he dropped the pace and began to turn away. That's when Valerius and Boltar turned south. As the booms swung further out to port, Boltar hobbled back to stand beside Valerius at the stern rail, watching the galley and waiting for a sign that it would turn back and resume the chase.

But Condor didn't take the bait. The galley continued turning north, then northeastward. Her mainsail dropped and filled and she began bearing away.

"Damn his eyes!" said Valerius.

"Shall we come about and follow?" asked Boltar. He was fearful of what that might mean, but terrified also, at seeing even more distance grow between him and Illana. What would be her fate if they didn't pursue?

"Can Illana swim?" Valerius asked.

"I don't know, Your Majesty."

"Masthead! Any sign of *Valadator* yet?"

"No, Your Majesty."

"Damn!" Valerius turned and studied his young captain, his eyes softening at the agony he saw in the young man's face. "Boltar," he said, "even if we managed to set her afire, and even if Illana could swim and managed to leap overboard, there would still be too many of them in the water for us to try and rescue her: we'd be overwhelmed."

"I know, my Lord. I had the same thought."

"I'm sorry, lad."

"Aye, sir. Thank you."

"Our best bet, I think is to run down Grumwald and set *Valadator* on her tail."

"Aye, my Lord."

"But right now, I think we should get you below before you fall overboard."

"I'm all right," Boltar gasped, but as *Kantar* dropped off the face of a wave, he staggered, winced as a sharp pain stabbed into his side, and collapsed into Valerius' arms. Two crewmen helped the King carry him below while astern, the galley bearing Illana sailed off towards the distant horizon.

Chapter 7

In all the excitement of the chase, Illana had been tossed into the captain's sleeping quarters and forgotten. She huddled there in a corner of the bunk, listening to the wild slamming of the oars, the curses of the men, and the protesting creaks of timber as the ship was driven through the tumbling sea. She was terrified, so terrified she could not even think, but wrapped herself into a ball and hid her face against her knees.

After a time, however-when the door did not immediately burst open to knife-wielding murderers, or worse-she opened her eyes and stared numbly at the rumpled linen coverlet on the bed. It was of a coarse material, loosely woven and stained yellow with age, not at all like the bed linens at home-linens, she thought with a sudden lump in her throat, she would likely never see again. But such thoughts would lead only to despair, and she forced her mind away, back to the insignificance of detail. Here and there, she noted prickly bits of straw poking through the mattress, and where she sat, there was hardly any straw at all. After a time, she shifted position, and steeling her determination, lifted her chin to her knees and began looking around her tiny prison.

It was a plain compartment of unadorned plank on one side and the curved hull on the other. Light came from a single candle, guttering in a holder by the door. Beside the bunk there was just room enough to stand and dress, and at the far end, where the stern flared out over the inward curve of the hull, was the captain's private head. At sight of this, hope flared and she hurriedly unlatched the watertight cover. But though she could look down through the hole to the sea surging past, there was no way she could squeeze herself through. Flopping back onto the bunk, she gave way to tears.

She started up again with a change in the motion of the ship. They were turning, it felt, and she heard the command to ship oars. In moments, an eerie quiet descended and the frequency of the ship's pitching decreased. They had turned around, she knew, and were traveling now in the direction of the waves. They had probably set the sail as well. Did that mean they had given up the chase? Suddenly her heart began to hammer as she heard someone enter the outer cabin and latch the door. Retreating to the furthest corner of the sleeping cabin, she wedged herself into the corner over the still open toilet hole and fastened her eyes on the door.

She had only a moment to wait before the door opened and the huge young man who had grabbed her squeezed himself through and sat down casually on the bunk.

"I hope I haven't caught you at an inappropriate moment," he said with a leer.

Illana had not really seen her captor before now, it had all happened so quickly. She had heard some commotion while she had been preparing the food down below, but there was always a lot of noise when *Kantar* tacked or changed sails, so she had thought nothing of it. When she climbed on deck, she had been startled to see the other ship closing alongside with armed men lining the rail. Then, there was this huge brute who leapt upon her and snatched her away like a sack and all she had really seen from then on was a confused kaleidoscope of upside down feet and flashes of deck and sea. There was no doubt that this was the man, however, and at the sight of him and his insolent grin, her anger flared.

"How dare you!" she spat. "Do you have any idea what you've done? Do you know what the King is going to do when he catches you?"

"What king would that be, my lady?"

Illana caught herself. Obviously, the fellow had no idea whose ship he had attacked. And something told her it would be better if she did not say. "King Reuters of Dulcai," she said in her haughtiest manner. "My uncle."

"Ah," he said, leaning back against the wall and casually stretching his massive leg along the bed, "so you count yourself a princess, do you? And I suppose you think that will make you so valuable I will ransom you off unharmed."

Illana could not help but stare at the leg, at the bulging muscles of calf and thigh, at the thick, curly hair along its length, and-before she could tear her eyes away-at what his posture had exposed under his tunic. A cold fear shuddered through her and constricted her throat. She could not speak.

"Well, my little princess," he said leaning forward and lowering his voice to a harsh whisper, "let me set your mind at rest about a few things. It will be easier for you that way."

There was something about his eyes that was strangely compelling. They were at once dark and brooding, yet flickered with a deep inner light, an intelligence that was cold and malevolent, yet projected a kind of searing heat. She had never seen eyes like these before and found she could not look away.

"You see, my lady," he continued, sliding closer along the bed, "I dare what I desire. Whatever I desire. If I want gold from your dear Uncle Reuters, why I'll go and take it. If I want sweet favors from you, why, I'll take those, too. And if I decide to make you a plaything for my men, or toss you into the sea, then that is what I will do. You see? Whatever I desire."

Illana was paralyzed. Her mouth was open, but she could not speak. Her eyes stared, but she could see nothing beyond the power of his eyes. And though she heard, she really only comprehended that she was totally, utterly at this man's mercy. She had no power, no will to resist.

"But you know what, my princess?" he said, reaching out his great beefy hand and sliding it gently along the length of her inner thigh. "I don't want to take you now like a bull mounting a cow. In fact," he said, his mesmeric eyes boring into hers, "I don't want to take you at all. What I want is for you to give yourself to me. In fact, I'm going to wait for a more appropriate time-when you will kneel to me."

It was nearly dusk when the lookout on *Kantar* spotted *Valadator* working her way north towards Zagorbia. Valerius came about alongside the great ship in growing darkness and sailed up close to confer with an anxious Grumwald. News that the princess Illana had been taken stunned the crew of the huge trireme-and Queen Eomer-and the evening's quiet aboard was instantly shattered as the men scrambled to their oars and began pulling in lusty pursuit.

In the light evening air, *Valadator* soon outdistanced *Kantar* and Valerius went below to check on Boltar. He found him conscious and in some discomfort, but anxious for news. There was not much comfort in that either.

"I'm afraid he's got too good a start on us," Valerius said

Boltar grunted and shifted a bit onto his side. It seemed he had cracked or broken several ribs when he hit the mast. It was very painful for him to draw breath. "With a good wind and *Valadator* under oars, we should be able to make up some of that," he said.

"Aye, but how much? And where is the fellow headed? It doesn't look like he put out from Zagorbia, and I doubt he'll lurk about Valeria. So that leaves the entire Inland Sea open before him. Of course," he said after a bit, "there is a chance he'll just hold her for ransom." But he didn't sound convincing.

Boltar nodded, a different kind of pain filling in behind his eyes. "Will you follow, my lord?"

"We'll do more than follow, lad. We'll set the whole fleet out after this rogue. But there's naught either of us can do this night. You're best setting your mind at ease as best you can, so you can mend. Hopefully, we'll get the chance to take another swing at this fellow."

"From your lips to the gods' ears, Sire."

"Aye. Well, you sleep now. Hasheb has the watch and everything is secure."

Valerius went to his own cabin then, but lay for a long time watching a patch of sea-reflected moonlight play about the deck beams overhead from the open port by his bunk. He blamed himself entirely for the incident. He should never have allowed an unknown ship to come so close. Two years of peace had made him complacent. But you couldn't be complacent at sea, or as High King. No matter what you had, there were always those willing to take it, always those who cared not a whit for what others had built, what peace others sought. The sea at least, as implacable as it was, was also impartial in its power. Only men pursued evil.

The patch of pale light skittered across the overhead as a stronger gust heeled the ship, and as his eyes followed it, they caught sight of the Eye stone hanging from a peg on the bulkhead. It looked dull and flat in the blue darkness of the cabin, like some piece of flint or chert you could pick up in a field, not a thing of power at all. Could he have foreseen this attack were he master of the Eye, he wondered? And how many other attacks to come?

At some point in his reverie, he passed over into sleep, and as often happens when we lay awake late worrying, his cares followed him into that other state, and he had a series of disquieting, oppressive dreams. At one point, he even called out a warning to someone and startled the watch on deck overhead. Later, he found himself walking through a dark wood and felt a presence, as if he were being followed. He saw shadows, then a dark figure lurking among the trees. Several times he ran after it, sword in hand, but there was nothing there. Then he was in a narrow defile-or was it the mines of Dulcai? -and suddenly the shadow was there before him, looming over him. He turned to run but the shadow was there behind him. Then the defile was a small cavern and the shadow like a great bird hovering over him. He held up the Eye, but it was powerless, a thing of stone. The shadow descended, blackness enveloping him, and he bolted upright in bed, panting for breath. There on the wall was the Eye stone, pulsing and flickering in the morning light. He stared at it, thinking hard, but the stuff of his dreams faded like darkness with the dawn.

The morning sea was clear of ships, except for a few fishing craft close in under the loom of the land, and there, standing proud off the starboard bow, was the tall gray promontory of Zagorbia. To the north and east, clear and sparkling under the morning sun, opened the vast Inland Sea, and farther to the north, not yet even a smudge on the horizon, lay the northern shore, and a half day's sail beyond lay Valeria, royal seat and capital of the Empire. They had passed *Valadator* again during the night, and the great trireme now labored along in their wake, her rowers exhausted from their long night's pull.

The breeze freshened from the southwest, bringing with it a few high cumulus clouds. Valerius took the helm again as the sheets were eased far out to starboard, and *Kantar* skipped away on a broad reach. *Valadator* folded her oars but began falling rapidly behind the fleet schooner, and after only a short break, the rowers bent back to their tasks. On her quarterdeck, Grumwald paced back and forth before the helm, his face grim. By the weather rail, Eomer and the children stood with Brenda the nurse, looking anxiously forward as if the mysterious pirate ship would appear at any moment. Eomer knew better than most what terrors her young cousin faced, and her heart went out to her over the empty waters.

When the great harbor at Valeria opened before them later that afternoon, they found *Kantar* already securely at anchor and a bustle of activity underway. The High King had not been idle. A barge bearing the royal pennant led them to an open dock where a fresh crew and a squadron of armed soldiers waited. Three other war galleys were being similarly manned, and as *Valadator*'s lines snaked ashore, Valerius himself vaulted onto her deck.

"Have the Queen's baggage taken ashore immediately," he ordered. "Commodore, I have a fresh crew here for you, fresh stores and water, and three other galleys at your disposal. I hate to send you off without so much as touching shore, but I want that pirate!"

"If he can be found, Your Majesty, I will find him," said Grumwald, and before the half-hour glass had been turned once more, *Valadator* and her consorts were back at sea, heading east.

The fleecy cumulus clouds of the morning filled in as the day progressed and by evening had overspread the western Inland Sea. As darkness descended, thick black cloud masses swirled over the waters of the river Sule, obscuring, then revealing, a bright, gibbous moon. In the intermittent light, the war galley *Steiger* snaked her way up river and nosed into the tiny stone jetty at the hamlet of Koth. It was a sleepy little town, a cluster of stone buildings and mud huts that served as the mercantile center for a scattering of outlying farms. Built around the shore of a small cove where fishing boats bobbed quietly at anchor, there was a salt works for processing fish, a grain warehouse near the jetty, what passed for a general store (though in that age and place, most common folk subsisted of what they could make, grow, or what lay ready to hand), a smithy, a neglected temple, a dozen or more houses, and on the northern outskirts, a small stone tavern.

It was late when several hands leapt ashore from the *Steiger* and secured her lines to pilings along the jetty. They did not speak and moved furtively, as if their scant shapes were more visible than their ship. With equal stealth, forty or so armed men quickly filed ashore and proceeded north behind their towering captain. They marched in silence along the deserted street, holding their equipment tightly lest any rattles give them away. If any saw them from the darkened windows along the way, they gave no sign but hid themselves instead.

At the tavern, Condor detailed a dozen men to go around back, and approached the front entrance with the rest. The place had not changed in the two years since he had fled in rage and disgrace from its door, and as he stood waiting for his men to take their positions, memories of that night surged fresh in his mind. The moon broke from the clouds overhead just then, bathing the rough-hewn door in pale light, and as it angled across the heavy features of his face, Condor grinned wickedly and his dark eyes flashed with a deep malevolence.

Inside the tavern, the scene was much the same as it had been that night, absent three principal characters. Small groups of locals sat in desultory conversation over their mugs, some already dozing, while the burly barman sat on his stool, wishing the night would end-a cruel irony. In the hearth, embers of the evening's cooking fire settled into ash, and a cauldron of mutton stew congealed on the grate. The events of that other night and its subsequent violence, which had so enlivened conversation in the town for weeks afterwards, had faded to an occasional 'remember when', and 'I wonder what ever happened to.'

They were all about to find out.

Suddenly there was a tremendous bang and the patrons leapt from their seats as the door was kicked open and slammed against the wall. Roaring in anger, they spun to accost whatever idiot had dared cause them such a fright. But their exclamations died quickly as a huge armed figure ducked through the door and stood, arms akimbo, on the threshold. Behind him, they could see other armed figures pressing forward.

"Here, what's this!" said the barman, coming down from his stool and striding forward with angry determination. But he stopped abruptly several feet from the intruder. "Condor?"

"You want to order me out of your sty now, Harkey?" Condor said, his head brushing against the ceiling beams. He was leering wickedly. "Why don't you fetch your axe, Harkey? We'll see how you fare in a real fight."

But Harkey did not seem inclined to fetch the woodsman's axe he kept on a shelf beneath the bar. He was not a cowardly man, far from it. He had served his time as a conscript in Fantar's legions, and had stood again with the resistance when Gamlarch had faced the Imperial Guard at Dunlor. But neither was he a fool. He knew bad odds when he saw them, and he knew from the strange elation lighting Condor's face that here was a situation requiring tact and diplomacy.

"Why Condor, lad!" he said forcing his own face into a grin. "We've missed the likes of you around here, lad. How long has it been? Let me draw you an ale, on me!"

The manic humor left Condor's face and a harsh glower dropped across his visage like a mask. "I said, 'get your axe,' Harkey."

"Ah, Condor," said Harkey, even his stout heart beginning to quail. "Old friends like us don't need weapons. If you've a problem, lad, why, let's settle it over a pint. Come now, what can I get you?"

But suddenly, the naked tip of Condor's sword flashed by, inches from his nose. He had not even seen him draw it. "Get your axe, barman, or die where you stand," its owner growled.

Grim determination now settled over Harkey's face, and without another word, he stalked back behind the bar and grabbed his axe. He had never actually used the thing-was seldom even called upon to brandish it these days-and over the years its hickory handle and double-bitted head had become discolored and rusty from neglect and spilled drink. Still, it would do a job and Harkey knew well how to wield it. A battle-axe had been his weapon on campaign and he was built with the deep, barrel chest and burly arms to use it.

How, was the question. As he turned back to face the massive intruder, he considered attacking quickly, trying to surprise his foe. But he rejected the strategy. Condor would be ready for that, and besides, there was still the possibility-slim though it was-that this standoff was mostly show; that after a blow or two, or even a sufficient show of force, matters might be resolved amicably. Then there was the matter of size and age. Condor was young, huge. Harkey was past forty and with a good deal more girth than he had carried in his prime. No, he thought, defense was the best strategy here. Let the young fool have his game and try best to survive it.

"All right, Condor," he said, taking his stand. "You asked for it and here I am. But there's still time to let this thing pass."

"Let it pass?" Condor laughed a harsh barking laugh and turned to grin at the dozen or so of his men who had slipped in behind him and now stood lining the wall. From the kitchen in the back, another squad filed in behind the bar. The other patrons, some holding stools and walking sticks and a few knives, huddled by the fire, their eyes wide and their faces sober.

"You didn't let it pass when I tried to stop those two lying about my father. You were pretty bold then, you sanctimonious bastard!" This last was spat, and Condor's face twisted into a savage snarl. With it, his sword arm flashed out, and before Harkey could move to parry, a stinging slice opened a gash on his right thigh.

"Arrgh!" he yelled and jumped back a step. "Lying about your father? What are you talking about, man? Those fools said naught about your father."

"More fool you then," snapped Condor and again, before Harkey could react, his arm snaked out, thrusting this time, and the point of his sword pierced the burly barman's left shoulder.

Harkey felt the blood trickling down his arm and the old battle rage rising up inside him. There was no chance for diplomacy here. He could stand

and get pricked to death, or he could fight: that was the choice. He let the rage take him, and with a loud bellow, launched a furious assault. He leapt at Condor, swinging madly. His blows were vicious, delivered with all his strength, left, right and across. But Condor danced away as light as an elf and laughed as the murderous axe flashed by, always inches from his frame. Then with a deft poke, he bloodied Harkey's other shoulder.

The blood rage took Harkey completely now and he redoubled his effort, seeing his mocking foe through a red mist. Again and again he swung, advancing left and right, whipping the axe around in a furious figure eight. But never was Condor there. He didn't block, didn't parry, he just moved, as lithe as smoke, as elusive as darkness. Try as he would, Harkey could not touch him.

Finally, he was spent and the axe head thudded to the floor. Harkey staggered, leaning on the handle, gasping for breath. Come death or what would, he could swing it no more.

"You've not faced the likes of me before, have you, barkeep?" Condor hissed, his own breathing unruffled.

Harkey tried to reply but could only rasp.

"Tell that to my father when you get to hell," said Condor, driving his blade deep into Harkey's chest, just below the sternum. "Tell him he would have been proud to know me." But it was unclear whether Harkey heard this last, for his body toppled sideways and crashed onto the floor.

The death of the barman was the signal for the rest of Condor's men and with a howl they rushed upon the other patrons. It was not much of a fight-a slaughter, really. One of Condor's men caught a flesh wound on his arm and another was sent sprawling by a blow from a stool. But the patrons-local farmers mostly, men with wives, children, and chores at home-were quickly butchered, and as the pirates turned their attentions to the well-stocked bar, their feet left bloody tracks across the floor.

But this was only the beginning. Inflamed by spirits and maddened by blood lust and the exhilaration of freedom after their long captivity, they soon burst from the tavern and set about sacking the town. Like a violent storm, they wreaked senseless havoc. Families were dragged from their beds, the men-and often the children-killed, the women ravaged, belongings ransacked for valuables, houses set ablaze. Condor's men leapt about in the roaring, flaming light like demons in a fiery hell, burning, pillaging, quenching lust and thirst and leaving behind an utter ruin. Some few of the townspeople managed to slip away and watched in horror from the shelter of a neighboring wood. But these were few, and as they watched their neighbors die and their own homes go up in flames, thought that they, too, might be better dead.

Condor himself took no part in the bloody sack. Sober, he watched for a time in the flickering light of the tavern, an amused smile playing across his face and an evil light glittering in his eyes. Then he called to a nearby group to accompany him and

135

set off down a darkened cart track for one of the outlying farms. It was a track he knew very well, for he had followed its muddy ruts since he had been able to toddle along on his own legs.

The farmyard stood quiet in the moonlight, the rape of the town a distant roar and a flickering glow in the sky behind them. There was the house, the barn and the two sheds, just as he had left them. There, under an open roof on the side of the barn, was the old plow, and in the barnyard beyond, the two oxen who pulled it lay quietly sleeping. In that shed over there, he knew, were chickens, in the barn, cattle and hay, and in the fields beyond-it being just shy of mid-summer-the grain was near knee high.

All this he saw and knew at a glance, but no warm feelings of homecoming rose in his breast, no longing for hearth and kin. Unknown to his real father (or simply ignored by him) and resented as a burden by his mother, he had been beaten and so worked like a brute by his step-father that this farm had become as much a prison to him as the bench and shackles had been to his crew. Now it was with a vindictive leer that he signaled his men into the house to drag out the hapless occupants.

The two were plainly asleep as evidenced by their sudden shouts of surprise and disheveled appearance when they were dragged into the yard. Condor was shocked at how much his mother had aged in the two years he had been gone. A stunning beauty in her youth, Enid had sought to trade on her charms for a high place at the new Emperor's side, and then had grown increasingly bitter and resentful after he had used her and tossed her aside. That her son by him might be equally valuable trade goods apparently never occurred to her-or she never found the means to capitalize on it-and as the years passed, she saw him increasingly as the reason for her rejection.

Desperate after Fantar dropped her-though she told herself it was to spite him-Enid had seduced and then run off with Coram, a palace guard to whom she had seemed a goddess at the time. He had not known she was with child, and at first, believed Condor was his. But feeling spiteful one night after a bit too much wine, she had hissed that he was not even capable of siring such a child. From then on, Coram turned increasingly hostile to the boy, blaming him for his mother's growing distemper, and as Condor himself grew more and more sullen and insolent, treated him ever more brutally in an effort-as he said-"to teach the boy proper respect" and "to make a man of him." Severe beatings were common, and his mother, who seemed to always have a wine decanter at hand, used them as a pretext to vent her increasing spume on Coram.

Thus, Condor grew up in the midst an ever rising spiral of bitterness, violence and hate. Even when he was large enough to resist Coram-indeed, by his early teens he had towered over his step-father, and that worthy, perhaps feeling somewhat at risk using only his naked fists, had taken to beating him with a lash or the staff he used to prod

137

his cattle-Condor had endured the beatings in sullen silence and had repressed his growing rage and resentment until it had eventually exploded that night in the tavern. Now Coram was about to see exactly what kind of man he had made.

"Condor!" his mother cried when she saw him, relief evident in her voice. "Oh, my boy, my boy! We thought you dead. Oh, Condor!" And when he did not reply but only glowered at the two of them, her voice became plaintive. "Condor? What's the matter? Tell these men to let us go."

"You'll wish I was dead," Condor snarled, and stepped past his mother to face the plainly terrified Coram. With all his pent-up strength, Condor smashed his fist into his stepfather's solar plexus. The force of the blow lifted the man completely off his feet and two or three ribs cracked loudly as the breath exploded from his body. He collapsed into a tortured ball and lay convulsing and making pitiful sucking, squeaking sounds as his diaphragm spasmed for air.

Condor stood over him, his face actually quivering with rage. "Now that I see you again, you're nothing but a worm! Kill him!" he spat, and began to stalk away.

"Nooo!" screamed his mother, fighting against the men who held her. "No, Condor, no! You can't!" But he could, and as two of the men plunged their swords into Coram's side, she screamed and sank to her knees. "You bastard!" she wailed. "You awful bastard! How could you?" and she fell forward, sobbing and moaning, onto her face, the dirt smearing her tear-soaked face with mud.

Condor looked down at the writhing, prostrate form, then turned without a word and began walking away.

"What shall we do with her, m'Lord?" asked one of the men who had been holding her.

"Do what you will," he said. "She's naught but an old whore anyway."

It was near dawn when the *Steiger*'s raiding party staggered back aboard, carrying or dragging their few wounded, and the ship dropped back down the river and out to sea. A spitting rain had begun by then which served to sober the men and helped cleanse them of gore. Most collapsed and slept where they lay, sprawled about the open decks, but in the pre-dawn blackness, others could see their chief pacing about on the quarterdeck. He seemed to be agitated about something and several swore they saw him in animated conversation with something that appeared to hover about him like a darker shadow.

With the dawn, the skies cleared and a bright sun saw them round the southern tip of the island and begin making their way back up the western passage. It took the lash to drive the most debilitated of the crew back to the benches, but a few hours at the oars served to sober even the worst of them and by the time they pulled into their berth in Palemia, *Steiger* again looked the picture of one of His Majesty's war galleys.

Bright and shiny in his best uniform, Condor repaired at once to the squadron commander. While on patrol, they had come upon a pirate galley sacking Koth, he reported, standing stiffly before Senior Captain Darios' polished desk, his helmet under his arm. They had given chase and had engaged the enemy, he said, but sadly had been repulsed and the devils had gotten away. Unfortunately, captain Malecium had taken an arrow while leading the boarding party and his body had been lost at sea.

Darios steepled his fingers and listened quietly to Condor's detailed report of the action. Smoke had been reported from across the river earlier that morning and seemed consistent with everything *Steiger*'s mate had to say. Too bad about Malecium, though no great loss to the service. This man, now, this Condor. There was something reassuring about his presence, something compelling in his eyes. Obviously a natural leader.

"A very thorough report," he said when Condor finished. "We've already sent a party to Koth to investigate, though I doubt they'll turn up much more than bodies. These pirates are a menace! Too bad about Malecium. Tell me, Condor, how long have you been aboard *Steiger*?"

"Over two years now, sir."

"And you would be comfortable commanding her?"

"Yes, sir. Very comfortable. And I would very much appreciate the chance to engage those pirates again, sir, if I may say so."

"Commendable, Condor. Commendable. Very well. I will need confirmation from the admiral, of course, but from now on, you may consider yourself as captain of the *Steiger*. Congratulations."

Condor didn't even blink. "Thank you, sir," was all he said.

"No need to thank me, man, you've earned it. Now I suggest your return to your ship and see to your wounded. I have no doubt you'll be after those pirates again very soon."

"Aye, sir. Yes, sir. And I do thank you, sir. Again." And Captain Condor turned on his heel and marched back to his ship.

Chapter 8

Vahla shifted uneasily on a straight, high-backed chair beside the throne and watched her cousin Eldred dispense justice. She had arrived only that morning after sailing from Thuringia in the north. Her plan, while Thorngere was off on his annual tour of the clans in Thule, had been to visit her brother's family in Valeria and see the new baby. But after learning that the High King and Queen were in Dulcai, she had decided to sail on to Palemia, and see how the recently appointed Eldred was faring as King of Palemia.

Now she almost wished she hadn't come. They sat in the great throne room of her grandfather's palace with all the court and members of the public in attendance, and she could feel the resentment in the hall as a palpable force. But it was not directed at her. As the only other person in the room whose rank entitled her to a seat on the dais, she could see the dislike on the faces and in the sullen attitudes of the crowd, and she watched the proceedings with growing discomfort.

Eldred seemed either unaware of the hostility or was provoking it deliberately out of some perverse delight in his own authority. The illegitimate son of Vahla's mother's younger sister, he was a short, scrawny fellow whom Vahla always remembered as a whiny, sickly child with a perpetually runny-and untended-nose. He had survived Fantar's various purges of old royalty simply by being too insignificant, and when Vahla had elected to go with Thorngere to rule Thule and not take the crown of Palemia herself, Valerius had placed him on the throne as the only other remaining scion of the old royal family. But while he had seemed a harmless little toady before his assumption, power seemed to be turning him into a rather nasty despot. And as Vahla listened to him render judgement and hear petitions, she was having an increasingly difficult time keeping her mouth shut.

To control her mouth, she let her thoughts run. The man had become insufferably infantile, avaricious, and vain, she hissed in her head. He had surrounded himself with a small group of sycophants as warped as he was, and already, though his reign was but two years old, was evidencing disturbing signs of moral decadency. He mocked petitioners, twisting everything to his own advantage, and made snide, insulting comments at which only his courtiers laughed.

When a man appeared to request a permit to set up a fish stall in the market, Eldred had sneered, "What's in that for me? Will I get a nice bit of cod from the deal?" And his courtiers had minced about and chortled. When another man was condemned to prison for robbery, Eldred ordered his left hand cut off. "Where he's going, he'll need his right hand for company," he quipped, and then laughed lewdly at his own joke.

And on it went through a long afternoon. Vahla was on the point of speaking out several times, but dared not interfere publicly. The High King himself had placed Eldred on the throne and only he could deal with him. But she promised herself that Valerius would certainly hear about this and that something would be done: the people of Palemia deserved far better than Eldred.

Finally, as evening shadows lengthened across the hall, a man was brought up for failing to pay his taxes. He was a small tradesman by the look of him, one who had plainly seen better times. It was also clear that Eldred did not like the look of him. "And what have you to say for yourself," he said, a sardonic smile curling the side of his face.

"If it please Your Majesty," the man said, visibly trembling and wringing his hands, "I just need a little more time. My brother-in-law died recently, Your Majesty, so now I have my sister and her six children in addition to my own four. I am only a poor tailor, as you can see, and I've paid last year's amount, but this new levy is just too much. If you could give me just another month or two... "

"So you've been feeding your sister's six children, you say?"

"Yes, Your Majesty."

"And with what?"

"With what? I don't under... "

"Yes, how have you been buying them food if you cannot pay your taxes?"

"Well, Sire, I cannot let them starve!"

"Oh, so you steal the money from your King instead, is that it? Do you think it my responsibility to feed your sister and her children?"

"No, Sire, but... "

"And what of your brother's taxes? Have they been paid?"

"He's dead, Sire... "

"And I'm to be penalized for that, too?" Eldred cast a smug look at his courtiers, several of whom twittered and sniggered in amusement.

"Your Majesty," said Vahla, unable to keep silent any longer, "may I ask a boon of you?"

"Yes, cousin Vahla," said Eldred, plainly irritated at the interruption.

"As a special favor in honor of my return to Palemia, I ask that you remit this man's taxes, or allow me to pay them for him."

Shocked silence filled the hall and Eldred's face went livid, twitching with repressed emotion. Interfering witch! How was he to answer this without looking the fool? Vahla was half-sister to the High King, Enchantress of the Empire. More, she actually had more right to his throne than he did. And the court knew it. He could not refuse her request. But to allow her to pay would make him look even more foolish.

"Cousin," he managed at last, his voice pouring out like oil, "your grace and generosity are well known to the people of Palemia, and you are justly loved by them as well as Ourselves. Would it be that taxes were unnecessary! That all of us could live our lives unfettered and free. Isn't that the dream of all men, even kings? But alas, it cannot be. Without law, there would be no peace, no security, and men such as this would face far worse than the taxman. Nor can one be allowed to shirk his rightful duties while others face theirs. What kind of justice would that reflect? But in honor of your visit, cousin, and in example of your goodness and generosity, we do hereby grant this man a stay of three months.

"Now," said Eldred, rising quickly from his throne so that the whole court had to clatter quickly to their knees, "that is enough for today. We are weary of judgement," and he stalked from the room. As royal guest, Vahla had no choice but to follow.

They were not quite out of hearing in the antechamber when he rounded on her. "How dare you! How dare you interfere with my justice?"

"That man had done no harm," Vahla hissed in return. "Why were you tormenting the poor fellow? Why were you tormenting any of them? And what's this about new taxes?"

"My business is not your concern," Eldred huffed and stalked off into his private apartments. But Vahla was not to be put off so easily. She followed hard on his heels.

"What do you mean it's not my concern? Of course it's my concern, you simpering dolt!"

"Oh, yes, you'd like it to be, wouldn't you? You'd like to Lord it over me again the way you used to. You'd like to Lord it over all of Palemia. Well, you had your chance! Now the crown is mine."

Vahla took a deep breath and tried to calm herself. "My dear cousin," she said, as reasonably as she could, "I am the sister of the High King, wife and Queen of the High Chieftain of Thule, and Enchantress of the Empire. I have already refused your place once, why would I want to take it now?"

"Oh, yes, you're high and mighty now, aren't you? Well, I knew you when you weren't so high and mighty, when you were a common little slut and twirled tassels on your breasts for your bread. You were very enchanting then, weren't you! I'll bet you weren't too proud to enchant a man's bed for the price of dinner, either!"

Vahla slapped him-hard-and Eldred staggered against a chair. "Be quiet, you little fool," she hissed, her temper blazing now, "or I will turn you into a toad!"

Eldred flinched, and behind the hand he held to his stinging cheek, a look of fear crossed his face. He knew he had gone too far. To act the popinjay in his own court was one thing, but to evoke the wrath of a sorceress as powerful as Vahla was something else. He had no doubt that she could turn him into a toad-and if he did have any doubt, the fire in the raven haired beauty's eyes would have convinced him-and his demeanor changed from haughty ruler to craven supplicant.

"Oh, Vahla!" he whined. "I'm sorry. I just don't know what's gotten into me today. I haven't been well, and your turning up so suddenly, and then the press of business at court... It's just... I've been trying to do too much, working so hard to earn the

High King's respect... I didn't mean to offend. And my head is pounding! But I don't want us to fight, Vahla. You know I've always loved you as a sister...

Vahla listened to this spiel in silence, the rage on her face settling into sour distaste. 'No need to turn you into a toad, even if I could,' she thought. But then she sighed and continued aloud:

"Nor do I wish us to fight, Eldred. We are family, after all. And I do apologize for interfering publicly. I should have waited and spoken in private. But Eldred, why must you... "

At that moment there was a commotion just outside the apartment. An attendant entered-rather like he had been shoved-and began to announce Commodore Grumwald, only to be followed by the man himself. Grumwald stumped purposefully into the room, followed by several of his officers and Darios, the local Squadron Commander.

"Your Majesty," he began, then stopped when he saw Vahla. "Princess Vahla!" he exclaimed, a smile brightening his grizzled visage. "I didn't know you were here! Is that reprobate, my lord Thorngere here with you?"

Vahla's face, too, lit up with delight-and relief-at seeing such a friendly and familiar face, and she gave him a warm hug.

"No, I'm afraid not, Grumwald," she answered. "He's off on his annual tour of the clans in Thule, so I took the opportunity to come south. But they told me in Valeria that you had gone to Dulcai with the King... "

"Aye, we've just come from there. His Majesty had some pressing business so we came back early..."

"Ah-hem!" said Eldred, standing in formal pose by the couch and waiting to be recognized.

"Ah, yes, sorry Your Majesty. Forgive me," said Grumwald, letting a quick bob suffice for obeisance-"it's the knees, you know," he grunted-"I was just so surprised to see My Lady Vahla here. But I do indeed have news-and directives from His Majesty, the High King. Reuter's niece, the Princess Illana of Dulcai, has been kidnapped and Valerius has directed that no efforts be spared in searching for her and bringing the brigands to justice." Quickly, Grumwald sketched in the details of the kidnapping and of his own pursuit eastward.

"How extraordinary!" said Darios. "One of my officers just reported a brush with pirates. It seems they sacked the town of Koth on the eastern shore. I've sent another galley to investigate, but I'll bet it's the same crew!"

"Is your officer available?" Grumwald wanted to know.

"I expect so, Commodore. He only returned this morning and had some wounded to attend to, and I expect, some repairs. They tried to board the pirate but were driven off."

"Well, let's fetch him and see if he can shed any light on this situation," Grumwald snapped, and then added lamely, "-with your permission, of course, Your Majesty."

"Yes, yes, of course!" said Eldred, suddenly the picture of concern. "Send for this man right away, er... ?"

"Darios, Your Majesty. Captain Darios."

"Yes, Captain Darios."

An awkward silence ensued. The various principals were seated, and refreshments served, but the conversation lagged. As King and host, it was Eldred's place to initiate a topic, or at least indicate that others were free to do so. But he sat in sulky silence with his hand shielding his face, trying to conceal the stinging slap mark that still glowed on his left cheek. Vahla had many things to talk with Grumwald about, but hesitated, not wanting to add insult to injury by further usurping Eldred. Grumwald, the old campaigner, sipped his wine and assessed the situation. The beautiful Vahla was in high color, her large, brown eyes still flashing, and though Eldred did his best to shield his face, the redness and slight swelling on his cheek were plainly evident.

Had he been presumptuous, Grumwald mused? As always, Princess Vahla was tempting enough to raise the newly dead, but somehow, he didn't think so. Eldred did not look the part. Yet he had obviously aroused her wrath in some way. Did he know so little of his own cousin, then; a woman who had duped the Oracle of Cartho and had faced down an entire army of Scythians and held them at bay for three months-by herself? He knew very little if he did not know the stories of the

Enchantress of Valeria. And if he crossed her knowing, then the more fool he.

Grumwald hid a smile behind his cup and watched as Vahla flashed several irritated looks Eldred's way, then turned purposely away from him.

"So, Grumwald," she said, "how are my brother and Queen Eomer?"

"Why, very upset by this incident, as you can imagine, Your Highness, but otherwise fine," the Commodore replied.

"And the children?"

Grumwald's face warmed. "Ah! That young Valerian, now there's a lad! Helps me sail *Valadator*, he does. Even yells out 'heave!' when the men are hauling the braces."

"And Alair?"

"Cute as a button. Favors her mother, I think, though Brenda-that's the nurse-says she's got her father's eye. 'Course, she's still just a babe, too little for me to hold, but... "

They chatted on amiably until, with another commotion, Condor made his entrance. He did not wait to be announced, but brushed past the guards and strode boldly into the King's private chambers. As Grumwald turned, he caught a quick glimpse of Vahla's face, wreathed in a shocked surprise, then his own breath caught in his throat at the sight of the huge young galley captain. If there was ever an image of Valerius from the days when he was a young rebel going by the name of Balazar, this man was it. Of course, no one knew who Balazar was

151

then, but this young man had that same massive frame and imposing countenance, coupled with an easy grace that had made young Balazar a leader even then. But no, Grumwald thought again, as the young man crossed the room, there was a difference about the eyes. Balazar's eyes-Valerius' eyes-always had a warmth about them, a kindness distilled from suffering. But there was no kindness in this man's eyes, despite the bemused smile he wore. There was something else about these eyes, something strange that made even Grumwald want to turn away.

Vahla, too, was startled by a resemblance, but it was not to Valerius. Her mind flashed back more than four years when, to use Eldred's phrase, she had indeed twirled tassels on her breasts for her bread. She had gone to Valeria then and had been summoned to dance before another king whose reign of terror had cost the lives of her parents and thousands upon thousands of others. What Vahla saw was the spitting image of the man she had tried to kill that night: Valerius' half-brother, the regicide Fantar One-Eye.

Condor ignored her along with the others in the room-including his own superior-and knelt conspicuously before Eldred. "Captain Condor of His Majesty's Galley *Steiger*," he said. "You sent for me, Sire?"

Eldred looked helplessly at Vahla, who in turn, looked to Grumwald. "Yes, we did, young man," he said, rising and moving quickly to stand over the still kneeling Condor. "I am Grumwald, High Commodore of His Majesty's fleet. Captain Darios

152

tells us you had a brush with some pirates last night. We wish to know more of the circumstances."

"Certainly, Commodore. May I rise, Your Majesty?"

"Certainly," said Eldred, summoning himself. "You are among friends here, Captain. There is nothing to fear."

"Thank you, Your Majesty," said Condor and rose to tower over Grumwald, who was far from a small man. He looked down at him, a flicker of a smile playing across his face. "What do you wish to know, Commodore?"

"We wish to hear your report, Captain," Grumwald snapped, beginning to bristle at the young man's impudence. "We wish to know the time and circumstances of the encounter, the kind and quality of the imposing vessel, the number and state of her crew, what actions you took to intercept her, what resulted... your report, man!"

"Commodore Grumwald," Eldred effused, trying to appear as regal as possible from his sitting position on the couch. "Surely there is no need for ire. Captain Condor has just returned from what I understand was a very harrowing mission."

Grumwald nodded, but did not take his eyes from the young captain.

"Please Captain," soothed Eldred, "just proceed at your own pace."

"Thank you, Your Majesty," said Condor, smiling like a gambler who has just been dealt a choice card. "We did indeed have a rather harrowing battle, during which my former captain, Malecium, died heroically. So I apologize, Commodore, for any incorrectness in my bearing-you see, I am but newly appointed to command."

"Noted, Captain," said Grumwald. "Proceed."

"Well, as I reported to Captain Darios, we were returning from patrol during the early hours this morning when we noticed several large fires in the direction of Koth, across the river. When we went to investigate, we saw a galley leaving port and heading down river. We gave chase and attempted to board, but we were clearly outnumbered and driven back by arrow fire. Captain Malecium fell leading the charge and we were unable to recover his body."

"What of the ship? It was a galley, you say?"

"Aye, sir. Single banked, about the size of *Steiger*, but beyond that she was unremarkable. It was quite dark last night, sir."

"Aye, I know. Which way did she head?"

"We shadowed her to the mouth of the river, Commodore. Then she bore off to the east and we returned up the west passage."

"Excuse me, Your Majesty, My Lord," said Darios, breaking off from a muted conversation with one of the men who had entered with Condor. "My other galley has reported the town of Koth is in ruins: every building put to the torch, at least two dozen inhabitants brutally slaughtered."

A shocked silence filled the room, broken finally by a grim-voiced Grumwald.

"Well, it's clear this kind of Vermin cannot be allowed to run free. I will proceed eastward then-with your permission, King Eldred. Princess Vahla. Will you be returning to Valeria or remaining here in Palemia?"

"I shall return. Much as I have enjoyed visiting my cousin here," and she shot him a look that might have pinned him to a wall, "I feel I should pay my respects to my brother and his queen now that they have returned-and see the children, of course."

"Captain Darios, you will see to it that the Princess's ship is suitably escorted?"

"Assuredly, my lord. I will send Condor here with the *Steiger*, and the *Recluse* as well."

"Very well. Then, by your leave, Your Majesty, I will return to my ship. There is no time to waste."

The meeting broke up, and as the naval officers left the palace, Grumwald summoned Condor to walk by his side.

"You look to be a very capable young man," he said, trying to make himself sound more kindly to the young captain than he felt. "But you would do well to study protocol, unless you want your superiors to send you to the benches. You committed some serious breaches in there, you know."

"Aye, sir. I see that now, Sir," said Condor, his face the picture of humility. "I'm sorry, Commodore. I've never been summoned to an audience before."

"Well, ignorance can be an excuse once, but I advise you to seek the counsel of Captain Darios-he's a very able man-and not to let it happen again."

"It won't, Commodore. And thank you."

"But you do look familiar to me, lad. Who is your father?"

"I don't know, sir. Fantar's men killed both my parents. I was raised on a farm. But then my step-parents died also and I've been in the navy since."

"I see. Well, you appear to be doing very well for yourself. I wish you well." Grumwald climbed into his barge and as he was rowed out to the waiting *Valadator* he thought, 'there must be some of the old King's wayward seed in that lad somewhere. He certainly has the arrogance to go along with it. But it's probably better he not know that. A young man like that could get ideas.'

Vahla returned to her chambers and ordered her servant, Chad, to repack everything he had just unpacked. She sent a message to Eldred that she was tired and would dine alone, then summoned an old girlhood friend to join her. They talked late into the night and it soon became clear that Celia-and to hear her tell it, most of the population of Palemia-shared Vahla's opinion of Eldred. As they parted, Vahla made Celia promise not to let their friendship lapse again: Celia must send her frequent letters, telling her everything that was going on in Palemia, especially the doings of the King.

Chad was just closing up the last of Vahla's clothing baskets when she entered her sleeping chamber. He carried it out into the passageway to be ready for the porters, then went back into his mistress' room. She had already removed her overdress and sat before a polished bronze mirror in her shift. In a long-practiced routine, he began to brush out her flowing, dark hair. But when she caught his eye in the mirror, he stopped and looked hard at her reflection.

"Yes, Chad?" She knew his moods by now and knew he would have his say.

"We go Valeria?" he asked. In the mirror, his pinched eyes looked as black and shiny as wet stones. He was a strange creature. Small and dark-complected, with a narrow face and deft, bird-like movements, he spoke little and often seemed of limited intelligence. But there was another side to him that was uncannily sharp, and he was always a superbly competent servant.

"Yes, Chad. His Majesty and the Queen are back from Dulcai." And when he did not look away, she added, "And no, I don't like it here."

"Bad here," he said, bobbing his head to emphasize his words.

"Have you been speaking to the other servants? Have they said things about Eldred?"

"Chad no speak. Chad know. Some bad thing here." And for a moment, Vahla had a strange sensation that the reflection of his face was not a reflection at all but something ethereal and disembodied, something speaking from the bronze itself. A quick shiver sent goose bumps down her arms and then it was gone.

"Yes, Chad. But we're leaving in the morning."

157

Condor, too, had a dinner companion in his tiny cabin aboard the *Steiger*. It was the Princess Illana, worn and disheveled, sitting across the cramped table from him like a mannequin dropped onto a chair. Though she had eaten but little since her capture, she picked at the food before her and touched her wine not at all.

Condor was in an expansive mood and told her all about his trip to the palace and his interview with the King and the Commodore of the High King's fleet. But in his version, things were a bit different. "The Commodore was out chasing some pirate, if you can imagine," he said and speared another slab of beef from the platter by his side. "I told him we had chased a ship like the one he described, but that it had escaped eastward. So that's where the Commodore is headed. He said the pirate had murdered some girl, a princess or something."

Illana looked up sharply at this and Condor stuffed half the slice into his mouth and chewed noisily. "Yes," he said in the same tone one would use to describe a stretch of unfortunate weather, "apparently they found her nude body floating near the mouth of the river." Illana's face went ashen and Condor swallowed leisurely. "Her face had been smashed in beyond recognition, the Commodore said, but they were sure it was her. He said he was duty bound to pursue the pirate, but didn't seem to think he'd have much luck. My guess is he'll sail east for a few days, then head back to Valeria and his cushy quarters. He didn't look like the kind of man to endure hard campaigning. But King Eldred, now, there's a man to lead! I think he and I will need to become much better friends, don't you?"

Illana stared at him, her face an agony of despair, her eyes devoid of hope. Condor saw the look and smirked as if he had just noticed her presence. "That's right, lass, no one's looking for you anymore. They all think you're dead. And no one is looking for me, either. They think I'm a hero. Chased those pirates right down the river, we did! Lost poor Malecium leading the charge. Ha! So you're mine, little lady. All mine."

His eyes bored into hers and he reached across the table and stroked her cheek. She sat unresisting, held by the dark power of his gaze. Carefully, he rose and came around to stand before her. Her face turned to follow his eyes, and when he raised her up from her chair, she came unresisting. His hands cupped her cheeks, slid down her neck and over her shoulders.

"Are you mine, now, little princess?" he whispered, his voice husky with desire.

But something in it snapped the spell. Illana flinched and shook her head violently and tried to twist away. She struggled, but Condor held her tight, his fingers digging into her shoulders, a sudden rage flaring in his face. He glared at her, his face positively twitching with passion, his lips curling and snarling. Lifting her like a doll, he tossed her onto the bunk in the sleeping cabin; and she, like a frightened crab, scuttled quickly into the corner over the toilet hole and cowered there, shaking.

Condor started for her but then stopped and drew back, his arms and hands shaking with the effort to control himself. "No," he rasped, his fingers still clawing the air for her, "not until you kneel to me. And you will kneel to me, little Princess. You will kneel!" And he backed out of the cabin and slammed the door.

Chapter 9

Vahla departed the next morning, accompanied by two galleys from the Palemia station, the *Steiger*, with Condor in command, and *Recluse*, with Darios himself acting as Commodore. It was unclear why Darios had taken personal command. Neither Eldred nor Grumwald had ordered it, and while Darios had little confidence in the regular skipper of *Recluse*, he was certainly capable of escorting a heavily armed Thuringian galley to Valeria. Perhaps Darios saw an opportunity to advance his career in Valeria, capital of the Empire. Perhaps, too, he was smarting a bit from being upstaged by Condor before Eldred and wanted an opportunity to shine. Or perhaps he simply wanted to see more of the Enchantress, Princess Vahla. She was a famous beauty, after all, and serving her would continue a tradition for him, since his family had been devoted retainers of Vahla's family for many generations.

Whatever the reason, it was Darios who stood on the quarterdeck of *Recluse* and piloted the three ships down the river Sule and out into the choppy waters of the Inland Sea. And a tough time they had of it. The wind blew hard from the southwest all day-which kept the benchers pulling at their oars without respite-and when the three ships turned westward to run along the coast, they began bashing head-on into steep, heavy chop which sent clouds of spray high over the bows and drenched everyone aboard. It also slowed their progress and by late afternoon they had covered less than half the distance they had hoped. With the rowers nearing exhaustion and a headland just to starboard offering shelter, Darios ordered the little fleet to drop anchor under its lee.

Cooking fires were lit and the crews fed and rested. But as evening came on, the wind dropped and Vahla became anxious to get back underway. She climbed from her tiny cabin to the poop deck and stood in the growing twilight, surveying the scene. The headland was blocking the sunset, but violet bands and swirls spread across the sky to the south of it. With the wind gone, the sea had flattened to calm and she could feel on one side of her the radiant warmth coming off the land, and on the other side, the damp chill of the sea.

The land was low and flat along this stretch of coast, a verdant plain extending to the sea from the distant mountains, populated with farms and vineyards. How different, she thought, from her new home in the mountains of Thuringia, where fiords cut deep among rearing cliffs and where snow was always visible capping the high peaks. A pang of homesickness touched her as she thought of the high meadows around Thorndale, and of her lord and love, Thorngere. And she felt, not for the first time, the quickening of life in her belly.

The other two ships lay quietly to their anchors, and she watched a thin ribbon of smoke drifting up from the galley fire of the *Recluse*. On the *Steiger*, she saw the ship's young captain,

Condor, standing on his quarterdeck, staring at her. The two ships were only a hundred or so feet apart and as their eyes met, she felt something very much like a shock. It was more than the recognition of his similarity to Fantar. There was a force in the young man's eyes, an intense, compelling force she could feel reaching out towards her, and for an instant, she felt a cold, encroaching darkness cloud her eyes like a mist. She shuddered and with a strong effort, tore her eyes away.

As she turned back towards the small companion ladder, Chad was hurrying up. His eyes, too, were searching hers. "I know," she said before he could speak, knowing he knew, too. "We're leaving now." Calling her captain on deck, she ordered him to weigh anchor.

"Shall we inform our escort, Ma'am?" The captain was a large man with the blond hair and blue eyes of his northern race, and their traditional disdain for southerners. He had not been happy to have an escort.

"They'll get the idea soon enough, Lars. Just start rowing and don't stop till we reach Valeria."

"Well, let's see how long it takes them to notice us going, then," he said with a wry grin, and with no other motive than to bedevil the naval galleys, he sauntered forward and had his men make their preparations as surreptitiously as possible. They did it well and when the galley's oars suddenly shot out from her sides and began churning froth in the quiet anchorage, no one was as surprised as Darios.

"Your Highness! Your Highness!" he yelled running forward to the *Recluse*'s bows. But Vahla, who was into the game herself by now, only waved gleefully as her ship sped away.

Recluse and *Steiger* scrambled to follow, but the Thuringian galley had weathered the headland and gained another mile before either got their heavy anchors back aboard. Then it became a race, north against south, freemen who rowed their slim Thuringian craft for honor and their Queen, against slaves who rowed under the lash. As the sun set and a rising moon cast a blue haze over the flat sea, the three ships sped on under long strokes. For mile upon mile, Vahla and her crew maintained their lead, while Darios and Condor strove in vain to shorten it.

Then they ran into fog. It was not unusual, when the wind suddenly dropped after a day of hot southwesterlies, and the skies were clear, for a thick blanket of fog to form along the northern coast of the Inland Sea. It would often extend several miles out to sea, and at night it was not uncommon for ships to suddenly run into it unawares, like they had been swallowed. One moment Vahla and company were shooting along under a clear, starlit sky, and the next they were enveloped by a dark, murky world where the helm could not see the bow. Faces and near figures took on an eerie, ghostly hue. Sounds had no source but seemed to come from everywhere, and any sense of direction or motion was totally lost.

Fog is unnerving. It so distorts and disorients the senses that even expert mariners can swear they know where they are headed and steer themselves onto the rocks. Thus, in that age, when the only navigational aide was line of sight, the proper course in fog was no course at all. The best thing to do was simply to sit and wait. If there was a current and a captain knew its direction and speed, he might bear on it and proceed cautiously. But if he simply ran into a bank of fog at sea, and thought he was sure enough of the land to head for it, he was as likely to shoot off in the opposite direction and in the morning, find himself far out to sea with no land in sight. If it was a sunny morning, he could find his way. But if, as often happened after a day of strong south-westerly's, the weather was overcast, he might well spend a week or more trying to find his way back to land (and if he was in the Outer Ocean, the gods alone knew where he might end). Far better to sit and drift the night away, then get back on course in the morning.

This was precisely what Vahla and Captain Lars prepared to do. They rowed on for a few minutes, just to be sure the bank was not a fleeting one, then shipped oars and prepared to wait it out.

Following in their wake, *Recluse* ran into the same dense fog a few minutes later. Fearful of running into Princess Vahla's galley, Darios ordered his oars shipped, sent a lookout aloft, and let his ship drift with the tide. In moments, another shape materialized in the fog from astern. It was *Steiger*. She rowed towards him, clearly intending to come alongside. Captain Condor was standing amidships, signaling for quiet. Darios repeated the signal along his own decks and motioned for his crew to secure the lines tossed over from *Steiger*, tying the two ships together in the swirling gray mist.

"What news, Condor?" he whispered hoarsely as the huge young captain vaulted over both rails and landed softly on the deck by his side. "Why have you come alongside at sea like this? What have you seen?"

"I have news," said Condor, stepping closer, his voice also a hoarse whisper. "I know who the pirate is and what he's planning to do."

"You do? Who, then? What?" Darios was all eagerness.

"He plans to kill you and release the slaves from your benches." Condor said this in a normal tone, his sudden voice, loud in the swirling mist, carrying the length of both ships. "Then he's going to take Princess Vahla."

"Well, let him come, then!" cried Darios. "We're ready for him!"

"I don't think you are."

"We're... ? What do you mean, man? Explain yourself at once."

Condor smiled and in the eerie half-light, his eyes seemed to shine with a demon light. His voice was a quiet hiss. "I mean, Captain Darios, that he's already here and you are already dead."

Darios' eyes flew open wide and he uttered a single grunt as Condor drove a dagger up under his sternum and into his heart. "At them, men!" Condor cried, and as Darios' body crumpled to the deck, *Steiger*'s cutthroats poured over the side and fell on the *Recluse*'s startled crew.

It was over very quickly. Only a few cried out as the cold, wet steel took them and Gunther, the ship's regular captain, only awoke in his cabin when a long blade sliced through his throat. Still, the cries were loud enough to carry through the fog to the Thuringian galley where alarmed and expectant faces turned this way and that, trying to pinpoint the sound in the murky gray around them. With a nod from Vahla, her captain motioned to his boatswain to out oars and pull. Suddenly, the normal rules for running in fog were superseded.

In Valeria, there was fog of a different sort, but it grew in Valerius' head as he sat late in his study, pouring over old scrolls and manuscripts dredged up from the palace archives. Immediately upon his return, he had gone down to the vaults under the palace where the old archives had been kept. They were still there-untouched by the fire from when Fantar had sacked the city-still massive, with row upon row of pigeon-holed shelves crammed with ancient writings, and astonishingly, still tended by the same staff of archivists. Valerius remembered the headman from his youth. He was ancient now, but still tall and gaunt, and still behaved towards the High King with a trace of disdain. For a man who had the legacies of so many high kings under his charge, this current occupant of the throne could hardly seem more that a new chapter, awaiting collation.

Valerius felt rather like a truant schoolboy in talking to him. He had paid scant attention to history as a lad, and a full two years after his return to power, this was the first time he had visited the archives. And since he could not tell the old man the true nature of his search, he was something at a loss what to say, finally blurting out that he was curious about court protocol and wanted him to find anything he could about the daily lives and routines of previous High Kings. It was obvious the chief archivist, whose name was Illardo, thought Valerius remiss in not already knowing these things (or at least in not having come to this source before now), but nevertheless, he nodded with serene condescension and shortly returned with several helpers bearing the Book of Kings, a many volume set of scrolls recording the daily doings and sayings of past high kings back into the mists of Valerian antiquity.

Valerius had no notion such a record even existed. He had the set-containing hundreds of scrolls-moved up to his own private study and had sat up into the wee hours since, studying it. So far, he had found little in it but horribly formulaic descriptions of ceremonies and state visits by personages great and royal, of gifts presented to "His Royal Majesty, Valerius Everreigning, High King of Valeria and all the Inland Sea," and of gifts given in return.

And while it was strange and almost unnerving to hear his own name and title repeated so frequently in reference to men and events of the far distant past, the compilation was neither entertaining nor helpful: the only mentions of the Eye were formulaic ones, of 'the Eye of Valeria, the Great Power Stone of the High King with which it is said he can see into the future and into the hearts of men.'

Now it was late. He had had too much study, or too much wine, which netted the same effect, and he sat slumped in his reading chair, the dregs of a last cup by his side and an errant scroll spilling from his lap and unrolling itself across the floor. His mind was too dulled with reading to be able to focus any more, and he drifted in aimless thought. His mind wandered back to the prophet in Dulcai, to the prophecy and to that extraordinary display in the mine, and he wondered what it could mean. How had his "ruby Eye" left him blind? What was this unseen deed of which he needed to beware? There was some threat, of that he was sure. His instincts warned him loudly enough. But what?

Idly, as one would think of a favored grandparent, long deceased, he thought of the old mage Volkmir. It was he who had rescued the Eye after it had burned out Fantar's eye and that worthy had tossed it into the sea. And it was Volkmir who had helped engineer Valerius' escape from the Hidden Valley and proffered the Eye after convincing him to reclaim his name. Valerius wished he were alive now, that he was still here to help. But even as the image of the man formed in his mind, simultaneously, across the room, a red glow began to form like a spotlight against a portion of the wall. And there, standing in it, was Volkmir, as hale and spry as ever he stood in life.

Valerius started up as if he had been poked, the scroll on his lap clattering onto the floor, and the vision-if that's what it was-winked out. Valerius shook his head violently and rubbed his eyes, but the wall was blank. He slumped back in his chair, the sudden energy draining from him like water from a pitcher. He rubbed his eyes again-with weariness this time-and yawned. He'd had too much wine, too many old scrolls for one night. But then again he thought, 'Though, I would that it were so,' and in a flash, the vision came again.

He stayed still this time and watched it, careful not to disturb anything, even with his thoughts. It was indeed Volkmir, standing there in a rose-tinted glow, looking at him-apparently as solid and real as life, except that around him was not Valerius' chamber at all, but Volkmir's own cave in the mountains south of Zagorbia. Valerius recognized a cupboard and a table from when he visited there. But as he did so, Volkmir nodded, as if he could read Valerius' thoughts, and beckoned to him. Again Valerius started to rise, and again, the vision dissipated. But this time, as he leaned forward, he could see the great gem on his chest glowing softly.

Valerius settled back in the chair and tried to calm his thoughts. Whatever had happened, he wanted to make happen again. Never, in the time since he had claimed the Eye, had it ever behaved like this. Had he willed it? Or was the thing acting on its own, reading his thoughts and displaying idle scenes? Either way, he could not calm his thoughts, and the stone lay cold and heavy against his chest, its deep facets dark, the light extinguished.

"Valerius?" The voice startled him and he looked up to see Eomer standing in the door. On the table by his side, two candles were guttering and another had burned out. "Are you all right? I've been waiting-it's very late."

"Ah, I'm sorry dear, I must have dozed. Too much reading for my poor brain."

"Well, come to bed, darling. It's late and you must hold court in the morning."

"Aye, I know," he said rising wearily and following Eomer's bare feet as she padded back to their chamber. "I may just be overreacting, anyway."

"Do you think so?" she said as they climbed into the imperial bed. "You mean about the curse?"

"Aye, that, and Illana, and well, this feeling I've got. Perhaps I'm only seeing shadows in the night. In battle-if you survive many of them-you develop a sixth sense of where your enemy will next strike and you move to parry automatically, without even thinking about it. That's how this feels now, but it may be fooling me after all these years. In truth, I don't even know what enemy, or where, how or if he will strike. I only sense that he's there."

At court the next morning, Valerius' senses were anything but sharp. He held court, as his predecessors had, in the great hall of the palace, seated on his great oaken throne. Before him, on a dais one step down from his own, was a row of lesser thrones reserved for visiting royalty. They were empty this day as the High King was reported to be away, but word had spread through the city and surrounding countryside, and the hall was thronged with petitioners, courtiers, and the simply curious.

Fortunately for the wooly-headed monarch, most of the matters were simple routine-petitions to be granted, contracts memorialized, petty disputes and offenses to be mediated or punished. In other days, under other kings, such matters would have been handled by administrators. But Valerius felt too keenly the nascency of his own reign-and the far too many years of brutal tyranny that had preceded it-to allow even such routine matters to be handled by bureaucrats. More important, he felt, was that the High King be seen, that he rule actively, and that the people feel he was there and accessible. The people needed to see in order to believe.

Perhaps part of it, too, was that he still did not feel comfortable with his crown. He was raised as a prince and educated as one, but had spent so many years as a common fighter that he no longer felt himself totally royal. In reading the Book of Kings, he had waded through all the descriptions of pomp and ceremony and wondered if his predecessors were comfortable in that role, or like him, felt like actors on a stage. His experiences had made him much more direct in his impulses, much more inclined to act than reflect. The scholarly delving itself seemed strange and, in a way, made him feel more like an imposter; like the real Valerius was the one in the book, and he himself was only miming the descriptions he had read.

He wondered if that made him a bad king. The others-and they were his ancestors, he reminded himself-all seemed so sure in their pronouncements. Did they know-or see-something he did not? Or was it simply the pomp and circumstance made it seem that way?

In the early afternoon, a group of merchants presented themselves before him to complain of another group that had begun setting up kiosks outside the city walls. These people were ruining trade for the established merchants they said, and ought not be allowed to set up out there, away from the market proper.

"But as I understand it," said Valerius, "the market is already overcrowded. Weren't some of you here a couple months ago, complaining there was no room to expand your stalls?"

The group acknowledged that this was so.

"Then where would you have these others sell their wares?"

"But Majesty," said their spokesman, "they get to the customers before we can!"

"I haven't noticed any shortage of people in the market. Are you left without customers, then?"

No, they acknowledged, they were not.

"So there is no room for them to set up inside the market proper; you are all still flooded with customers; and yet you object to others doing business as well. How would it be if we tore down the palace here and built another outside? That way, you could expand your stalls, and there'd be more room for the others to set up inside as you seem to think is proper."

There was no reply to this and the contingent would no longer meet the King's eye. "Then I may keep my palace?" Valerius asked as a sprinkle of laughter pattered about the hall. "Gentlemen," he said, serious again, "the reason there are more vendors is because there is more trade. More trade means more customers. People are coming to Valeria from all over because peace brings prosperity. It is a sign of good times that you would even think to voice such a complaint. If you feel hampered in your ability to do business, I suggest you, too, set up kiosks outside the walls: that way you can enjoy the benefits of both locations. But please don't ask me to deny to others the freedoms you enjoy."

At least, he had not read of an incident like that in the Book of Kings, he thought, as the merchants shuffled away and the next set of petitioners began reciting the terms of a lengthy contract they wished him to bless. Valeria was beginning to prosper. There was more trade, more ships, more travel. So perhaps he was not a bad king.

But either way, he told himself as the lawyers droned on, he was the High King. There was no other, and if old Volkmir was to be believed, even the Eye had acknowledged him as the rightful one by not burning out his eye as it had Fantar's. So good or bad, simpleton or sage, his was the rule. It was up to him to deal not only with these petitioners, but with the more sinister things as well: like a young girl kidnapped before his eyes, like a strange prophecy intoned from a rooftop and dark forebodings of evil flashed in a cavern. And if his "ruby eye" had left him blind, it was up to him and only him to find a way to see.

Again he thought of the russet image of Volkmir, appearing on his study wall. Had he simply imagined or even dreamed that? The Eye had never done such a thing before. But if it had, it was surely no coincidence. There was something the Eye, or Volkmir-or whatever power moved them both-was trying to tell him; something he needed to understand. And somewhere among those dusty remainders of past glories that littered his private study, the answer must lie.

A trumpet fanfare at the end of the hall startled the crowd and interrupted his reverie. The great double doors swung open and a buzz of excitement rippled through the throng. Men at arms pushed forward, clearing a path down the center aisle, and even Valerius craned his neck to see who was about to enter. After a suitable pause to allow an expectant hush to fall over the crowd, the High Chamberlain stationed himself in the center of the doorway and in smooth stentorian tones (indeed, a stentorian voice was the chief qualification of his office) announced the Princess Vahla, Wife of the High Chieftain of Thule and Enchantress of the Empire.

Chapter 10

It was early afternoon by the time Vahla arrived in Valeria. Her ship had broken from the fog in early morning, and with the coast still miraculously in sight, they had sailed on under a comfortable southerly breeze with no sign of their escort. At the palace, an obviously delighted Valerius used her arrival as an excuse to adjourn court, and lead her back to his study.

"What a delightful surprise, sister!" he said, giving her a big hug. "I had no idea you were coming. I must call Eomer. Where's that rapscallion of a husband of yours?"

"Oh, he's off to the north at a clan gathering. He takes his job as High Chieftain way too seriously, so I thought I'd come south and meet my new niece. But what's this?" she asked, indicating the piles of scrolls and ancient bound manuscripts which littered the room. His desk was heaped with them, as was the low table by his reading chair, where several candles and oil lamps gave evidence of late night study. "Have you decided to add Scholar to your titles, or are you trying to take over my job as mage?"

"Oh, neither," said Valerius, rubbing his eyes, which she noticed now were red-rimmed. "Nor am I making much progress, I'm afraid."

Vahla's expression turned business-like. "What's going on? Does this have anything to do with Princess Illana being kidnapped and Grumwald off chasing pirates in the east?"

"How do you know about that?"

"I've just come from Palemia," said Vahla, and then quickly filled him in on her travels and the situation there. He nodded and pursed his lips as she described Eldred's antics.

"Aye, I've had my reservations about that one for some time, and I wouldn't be surprised if the discontent he's sowing is behind this piracy. But-to answer your question-as tragic as Illana's capture is-and I must tell you, young Boltar is devastated-there are other concerns as well. But here, where are my manners? Come sit down, let me pour you a glass of wine. Have you eaten?" He led her over to a small couch and moved an armload of scrolls so she could sit.

"I'm fine, really," she protested as he poured her a goblet. "Tell me what's going on."

Valerius moved to the chair behind his desk and assumed a more regal expression. "Very well, then, let me solicit your official advice as Enchantress." Carefully, he related the events since his arrival in Dulcai, providing as much detail as he could remember. One never knew, with a Mage, what little mote of information would provide a clue. "So what I need," he concluded, is to learn more about the Eye. Koltar promised to search his archives, and since I've gotten back, that's what I've been doing here."

"Well, it looks to be quite a task! What have you found out?"

"Not much, I'm afraid. About the only thing I have learned is that this tradition of the High King always being named Valerius is ridiculous! I can't tell one from another, or who did what when! It's all bloody 'King Valerius Everreigning this' and 'Valerius Everreigning that.' I'm thinking of changing young Valerian's name to Phred just to amaze future scholars!

Vahla laughed, but then Valerius turned serious again.

"But from what I've read, even in the earliest records, the High King always had the Eye stone. He also always had a mage, you'll be pleased to note, and I even saw a reference that one of the mage's servants was named Chad. There's a coincidence for you, eh? Chad and Valerius marching through time, hey!"

"Any other brother-sister/king-mage combinations?" Vahla wanted to know.

"None that I've found. But I did learn there was apparently some kinship between Valerius the first High King and the king of Palmeria, whom he defeated on the Plain of Darlung-where we faced off against the Scythians and you terrified my army with your shoddy tricks! Anyway, they were distant cousins, or something. The Book said the world then was divided into two camps that it said reflected a schism among the gods. The Palmerians and the Empire of the East worshipped a cruel serpent god who demanded human sacrifices and kept the people in bondage. It was only through the power of the Eye that Valerius was able to defeat them, and that was apparently a very near thing."

"Yes, I heard the story of Darlung from Volkmir. But where did the first Valerius get the Eye?"

"That I don't know yet. And I've found no descriptions of any king using it, or telling of having used it: most mentions are simple pat phrases about the Eye allowing the King 'to see into the future and into the hearts of men.' That sort of thing. I have seen two references to a 'Scroll of Dimmian', which might shed some light, but I've found no such scroll."

"Dimmian," Vahla said, sipping her wine and squeezing her eyes in thought. "Do you know who Dimmian was?"

"One of the Mages, I believe."

"Hmmmm. The name does sound familiar. I think maybe Volkmir was looking for that same scroll the year before he died-or at least, was looking for something regarding Dimmian. But, of course, he couldn't get to the archives here then, so maybe you'll turn it up."

Valerius nodded as if this confirmed his own thoughts. "That's what I'm hoping. And that in it might be some instructions on how to use the bloody thing!"

"And if it occurs that there is no power other than to see... ?"

"Well, so be it, then. To see is better than to walk in blind. All I sense now are dark shadows... Light would at least show us where we stand. But if

Volkmir was looking for this 'Scroll of Dimmian,' he may have left some record of it, or there may be other references among his archives. He had quite a horde of documents, as I recall. Do you know what happened to them?"

"They're still in his cave in the mountains, as far as I know," said Vahla.

"How did Volkmir get all that stuff up there, anyway?"

"You know, I asked Chad that very question once," she laughed.

"And he said?"

"He said, 'Chad carry,'" doing a very credible impersonation of her strangely talented, though curiously limited servant. "'By yourself?' I asked" "'Chad had donkey,' he said. And that was all I could get out of him."

"Might not be a bad idea to go collect that stuff and bring it back here one day," Valerius mused. "We could even put it back in Volkmir's old cave in the hills west of here where we can keep an eye on it."

"And where I might be able to learn something from it!" said Vahla. "I am supposed to be an Enchantress, after all."

"You've done pretty well so far."

"So far... But I don't know what I did!"

"That's how I feel about the Eye."

"You know," said Vahla, "just before he died, Volkmir said something very interesting... he said he was a fraud."

"I think we're all frauds to some extent," said Valerius. "Especially High Kings! But still, we must do the best we can... I just can't help thinking there is some purpose here, some reason why my father lost the Eye and the Empire was overthrown and why it took me nearly twenty years to win it back... "

"You mean beyond the effects of evil acting on chance?"

"Yes, my father-our father-did not believe in the Eye. I heard him say so and he told your mother so. But I know there is power here. I've seen it, and certainly felt it. But I don't know how to use it. It's not an evil power, else it would not have burned out Fantar's eye, and it is not a mindless power, else it would not have put me in my place the way it did in Darlung. No, it has a purpose. I can feel it. And I can't help but feel that my job as High King is to serve this purpose, that the Empire depends on it.

"But enough business for a while!" he said, his mood suddenly turning gay. "We haven't seen you in an age. You've yet to meet our young Princess Alair, and we need to hear all about you and Thorngere and your new home. Come, let's go find Eomer," and he dragged her off by the hand, down the hall to the nursery where Eomer was just putting little Alair back in her crib.

"Here's a surprise for you, my dear," Valerius announced.

"Vahla!" Eomer squealed and the two women rushed to embrace.

Later, after the gush of greeting, and the ohhing and ahhing over little Alair, and after young Valerian was suitably petted and admired-he told his aunt Vahla a rather long and complicated story about steering the ship in a toddler language she could not begin to understand, though she nevertheless marveled at the tale-the three adults settled in for a quiet family dinner on the royal veranda and chatted comfortably as the shadows lengthened into evening and the servants lit lamps and candles. Vahla talked about her new life with Thorngere in the wild highlands of Thuringia. Eomer countered with talk of life at court in Valeria, and of their trip to Dulcai and her worries about her father.

Valerius found little room to fit into the conversation and little need to do so, but sat smiling benevolently as the two sisters-in-law chatted volubly. For a man who had been ripped violently from home and family at fifteen and who had for years expected to die in battle without anyone even knowing his real name, much less have a family of his own, this little domestic scene was bliss beyond words, and for a time, banished the dark shadows that had been haunting him. Finally, however, he felt he must say something, even if only to remind the two women he was still at the table.

"So," he broke in when both women happened to inhale at the same instant, "Vahla may be taking a little trip with me back to Volkmir's old cave."

His announcement was met with two rather surprised looks.

"I don't think so," said Eomer.

"Excuse me?" said Valerius and the two women shared a look.

"Well," said Vahla, "I won't be able to travel much at all in a few months, and then I shall be quite busy."

Valerius furled his brow and looked from one to the other, trying to puzzle this out. "Busy with what?"

"Oh! You men are all alike!" Eomer giggled. "Dunderheads, all of you. Can't you see she's pregnant, you silly thing?"

Condor searched through the night for the Thuringian galley, at one point nearly running his own ship up on the rocky shore in the dense fog that clung all along the coast. Then, when the next day's sunburned away the mist, he joined company with the *Recluse*, and after a lengthy confab with her newly released captain and crew, the two ships set a leisurely course back to Palemia. There, a freshly scrubbed and starched Condor, his red cloak of office draped over his shoulder and Malecium's ceremonial sword at his side, made his way to the palace and begged an audience with the king.

It was a solemn-faced Condor who was ushered into Eldred's presence, and a deeply saddened Condor who-seated knee to knee with the monarch in his private apartments-reported the tragedy of a battle at sea: of thick fog that separated the fleet in darkness; of a treacherous enemy falling on the *Recluse* unaware; of a heroic defense by her crew until the *Steiger*, blindly following the sounds of battle and pain in that murky hell, stumbled on her and was able to drive the attackers off; of the ship's decks slippery with blood, and of both her gallant captain and Commodore Darius, fallen where they fought, their bloody swords still clutched in their lifeless fists; but of their charge nevertheless delivered safely to Valeria.

"Both captains?" asked an ashen-faced Eldred, aghast at this tale of horror. "Both dead?"

"Aye, your majesty," said Condor, the sorrow heavy in his voice, "along with about a dozen other good men."

Eldred sat in silence for a moment, shaking his head. "But my cousin Vahla-you know she's safe?" he asked, looking up.

"Aye, sir. We saw her ship safely at the dock."

"And the pirate?"

Now Condor shook his head. "Got away in the fog, Sire. I'm sorry. It was my fault."

"Your fault!"

"Yes, sir. He had come up along *Recluse*'s starboard side. We happened on them from the other side and in my haste to help, I simply came alongside her to port and boarded. Had I my wits about me, I'd have come up along the other side of the pirate and we'd have had him sandwiched between us. We could have bagged the whole lot, sir." A surge of emotion shook Condor's frame and for a moment, Eldred thought he would cry.

"Ah, you can't blame yourself for that, man," he said, patting the huge sailor's clasped hands. "Anyone would have done the same. You were just trying to help. But at least my cousin's safe. They can't blame me for that... 'Tis a pity, though. I'd like to have handed this pirate over to His Royal Majesty the High King." This last was said with a slight sneer that raised an eyebrow on Condor's otherwise crestfallen face.

"I want him badly myself, Sire," he said a new urgency in his voice. "Captains Malecium and Darios were good friends to me, sir."

"I know they were. They recognized your talent is why. But what am I to do now without them? Who's in command of the *Recluse*?"

"I put my mate, Hagreb, in temporary command, Sire, pending your and Lord Grumwald's approval."

"Lord Grumwald! What has he to do with it? I rule here, Captain Condor, make no mistake of that."

"Yes, Sire. Pending your approval, then."

"And who is this man, Hagreb?"

"A good man, Sire: twenty year veteran, good disciplinarian, respected by the men. Loyal as can be and a fine seaman, sir."

"You're sure he can do the job?" And here, for the first time, King Eldred met Condor's eye. It was meant to be a sharp, commanding glance, but as he met Condor's dark, absorbing gaze, it was as if his own eyes were suddenly caught and held there. The muscles around his eyes went momentarily slack. His mouth fell open a bit and his face went blank.

"I'm very sure he can do the job," said Condor, his voice soft and reassuring.

"Very well, then," Eldred murmured, his eyes now drifting aimlessly towards the window.

"But may I make a suggestion, Sire?"

"Certainly, Condor," said Eldred, his face resuming its normal pinched expression. "What is it?"

"Well, it's just a feeling I have, your majesty, but I don't believe this pirate is lurking along the coast at all."

"You don't?"

"No, sire. There really isn't any place for him to hide along there, and he certainly can't be staying at sea all this time, not in an open galley. He must have a base, some hole he can crawl into, someplace he can provision."

"And you think you know where it is?"

"Well, not precisely, sir. But I think he's up river somewhere."

"Up river!"

"Aye, sir. There are hundreds of creeks and inlets you could tuck a galley into, and any number of little towns where he could provision. As long as he behaved himself in port, the townspeople would be none the wiser: they'd just think him another imperial war galley."

"So, hiding under our very noses, eh? Very clever. It makes sense when you think about it."

"Yes, sir, it does. And what I'd like is your permission to take the *Recluse* and the *Steiger* up river and smoke him out."

"By all means, Captain Condor! By all means." A suddenly excited Eldred hopped up and began pacing about the room. "And you shall command, too, by the gods. Initiative like this does not go unrewarded in my realm, not by half. Take your expedition and route this viper out. Bring him here to me and we'll execute him on the steps of the palace for all the people to see! Then we'll send his head to Valeria. That will show Lord Grumwald and the High King who rules in Palemia!"

It was a less than somber Condor who made his way back down to the harbor and the tiny naval base. In fact, it was a Condor barely able to repress his jubilation. His face kept breaking into a wicked grin and his eyes fairly sparkled with glee. Hagreb, who still feared for his life after their audacious return to port, met him at the jetty and nearly toppled off into the river when he learned he was now officially captain of the *Recluse*.

Condor laughed heartily at the man's shocked expression, then draped a companionable arm about his shoulder and led him on board the *Steiger* to his tiny aft cabin. Wine was demanded of the steward to toast Hagreb's promotion, and food, and then the hapless servant was hustled out and the cabin door securely fastened behind him. "We have some things to discuss, my friend," said Condor turning back to the table, his glittering eyes and imposing frame seeming to fill the entire cabin. "And plans to make."

In the cramped sleeping compartment next door, Illana lay stretched on the bunk. As a precaution, she had been bound and gagged when they entered port, and now, having given up fighting against her bonds, lay despondent while the deep voices of Condor and another rumbled on beyond the thin partition. For a time, she tried to make out what they were saying, but only the occasional word came through. Instead, as the late afternoon turned to evening, the deep droning lulled her senses and gradually, she drifted off into a dull, dreamless sleep.

Chapter 11

They split up and worked both sides of the river, raiding and plundering one day, crossing paths at night and going back the next day as hard working naval galleys, in hot pursuit of the pirates. They did not even have to disguise their ships as the renegades were supposed to be former navy. So it was easy. They worked their way north, one portion of each crew raping and pillaging one night, the other part, buffed and polished in their Imperial finest, investigating the depredations the next day. Then they switched. For men who had spent the better part of the last two years chained to rowing benches, it was, said Condor, some well needed rest and relaxation.

And as raiding and plundering goes, it was not that bad. Not as bad as it could be, not as bad as Koth. The men drank what they wanted, took what they wanted, and who they wanted. Rape, theft and mayhem were the chief offences. Women of all shapes, sizes and ages were taken where and when they were found. But force was used only against resistance and there was little wholesale slaughter. Indeed, after a week-when even the hardiest of revelers had been sated-the number of dead barely topped a dozen. The men actually fought more among themselves than against the citizenry.

But the psychological effect of this scourge was like a tidal wave of terror rolling up and down the river. Rumors of mass devastation and atrocity flew like the wind and after a few days, people fled at the merest glimpse of a galley-any galley-so that the rovers found increasingly slim pickings.

Still, the men had their fling, and for Condor, that was the main point of it all. He had promised them freedom and with it-in the minds of these men, at least-came license. He could not have held them otherwise. He himself took little part in the festivities. While his men ran riot, he stayed quietly in his tiny cabin with Illana, without so much as a glowing candle to give away his presence. But in the mornings, when they crossed the river to 'investigate' the other galley's crimes, he was always at the forefront, his hair and beard neatly trimmed, his breastplate and helm glistening against the impeccably bright white of his toga, his swirling red cloak draped neatly from his massive shoulders. He was the picture of the Imperial Naval officer and the bruised, battered and violated residents took comfort at the sight of him.

It could have been far worse, they told themselves-indeed, many remembered far worse when Fantar reigned-but with a man like this on the job, the pirates would no doubt soon meet their deserved end. Not one realized they were being duped.

But Condor was also looking for something. As the pair of galleys moved north, they poked into every creek and inlet they passed, exactly as if they were searching out pirates. Then, late in the afternoon on the sixth day out, he found it.

The *Steiger* was working the west bank of the Sule, about thirty leagues north of Palemia. The country hereabout was hilly, heavily forested, and sparsely populated. The river had grown increasingly narrow and fast, fed by the many tributaries that tumbled down from the mountainous regions further north. *Steiger* was working past what appeared to be a low, swampy area with dense stretches of bulrush interspersed with stands of huge old willows and chestnuts crowding the bank along the water's edge. Just ahead, the flank of a low, heavily wooded ridge signaled the end of the lowlands and beyond that, the river took a sweeping turn to the right.

Condor was focused on the water at the base of the ridge, scanning intently for evidence of rocks or snags that could endanger his ship, when, from the corner of his eye, he saw a small passage opening to his left. It was nearly concealed by the arms of a great willow dipping its long fingers into the swirling water, but it ran right along the base of the ridge, and looked both deep and wide enough to float a galley. Condor signaled *Recluse*, then spun the *Steiger* around and nosed cautiously into the inlet, a man forward plying the lead and calling back the depths. The channel ran straight and deep for nearly a quarter of a mile, just wide enough to allow a galley and her sweeps. Then, as they passed another large stand of willows on the left, the stream opened out into a large pond, nearly a half-mile across.

The two ships found deep water all around the circumference and a steep, shelving beach at the western edge where they could run their beaked prows right up onto the pebbly sand and step ashore dry-shod. It was perfect, exactly what Condor had been looking for. You could moor a hundred galleys in the cove and ships could pass by in mid-channel none the wiser.

But it got better. Just up from the beach, they found a small, abandoned settlement of about a dozen buildings. A few of the houses had been burned and the bones of several inhabitants lay scattered about. The rest of the buildings had been ransacked but were still intact, right up to the thatch on their roofs. Whatever had happened to kill the town-a roving band of brigands at the end of the war, or even a deliberate act by some local minion-had not happened so long ago that thatch would rot.

Whatever, the place was perfect. Made to order. A lair, a hole to crawl into should the need arise. Condor set parties to work clearing away the bones and rubble and hauling supplies up from the ships. He took another party to scout out the vicinity, working his way through the abandoned fields stretching west and south of town and up into the forested hills to the north. A single cart track meandered westward along the forest's verge, overgrown and obviously unused for some time. Nevertheless, a cautious Condor set flankers out on both sides and walked until the track petered out in the underbrush of an abandoned woodlot. It appeared that whatever commerce the town had with the outside world had been conducted from the river.

Condor was about to signal his men to turn back when a scream pierced the verdant stillness of the woods. The sound was loud with surprise at first, then rose with terror, then stopped abruptly. Sword in hand, Condor rushed towards the scene. A group of men were clustered around a dense thicket of trees, swords and spears leveled. Several had drawn bows and were angling for position. In the midst of the thicket, a large gray wolf had taken one of the men as he squatted to relieve himself. Now, the creature crouched over his body, snarling and snapping its bloody fangs at the encircling men and showing no intention of fleeing.

It was strange for a wolf to attack a full-grown man, especially in broad daylight and with other men around, unless it was starving. And this one didn't look starved at all. More probably, it had gotten a taste of human flesh after the town was sacked and decided it liked it.

Condor signaled the bowmen to lower their weapons and stepped into the circle. The wolf had ripped out the man's throat and he lay sprawled in his own blood and muck, obviously beyond any help Condor could provide. But it was not on the man that Condor focused his gaze as he entered the thicket, but the wolf.

Seeing him, the animal tensed, the long hair rising along its back, its ears flattening, fangs bared in a low, steady growl. Condor advanced slowly, placing one foot carefully ahead of the other, his sword at the ready, and his dark, flashing eyes holding the creature's gaze. The encircling men held their breaths, not knowing what to expect or what their huge commander intended.

Condor intended what he did. He moved closer and closer, the wolf crouching ever lower as he came, preparing to spring. Its eyes glowed with a fierce red, blood and saliva dripped from its fangs, and it snarled in steady, panting bursts. Condor held the beast's gaze with his own and moved closer still. He did not speak, did not relax his posture, but slowly crouched down so that, to the beast, his face and dark, compelling eyes must have seemed to swoop down onto him.

As he got within striking distance, the wolf seemed to flinch and as Condor's staring face came ever closer, the muscles around its eyes seemed to lose their hard tension, the pupils fading from red to black. Without moving, its posture settled and relaxed and its lips slowly extended, encasing its fangs. The creature flicked its eyes away for an instant, looking this way and that as if seeking escape, then looked back into Condor's face. Its eyes caught and compelled by his, it lowered its head and whimpered.

Later, one of the bowmen in the encircling ring-the one who had the best angle and stood ready to shoot-swore that as Condor's face loomed over the beast, something dark and shadowy had passed between them, and that it was then that the beast had cowered. And cower it did. It lowered its bloody muzzle between its paws, thumped its tail and whined with a soft, pleading sound.

Condor held its gaze for a few more seconds, then abruptly stood and walked away. After several steps he stopped, turned back and slapped his hand twice against his thigh. Instantly, the creature leapt from its prey and came to heel beside him. Condor stalked on, through the line of stunned and gaping men and back along the track to the village, the wolf trotting obediently beside him.

Condor moved into the main building in town, a solid stone edifice of two stories with a flat roof and a parapet. The former owner had used the second floor as living quarters. Its opulent furnishings had been ransacked and overturned, but were otherwise undamaged, and Condor was soon ensconced in more comfort and luxury than he had ever experienced in his life. There were oil lamps as good as Eldred had at the palace, china plates and metal utensils to eat with, and even a goodly supply of firewood, ready stacked beside the main hearth.

After dinner, Condor had his steward, Sardin, make up a small fire-for effect more than heat-and as the evening shadows lengthened into night, he sat before the flickering blaze, drinking freely from a large flagon of wine. The wolf lay at his side, as contented as any rural hound, while across the hearth, huddled in a large, cushioned chair, hugging her knees to her chest, sat Illana.

Her near two weeks of captivity had not been kind to her. Her flesh had wasted away so that her shoulders and cheekbones seemed about to push

195

through her skin. Her eyes were sunken and dull and her face had taken on a sallow pallor that even the flickering firelight could not conceal. Mentally, there seemed little left of the spirited girl who had boarded *Valadator* in Dulcai, and even less of the budding woman whose gaze had so captivated Boltar. Her friends, she believed, thought her dead. She could see no way of escape, and her will power-which was all that kept her from debasement by her captor-was nearly gone. Even her memories of home and of her recent past-of Boltar and Eomer and the King and all the voyage north-were but vague shimmerings in her mind, like bits of half-remembered dreams that she was no longer sure were even real. Day and night Condor had assaulted her with his presence, with his commanding eyes, and his implacable demand that she kneel before him. And her resistance was fading.

Now there was this wolf-the most terrifying creature she had ever seen in her life-wild and bloody, fresh from its kill, lying at his feet like some domesticated daemon. And his eyes were worse this night. Whatever power was in them-and power there was; in her more lucid moments she was aware of some extra-human evil-had been enhanced by his subjugation of the wolf, and as he drank, he leered at her with them. She could feel his eyes roving up and down her body, intruding at every curve and joint, could feel the mounting lust behind them. She curled herself tighter and tighter, trying to become as small as possible.

But then those eyes locked once more on hers and she knew it was the end.

"Stand," he said and she could not but obey. She stood.

"Turn," he said, and she pirouetted slowly before him, trembling in every limb as she felt his eyes travel over her. Then, when she was facing him again, his eyes locked on hers like a physical force.

"Undo your shirt." Her own clothes had been replaced by rough seaman's wear, and though she willed her hands be still, her fingers crept up her chest and began undoing the ties, one by one. When the last one was undone, her hands fell back to her sides and she stood, her shirt hanging open before him.

"Show me," he said. There was a different quality in his voice now, a huskiness she had not heard before. And she watched, helpless, as her own hands pulled open her shirt, exposing her naked breasts. His glistening eyes caressed them, lingering slowly over each delicate mound and circling each areola. She could feel the wetness of them, suckling her like tiny tongues.

"Now the trousers," he said, and though she trembled with the effort to hold back, her fingers plucked the drawstring, and the loose pantaloons dropped to the floor. She wore nothing beneath them.

Now those insidious eyes were probing her most secret, most intimate parts. She wanted to cringe, tried to turn away, but some contrary force impelled her hips forward. She spread her thighs and opened herself to him more completely. A prickling heat danced all around her groin and pierced her flesh like a tongue of fire. She caught her breath once, twice, then began to pant as a flush crept up from her loins. It encircled her breasts, infused her cheeks and misted her eyes. She felt she might swoon, but still opened herself further to his engorging eye.

"You are very beautiful, my little princess," he gasped, a flush spread wide now across his own cheeks. "Will you kneel to me now?"

She looked down and saw that he had loosened his own small clothes, exposing his rigid member. A trembling came over her as a distant part of her brain fought against this last total violation of her will. Her mind swirled with dizziness and disgust, but the struggle was short. Again, his eye commanded and she fell to her knees, blind with a ravenous desire.

But on the instant, another voice interrupted, a sibilant, hissing voice, laughing. At the sound of it, Condor leapt from his chair, and sent Illana sprawling. In the corner of the room furthest from the fire, a dark figure could just be seen emerging from the shadows.

"It's you," said Condor, his voice alarmed, yet still slurred and heavy. "How did you get in here?"

"I entered," said the figure.

"Well, you can exit again. I don't need you here!"

"I think you have missed the point," said the figure. "Without me you would not be here."

"Well, I am now, so bugger off."

The figure did not reply but began to approach, sliding effortlessly across the floor.

"Stay away from me," said Condor, his voice menacing.

But the figure ignored him and came on, drifting like a black cloud.

"Sick him!" Condor hissed to the wolf and pointed, but the wolf cowered on the floor, its head down, ears back. Illana, too, sat in a stupor, her back against the woodpile, her naked buttocks pressing against bits of bark and wood chips that littered the hearth. Her mind seemed to be encased in fog, her vision clouded, and though her eyes followed the scene before her, she made no sense of it. Her brain did not record it.

The figure stopped in the center of the room. Condor grabbed his sword and tried to attack, but his arm was arrested in mid-swing. He stared at it, his muscles bulging and his face straining as if he were trying to pull the sword out of solid rock, but his arm wouldn't move. He glared at the figure, fear beginning to flicker in his eyes. Slowly, his mouth came open and his head began to twist to the side, but like Illana, the act was not done at his volition. His mouth opened further and further, as if two fists were forcing his jaws apart, and his neck was twisted nearly to the snapping point.

He gurgled, his eyes wide now with panic and pain: "Arrrrrrgh."

"The point, you see," said the figure, its voice calm and modulated, "is that all you have has been given by me. Your power is mine as you are mine."

Suddenly, he released him and Condor collapsed back into his chair. He sat there, working his jaw and rubbing his arm. He wore a sullen, petulant look like a child who feels unfairly disciplined.

"And why do you suppose I have given you these things?" said the figure. "Did you suppose it was so you could sit here in this backwater and dabble with your little plaything there? Is that why you think I have been to all this trouble over you? I doubt even you are such a fool as that, though you surely have no idea what value you have there. So, tell me, what is your purpose, holed up here?"

Condor stared, his eyes hard and offended, but it was clear there was no cogent answer behind them.

"So it is as I suspected," said the shadow. "You thought no more than to put your back against something, to protect the little you have gained with no thought as to what purpose you could put it to. You have planned nothing, have you? You're like this wolf, acting on instinct with no thought for the future beyond your next meal.

"Well, unlike you, my friend, I do have thoughts for the future. In fact, I have a little job for you. And if you complete it successfully, you will have more future than you ever dreamed of, and more power even than that bastard of a father you so envy."

"What is this job?" said Condor, his voice still sullen but betraying interest.

"I want you to fetch something for me. And when you've fetched it, I want you to wear it."

"Wear it! Wear what?"

"Oh, just a little bauble. It's called the Eye of Valeria."

"That's the power stone of the High King!"

"Very good! Your erudition surprises me."

"But how can I get such a thing from the High King? And what good will it do me if I could? When my father had it... "

"Yes, I know very well what happened," the figure interrupted, its shadowy face actually seeming to smile. "In fact, I know all about it. But fear not, my young friend. As I said, I have a plan, and I will be with you all the way."

It was an apparently downcast and disappointed Condor who sat in King Eldred's private chambers several days later and confessed that he had been unable to catch the pirates. He had brought along a young woman, whom he introduced as Marla, and a large wolf that trotted by his side as obediently as a well-trained hunting dog. Marla, too, stayed close by his side, barely acknowledging the King and saying very little. She had a strange, rather vacant expression but, nevertheless, was exceedingly attractive. She wore a low-cut gown of some diaphanous material that revealed more of her physical charms than it covered, and despite his terror of the wolf, Eldred could not take his eyes off her while Condor gave his report. The brigands had gained strength, the latter said, and seemed to have acquired a second ship. He had followed doggedly in their wake, he claimed, but had not been able to find them.

"There are creeks and inlets by the hundreds up there, your Majesty. It would take a fleet to search them all. Perhaps when Lord Grumwald returns, he will accompany me back up river and we will have more success."

"Ah," said Eldred, pulling his hungry eyes away from Marla, "you just missed Grumwald. He came back through here yesterday."

"That is surprising," said Condor, stroking the still fine tendrils of his beard. "We saw another pair of His Majesty's galleys up river two days ago. But when we attempted to come up with them, they waved us off."

"How could that be?" said Eldred. "Grumwald said he was just on his way back from the east and stopped to see if we had made any progress here. When I told him about your confrontation on the way to Valeria, he left immediately."

"If he ever went east," said Condor.

"What do you mean?"

"Well, all the reports say this pirate is sailing a naval galley-or now, as it appears, a pair of naval galleys. And what naval galleys are here? Four: two of which have been in port here in Palemia, and two of which-the *Recluse* and my *Steiger*-we know have been chasing the pirates. Yet here we see two other naval galleys up river at the same time Lord Grumwald is here, 'reporting' to you."

202

"I don't follow: why would Grumwald send ships up river and not tell me?"

"Well, I'm only speculating here, your Majesty, and would be loath to speak ill of any superior, but suppose-just suppose-this whole pirate thing is a plot by Princess Vahla and the High King to make you look bad."

"By the gods!" said Eldred, glimpses of Marla's saucy breasts suddenly forgotten. "How could this be?"

"Well, again your Majesty, I'm not one to tell tales, but it's no secret that relations between you and your cousin have been less than cordial. So just suppose they want to replace you, but don't have the nerve to just do so without cause. And surely there is no cause! But, if they could show you as ineffective in cornering this pirate, they could start building a case."

"Well, then it's clear we must get this pirate!" said Eldred, his anger suddenly aroused.

"Ah, not so fast, your Majesty. Are we sure we know their entire plan?"

"What do you mean?"

"Well, if there really is no pirate, then who sacked Koth? Who killed Malecium? And Darius, and Gunther of the *Recluse*? It must be one of the High King's own galleys, acting in disguise under orders from Grumwald. So if we take the bait and attack and kill them, what's to stop them from turning around and saying we're in open rebellion? Don't you see, Sire? That's the real trap!"

"What do we do, then?" said Eldred, his face in open alarm, his eyes darting between the wolf and the girl Marla as if they were the symbols of his dilemma. Then Condor caught those eyes with his own and fixed them with a hard, penetrating stare. Under it, Eldred's face went slack, his jaw sagged and he slumped against the back of his chair.

"Just leave it to me, your majesty," said Condor, his voice deep and soothing. "I know a way we can make them twist their own tails."

Chapter 12

Valerius stood on the walls of Valeria, looking out over the plains to the north. They were all cultivated now, the crops a mosaic of green lines sketched against brown earth. In the distance, the hills rose as dark smudges, shimmering in the heat haze. It was high summer, just the time of year, he thought, that Fantar had descended on the city from those hills. In his mind, he could still see the endless flood of men, streaming out of the forest and spreading across the plain. How many did he have, he wondered? It could not have been that many then. Ten, perhaps fifteen thousand? It had seemed like a vast host then, and was certainly more than the city could muster.

Young Valerius-he was Valerian then-had been just shy of fifteen, too young to bear arms, though even at that age, easily large enough to wield them. The generals had counseled caution. "Bar the gates and summon your allies, Majesty. We can protect the harbor and he can do nothing against us otherwise. A week tops and we can muster twenty thousand to take the field against him."

But Valerian's father, then King Valerius, would not listen. "Cower behind my walls in the face of such rabble? I won't hear of it! They won't stand against disciplined troops." And out he went, with fifteen hundred Imperial Guard dressed in their finest. Young Valerian went too, against his father's direct orders. He was supposed to stay with the women-"to protect them," his father had said. But Valerian had ordered a young companion to switch places with him and had marched out with the Guard in that young man's place and answering to his name-Balazar. Little did he know then that he would answer to that name for the next fifteen years.

Fantar's rabble had done more than stand against the city's disciplined troops. They had crushed them utterly, then had sacked and burned the city. Valerian-Balazar-had fallen early in the fight, knocked unconscious by a heavy blow to the helm, and had awoken that night to the hellish scene of rebels, silhouetted by raging fires within the city, cavorting along the walls, murdering ancients and young children and flinging their bodies down into the blackness below. But that was not all. Crawling and stumbling among the corpses on the field, Valerian had sprawled face to face with his own father's severed head. Fantar-who was the King's own bastard son and Valerian's half-brother-had hacked it off to more easily remove the Eye Stone, symbol of Imperial power. Valerian, who from that moment on would even think of himself as Balazar, had vomited his horror and fled into the hills.

How many years ago had that been, Valerius now wondered? Twenty-five? More? Too many to recall, and too many lived in hopeless desperation, in a raging self-loathing that drove him to the forefront of every succeeding battle as Fantar conquered the Empire, city by city, hoping to find

206

the death that had passed over him at Valeria. Only when he finally accepted the challenge of leading the tiny Kantaran against their cannibalistic enemies, the Iblis, had the great tear in his psyche begun to heal, and only with the help of Thorngere and then the old Mage Volkmir, was he finally able to acknowledge his true name and reclaim the title-and the Eye Stone-that was his rightful patrimony.

That had begun the process of reclaiming the Empire and he had thought that the fall of Fantar in the hills beyond Palmeria had ended it. But now he knew that was not so, that the struggle to retain the Empire was far from over, and would never be as long as there was an Empire to defend. No matter how powerful his armies, how numerous his fleet, he could never really rest secure. A single false move, a single vainglorious act or foolish bravado, and he could end like his father, sprawled in a bloody heap. And the Empire would end with him. As grand as it was, it was as fragile as life itself.

And now he faced a threat that seemed beyond life. There was no host spreading across the verdant plain before him, no fleet blockading the city, no states rising in rebellion, no Scythian hordes sweeping down from the distant steppes. Apart from a handful of renegade pirates and the usual mildew of crime, the Empire was at peace. Trade and business were flourishing. Fields were tilled, forges were turning steel into plow shears, young people were starting families, babies were being born.

The Empire was as green with rebirth as these plains stretching before him, and yet he sensed a darkness hovering on the edge of vision, an evil he could not name, could not see, but which was as insidious as a plague. How could he fight a threat he could not see?

The circle of his thought came back again to the Eye. Always the Eye: a weapon his forefathers had born for nearly a thousand years; a weapon that was as familiar to him as his own sandals, or the great falchion he had chosen as his personal weapon and which had earned him the nickname, 'Balazar the Butcher'; but a weapon he did not know how to use. Somewhere in that eons long trail of familiarity, the knowledge of how to use the great red gemstone had become lost and the Eye became blind, a symbol lacking substance. And nothing he had found to date in the Book of Kings or any of the other ancient scrolls, which occupied his nights, had shed any light. Again and again he read that "the Eye was the symbol of the High King's power," that with it he "could see into the future and into the hearts of men." A simple, formulaic description repeated endlessly through tome after tome, generation after generation with never a hint or clue as to how the High King could 'see into the future' or into 'the hearts of men.'

His father-and perhaps many High Kings before him-had thought the thing a mere bauble. And Valerius could see where he had ended, and remembered only too clearly how he had ended. But he himself had also doubted at first, refused to believe that it was the stone which had burned out Fantar's eye when he tried to use it, humored Volkmir when the old mage said the Eye had "allowed" him some limited use of its powers, that by merely "gazing into it" he had been able to track Balazar's whereabouts for years. Those visions, he had thought, were merely an old man's imaginings.

Yet, still, he had wanted to believe. A king in name only, facing an Empire-who would not want to believe in such a thing? And so he had tried and tried again, with Volkmir there in his mountain cave, then many times in the years since-regularly in fact-with little concrete results beyond vague imaginings and associated coincidences. And were it not for the stone itself, he might, too, have come not to believe. But that there was power there was as sure as the weight of the thing, hanging on its golden chain. He had seen that power, felt that power. It had flashed out, seemingly of its own volition a number of times, striking down a frenzied maenad, servant of the god Balaam, and on the mountain overlooking the Plains of Darlung, the Eye had blasted him a full fifty feet, nearly blinding him and starting an earthquake when he had tried to use it for personal, vengeful ends.

So there was power there. And apparently, some overall, guiding will, some power behind the power. But all his efforts to use it at his will-even for good-had come to naught. Was it not a thing he could use? Was he a bearer only, the mere point of a mightier spear, to be used at its behest, with no say for himself in where, how or when? Was he the tool, then, the chariot upon which the power of the god rode? For what else would you call such a power, if not god?

But if that were so, then why make him and his line High Kings? Why not a Mage? A man-at-arms, could carry a stone, could move at the god's behest, and dumb and unknowing, project its power. So why a king? Why a High King, with volition over an Empire, if not to share that power?

Perhaps he was not ready, an acolyte unfit, as yet to bear a master's burden. Perhaps there were other things he had to learn, other tests he had to pass. But what? And where? And how? And how many times, in the past how many years, had his mind run this same course, reached this same end, and got not one inch beyond it?

In his frustration, he had unwittingly begun pacing the battlements, guards and citizens skipping out of his path, their salutes and greetings unseen and ignored. But now, something caught his eye and he emerged from his reverie to find himself staring down at the quays, at the *Valadator*, which had apparently entered the harbor without his notice and was even now securing her dock lines. Thinking that Grumwald would soon be making his way up to report, he turned to find a messenger waiting to speak to him.

"Ah, yes lad, I see *Valadator* has just come in," he said, preempting the boy.

"Yes, your Majesty. But I'm to tell you there is a messenger here from Dulcai."

The messenger was from Rondo and the news was not good. King Reuters had died within a week of their departure. Valerius, Eomer, and Vahla listened to the report in the private family room of the palace. He had seemed to rally, the messenger recounted, but then almost overnight, he had become lethargic, fallen into a deep sleep and passed away. It was so sudden, Rondo wished them to know, the whole kingdom was in shock to lose such a beloved king, especially so soon after the hope and excitement of the Queen and High King's visit. He was having King Reuter's body embalmed, the messenger said, and making the other usual preparations, but awaited instructions from Her Majesty.

The messenger fell silent and Valerius looked to Eomer. She seemed stunned she sat so stiffly in her chair, so he quietly thanked the messenger and dismissed him. "I'm so sorry, my dear," he said when the man had gone.

"I knew," said Eomer, a single tear running down her cheek. She swiped at it quickly with the back of her hand. "I knew when we left I would never see him again." She began to tremble, sitting so straight and fighting so hard for control. Other tears fell unheeded. "Oh," she cried suddenly, "I wish we had stayed so I could have been with him!"

Both Valerius and Vahla moved to comfort her, but Vahla, being closer, got there first and Eomer clung to her, sobbing softly. Valerius stood helpless, stroking aimlessly at her shoulder. "We didn't know," he said. "We just couldn't have known."

Eomer shot him a hard look, but whether of anger or sheer pain, he didn't know, for she turned away and buried her face in Vahla's dark flowing mane and began to sob.

It was this scene that confronted Grumwald as, accustomed by long habit, he strode into the palace's private quarters. But he stopped short just inside the family room door when he saw the weeping Eomer. "Oh, I beg your pardon!" he exclaimed and made to withdraw, but Valerius motioned him in.

"We've just gotten word that Reuters has died," he said quietly.

The alarm and concern, which had etched the old warrior's face, sagged suddenly and he shook his head sadly. "Ah, I'm sorry to hear that. He was a good man, King Reuters, and a more loyal and stalwart ally you could not find. My condolences to both Your Majesties."

"Thank you, Grumwald," Eomer sniffed and held out her hand. But when he went to kiss it, she hugged him instead. "I know he felt the same about you and appreciated all you've done."

"Thank you, Ma'am. I'm proud to have known him. You'll be going back down for the funeral, then?"

"Of course," said Valerius. "Reuters was a friend long before he was family. And Rondo is having the body embalmed, so there's time. But we'll also need to have a coronation."

"Aye, that's right! My felicitations to you, Your Majesty," Grumwald said, stepping back and bowing-not without grace-to the new Queen of Dulcai. "May your reign be long and prosperous." Now Eomer did hold out her hand, and Grumwald gently kissed it.

"Thank you, Grumwald. And if his Majesty will permit, we would be honored if you would ferry us south in your great ship and carry my father's sarcophagus up river to the valley of tombs." Valerius quickly nodded his assent.

"Nothing less would suit him, my Lady," said Grumwald and bowed again, a short military bow this time, from the waist. "I'll begin preparations immediately."

"Now, if you'll excuse me," said Eomer. "I know you have business to discuss... "

"No business that does not concern you, my dear," said Valerius.

"That's all right. I'd better check on the nursery anyway."

When she had withdrawn, the three sat in silence for a few more moments. "Well," Valerius said at last, "we can still do our best to find his niece. What did you turn up, Grumwald?"

"Not the least shadow of the fellow," Grumwald growled. "Sailed east and south as far as Palmeria and nobody'd even heard any reports of a pirate. Then, on the way back, Eldred tells me one of his ships was attacked while escorting you, Princess Vahla. Two of his top commanders and a dozen more killed before the other fellow drove them off. It was that saucy young commander we met before. Eldred said you were safe and that he had sent him up river to search, so I scoured the coast on the way back here. There's not a trickle of a creek we didn't look into, and found nothing. But tell me about the attack, my Lady?"

"You didn't tell me you were attacked," said Valerius.

"Well, we really weren't," said Vahla. "We' ran into fog and heard sounds of attack, so I ordered my captain to row on. But we didn't see anything."

"What did your escort report?" Grumwald wanted to know.

"We didn't see them again, either."

"But Eldred said they reported you safe in harbor."

"Maybe they pulled in later, saw us docked and headed back to Palemia."

"That's strange. Doesn't seem in character for that impertinent young buck to pass up a chance to make himself known at court."

"Well," said Vahla, "he's doing all right in Eldred's court, I can tell you. I've just had a letter from my old friend Celia and it seems Eldred has made this fellow squadron commander. The two are quite chummy, she says, and the new commander parades around town with a pet wolf! She says half the people in town are terrified at the sight of him and that Eldred loves it."

"Well, I'm not surprised," said Grumwald. "I knew when I saw him there must be some part of the old King's seed in that young fellow."

"What?" said Valerius.

"Oh, it's as clear as can be," said Vahla. "We didn't say anything to him, to give him ideas, but the resemblance between both of you-and especially Fantar-is uncanny."

Suddenly, Valerius saw again the images he had seen in the cave in Dulcai, the dark figure looming, the sudden face, a beardless, then a newly bearded youth. Then he saw the Eye throbbing on his cabin wall that day aboard *Kantar* and the face of the hulking, bearded youth as he barreled his way down the deck, Illana over his shoulder.

"That's him!" he shouted, startling the others. "A great, huge fellow, my size or bigger, right?" The others nodded. "That's the pirate, then! I didn't realize it until now, but he was the fellow who took Illana. It happened so fast I only got a glimpse of him, but something about it kept bothering me. It was that he looked like me! By the gods, what a cheeky bastard! Pirate at sea, loyal commander ashore.

But he's no seed of the old king, I'll wager. He's Fantar's bastard! The bastard son of a bastard son. And it was this fellow in your escort, Vahla. Who commanded?"

"A man named Darios." She said, her own mind going back to that moment at anchor when she and the young commander locked eyes across the quiet water.

"Aye, I remember him from Zagorbia. But before you ran into the fog, you didn't see any other ships?"

"Well, no. But it was dark."

"Yet a pirate was supposedly able to find you in the dark and the fog? I'll bet it was this same fellow, falling on his own commander unawares. You're lucky he didn't see you. What did you say this fellow's name was?"

"Condor," said Vahla. "His name is Condor."

Young Valerian was napping in his big boy bed and Eomer was just putting Alair back in her crib when Valerius entered. The nurse, Brenda was off duty. Eomer came to her husband and he held her quietly, feeling her body tremble and the wet of her tears on his tunic. He stroked her hair and watched over her head as the afternoon light flickered across the bed and across the face of young Valerian. And he had this sense of time rolling on like a great wheel, raising up generations of men only to throw them down again and crush them. How quickly it moved, when you looked back on it. How soon would young Valerian here be mourning the passing of his parents? And what of his children? Or little Alair's? Would he and Eomer get to watch them grow, or like poor Reuters, would they fall beneath the wheel?

Eomer sniffed and blew her nose, then leaned back to look up at her husband. "I feel so guilty, weeping like this," she said.

"Guilty?" The comment surprised Valerius. "What on earth for?"

Eomer shook her head. "I'm not sure. It's just that so many died over the years, fighting Fantar, it seems kind of selfish just to grieve for one."

"It's never selfish to grieve for someone you love. Besides, death in battle is something we all face. It's almost expected. But Reuters had gotten past all that, that's what's so sad to me. It's like he was cheated. I mean, he'd just seen his grandchildren for the first time."

Eomer's face crinkled up and she began to sob again. "I didn't want him to die!" she wailed and threw herself against Valerius' chest. "I wanted the children to know him, what a good man he was, and I wanted him to know them!"

Valerius led her to their own room so as not to disturb the children. They lay on the bed and he held her for a long time. Finally, she blew her nose again and propped herself up on an elbow. "What did Grumwald say? Is there any news of Illana?"

Valerius shook his head. "No news of her, but we think we figured out who the pirate is."

"Really? Who?"

"Well, nobody we've met. He's a young officer of Eldred's in Palemia. It seems he's been acting the pirate at sea and masquerading as a loyal officer ashore. Eldred has made him commander of the squadron, and he's apparently parading around like quite the cock of the walk. Grumwald thought he might be another wayward bastard of my dear departed father."

"Another half-brother?"

"I think he's too young for that. It's more likely he the spawn of Fantar."

"Fantar! What are you going to do?"

"Do? I'm going to send some people to Palemia and have a talk with this young man, that's what."

"You've got to go yourself, especially if he's Fantar's bastard son."

"He's only a single renegade. I've many others who can handle him. Besides, we've got Reuters and Dulcai to think of."

Now Eomer sat up cross-legged on the bed and looked hard at her husband. "Those are my responsibilities, Valerius. You go to Palemia and find my niece! Besides, I think it will be better if I go to Dulcai by myself anyway. I need to establish myself as Queen there, not just as the High King's wife. That's assuming I can still have Grumwald and *Valadator*, of course."

Valerius smiled up at his gorgeous, golden wife. "You can have Grumwald and all else that I possess, my love. But none of them will make you any more of a queen than you already are."

Down in the market, Grumwald made his way among the stalls, his rank offering no protection from the buffeting of the crowds. But he paid scant attention to the bustling throng, or to the many vendors who called out to him and held up their wares. Rather, he worked his way this way and that-seemingly always against the flow of the crowd-craning his neck to look down side aisles, his seamed and scarred face pursed as if he were searching for something. And indeed he was, for suddenly he spotted his quarry and began thrusting his way through the jostling bodies until he came up with her.

"Why, Nurse Brenda!" he exclaimed as he reached her side. "What a surprise meeting you here."

"Commodore!" she said, her cautious buyer-beware expression breaking into a wide, welcoming smile. "Whatever are you doing here?"

"Oh, just looking for a few things, you know. Here, let me help you with those packages. What have you bought?"

"Oh, just some cloth and sewing things. I've been thinking it's time to make myself a new dress."

"Well, it's a lovely fabric and I must say, I can't think of anyone it would look lovelier on."

Chapter 13

Condor and Eldred were playing Harat in Eldred's private chambers. Illana-or Marla, as Eldred knew her-stretched languorously on the couch beside Condor, while the wolf dozed fitfully on the floor by his side. Eldred sat opposite on a straight-backed chair, dividing his attention not quite equally between Marla, the game, and the wolf; which perhaps accounted for the fact that over the course of the afternoon, and despite Condor's efforts to make things appear fair, he had lost more than he had won.

The Harat board on the low table between them had been imported from the distant provinces to the east and was elegantly made of hand-carved wood and inlaid ivory with a little drawer at one end to hold the gaming pieces. These were of black shale and white ivory, seven to a side, each inlaid with five white or black dots of shell. The same dot pattern was repeated on five squares of the board, which was a curiously shaped arrangement of twenty squares, laid out in three rows. Two squares were cut out of the board on each side, marking the entry and exit points for the game pieces. A rosette pattern and what appeared to be a geometric arrangement of four eyes, decorated an additional five squares each, and the remaining five squares were divided into three patterns, two, two and one.

Each pattern affected some movement of the pieces that landed on it. For example, under the rules Condor and Eldred were playing by, each time a piece landed on a rosette, it had to go back to the beginning. Land on the eye pattern, however, and you got a free move. If a piece landed on an opposing piece, that piece was 'captured' and had to start over at the entry point: that was unless that piece was on a five-dot square, in which case, the landing piece had to start over.

Moves were determined by throws of three pyramidal dice-Eldred's were carved of black onyx-each with two of their four points tipped with white ivory, and the purpose of the game was to race the pieces clockwise up and down the board. The winner was the first player to get all his pieces around the course and off the board at the missing square next to where they entered.

Eldred, as noted, had not been playing well. He lacked the attention span for concentrated efforts, and after sporting Condor a small pile of gold to cover his initial ante-Condor, being only "a poor naval officer," who could hardly be expected to front his own cash-had quickly lost that and several of his own as well. Now, as the afternoon shadows stretched long across the veranda and the rectangle of light from the open double doors angled eastward, he was showing even more impatience as Condor once again skipped his last piece five squares down the board, got a free throw and won.

"You know what you need, my Lord," said Condor, setting the pieces for another game before Eldred had a chance to protest. "You need something to make the game interesting. How about we play for something better than gold?"

"Like what?" said Eldred, rolling his eyes up from Marla's legs.

"Well, how about Marla, here?"

Eldred inhaled so sharply the wolf twitched at the noise. "Marla! But how could you... ?

"Oh, I'm sure she'd go along with it, wouldn't you, Marla?"

"Hmmmm?" said Marla, stretching like a cat and looking dreamily up at Condor.

"You like his Majesty, don't you? Wouldn't you like to go play with him?"

Illana smiled and gave Eldred an appraising look. "Mmmm," she said in a tone that made his heart hammer.

"But," he said, blood rushing to his face, "how could I... What could I wager in return?"

"Ah, that's easy," said Condor, his voice soft, his smile disarming. "Wager the command of all the forces in Palemia."

Eldred's eyes went sharp and a knowing smile creased his face. "Ahhha. So that's your game, is it?"

"You can't fault a man for having ambition," said Condor with a warm smile of his own. But his eyes locked Eldred's in their grip. "Besides, your Majesty, you know I'm more capable than old Gainor. He's a good man, but he is getting on."

Eldred met Condor's gaze but did not succumb. Instead, his eyes squeezed hard in calculation, then darted to Marla. "Done!" he said. "But I start this time," and snatched up the dice.

The game of Harat was not all luck, but required skill and not a little strategy. Skill in marshaling your pieces down the board, and strategy chiefly in how you launched your pieces and countered your opponent's drive. Eldred, now that his attention was fully on the game, was a blocker. He wanted to get as many pieces on the board as he could, then move them in as tight a formation as possible. This was not so much for protection-for there really was none-but to enable him to maximize the effect of every throw.

Three dice with two white tips each could land in any of four combinations: no white tips up, or one, two, or three white tips up. Under Palemian rules, throw a zero, you got no move; throw a one, you could move a piece one square. Roll a two, however, and you could move three squares. Roll a three and you went five squares. Rolling either a two or a three gave you another throw. Thus, with a number of different pieces on the board, Eldred could better choose which piece to move. Theoretically, this would allow him to avoid trouble spots, and since an exact throw was required for a piece to exit the board, gave him better odds at the finish. On the other hand, as a player's pieces could not land on each other, too many pieces also tended to get in each other's way.

They also afforded Condor more chances to pick them off. Condor was a stalker. His strategy was to hold back and use his pieces sparingly-

usually in pairs-and to attack his opponent at every opportunity. This meant that while Eldred was massing pieces on his entry row, Condor could skip two or three pieces all the way around the course to await a convenient exit throw. Then, when Eldred began moving his pieces onto the center row, where conflict was possible, Condor had reserves in hand to capture them from behind and send them back to the beginning. He also had seemingly uncanny luck in throwing the dice.

This strategy had worked well thus far, and during the course of the afternoon, Condor had won enough gold to buy a small estate. But now that an important prize beckoned, Eldred began paying more attention to what Condor was doing. When Condor got his first piece out into the center lane, instead of focusing on his own pieces, Eldred took a lucky throw to snap it up. More, he skipped his own piece right down the board on his next two throws and was the first to have a piece finish.

Thus the battle raged far longer than any of the previous contests, with both sides scoring and both sides taking hits and having to start their pieces over. Outside the shadows lengthened into dusk. Servants came in to light the oil lamps and then brought in hors d'oeuvres. And after watching for a time, Illana stretched full length on the couch and fell fast asleep.

Condor, however, never lost focus but watched every move with dark intensity. In the days since his return, he had been working assiduously to extend his influence over Eldred, and now the fruition of his plan seemed at hand. In her repose, the bodice of Illana's gown had fallen open, revealing all but the rose-tinted tip of her left breast. Condor watched as Eldred's eye sought this delight with increasing frequency as the game progressed, and at several critical moments, when that eye strayed, Condor's fingers played. The tiniest flick could tip a die from black to white or white to black, and change a move from defeat to attack.

Thus, though Eldred jumped out to an early lead and seemed several times to be within a few moves of achieving his desire-the object of which lay just beyond the reach of his twitching fingers-Condor kept coming on, taking a key piece here, leaping over a lurking trap there, so that the impending victory never quite materialized. But neither did hope fade, for as they came down to the final pieces, the race remained neck and neck.

Then, a lucky five got Eldred's last piece but one around the final corner and off in a single throw, and his additional throw brought his last piece within three. Condor had a piece one square ahead-which meant he had to roll two ones to finish, since no combination of the dice allowed a two square move-and another piece back six places down the center lane with a rosette in between. Thus, thought Eldred as he calculated the odds, Condor would need to throw four more times at the very least, while all he had to do was throw a single two. Then that lovely breast lying there-oh, so delicately-and the rest of the lovely thing attached to it, would be his.

He looked back and Condor's throw showed three white tips and he moved his piece down the center lane, right over the rosette, and landed right behind Eldred's remaining piece. Here was risk Eldred had not foreseen, as Condor also got an extra throw. Eldred glanced once more at the sleeping Marla, then squeezed his eyes tight shut and whispered a small prayer.

But the gods were not with him. When he opened his eyes, Condor's dice showed but a single white tip. Eldred's piece was sent back to the beginning and the game was effectively over. Eldred slumped in his chair and covered his face with his hands.

"Do you want to play it out, Your Majesty?" said Condor victory lighting the darkness in his face. "Who knows how the dice will fall?"

"No, it's impossible. There's no way. You've won-Commander."

A broad grin split Condor's face. "Thank you my lord. You will not regret it, I promise you. Ho, Marla, did you hear that? While you were sleeping away, his Majesty here has made me Commander of the City!"

Marla stirred and yawned and pulled her clothes together as she sat up. "You won?" she asked, her eyes still distant with sleep.

"Yes, my dear. I've won. But you sound disappointed. Doesn't she sound disappointed, my Lord?"

There was something in Condor's tone and the wry look in his eye that checked Eldred's pulse.

"Why would she be disappointed at you winning such honors, Commander?" he asked urbanely, holding in check the surge of excitement that throbbed just beneath his skin.

"Why disappointed? Why, to have missed out on trading me in for one better, of course! Ah, look! Look at how she blushes! I believe we've caught her out, my lord. She's disappointed not to have been won by you."

Illana said nothing but sat demurely, her hands clasped between her knees.

"Well, my lord, you're obviously one for the ladies, you are. I didn't realize! Now, a deal's a deal, and as you said, your Majesty, I've won fair and square. But that's not to say we can't make another deal is it?"

Eldred was on the edge of his chair now and Condor's face was glowing with amusement.

"Yes, I think if his Majesty wants to win Marla, and Marla wants to be won by his Majesty, it should be up to me to arrange a contest to make that happen. Wouldn't you say so, your Majesty?"

Now for the first time, a hint of suspicion crept into Eldred's face. "What kind of contest?"

"A simple one, my Lord. A test of courage, if you will. Don't you think that would suffice, my dear? All King Eldred has to do to win you is pet the wolf. Isn't that easy?"

"Yes," said Illana, her voice a monotone. "King Eldred must pet the wolf."

But Eldred was terrified of the wolf and at the very thought, his stomach turned to jelly. Still, he made an effort, crouching down and reaching his hand out towards the great gray-headed beast. As he caught the scent of Eldred's hand, the wolf opened its eyes, laid its ears back and growled low in the back of its throat. Its eyes were yellow and hard and glowered with malevolence. Eldred's hand began to tremble.

"Be careful, Eldred," said Condor. "He can sense your fear. If you're fearful when you approach, he feels threatened and might attack. I've seen him rip a man's throat out as quick as that!" and Condor snapped his fingers so loudly that the wolf flinched and Eldred leapt back to his chair.

Condor threw back his head and roared with laughter.

Valerius sat in his study, reviewing provision manifests for the expedition to Palemia. But his mind would not focus on the business at hand, and kept drifting back to the departure of Eomer with *Valadator* and two escort galleys earlier that morning. Though it had all be agreed and decided, seeing his wife and children board the great ship and knowing it would be some weeks at least until he could see them again almost made him change his mind: that and Grumwald who was not at all pleased when he discovered he would be sailing south with the Queen while Valerius headed east to run down the pirate.

"Why, I thought you'd have been pleased with a bit of light duty," Valerius teased when Grumwald confronted him in the great cabin of

Valadator. "I hear Eomer has even arranged for a nurse to take care of you in your dotage."

"I see there are no secrets in this court!" Grumwald retorted, grinning sheepishly. "But seriously, my Lord, do you think it wise to confront this fellow without *Valadator*?"

"Well, it's not as if the whole city has risen against us. He's only got-what? -two ships? And I'm taking six. I think we'll be fine."

"Aye, but for the matter of a couple days, why risk it? If the force is here, why not use it?"

"Because it's also important for Queen Eomer to get to Dulcai. Besides, I'm not even sure how well *Valadator* would do against ramming galleys: she's not exactly nimble you know."

Grumwald bristled at this insult to his ship, but he also knew the charge to be true: as huge and impressive as the great triremes like *Valadator* were, they were also easy targets for smaller, more agile galleys which could dart in, pierce the great ship's bellies with their bronze-sheathed rams, and dart away again before the others could begin to turn away. That was why so few had been built and why Valerius would not build any more. *Valadator* and her few sisters were products of Fantar's inflated sense of glory.

"Still, I'd feel better coming along." Grumwald muttered.

"And I appreciate your feelings, but it makes me feel better knowing you're accompanying Eomer to Dulcai. You know, we're assuming all will be well when she gets there, that the populace will welcome her as the new monarch and all will go on as before. But there may be things going on there we don't know about. And while I certainly have every faith in Eomer, I'm very glad you and *Valadator* will be there to back her up."

This had mollified the old warrior, but it had also started Valerius worrying, and he sat-the manifests unread before him-mentally searching the streets of Dulcai for the slightest sign of trouble.

"My Lord?"

The voice startled him and he looked up to see Boltar hesitating in the doorway. "Ah, Boltar!" he said getting up and ushering the young man in. "How are you? You look like you're starting to come around."

Boltar looked anything but. His face was pasty white, his rib cage tightly bandaged, and he walked as gingerly as an old man with shin splints. Valerius led him to the couch and he sat down with a grimace. "Aye, my Lord," he said. "I'm still a bit stiff, but otherwise, I feel fine."

"Good, good! I'm glad to hear it, lad. You took a nasty tumble. Now, what can I do for you?"

"Well, sire, Grumwald told me about King Reuters and his trip east and that you think you know who this pirate is, and I was just wondering if perchance you'd heard any news of Illana."

Valerius shook his head and sighed heavily. "No, not a thing, I'm afraid. But don't lose hope yet. I'm putting together a fleet right now to go and pay a visit to our sneaky friend in Palemia."

"Aye, sir. Grumwald told me that, too, and well... I was hoping to come with you, sir."

Valerius looked up sharply at this and saw much more than physical pain in Boltar's eyes. "Boltar," he said, rising to pace about the room and noticing how the young man grimaced as he, too, leapt to his feet, "you're a fine young man and an excellent officer, and I know your personal life is no business of mine. But do you really think it wise to pursue this course you're on?"

Boltar hung his head and anguish etched his face. "I know she's royal, Sire, and that I can hope for nothing. At this point, I hardly even dare hope she's alive. But I swear to you, Your Majesty-as my life is yours to do with what you will-so my heart is hers. I could not make it any other way if I wanted to, and frankly, Sire, I do not want to. All I can think about is that bastard-pardon my tongue, my Lord-making away with her, and me helpless. The image haunts me. I dream of it at night. I know there is no hope for me in the way you imply, but all I ask is the chance to help; if I can get her back safe from, from him, I don't care what becomes of me."

Valerius studied the young man before him, saw the earnestness there. "Believe it or not, Boltar," he said at last, "but I do know exactly how you feel. Get your kit and take command of the *Kantar*. And don't let me see these little bruises of yours causing you to slack on your duties!"

A broad grin swept across Boltar's face and for a moment, Valerius Everreigning, High King of

231

Valeria and all the Inner and Outer Seas was afraid he was going to be hugged. "Aye, aye sir!" Boltar snapped instead, and with a spring in his limp, went off to gather his gear.

Chapter 14

A strong southwest breeze kicked up white caps on the Inland Sea and tumbled fleecy puffs of cumulus clouds across the deep blue vault of the sky. Close hauled under full sail, *Kantar* heeled sharply to the wind and dipped her lee rail as she rounded the breakwater at the harbor entrance and began beating her way clear of the land. A short, steep chop sent spray high over her bow and the men who had been added to her crew-none of whom had seen such a craft in their lives-clung to any purchase they could find on the canting deck and stared about wild-eyed, sure that their last hour had come. At the helm, the High King braced himself sideways with a foot on the cockpit coaming and drove the ship on, a huge grin spreading across his face. The regular crew, including Boltar, found secure niches for themselves against the windward deckhouses and enjoyed the discomfort of their new fellows. Behind, the other five ships of the fleet, including Vahla's Thuringian galley, struggled to keep up.

The struggle grew worse as *Kantar* turned eastward and spread her wings before the wind on a broad reach. The other ships also set sail on this tack but were unable to keep up with the bounding schooner until Valerius dropped his main and sailed on under foresail and jibs. Still, the little fleet fairly flew along under the scudding clouds and the coastline passed at a gallop. Aboard *Kantar*, the new crewmembers relaxed as the decks leveled out on the downwind tack, and once they realized death was not imminent, began to marvel at the ship built by King Koltar and his tiny Kantaran craftsmen.

One of these new crewmen was none other than Chad, Vahla's personal servant. When Vahla and Valerius came down after sacrificing a young bull at the temple, they had found him at quayside, staring intently at the ship. "Do you like her, Chad?" Valerius had asked.

Chad had given him a curious look. "How boat go?"

"The wind," said Valerius, but this only seemed to confuse Chad more.

"Would you like to sail with the High King to Palemia and see how it goes?" Vahla asked. Chad nodded sagely.

"Are you sure?" asked Valerius. "He's kind of your right-hand man, isn't he?"

"Well, he's not so indispensable I can't get along without him for a day or so. Besides, you need a cook and you know yourself he's excellent."

"Well, he is that. So be it, then. Get your dunnage, Chad, and welcome aboard."

Chad had little dunnage, being one who always traveled light, but never seemed to lack for anything that was needed. Nor was he alarmed like the others at the ship's strange antics, but scurried about as nimble as a squirrel, puzzling intently over every sheet and shroud as if the ship's rig were some giant cat's cradle and he about to take it on his own fingers. Satisfied, at last, that he had plumbed the mystery of it, he dropped down to the tiny galley amidships, and seemingly from nothing, began to prepare lunch.

Valerius meanwhile, had turned the helm over to a crewman and taken up his favorite position, standing on the fantail behind the helm, leaning against a stanchion of the boom gallows. From here, he could see the entire sweep of the deck as *Kantar* surged along, and first feel the rise of the following seas. But his mind had drifted and when Chad handed him a thick sandwich, he took it without comment and began munching absently.

He was surprised to realize how lonely he was. Though it had only been a few hours, he already missed Eomer and the children and was worried about her traveling alone to Dulcai. Of course, she wasn't really alone, and she was a grown woman, brilliant as well as beautiful-a queen born if ever there was one-and fully capable of assuming the throne. Nor could he ever recall hearing or reading about any succession problems in Dulcai. Reuters had been well loved and Eomer was, too. Still, he was troubled, and when the thought occurred that he should try to use the Eye to look for any problems, he pushed the thought aside as unworthy. It would be like spying on his own wife.

Instead, he focused on the grace and power of *Kantar*'s motion and on the pristine beauty of the day. It truly was a relief to be away from the palace and all the business of ruling, and from the thick tomes of The Book of Kings spread around his study. This little excursion would be like a tonic, and his pulse quickened at the prospect of action, though he really didn't think there would be any. The plan was for Valerius and Vahla to arrive in Palemia on a "state visit." Once they had informed Eldred what kind of game this Condor was playing, it would be all over, he was sure. They would summon the fellow up to the palace and nab him quietly while he was away from his ship. His crew would then be rounded up and the other galley's as well, if they were implicated, and the lot dealt with summarily. And they would find out what had happened to poor Illana.

But then what? Off to Dulcai? No, not yet. If he took off now-or within the next couple days, whenever they had disposed of this Condor fellow-he would overtake *Valadator* and Eomer would not get her opportunity to take command in Dulcai. No, he would have to wait at least two weeks. Doing what? Reading dusty tomes back in his study? Ugh! The very thought gave him a headache. How about a quick visit to Zagorbia to see how Ragnar was getting on? That was certainly possible. How about going from there up to Volkmir's old cave as he and Vahla had discussed? There, he thought, was an idea that had definite merit.

The little fleet made excellent time and by mid-morning of the following day, were well up the river Sule and in sight of the city. But their progress against the river current had not been nearly as swift as along the coast, and there was plenty of time for a horseman to outdistance them and bring word of their approach to Condor.

"You see, my Liege," he told a disheveled Eldred whom he had rousted out of bed well before his time. "It is as I suspected: this whole thing has been a ruse by Vahla and the High King and now they come to displace you."

Eldred was frantic. He turned this way and that, wild eyed, as if some way out of this difficulty would appear on the walls of his chamber like a new doorway. "What am I to do, Condor?" he stammered.

"You must stand up to them, my lord."

"Stand up to the High King? That's madness! He has armies and fleets. We have four ships and a couple thousand House Guards. We can't stand up to Valerius."

"I don't mean we should try to fight him," said Condor, his deep voice as soothing as a cool breeze. "I simply mean we stand up for your rights, Majesty. We meet him at the river in full public array and demand, not war, but justice. Don't you see? Their whole plan is based on lies and deception: it won't hold up to public scrutiny. And before they allow themselves to be exposed, they'll back down. The whole problem will evaporate. We'll have a private parley with Vahla and the High King and let them know we're on to their tricks, and that will be the end of it."

"Do you think so?" asked Eldred, his voice quavering, but his eyes desperate with hope.

"I know so," said Condor, and thought to himself, 'and it will also get me just close enough to the High King.'

The city of Palemia splashed white across a low brown hill and dribbled down to the river like milk staining a cloth. Primarily an agricultural trading port, it had never been fortified, and as a consequence, had grown willy-nilly between the quays and warehouses along the river and the palace complex on the hill. The administrative buildings were, of course, on the high ground near the palace, and the wealthier merchants had built stately homes there, while tradesmen, innkeepers, ships' captains, laborers and the rest of motley humanity had settled in between among a hodge-podge of streets and alleyways off a broad central avenue. In total, the metropolis housed some twelve thousand souls.

To Vahla, watching the distant city from her approaching galley, it seemed that most of these souls were on the move this morning, scurrying down the hill and gathering about the harbor like ants on a sugar stick. But as the galley drew closer, she could see the flash and glint of arms, and that a solid, military formation lined the waterfront, behind which the townspeople gathered in their thousands like leaves blown against a fence. In the center of the line, beneath the banner of Palemia, stood Eldred himself, fully armed and surrounded by his personal guards. By his side stood the huge young captain, Condor-Commander of the Guard now, by the look of his arms. What was this then, a battle line? Eldred standing in full array against Valerius?

At first, she could not believe her eyes. It could not be that Eldred was taking arms against the High King. It must simply be his perverted idea of an honor guard. But no, as they drew in towards the quay, a line of archers stepped out from between the pike men and stood at the ready, arrows knocked. Valerius had given her the honor of the lead. Now, as her crew backwatered, the High King swept by in his strange craft and their eyes met over the narrow strip of water between them. His were questing, hers furious. There was no need for words. He nodded and jibed away.

Vahla guided her galley in close along the quay opposite Eldred and stopped about two boat lengths from shore. Looking more nimble than she felt, she climbed up on to the rail by the main shrouds and stood in full view of the people.

"Eldred, my cousin," she yelled, her voice carrying easily over the thousands of faces before her, "is this how you welcome the High King, your liege lord; armed and threatening? Why stand you so?"

After a hastily whispered conference between Eldred and Condor, the former-his voice seeming to quaver slightly, though it may have been a trick of the wind-yelled back: "I stand for my rights, Cousin Vahla! And neither you nor your duplicitous Lord shall enter Palemia until I have them!"

"You defy the High King?" Vahla let the question hang for a moment over the stunned crowd. "Fie and shame, Eldred! And do you also now countenance the company of pirates? Do you thus condone abduction and murder? Shame on you, Eldred. Stand down this instant, I say!"

There was a ripple of motion along the front ranks as soldiers turned to look at their king, and another flurry of conversation beneath the royal banner. "I stand for my rights, I say," returned Eldred, his voice definitely unsteady now. "I know how you've been plotting against me and you must answer for your deeds."

"We must answer! Our deeds!" Vahla was astounded at the effrontery of this and her blood so rose in her gorge that for a moment she could not speak. Then she did, her voice ringing in a clarion call. "Shame on you, Eldred! You are no King! You are a parasite on your people! Hear me now, Eldred! I am Vahla, daughter of Vauhna, daughter of King Eldorim and rightful heir to the throne of Palemia. I, Vahla, who crowned you king, now uncrown you, Eldred! I declare you King no more. You are deposed. You, Gainor, Commander of the Guard, take him into custody!"

The people listened in absolute silence and when she finished, not a shuffled foot or muffled cough could be heard among the entire population. Many expected her to turn into the god, as she was supposed to have done in the east, but all they saw was a very angry woman, a woman in whom not only did magic flow, but the blood of generations of Palemian monarchs. Not a one among the rank and file facing her or the masses behind them did but wish that she and not Eldred ruled Palemia, and now this seemed possible. From the back ranks, someone started a chant: "Vah-la, Vah-la, Vah-la." It was taken up by more and more voices until the whole city was chanting her name. Without a word, Gainor and another officer stepped up beside Eldred and gently took him into custody.

Condor looked as though he had just been shaken from a dream, and as the crowd chanted, his eyes went momentarily wild as he looked down the river at the five galleys closing with the shore. Suddenly, he bolted from his position, ran along the quay and vaulted the rail onto the *Steiger*. For some reason, his crew was still aboard, as was Hagreb and his crew aboard the *Recluse*. Now as if by some pre-arranged contingency plan, both tossed their lines and swept away from the dock.

One of Valerius' galleys drove forward to intercept the *Steiger*, but Hagreb swung out from Condor's wake, and with a well-practiced burst of speed, rammed the High King's vessel amidships, splintering oars and planking and flipping rowers into the muddy waters like dolls. The ship's mast toppled sideways into the river and as *Recluse* backed away and sped after the fleeing *Steiger*, the breached hull filled quickly and began to sink. The crew scrambled to grab anything that would float while the officers and marines among them furiously sliced away at the leather straps that held their armor lest it drag them to the bottom.

Valerius had continued upriver while Vahla dealt with Eldred. Now he spun about and headed back down. Vahla and a second galley quickly came alongside the stricken ship, and as he passed,

Valerius yelled for Vahla to take control ashore while he pursued Condor with the remaining two galleys.

These had already given chase, angling out toward mid-river after the fleeing pair, but Valerius quickly outpaced them and began closing on the trailing *Recluse*. He was sailing close-hauled on starboard tack, but as he drew near, Condor and Hagreb bore to the right, adjusting their course to head straight down river. This put them directly into the wind, a direction Valerius and the *Kantar* could not sail, and he quickly saw that the closest he could come would be to cross the *Recluse*'s stern at a long bow shot range. Boltar stood forward with his crews manning the slings, but he shook his head at Valerius' unasked question: no, they would not be able to shoot their fire-bombs with the ship heeled over like this.

"How about if we head up?" Valerius yelled. This would remove wind pressure from the sails and allow the ship to come back to an even keel. But it would also stop them.

But Boltar shook his head again. "The angle will be wrong!"

Valerius studied the speeding *Recluse* and his own angle of sail. She was rowing well at a good thirty strokes per minute, and aided by the following current, was coursing down river at a good clip. He was approaching at an oblique angle, already behind her stern quarter and knew that within a very few moments, he would cross her wake and their courses would diverge. He would then have to sail all the way across to the eastern shore and tack back before their courses crossed again to give him another chance-assuming he was still traveling faster through the water and could get close at all.

Then he looked up at the rig and on a sudden impulse yelled out, "Let go the peak halyards!"

The sails on *Kantar* were not triangular, but quadrilateral, with the head of the sail supported by a short spar King Koltar had called a "gaff" ("Why?" Grumwald had asked when he heard. "Is it a mistake?"). The gaff was raised by two lines or halyards, one attached at the throat, which slid up the mast, and the other at the outer end or peak. These two could be adjusted to provide even tension across the sail, giving it shape and power to catch the wind. Letting go the peak halyards spilled the wind and depowered both the main and foresails. *Kantar* immediately rose to an even keel, though she was still driven along her course by her two jibs, and Boltar's crew quickly slipped grapefruit-sized clay canisters into the pockets of the four sets of firebomb slings along the starboard rail.

"Fire as you bear!" Valerius roared, and one by one the double sets of bow staves were drawn back and released, flinging their explosive canisters high into the air, arcing towards the *Recluse*. One went wide to the left, another wide to the right. A third fell short, but one fell directly into the open hull and exploded among the benches.

Aboard *Kantar* they could see the bright flash, then the long oars flailing as men scrambled out of the way. Then fire took hold in earnest and exploded to engulf the mast and rigging and raced fore and aft. Men flung themselves overboard in wild panic, some dark figures leaping, others human torches thrashing and wailing as the fire roared around them.

Their screams came down to *Kantar* on the wind and the crew stood transfixed at the sudden and terrible destruction they had wrought, until the High King's harsh voice brought them back to duty. "Hoist those halyards, there!" he yelled. "There's another one yet." And as the mast on the *Recluse* fell sideways into the river and the ship began to break apart into bits of flaming driftwood, *Kantar*'s sails filled with a snap, she leaned her shoulder again to her work, and charged off towards the eastern shore. "We'll let the Bremmer take care of anyone left," Valerius said loud enough for the whole deck to hear, and waving his arms at the following galley, pointed to the stricken *Recluse*.

"That ought to put the fear of the gods into our friend up there," said Boltar as he made his way back along the tilting deck to stand beside the King. "I had no idea those things would work so well!"

"Nor I! And I'm very glad wee King Koltar is our friend and not our enemy."

"Aye, sir. I'll drink to that! But when we close with *Steiger*... ," he started and then left the question unfinished, knowing both that Valerius was as aware of possible danger to Illana as he-if she still lived-and that there was nothing either of them could do about it. The two stood quietly, watching the smoldering wreckage of the *Recluse* as the Bremmer picked its way carefully among the still burning flotsam, hauling aboard survivors and pushing aside the drifting dead.

Downstream, Condor and the *Steiger* were pulling southward, gaining distance as *Kantar* beat eastward. But Valerius' third galley, the Rory, was coming on strong. Valerius and Boltar counted the rhythm of her oar strokes as she sped by the Bremmer and sprinted down river.

"I don't know how long she can keep up that pace, but she looks to be gaining," said Boltar.

"Aye, it looks so. Sengar has a good crew there, though, and he trains them hard. I wouldn't be surprised if they could keep it up for quite a while."

The two men fell silent again as the graceful panorama of the race unfolded before them. Upstream, the city was falling away into the distance, the crowds which had cheered Vahla as she went ashore no longer visible. Overhead, the sky was a deep blue and empty of clouds. On either hand, the verdant green shores stretched like hedgerows, bounding the river's domain, and to the west, a patchwork of farms checkered the sloping hills. It was a gorgeous summer day.

Chapter 15

Aboard *Steiger*, Condor paced his tiny quarterdeck, seething. His plans, it seemed, had all come to naught and here he was, a single renegade ship again, fleeing for his life. And from that same, silly contraption of a ship with two masts and no oars! A ship that had somehow used magic to set Hagreb afire and would no doubt do the same to him if it got close.

Condor spun at the sudden sound of a raspy voice close by his ear, but there was no one there. Then he saw a bit of shadow aft by the rail, a light smudge in the air, no darker than a bit of smoke yet somehow holding form and substance. He did not need to ask who was there, nor close with it to speak, for its voice now came softly to his ear as if it were in his own head. And it was laughing.

"Oh, you silly fool," it hissed. "You think you've lost it all when it's desperately trying to fall in your lap!"

Condor stalked to the taffrail and stared across the muddy water to the tall masts and tilting sails of his main pursuer. Yes, it was the same ship he'd stolen the girl from and which had then tried to lead him to Grumwald's great trireme. "Bring me the girl!" he snapped to a crewman who happened to be standing near. "What ship is that?" he demanded when she approached, as vague and lissome as a spirit herself.

Dreamily, her eyes drifted across the span of the river, finally focusing on the distant schooner. "That?" she asked. "Why, that's His Majesty's new ship. His Majesty the High King."

Condor's face lit up with a fierce joy, his black eyes glittering like obsidian. In the distance, he could see a large man shape looming at the stern of the tall ship, and for an instant, a tiny red flash from the great gem that hung upon his chest.

Kantar closed with the eastern shore-which was actually the western shore of the long island that split the river from just south of Palemia to a league or so up from its mouth-and came about gracefully. The wind being just west of south (though funneled further south by the long river valley), their westward leg was shorter. But still, when they crossed Condor's track in mid-river, they saw that they, too, were gaining ground on him. They cheered as they passed just behind the racing Rory and though Sengar's crew was much too busy to cheer in return, Sengar himself waved and bowed to the High King before turning his attention back to their quarry.

Condor's crew, in contrast, seemed to have slowed their pace a bit, and their stroke suddenly looked ragged, as though the oarsmen were beginning to feel the effort of the chase.

"Looks like they've spent a bit too much time debauching," said Boltar as a crabbed oar on *Steiger* suddenly threw the whole starboard bank out of synch and momentarily slewed the ship sideways.

"Mayhap, though he could be faking. We've played the lame game ourselves a time or two."

"Aye." But fake or no, Sengar took advantage of the slip to make ground with another burst of speed. From *Kantar*'s angle, the prow of the Rory now appeared nearly even with the *Steiger*'s stern, and as archers aboard both craft began plying their trade, Sengar began steering his ship wide, his intention clearly to swing around and ram. Valerius anxiously checked the distance to the western shore and the angle between *Kantar* and *Steiger*, and then when he judged the moment exactly right, gave the order for *Kantar* to tack back to the east. She came up smartly, her sails flapping wildly as she came through the wind. Then her booms slammed over to port and as the crew raced to haul taut the jib sheets and running backstays, she began to accelerate again on a southeasterly course, her bowsprit aimed at a converging point just south of the pair in mid-river. When Rory and *Steiger* came to grips, Valerius wanted to be there as quickly as possible.

"Your Majesty, look!" Boltar had started to make his way back forward to his station, but stopped at the gap between the fore and mainsail and pointed.

In mid-river, the Rory had now drawn abreast of *Steiger* and began turning back towards her. But the air around *Steiger* had suddenly become dark and misty. Black smoke was billowing up around her mast, as if she, too, had been set afire. But there was no appearance of flame and the smoke did not dissipate or stream upriver with the wind: it hovered about the pirate galley and grew thick like a cloud until the *Steiger* was totally lost to sight.

Boltar had hobbled back to stand beside the king and as the two watched, Sengar's galley darted in to enter the cloud, then slowed and stopped, its oars working the river into a froth, but making no progress. It was as if the ship was trying to penetrate a solid wall. "What the hell is that?" Boltar wanted to know.

"Damned if I know," said Valerius, shaking his head.

Sengar backed Rory off then, and turned down river to skirt the edge of the cloud. Suddenly, *Steiger* shot from the cloud with a terrific burst of speed, and as the crew on *Kantar* shouted in helpless surprise and alarm, her beaked prow slammed into Rory with such force it broke Sengar's galley in two.

Seeming to gain speed even from the impact, *Steiger* drove right through the stricken remnants of Rory and, leaving its thick cloud behind, sped on down the river while an astonished Boltar and Valerius stared after it open-mouthed.

"What in the world is going on here?" Boltar exclaimed.

Valerius watched the fleeing *Steiger*, its oar banks rising and falling now in cadenced union, and muttered, "More than we know, I'm afraid. More than we know."

After picking up the few surviving members of the Rory's crew-the captain, Sengar, was not among them-Valerius and *Kantar* continued the pursuit, zigzagging back and forth across the river behind the fleeing *Steiger*. The winds remained light but Boltar and his crew readied the lethal slings at every pass. *Steiger*'s oarsmen maintained their stroke with uncanny endurance, but Valerius narrowed the gap on every tack, getting closer and closer to effective range.

Then *Steiger* set her mainsail and the crew aboard *Kantar* began laughing and jeering. Didn't the fool know he couldn't sail upwind? But then, the sail filled with a resounding pop and an uneasy silence fell aboard *Kantar* as *Steiger* began slipping away. She seemed to be driven by a cloud of grey mist and her hull slipped through the light chop like a skipping stone.

Boltar made his way aft again, and speaking low so only Valerius could hear, pointed to the *Steiger*'s quarterdeck. There, in addition to the helmsman and the huge figure of Condor, a dark shadow seemed to obscure one corner. Valerius nodded, but did not respond.

Down the broad river they raced all through the morning and into the afternoon. As the shoreline fell away on either hand, they beat their way out into the deep blue expanse of the Inland Sea. Here, *Steiger* turned more westerly, sailing-somehow-directly into the wind. Valerius tried longer tacks-southward first, then as they gained offing, northwestward as well-hoping his superior boat speed would help him gain on his quarry when their paths next crossed. But though they seemed to come ever closer, it was never quite close enough.

Then in late afternoon, the wind began to freshen. *Kantar* leaned, butting her shoulder into the rising chop and kicking a fine spray up over her bows. Valerius could feel her surge ahead and when next they crossed *Steiger*'s track, they were perceptibly closer. Boltar tried a ranging shot with his slings. It fell short, but not by much. And at this range, against the westering sun, the shadow on the quarterdeck bore a distinct shape and moved like a living thing.

The entire crew aboard *Kantar* saw it, but as the ship pounded past on her southerly leg, no one dared speak of it.

When *Kantar* came about again it was with a thunderous flapping of sails. The booms slammed over against their sheets and as she steadied on her course, foaming white water coursed along her lee scuppers. Valerius closed one eye and sighted on the *Steiger* across the main shrouds, then nodded to Boltar. This time they had her: their courses were definitely converging.

Down on the wind came *Kantar*, swooping like an eagle onto her prey, spray flying high, her crew clinging to any possible purchase. *Steiger* was in her sights, dead ahead, just to the right of their spearing bowsprit, looming closer by the second.

"Stand by the peak halyards!" Valerius yelled against the wind and half a dozen men crawled precariously to their stations across the sloping, pitching deck. Then he cupped his hands and yelled to Boltar: "Aim forward of her mast!"

Boltar signaled thumbs up: if Illana was aboard, setting fires up forward would give her the best chance of escape.

On came *Kantar*, closing within sling range and more, so close it seemed they must crash into the other's bow at any second. But aboard *Steiger*, none paid them the slightest heed. She sailed along, enveloped in mist, as if alone on a broad and empty sea, her afterdeck crew-Condor included-as intent upon their course and the rhythmic stroke of their oars as if they were transfixed.

"Let go!" yelled Valerius, and as the peak yards dropped, *Kantar*'s lee rail rose and all four of her starboard slings let go at once, their vicious contents arcing across the short space between ships.

But then, nothing. The firebombs entered the mist... and disappeared.

"Again!" Boltar ordered, and again the four sling sets were loaded, drawn back and released. And again the canisters entered the mist and disappeared. No explosions, no fire, not even the splash of a miss.

The crew stood, stunned, watching *Steiger* draw serenely away until Valerius yelled to haul peak halyards and get the ship back underway. But no sooner did the sails fill than the wind headed them and *Kantar* came up in irons, all her canvas flapping wildly. Valerius ordered the jib backed, but as the bow began to fall off, the wind veered with it, keeping them in irons. They tried backing the other way, but the wind veered with them again.

Kantar now sat dead in the water while ahead of them, *Steiger* swung gracefully around and with the evil mage wind steadily filling her sail, bore back down on them. In her bow now were a score of armed pirates and the hooks of a half-dozen grapnels. In their midst, stood the huge leering bulk of Condor himself.

"Out oars!" Valerius yelled, but even as the crew scrambled to unleash the long sweeps from their racks along the bulwarks, it was clear there would be no time to man them. Another crewman dove below and began passing up arms-Valerius' great war falchion first among them-but it was also clear they were vastly outnumbered.

Steiger swung around to come alongside upwind. A hand leapt up onto her starboard rail, swinging his grapnel. *Kantar*'s crew took what defensive stations they could, raised their swords and spears and grimly awaited the inevitable.

Then Chad came on deck carrying a small plate of pastries and a mug of hot tea for Valerius' afternoon snack. He had been below during the entire latter part of the chase and was oblivious to the fate about to come crashing down on them. He stopped before the High King, and with head bowed and eyes averted-all the proper etiquette-offered up the plate and mug.

Valerius shot him a single, incredulous glance, then sprang to the rail, his great falchion bared and ready.

Chad looked up, curious that his offer had been spurned, then dropped plate and mug with a crash when he saw *Steiger* and a hundred armed men looming close alongside. "Aie-ye-lah!" he yelled and threw his arms wide. Valerius glanced back when he heard the plate drop and saw Chad fling out his arms. He felt a sudden gush of force, like a blast of hot air, and for the merest fraction of an instant, Chad appeared twice his size.

Aboard *Steiger*, the shadowy form by the wheel suddenly recoiled as if it had been struck. The headwind, which had been holding them in irons dropped suddenly, and the fresh southwesterly breeze, as if it had been pent-up, slammed into *Kantar* broadside. The ship heeled violently, her booms slamming out and most of her crew tumbling to the deck, then shot off northward like an arrow released from a bow, the helmsman just managing to control the wheel.

Steiger meanwhile, spun around in the opposite direction and with the mage wind again filling her sail, fled away to the south.

Valerius, clung to the running back stay and watched the *Steiger* depart, then glanced down at the great red gem on his chest. It was pulsing with a deep russet glow. Boltar appeared, his face still rimmed with the aftereffects of shock and fear. But Valerius did not order pursuit. Instead, he watched Chad, now studiously cleaning up the shards of pottery and remains of pastry.

"Make course for Palemia," he ordered the still speechless Boltar. Then, heading for the companionway, he turned back and added with a casual air: "Chad, when you're done there, would you please attend me in my cabin?"

Chapter 16

"Why did you come on deck just then, Chad?" Valerius asked. Chad sat across the tiny work desk in his private compartment, staring down at the tabletop and looking ill at ease.

"Master food ready," he said.

"But why else did you come on deck? Why just then?"

Chad looked at him, his head cocked to one side, bird-like, his dark eyes questioning. "Food ready then."

Thus far, the interview had not been very productive. Communicating with Chad was difficult. Valerius' initial expression of gratitude had yielded only a blank stare, and subsequent questions about what he had done failed to illicit any response at all. Now Valerius was trying a more circumspect approach.

"Did you see the other ship?"

"Bad man ship."

"Yes, Chad," said Valerius, "there were bad men in that ship," and thought to himself, 'this is like talking to Valerian!' "But did you notice anything when you came on deck? Did you notice the wind?"

Chad dropped his gaze and shifted uneasily in his seat. Valerius leaned forward, his own eyes boring into the slender figure.

"What else did you see, Chad? Did you see that shadow on the other ship's deck?"

Chad looked away and his narrow shoulders turned, as if he were about to flee.

"Chad?" Valerius repeated, his voice holding him.

"Chad do bad?" The little man looked up, meeting Valerius' eye, his face contorted with fear and guilt.

"What did you do, Chad?"

"Shadow not good," Chad blurted. "Chad stop wind. Wind bad. Chad not do good?"

"No, Chad, you did very well," said Valerius, a strange sense of pity mingling with the awe he felt at what he had just heard. "But how did you stop the wind?"

Again came the bird-like stare. "How?"

"Yes, Chad, how?"

Suddenly, Chad squared his shoulders and his narrow face assumed a look of infantile determination. "Chad stop," he said, as if that explained it. And then, as if it were a plainly obvious counterpoint, "Chad say 'stop'."

"How did you say, 'stop,' Chad? What language was that?" But try as he might, Valerius could get no more out of the man on that point. It would be as easy, he thought, to ask a bird how it could fly. He switched to another tack.

"Chad, do you remember Volkmir using the Eye, this Eye?" he asked, holding up the great red gem by its golden chain.

"Oh, yes," Chad said, "but master afraid. Eye not his."

"Yes, I remember him saying so," said Valerius. Volkmir had also said he could only use a bit of the Eye's power, that he could see what was, but not what would be. 'And I can't even do that,' Valerius thought. "Do you recall him ever saying anything else about using the Eye? Do you know how it is used?"

"Used? Eye not used," said Chad. "Eye see. Look out of Eye, see."

"Yes, I know," said Valerius, his eyes flaring with a sudden excitement. "But do you know how?"

"How? Look out is all Chad know."

This made no sense to Valerius and as he looked at Chad's clouded face with its narrow set eyes and furled brow, it seemed he would get no sense to it from there either.

"Vahla, what is this fellow?" *Kantar* had returned to Palemia and Valerius had just finished describing the incident to her in the privacy of Eldred's former-and now her-royal chambers. Eldred, an emotional wreck after his deposition, had been relegated to a small apartment at the far end of the palace, where-though probably harmless-he was nonetheless being closely watched.

"Did you ask him that?" Vahla countered, a wry smile spreading across her face.

"I did."

"And he said?"

"He said he was a servant, and from his tone, I got the decided impression he thought I should already know that."

Vahla laughed. "Yes, I know that tone very well. I didn't tell you this, but when I escaped from the Scythians after Asperides was killed, it was Chad who did it. Karghan had me in his tent, all ready to... well, never mind that part. Anyway, someone called him from outside and when he went out, Chad walked in, just as casual as if he were going to the market, and said we should go now. I couldn't believe my eyes, but when we walked out, I don't know what he did or how he did it, or what was going on, but it was like everything was frozen but us. Everyone was standing around like trees, and we just walked to the picket line, got on our horses and rode away."

"I thought you used a trick you learned from Volkmir."

"I never learned any tricks like that from Volkmir. And I got no better explanation from Chad than you did. I'll tell you something else as well: just before he died, Volkmir told me he was a fraud. He said that all he could do was observe the gods' will and that Chad would guide me."

"Chad again. You know, on the way back here I got to thinking. In the archives I've been digging through there are very few mentions of the Royal Mage's servant, but curiously, the few I came across were all 'Chad.' I assumed this was just coincidence-well, actually, I didn't think anything of it at all-but then I remembered when I was a lad and Volkmir was my tutor. I thought him an old man then, of course, but Chad was his servant then, too, and I truly can't say he seems any different now. And that's thirty years ago and more."

The two looked at each other, neither wanting to voice the implication. "That's ridiculous," Vahla said finally.

"I know. So, What is he?"

"I don't know. I'm not sure he does, either. He doesn't respond well to questions."

"Well, there's another guy out there who doesn't respond well to anything I can throw at him either. I don't know what he is-or what's helping him-but frankly, it scares me. Whatever Chad did sent him packing like a cur from a flung rock and I'd like to know what it was!"

"How about we try it again, then-the two of us this time?" Vahla went to the door and summoned Chad who, as ever, appeared immediately. "Chad, sit down here," she said, ushering him into the room and placing a chair near theirs. "And don't worry, you're not in trouble. His Majesty and I would just like to talk to you."

Chad looked nervous, but did as he was bidden.

"Chad," Vahla said, her voice soft and calming. "If you are a servant, who is your master?"

Chad started at the obviousness of the question. "You, mistress. You Chad's Mistress."

"And who was your master before that?"

Chad's face clouded for a moment. "Master was master then."

"Yes, but what was your master's name?"

"Master."

"His name, Chad... What was his name?"

Chad looked at her suspiciously, as if this was something she should already know. "Master's name Master," he said patiently.

"Let me try," said Valerius, smiling despite himself. "Chad, do you remember when I was small and we all lived in the Palace in Valeria, and your master gave me lessons?"

Chad thought hard for a moment. "Yes, Master say you thick."

"Yes, but I don't mean that," said Valerius, reddening as Vahla sniggered. "Do you remember my father who was High King then?"

"His Majesty?"

"Yes, His Majesty the High King."

Chad nodded. "Yes, Chad remember."

"Do you remember when he was a boy?"

"High King not a boy. High King a man."

"Yes, I mean before he was High King. When he was a boy. When he was Valerian. Do you remember?"

Chad's dark face clouded with effort and he sat in hunched silence for some time, working at what was apparently a difficult problem for him. Finally, he recited the facts, as he knew them. "Master is master. High King is High King. Boy is boy."

Valerius and Vahla exchanged hopeless glances. Then Chad spoke again. "But master not like that boy."

"All right, Sister Enchantress" said Valerius when Chad had been dismissed, "what have we got?" Despite its comic aspects, the interview had proven completely futile and two were now sipping large glasses of wine. They were feeling rather drained.

"Well, we've got Chad."

"Yes, may the gods love him-and they obviously must-we've got Chad. But I think it's clear we're not going to be able to use him."

"True. You've got the Eye... "

"Which I can't use either. It does what it wants, when it wants, and apparently uses the Royal Line of Valerius Everreigning as convenient pack mules."

"You've got me."

"Yes, thank the gods again. But you're pregnant."

"And a self-confessed fraud."

"Who nonetheless manages to make a pretty convincing Enchantress."

"Maybe," said Vahla. "But not the kind who can stand up to this pirate of yours; not from what you've told me."

"No, and that's the problem: nothing we've got-or at least nothing we've got that we can use-can stand up to Condor's Sorcery." Valerius began pacing the room. Vahla watched the stress and frustration working in his features. His face looked haggard and drawn, the streaks of silver in his hair and beard more prominent. They seemed to have multiplied in just the last day. It was clear the sea battle with Condor had shaken him.

"True," she said. "So, what do Chad, the Eye, you, me, and sorcery all have in common?"

"Volkmir."

"Yes, but he's dead."

"Yes, but his cave is crammed with musty old tomes... "

"Which are full of arcane knowledge... "

"Like this mysterious Scroll of Dimmian!" Suddenly Valerius recalled the image of the old mage appearing to him in Valeria. Was that what he was trying to tell him? He looked at his half-sister, the realization dawning on them both at the same instant. The answer, if it existed at all, was to be found in Volkmir's cave.

"There's also knowledge there that may help a 'phony' Enchantress become real," Vahla added.

"It might. But you certainly don't think you're coming with me, do you? In your state?"

"My dear Royal Majesty brother," said Vahla, her color rising, "just you try to get away without me!"

Chapter 17

Volkmir's cave lay high in the fastness of the mountains south of Zagorbia. From the mouth of a river that drained the swamps behind the city, a single tortured path led upwards through a vast forest, to the barren, rocky peaks beyond. Along this trail, a week later, Valerius led a little party in single file: Vahla, the ubiquitous Chad, Boltar, and two men at arms, along with their gear and supplies packed on a pair of mules. It was late on their second day out, and although the thin air was already growing cool from the elevation, their faces glistened with sweat and their breath heaved as they toiled up the steep forest slope.

At a small clearing along a fairly level stretch, Valerius called a halt for the night and they went about setting up camp. As was his habit, Chad disappeared into the undergrowth in search of edible delicacies-he had an uncanny ability to turn the most rudimentary camp meal into a sumptuous feast-while the others gathered firewood, smoothed out sleeping places and lined them with soft ferns. Around them the vast forest loomed majestically, the great trunks rearing high into the growing gloom, their canopies rustling quietly in the gentle evening breeze. There was a solemn, forbidding air to the place and there was little talk as they went about their chores.

They had sailed into Zagorbia where Valerius had taken King Ragnar-an old and trusted comrade-into his confidence. Given the situation with the pirate, Condor, he didn't want anyone to know where they were headed, he told Ragnar. Nor did he want to take a large party. Put it out, he said, that the High King had decided to sail back down to *Kantar* to affect some modifications to his fancy new sailing vessel before going on to Dulcai for King Reuter's funeral. Instead, once the *Kantar* had sailed around the headland south of the city and out into the Outer Ocean, they had slipped back into the river, which drained the vast Zagorbian, swamps, rowed upstream to the trailhead, and left *Kantar* and the rest of her crew snugly moored in a secluded creek.

Valerius felt the two days of hiking rather acutely and tried not to groan as he bent to dump an armload of branches onto their woodpile. But a pained grunt did escape him as he sank down onto his spread out bedroll beside Vahla. "How's my little sister feeling?" he asked.

"Like you sound," she smiled. "Stiff and sore, aching in every joint. I'm not sure I'll be able to climb out of this bedroll again in the morning."

"I mean other than that... with the baby and all."

"Oh, the Royal nephew, you mean," she said, smiling more broadly now and patting her tummy which as yet showed only the most imperceptible swelling. "I think all this exercise is probably good for me in that regard. The midwives always say it's a mistake to take it too easy during pregnancy.

They say you need to build up your strength for birthing."

"Well, I worry. I don't think the midwives are referring to this kind of trek."

"Oh, you men think you're so gallant!" Vahla teased. "You let us poor women drudge eighteen hours a day, keeping your houses, feeding your bellies and warming your beds, and then, the minute you think we're carrying one of your heirs-well! -then we need to sit on soft pillows and sip lemonade all day!"

"Oh, I'll just bet Thorngere makes you 'drudge' away eighteen hours a day! And what will he say when he finds out I let you come along on this silly expedition?"

"He knows me well enough-and you-to know how things were decided."

"Hah! You mean he knows you're as stubborn and unruly as a mountain cat," said Valerius, referring to the rather loud discussion they'd had in Zagorbia about her coming along-a discussion that could be heard from the palace to the city walls.

"Something like that," said Vahla, grinning. "Though he's usually a bit more compliant than you."

Boltar's men-at-arms had found a spring and came into camp carrying a leathern bucket of water between them. Vahla and Valerius watched companionably as the two soldiers rigged a tripod to hang it from. Boltar crouched over the fire pit working his flint and steel, and then blew softly on the tiny flame. A further rustling along the trail was presumed to be Chad, returning with whatever delicacies he had managed to find in the forest.

But it was Condor. Suddenly, he was standing there at the edge of the clearing with a broad grin on his face, the leash of his straining wolf in one hand, a naked sword in the other. Behind him cowered a nearly naked Illana.

Unbeknownst to Valerius and company he had followed the *Kantar* into the river, and moored his own galley downstream. Leaving his crew, he had tracked Valerius' party up the forest trail, and for reasons of his own, had passed them during the previous night and lain in wait on a nearby cliff's edge for most of the afternoon, watching his quarry's slow assent.

For a long instant, the company stared open-mouthed at this sudden apparition, then erupted in a flurry. The two men-at-arms-who were closest to that side of the clearing-snatched up swords and shields and advanced in a defensive posture. Condor laughed at the sight and let go the leash restraining his wolf. Instantly, the creature leapt at one of the men-at-arms, the attack so sudden and furious the man had only a chance to make a single, ineffectual swipe with his sword before being borne to the ground, the jaws of the huge snarling beast snapping at his face and neck. He screamed as the teeth sank into his throat, then gurgled and flailed helplessly as the jaws tightened into a strangle hold.

The attack happened so fast, the second man-at-arms barely had time to react. He swung wildly as the wolf attacked, but the blow went high as the beast bore his companion to the ground, and by the time he drew back his arm to strike again, Condor was on him. Condor's sword caught him high on the left shoulder as he turned to strike the wolf, and like a woodsman's axe biting into soft pine, clove deep into his chest cavity, nearly splitting him in two. The man crumpled under the force of the blow, gushing blood. But his body twisted, wedging Condor's sword and dragging it down.

Boltar saw the opportunity and leapt to take advantage. Screaming, "Illana!" he came in on the run as Condor yanked at his blade, and swung his own sword two-handed in a vicious swipe at Condor's defenseless head. But Condor was very fast. Dropping into a crouch, he let the swishing blade pass over his head, then countered with a massive left upper-cut that lifted Boltar off his feet and dropped him in a clattering heap onto the just erected tripod and water bucket. The bucket's contents gushed out, drenching Boltar and drowning out his nascent fire.

At the sound of her name, Illana's head perked up. She watched curiously as Boltar fell, and then stared at his sprawled form, her head cocked to one side, a slight frown on her otherwise impassive face. She looked as if she were trying to remember something from the distant past and absently took a step in Boltar's direction before the massive arm of Condor swept her back.

But now Vahla and Valerius were on their feet, Vahla circling to her left, Valerius adjusting the buckler on his left arm and testing the heft of his great war falchion. At a bark from Condor, the wolf left the gristly remains of the man-at-arms and took station before his master. He crouched there and snarled death at Valerius, his bared fangs drooling blood, his ears laid back, and the hackles around his shoulders bristling. Condor flicked his glance from Vahla to Valerius and back, and smiled softly.

Suddenly Vahla flung one of her flash bombs at Condor's face. It exploded with a bright green flash. The wolf yelped and leapt aside and Illana flinched and cowered, but Condor only laughed, and then flung something of his own in reply. It was like a tiny bit of cloud or mist, which grew as it flew and darkened from grey to black. It seemed to move slowly from his out-flung hand, like a toy boat drifting on an idle current, yet actually sailed so fast that, though they both saw it plainly, neither Vahla nor Valerius had an instant to react. The thing struck her in the face, a black ball, slightly larger than her head. It enveloped her head and Vahla collapsed in a heap, the thing covering her head like a hood.

Valerius screamed. "Now you've done it, you Bastard!" and leapt forward, his falchion raised. The wolf met him, leaping as he leapt. But Valerius had anticipated that and as the animal's forefeet stretched out towards his chest, the great cleaver blade smacked down onto its skull, splitting it in two and swatting the carcass down with a thud.

In the same move, Valerius ducked left to avoid Condor's following charge, then swung his falchion up and over in a high windmill stroke that

Condor just managed to parry. The two locked swords, and for a long instant, locked eyes as well. Condor's smile was gone now, and as they stood, forcing blade against blade, contending will against will, so alike in their forms and features, old and young, that they could have been father and son.

But Valerius also felt the younger man's strength, and for one of the few times in his life, realized he was up against an opponent more powerful than he. Pushing off the blade and leaping away, he began a furious assault. Against an enemy both younger and stronger, his best chance was to overwhelm him quickly. Swinging his broad blade two-handed, he waded in, raining blow after blow onto Condor. He struck high and low, swept at Condors feet, beat at the man's sword from left and right. Condor parried awkwardly, backing away. Valerius could see that despite his power and native ability, he was not a trained fighter. Still parry he did, his speed compensating for his lack of technique, and Valerius' fury found no hole in his defense.

But within minutes, Valerius' lungs felt like burning holes in his chest. His breath came in ragged gasps and his blows lost some of their speed. Now it was Condor's turn. Sensing his opponent weakening, he stepped nimbly to the side of a wild overhand slash, and as Valerius lurched slightly when his sword met no counter, went on the attack himself. Valerius caught the first blow on his pommel, but the force of it jarred his arm to the shoulder and nearly caused him to drop his sword.

He leapt back and away from the next blow, but Condor followed, mimicking Valerius' own charge, slashing cut after cut at him. Valerius parried, his own lifetime of experience in battle coming to his aid, and caught his breath as he watched for an opening. But Condor was coming in fast, faster than anyone Valerius had ever faced, and he showed no sign of slackening. Valerius could hear the rhythm of his breathing, steady and even like a seasoned woodsman plying his axe, and as he backed away step by step, he knew he was losing the fight.

His attack had driven Condor a dozen or so yards along the path to the main trail and now, as Valerius backed again into the camp, he glanced to see Vahla, still lying where she had fallen, the shimmering cloud covering her head like a sack. He could not tell if she breathed, but the thought did flash that if she did not, the cloud would probably have gone. From the corner of his other eye, he could see Illana, standing perplexed over the still senseless Boltar, but he had no time to spare thoughts for them either: though his defense was practiced and sure, it was all he could do to avoid swishing death.

Nor, he realized, would the outcome long remain in doubt. He was no match for this marauding monster, either in strength, speed or conditioning, and unless he could pull something soon from his bag of battle tricks, the thousand-year long line of Valerius Everreigning would end here, in this tiny clearing, in the foothills south of Zagorbia.

There was one thing that might just work. Unconsciously, the less experienced Condor had fallen into a steady rhythm with his blows, and although they fell as fast and furious as ever, they had also fallen into a pattern-a predictable pattern. Timing his move to Condor's next right-handed swing, Valerius twisted left, and instead of parrying the blow directly, swung his falchion in from the side and whacked Condor's blade on the flat, just above the pommel. The blade snapped and in an instant, it was Condor who was defenseless.

Now it was Valerius' turn to laugh as Condor stared in shock at the useless stub in his hand. "I am normally one to grant mercy in situations like this," Valerius growled, "But you, young bastard, have forfeited any claim to that."

Condor tossed the useless pommel aside and stood straight before Valerius, his black eyes still seething. "You think you are man enough to kill me, old man? Even unarmed as I am? Go ahead, then, take your shot!"

Valerius felt the dark eyes boring into him, felt their power, as a black mist seemed to creep like fog into his limbs. He went to raise his sword but his arms felt suddenly heavy, the falchion almost impossible to hold. Some other part of his brain told him this was a trick, that he should fight against it, but even as he thought this, even as he summoned his will to resist the blackness swirling through him, he saw another thing: a great balled fist swinging up at him from somewhere far away. It seemed to come slowly, like smoke drifting up from a distant fire-so slowly that as it approached he could even see smudges of dirt and tufts of black hair on the knuckles-but there were so many other things crowding his mind at that moment, so much he had to do to move his own arms, that he could not summon himself to react. Then, in a very brief instant, he realized the fist was not traveling slowly at all. It smashed into his face with a blinding flash, knocking him off his feet. He sprawled in a heap amidst the sodden ruins of the fire and lay still.

Condor spat at him. "Call me a bastard, will you? I'm more than enough bastard for you!" Bending over the still form of the High King, he yanked the glittering red Eye Stone with its golden chain from his neck and stalked off into the woods, Illana hurrying along behind.

Condor returned to the main trail, and then branched off to the right towards his camp on the high tor where he had lain in wait. Darkness was fast settling in, and he had nearly reached the rocky eminence when something snapped on the path behind him. Spinning about and yanking the dagger from his belt, he scanned the trail and murky depths of the woods on either hand, but saw nothing. He shot a questioning glance at Illana, but she, as usual, was drifting about in the fog he had placed on her. Grunting, he turned back towards his destination, only to see Chad standing quietly on the path before him, his arms loaded with fresh herbs, wild cabbage and a large yam.

"You have Master's Eye," said the servant, his tone calm and ordinary as if somehow, Condor had wandered off with the thing by mistake.

"And you have a problem, little man," said Condor and lunged at him with the dagger.

But Chad was not there when the dagger struck. He was several feet off to the left, standing as calmly as before, his vegetables clutched in his boney arms. Condor swung hard at him this time, slashing out viciously and following the blade fast with a blow from his other fist, from which swung the glittering Eye stone on its golden chain. But blade and blow met only air: Chad was off to the right this time, still holding his groceries.

Rage exploded in Condor like molten lava and he leapt at the little man with a savage cry, swinging wildly this way and that, twisting and striking, lunging and slashing like a madman trying to drive off a swarm of biting flies. And through it all, Chad calmly sidestepped every blow. Though Condor moved with blinding speed, Chad slipped away like smoke and wherever blade or fist struck, Chad was not.

Then another voice called his name and Condor drew up short. It was a soft, sibilant voice, coming from the murky depths of the trees beside the trail. "Stop being such a fool," it said, the speaker emerging from the shadows, a shadow still, but darker and better defined. "Can you not see what you're up against? Put on the Eye!"

"No," said Condor, "it will strike me down. Here, you wanted it, you take it!"

274

"I cannot. You must. Don't try to use it, just wear it."

Condor stared at the thing for a long moment, then back at Chad, who stood as calmly as before, his dark eyes watchful. Then he refastened the twin loops of the chain and raised the great Eye stone over his head.

In that instant, Chad moved. His herbs and cabbages flying loose, he darted in like a humming bird, his outstretched hand reaching and grabbing the glittering gem. At his touch, it exploded with a blinding red flash and a sound that was no sound at all, but shook the earth. Condor was flung several feet and landed in the brush like a rag doll.

And Chad was left, standing as before, his head cocked curiously to one side, the Eye stone swinging in a gentle arc from his outstretched hand. For a brief moment, he looked over at the shadowy form, and the expression on his face, which-if Chad's face could be said to support such an expression-looked very much like a smirk. The figure hissed in frustration, and in a flash of darkness, disappeared.

It was then that Illana awoke. She had been standing on the trail, staring vaguely into the distance while these events occurred, neither responding nor showing any sign of awareness. Now her head snapped around, her eyes flashed into sharp focus, and her whole body tensed as if she, too, had heard a sudden noise. Searching about, she saw Condor sprawled in the bushes and with a wild shriek, leapt at him. Snatching up the dagger fallen by his side, she plunged it into his chest with all her strength.

Then, screaming, she ran off towards the high cliff's edge at the far side of the tor.

Boltar appeared then, laboring up the path from the camp, his step still unsteady, but his face grim and a bright sword gripped tightly in his hand. He was just in time to see the dagger strike and as Illana fled, he flung the sword aside and sprinted after her. He caught her just before the edge, just as she leapt. As her body sprang into the void, his arms wrapped around her from behind, catching her in mid-air. He skidded to a stop on the rocky verge and gathered her to himself like a child.

Illana turned and screamed, her arms flailing at him. "Let me die! Let me die!" she wailed.

But he held her tight and suddenly the fight went out of her and she collapsed, sobbing, into his arms.

Chapter 18

The trireme *Valadator*, carrying Queen Eomer, did not stop at the Hidden Valley of Kantar along the way to Dulcai. But as they passed the cliff bound entrance late one afternoon, Grumwald's signalmen exchanged messages with the Kantaran lookouts high atop the cliffs. It was a quiet evening, the sea flat calm with barely enough breeze to lift the signal flags from their halyards, much less fill the great sails that hung limp from their yards. Below decks, the benchers pulled their oars to the slow, steady thump of the boson's mallets and the ship plowed along, furrowing white the deepening blue of the evening sea.

From the weather side of the quarterdeck, Queen Eomer watched bands of rose and purple spread out across the western sky as the yellow ball of the sun dropped towards the sea. She could almost see it move, and as it settled, a great golden pool spread out across the water, shimmering on the wrinkled waves and stretching towards her like a path to the very heavens.

"Ma'am?" said Grumwald coming to her side and bobbing his head in quick obeisance. He had been much more deferential to her this trip, much more formal than when they sailed with Valerius.

"Isn't it gorgeous?" she said, nodding towards the sunset.

"Aye, Ma'am. No sunsets anywheres like in the western sea. But beg'in your pardon, Ma'am, King

Koltar sends his condolences and says he'll join you in Dulcai to honor King Reuters' memory, Ma'am."

"Thank him for me if you would, Grumwald? And say I look forward to his comfort and his counsel."

When the message was sent the grizzled Admiral returned and stood by her side, watching the sun settle into the sea. "I should go below to check on the children," Eomer said. "But it's so beautiful up here."

"Stay and enjoy the evening Ma'am," said Grumwald. "I'll go and check on the babes. I'm sure nurse Brenda has them well tucked in."

"Would you mind?"

"Not at all, Ma'am. It would be my pleasure."

She could definitely see the sun moving now, the great orb dropping, touching, and disappearing into the sea. Twilight settled quickly about the ship, the hazy warmth and brightness of the day fading into the cool, aloofness of the evening.

As they had for days, Eomer's thoughts raced ahead to what awaited her in Dulcai. Her mind skipped across a hundred things: how she would be received, how she would carry herself, how the funeral ceremony would go, what she would say. She felt very unsure of herself. At first, she had been angry when Valerius so blithely sent her off on her own so he could go chasing after some pirate. But then, she had realized she was being ungenerous: he was trying to rescue her niece, after all. And she was now coming to see what a gift he had given her: autonomy. And trust. How many women in this world were accorded that, she wondered? He had even said as much the night before she left when, in her pique, she had thought him only trying to humor her for his own ends. "No one I can think of is more fit to rule Dulcai than you, my dear," he had said. "Besides, it is your right, and I would not rob you of that; least of all of that."

But the gift of autonomy was an awesome thing, a thing she had no experience of. Oh, she had played at independence as a girl and in her imagination had wielded a haughty scepter. But then, as Glaucon's hostage, threatened daily with violation and worse, she had been brought face to face with her own fragile reality and later, when Valerius declared himself to her, she had flown to him as a bird to the nest.

Now she was on the wing again with no nest for succor but that of her own making. How well, she wondered, would she fly solo?

The starboard aft cabin of *Valadator* had been turned into a nursery and Grumwald and Brenda sat by the open stern windows, enjoying the quiet breeze and watching the final glories of the sunset. Both children had been tucked in and were sleeping quietly. "Do you think young Valerian misses his Da?" Grumwald wanted to know, his voice a quiet rumble.

"I think he does, yes," said Brenda. "He's asked for him several times, but I don't think he understands that he's not here. You're very fond of the lad, aren't you?

279

"Me? Oh, Aye. He's a corker, he is."

"Did you ever have babes of your own?"

"Once, yes. Years ago, before Fantar rose. A boy and a girl. He was just about Valerian's age."

"What happened?"

Grumwald shook his head, the memory still troubling. "I was at sea," he said. "I skippered a small trader then, out of Dulac. Fantar's horde came ravaging through, burning and pillaging-the usual story. When I got home there was nothing left of the cottage but charred timbers. That and a few scattered bones left by the wolves. Small bones," he added quietly.

Brenda reached out and put her hand over his, her eyes searching his scarred, ravaged face. "I'm sorry," she said. He nodded, not looking back.

"I joined the fight then," he said. "Stood in the line first before Palmeria, then got driven back through every town around the Inland Sea. After Zagorbia, a bunch of us went roving-the king among us, though we didn't know he was the king then-and preyed on Fantar's shipping. Then, fool that I was, I took an amnesty Fantar offered and promptly got chained to a galley's bench for three years. Then his majesty and Lord Thorngere rescued me one day and here I am! But what of you, Brenda? I know your husband died fighting, but had you any children?"

"I had a daughter, " she said. "Kayla. She was but a babe when her father left. I was very young then myself as we'd only been married a year or so. I stayed with his folks, but then, when she was five,

Kayla died of the fever. I've made my way as a nurse ever since. I couldn't believe it when the Queen chose me. It's been the best thing to happen to me in a long while."

"Well, you deserve good things!" said Grumwald, a smile warming his crooked face and a twinkle lighting his eye. Brenda blushed and dropped her eyes and a silence fell between them. When she looked back up, the smile had faded from his face, and there was something else in his eye, something very compelling indeed. Without really willing it, she felt herself lean towards him just as he was leaning towards her, his head tilting just so.

And it was just then that the door opened and the Queen came in to check on the children.

The counting room in the palace at Dulcai was deep in the basements, adjacent to the treasure vault. It was a fully enclosed room of solid stone walls, no windows, and but a single heavy door. That door was closed and bolted this evening, and sitting at the massive counting table, working by the flickering light of a single pair of candles, was Rhondo, former Dulcaian ambassador to the High King and lately manager of the city's business affairs.

He had no scribe with him this night, but labored alone on the high stool, counting out the various piles of markers-each one representing a quantity of gold, ore or other precious metal refined, transferred, expended or stored-and marking the totals onto one of several scrolls unrolled along the table and held down by weights.

Some entries were made on multiple scrolls, some were broken down into disparate amounts, and others-in apparently large sums-were made on another, smaller scroll spread off to the side. Whenever Rhondo made an entry here, he looked up furtively and quickly scanned the room.

But of course, there was no one else there, and the door was securely bolted-which is perhaps why he jumped so when another voice spoke out from the shadows behind him.

"That's quite the pretty system you have there," it said with soft insinuation. "I expect it would take a team of scribes weeks to figure out how much you've stolen."

Rhondo's life nearly ended on the spot, so violently did his heart jump. He spun wildly about on his stool and tried to shield his work with his body, but as the immediate effects of the shock passed, his body sagged so he had to hold the table for support. It was some moments before he could regain breath enough to speak.

"Who are you?" he gasped at last. "How did you get in here?"

"I'm someone with your best interests in mind," said the voice quite merrily. "Someone who wonders why you would waste your time on such petty larceny when there is so much more within reach."

"What do you mean?" Rhondo's voice was stronger now and he searched the shadows for a clearer view of the intruder. "And what business do you have coming in here?"

"Your business," said the voice with what seemed to be amusement. "And I mean a kingdom: why pilfer the treasury when the whole palace could be yours?"

"Are you insane speaking such treason?" Rhondo's natural assertiveness was coming back to him now, along with a considerable pique. He grabbed one of the candles and thrust it out before him "Come forward here into the light where I can see you!"

Something moved in the shadows, but it was only a shifting of the darkness. "It is not me you need to see, my friend," said the voice, closer now but no more visible, "but the opportunity that is there for the taking."

"What opportunity? To be Regent? I am that in all but name already. And as for this 'pilferage' as you call it, it has already made me the richest man in the kingdom." Rhondo hadn't meant to say this last and was surprised to hear it blurting from his mouth. It was as if he were somehow being compelled to voice his innermost thoughts.

"Very amusing. And will you spend the rest of your days counting it then? Don't try to make me think you're such a fool, Rhondo. You know gold is nothing without power. I'm talking about the opportunity to be King!"

"Oh, that would be bright, wouldn't it? Seize the crown with the Queen and her dear husband the High King no doubt on their way here right now! Whoever you are, you must be mad."

"What if I told you that the Queen was on her way, but in company with only her two dear little children, and that the High King would not trouble anyone ever again? Or if I told you there was a new power rising in the Empire, one that would be very grateful to someone who took the trouble to remove the last vestiges of the Line Everreigning?"

"You talk high treason! Treason and murder! Who are you? Come here, into the light I say, where I can look at you!"

The shadows shifted again and something glided closer from the darkness. "What is murder for a man like you, my friend, but another form of state craft? Is it not just war on a smaller scale? The inevitable struggle of the strong to gain their rightful dominion? And is not treason but the victor's sentence upon the vanquished? Come, my friend, you know the truth I speak, you feel it in your heart. Join with me and together we can achieve more than you ever dreamed."

Something in the darkness began to solidify and take human shape. As it neared, the candle in Rhondo's hand began to gutter and dim as if the wick were suddenly starved of wax. Rondo's eyes opened wide as he realized the thing had no features and he sat mesmerized like a rat before a rearing snake. In the fluttering light the thing loomed as it approached, and Rhondo's mouth opened in horror as a shapeless arm stretched towards him, tipped by an equally shapeless, yet pointed finger. It was within an inch of his eye when he suddenly flinched and flung his arm up over his face, and screaming,

"No, no, no!" tumbled off the stool and scuttled away under the table.

At the other end of the basement complex, where a mortuary had been set up to preserve the remains of the former king, different events were transpiring. Here, in a vaulted chamber, brightly lit by torches around the walls, two attending morticians also worked late, the needs of preparing King Reuters for his journey to the afterlife keeping them from home and their suppers.

The funereal science had developed to a higher degree in Dulcai than in just about any other spot in the Empire, and on none was it practiced more assiduously than members of the royal family. Thus, Reuters was indeed getting the 'royal treatment.' Immediately upon his demise, he had been stripped of all worldly adornments and placed in a highly concentrated salt bath. Here, weighted down by golden icons and attended constantly by chanting priests, he had stewed for two weeks. This time having now expired to the minute, the priests had retired and the city's leading mortician and his assistant had begun the more technical part of the process.

They had hauled Reuters out of the salt bath and laid him on his back on a large stone slab. His skin was white and wrinkled from the long immersion and his eyeballs shrunk in their sockets. His jaw was slack and his cheeks sunken, but his mouth was puckered as if he were sucking on a straw. The senior of the two morticians, a grizzled fellow, stooped with age, whose sparse white hair stood out at all angles, had unceremoniously slit open his gut from sternum to pudendum and the two were now in process of scooping out his internal organs, wrapping them in linen and packing them in special jars filled with an even heavier concentration of liquid salts.

But the job was not an easy one and the old mortician swore loudly as a section of small intestine escaped the assistant-a frail, dull-eyed fellow of about thirty who went by the name of Scarf-and went slithering off the slab and away across the floor. He chased it down and wrestled it into submission, but not before its contents had squired about wildly, fouling the air with a nauseating reek.

"Faugh!" said the old one, fanning the air. "Mind what you're about there, can't you?

"Sorry, Emmet," said the younger, securing the slimy bundle with a double wrap. "It's bloody slippery stuff, you know?"

"Or you're just slippery-handed, you bugger! And make sure you scrape all that mess up. We don't want to be leaving any of His Majesty lying about or he'll be stuck here, you know. You don't want to be haunted by a king, do you?"

Thoroughly startled by this, Scarf scurried about, scraping up all visible traces of spilled material with a wide-bladed putty knife and wiping them on a linen rag which went into the stone jar with the rest and was sealed for its journey to eternity. Contrite, he went back to the slab and helped Emmet remove the stomach, being very careful this time to tie off both ends where it had been cut free.

"I saw your son out doing his exercises the other day," he said by way of amends. "He's looking quite the young man."

"Yes, he's getting in shape for the funeral games, thinks he can take the wrestling prize."

"Well, he's a rugged boy."

"Aye, and if he had as much in brains as he does in brawn I'd have been able to retire by now. And I surely wouldn't have to be working with the likes of you!" But this last was said with a wry grin and Scarf knew he had been forgiven.

"What, and miss the job of a lifetime, preparing His Majesty here for his journey?"

"Well, I did his wife, too, you know, so it's actually the second job of a lifetime. That's how he knew me."

"You knew the King?"

"Well, I say 'know' but it's more like he knew of me. Hand me that short knife there, will you?" Turning Reuter's head, Emmet stuck the blade deep into his neck at the base of his skull, then broke through the cranial cavity with a chisel and began scooping out globs of gray brain tissue. This went into a special round container, shaped to resemble a skull. "I did meet him once when his wife passed," he went on. "Never saw a man more broken hearted. Course, if you'd a seen her, you'd a knowed how he felt. The girl is like her, but no match to my mind."

"The Queen, you mean?"

"Well, aye, I suppose she is now, yes. I still think of her as that long-legged filly who used to go galloping about the town, with her attendants fluttering after like a flock of starlings. She was lively, that one."

"Well, I seen her when she came with the High King here this spring, and she's no girl anymore, I'll tell you that. And if as you say she's no match for her mother, then I can see where old Reuters here would pine like the blazes," Scarf said, giving the former king's cold haunch a friendly slap.

Just then a muffled scream was heard from somewhere and both men looked up. "What was that?" asked Scarf.

"Probably old Reuter's soul writhing in torment from being abused by the likes of you," said Emmet and went back to his task.

"Don't say such things!" said Scarf, a second fright settling uncomfortably atop the remains of the other. "It's bad enough as it is, working down here like this in the dead of night."

"Oh, you believe the priests, do you, that the King's soul is hovering about watching us?"

Scarf scanned the room nervously. "Don't you?"

"Well, I been handling the dead for over forty years now and if there was any souls hanging about, they never said nothing to me."

"You believe in the afterlife, don't you?"

"I reckon I'll find out soon enough not to worry about it now... And so will you if you don't get a move on. Here, help me with the King here. I need to get a better angle on this."

The two had just hoisted Reuters up into a sitting position and Emmet was just swabbing out the last bits of brain with a rag and stick when the door burst open and Rhondo rushed in. His eyes were wild and his face white with fright and he skidded to an abrupt halt when he realized where he was. His eyes widened even further when he recognized his former king, sitting slumped over before him, his head hanging down onto his left shoulder, his arms dangling and his glazed eyes seeming to stare wearily. His abdominal cavity gaped open and empty like a gutted fish, and his legs had slid off either side of the slab, exposing his shrunken genitals. Rhondo stared in horror at his former master, then with a retching sound, turned and fled the room.

"And there, my friend, goes our future regent," said Emmet, yanking out his swab and stuffing the slimy rag into the skull-shaped jar.

"Regent? Really?"

"Aye, and if what I hear is true, he'll steal us blind before he's done."

"Oh, I don't think the Queen would let him do that, do you?"

"And just how do you expect the Queen will find out? She'll come on down to send our friend here off to eternity, then away she'll go back to her fancy court in Valeria. She could care less what goes on here!"

Chapter 19

It was a very weary King Valerius who stumbled the last few yards into Volkmir's mountaintop cave and flopped down onto one of the old, overstuffed chairs. The place did not appear to have been touched. Except for a bit more dust, it looked exactly the same as it had nearly four years before when he had left Vahla there to apprentice with the Mage. That sameness seemed strangely disorienting, though perhaps his weariness and the thin air of the mountaintop also had something to do with it. So much had changed in those intervening years-a tyrant toppled, an empire revived, a Queen anointed, a prince and princess born, the old Mage himself gone and resting under a carefully built cairn at the other end of the small dell which enclosed the cave-and yet here were these same rooms, carved from living rock by an unknown hand (or means), these same worn chairs and tables, the same racks of scrolls and dusty volumes, the same cupboards of utensils, the same half-burned candles, the same open hearth. Chad, in his inscrutably efficient way, had even left a supply of firewood stacked neatly against the wall and fresh kindling lay in the grate. It was as if Valerius had been out for a walk instead of a near four-year odyssey.

Rising again with a groan and twisting to stretch the aching muscles in his back, Valerius went out to unload and tend to the two pack mules, then hauled his supplies inside and set about preparing some food. It was also strange tending for himself: that and just being alone. It had been four days since the fight with Condor, four days since he'd had a living soul to talk to, other than the mules.

He had sent the others back. Vahla had objected, of course, but the woman was plainly feeling the effects of whatever it was Condor had hit her with-and she was pregnant, after all. Nor was Boltar in much better shape. He had not been that strong to begin with and the blow he took had also taken a toll: all that night he'd had an excruciating headache, and by morning was vomiting. Chad brewed up some herbal potion that quieted his stomach, but he was plainly in no shape to climb a mountain. And then there was Illana: reed thin and emotionally devastated after her ordeal, she was in no shape for further adventures either.

There had really been no choice in the matter: none of them were fit to accompany him, and plainly needed Chad more than he did. So he had left them with instructions to get more men and mules from Ragnar in Zagorbia-there being no more need for secrecy-and to follow him if and when they could.

So here he was, back in the very place he had begun his odyssey when Volkmir had returned the Eye of Valeria and made him see that not only was it his duty to reclaim his rightful place as High King, but that he really had no other choice. Now, it had become clear he had to figure out how to use the Eye if he was to remain High King. The renegade Condor might be dead, but whatever power it was that drove him was as potent as ever. The secret to fighting that power was the Eye, and the secret to that was, he felt, right here, in this very cave.

Gnawing on a crust of stale bread and sipping from a cup of wine, Valerius wandered about the cave's chambers, idly scanning the rows upon rows and shelves upon shelves of scrolls, manuscripts and dusty, leather-bound volumes of lore. In the chamber that had been Volkmir's work room, he idly pulled a manuscript of thick parchment down from an upper shelf and scanned its yellowed cover under the light of his candle: it was written in some crooked, rune text, nothing even like the squared and symmetrical Valerian characters he understood. Replacing it carefully, he pulled another down at random: that, too, was in some strange text, one utterly different from the first.

Sitting down at the old Mage's worktable, he scratched his beard and looked around, bewildered. Where to begin? Volkmir had spent a long lifetime collecting and studying these tomes, yet had claimed there were only a few scraps of information that related to the Eye; claimed he knew no more about the use of it than Valerius himself. And here Valerius was, unable to even read what Volkmir had. Had he come on a fool's errand?

The plan had been to look for a 'Scroll of Dimmian,' but if Volkmir had it, and if it had Eye related stuff in it, wouldn't he have said so? Unless he couldn't read it. Volkmir always told Valerius to use his head, to think things through, assemble the things he knew like the pieces of a puzzle, then look at them and see what was missing: test his assumptions. Well, what if Volkmir could not, in fact read all the manuscripts in his library? Then, obviously, there could be information there that related to the use of the Eye that he did not know.

But so what? If Volkmir couldn't read them, how was Valerius supposed to? And how could he even tell which manuscripts might contain information? If Volkmir had spent his life studying these manuscripts and hadn't mastered them all, how was Valerius to succeed who had never been a scholar and was otherwise rather busy being High King?

Well, he thought, as if this were a problem posed by the Mage himself, as High King he had resources Volkmir did not. He could have all these tomes moved back to Valeria, assemble a team of scholars from around the Empire and charge them with deciphering them. In fact, there might already be such a team-or at least the means to find and establish one-right in his own palace among his archivists.

But would that be wise? Volkmir would not have taken the trouble to bring common, everyday manuscripts up here. He was a Mage, not a scholar. More, he was Mage to the High King. The information contained in these volumes was probably not only privileged, but possibly dangerous if it got into the wrong hands. This was not the kind of stuff he could simply throw open to public access. Whoever he turned loose with it would have to be someone he trusted implicitly. Other than Vahla, he couldn't think who that could be, and she, while certainly a very credible Mage-or Enchantress, as she preferred to call herself-was no scholar, either. Plus, she was pregnant, and the wife of the Atheling of Thule-not exactly a candidate for a lifelong scholarly quest.

So, what else? Another thing Volkmir said came back to him: that many of the most recent High Kings had not believed in the Eye, and the ancients who did were not particularly inclined to impart its secrets to their Mages, for obvious reasons. Knowledge of the Eye was power and power must be guarded jealously.

Thus, anyone who helped him learn how to use the Eye became a potential threat. They might not be able to use the Eye themselves-Fantar had clearly demonstrated that only the rightful High King could use it when the thing burned out his eye-but even the knowledge of how to use it could prove a danger.

So it came back to him. Alone. Sitting here in a cave in the mountains, surrounded by manuscripts that in all probability would be of no help and which he was unable to read in any event. Where was the exit from this circle of reasoning?

Chad? An enigma there, certainly, and one apparently as impenetrable as the Eye itself. Chad-as he often said of himself with utter sincerity-was a servant. But a servant of whom? Or what. Like the Eye itself, he was apparently an instrument of a higher power-Volkmir always said the Eye was a tool of the gods-but Chad himself was seemingly as ignorant of the use he was put to as a flute is ignorant of the music it makes.

What did that leave? If Chad was a tool of the gods, and the Eye was a tool of the gods, was he, Valerius, also a tool? Valerius had never paid much serious attention to the strictures of established religion. As High King he was also High Priest, of course, and officiated at important ceremonies like the Harvest, Solstice and the Rites of Spring. But the priestly caste was a shallow, grasping lot, not much better than those manipulative priests of Balam he had confronted in Telos. And the people knew it: they attended the ceremonies, gave their votive offerings, mouthed the appropriate phrases. But nothing was ever really expected of the priests, and there was no serious belief they were actually connected with the gods they claimed to represent. Neither was Volkmir a priest, nor to Valerius' knowledge, had he ever associated with them.

But on the other hand, since the power of the Eye existed, did that not also prove that gods, or some other powers also existed? How could the stone have power otherwise? As an extension of his will? Was it he as High King who-theoretically-was able to tap into some cosmic power source, pull it down and use it for his own ends? Could he wield the Eye as he wielded his sword?

He had never felt so, and on those few occasions when the Eye had opened to him, it had never seemed so. It always felt there was some other entity involved, someone or something that lent the power; some complicity of wills. He, Valerius, was more an intermediary than a source or progenitor. In that, he was more like Chad, more like the flute than the flautist, though he balked at thinking of himself as a simple tool.

So was the key for him to approach these gods or powers directly? Ask them for guidance? How did he do that? 'Look at the pieces as if they were a puzzle,' Volkmir had said. 'Study them and see what is missing.'

Valerius' head was spinning. This was too much thinking. Rising, he wandered about the cave again, scanning the shelves. Maybe some of that knowledge was here: if not how to use the Eye, then perhaps how to approach those who did know. Perhaps Volkmir even knew that but did not apply it to Valerius' problem. Volkmir had his own problems, as Chad had his and Vahla had hers. Each saw with their own eyes, thought in their own directions, looked to their own ends. A hunter would walk past a stone a sculptor would treasure; and a sculptor ignore stones a fisherman would gather to sink his nets. He, Valerius, might see in these tomes-at least, the ones he could read-things that were of no apparent value to Volkmir.

So that, at least was something to do: find out which ones he could read; see if perhaps there was any rhyme or reason in their organization; if perhaps that in itself could help guide his quest. If these were the pieces, he could start by seeing if and how they fit together. From there, who knew? He would have to follow the path and see where it led.

There were, he estimated, well over 4,000 manuscripts stored in the cave, and for the first couple of days, he concentrated simply on seeing what was there and how it was organized. He found no Scroll of Dimmian, but was surprised to find that not all the texts were indecipherable. In fact, a goodly portion of them-even some evidently ancient ones-were written in Valerian. Much of it was not Valerian as he read and spoke it-curiously, it appeared the language had changed considerably over the centuries-but it was close enough for him to understand what he was reading. In fact, the syntax and use of words reminded him of the old songs and stories he had heard as a boy, and in his efforts to simply scan and catalog, he often found himself engrossed in one tome or another, reading for simple curiosity.

It also quickly became apparent that Volkmir had organized the material by subject, and that the scope of it was much broader than he had expected. He was expecting books on magic and spells, incantations, potions and such. But what he found was husbandry and history, drama and poetry-some of which had apparently been penned by Volkmir himself, the sly old bard-herbology and medicine, military engineering, philosophy, mathematics and law, even a number of volumes on court ceremony and diplomatic protocol. Much of it reminded Valerius of his own studies as a young prince and he realized that if the normal course of succession had been allowed to proceed-if Fantar had not cut it off at the neck-these would have been the materials the Mage would have used to tutor and counsel him.

But there was also a large section on occult topics, which took up the entire back wall of Volkmir's workroom, and it was here where Valerius found the highest proportion of foreign texts. He also found-on a lower shelf where it was ready to hand-a partial translation key written in Volkmir's own shaky scrawl. Obviously, the old Mage was working at deciphering the ancient texts right up till the end. Intrigued, Valerius sat down with one of the old texts and began trying to puzzle out some of the runes using Volkmir's key, and after an hour's work, was rewarded with an incantation that would give his enemies chilblains.

He doubted it would be of much use for his purposes. But what would? What was the next step, the next piece? He now had a sense of what was here, but felt more at sea than ever. Should he just continue puzzling out random bits of manuscript in hopes of stumbling onto something useful? That seemed rather silly. He had to think this through, not wander aimlessly. But what else? What had he learned that could be of use?

Well, he thought, information on the Eye was probably not in the section on herb ology. In fact, there were probably a number of sections he could eliminate: diplomacy, military engineering, court ceremony. Poetry might have a clue, especially Volkmir's own stuff. History would be good, though he had tested those waters pretty thoroughly in his own archives. And, of course, the occult. He could also probably assume that even if Volkmir had not read everything in the library, he had probably gone through the occult section pretty thoroughly. So unless there was something relating to the Eye the old mage would not have recognized, Valerius could probably eliminate everything occult written in Valerian. And since Valerius had come to Volkmir with this very problem, it was probably also safe to assume the old man had redoubled his efforts afterwards. That probably meant Valerius could eliminate anything written in Valerian in any of the sections that might apply.

What did that leave? At a quick guess, perhaps two hundred volumes of material, written in any of several different languages on topics he could not even fathom. No, that last wasn't quite true. Volkmir had organized all the material, even the foreign tomes. That meant he had deciphered enough of them-even if only the titles-to know what they were about. And he had placed them, individually, in specific spots on the shelves, not just lumped together as 'foreign military,' or 'foreign ceremonies.' That probably meant Valerius could get a sense of their content by checking the Valerian titles around them. That could at least help narrow the list of candidates.

Feeling energized again now that he had something specific to do, he set off to search the stacks again, finding foreign volumes and guessing their content from their surroundings. Those that appeared even remotely likely to have something relating to the Eye, the early kings of Valeria or Palmeria (where the Eye supposedly came from) or anything even curious, he pulled slightly out from their companions so he could find them again at a glance.

It took him most of an afternoon, but when he went back through and counted, he found he had narrowed the possibilities down to eighty-six volumes. He felt he had made progress: eighty-six was a lot better than four thousand. There were also several volumes that seemed to be very good prospects. They were together in a section with a single Valerian title, "Ancient Power Rites." He found a quill and some parchment, mixed some fresh ink, and went to work, puzzling out their titles and front matter.

But the work was hard. First he had to comb through Volkmir's key to determine what language the runes represented, whether letters or phrases, and whether they read left to right, right to left, or vertically down the page. Then, again with Volkmir's help, he had to decipher out what the words or phrases meant. He had often wondered what the old Mage had done to occupy himself. Now he was beginning to realize the monumental task Volkmir had set for himself.

Then a sudden brainstorm spread a grin across his face: if he could use the translation guide to identify a few key words in the various languages-like 'Valeria,' 'Eye,' 'power stone,' and 'gem'-he might be able to simply scan the volumes for them and would not have to translate all the text! That made the task suddenly seem possible and he set to work immediately.

Still, the work was tedious and long. He labored late into the night as day followed day, until his head ached and his eyes blurred from the strain. And as one part of his brain focused on the tomes before him, the rest of his mind wandered. He suffered from the solitude and pined for Eomer and the kids. It was very different for him, being alone like this after the usual attention of being High King. It reminded him of when he was cast away in the Hidden Valley of Kantar, out of touch with the outside world and was alone for days at a time. He began talking to himself and sang old songs just to hear a human voice.

He also felt very close to old Volkmir during these days and sensed his spirit wandering about the cave. Once or twice, in the evenings when the candles began to gutter, he even thought he could see a fleeting image of the old mage, beckoning to him. At other times, he was assailed by a bad odor but could find no source. He put these things down to his growing weariness and solitude and went on with the work.

At the end of a week he had finished fifteen volumes. But his head swam from the close study and his back and neck ached from long hours at the desk. That night, as he relaxed in one of the pillowed chairs, sipping a cup of wine, Volkmir's spirit appeared again, directly in front of him. It was very agitated this time and more visible than usual. It beckoned and he followed it to the other side of the cave where it hovered before a small cupboard.

The visage vanished as Valerius reached to open the cupboard, but inside he found only some dried foodstuff and rodent droppings. But as he closed it again, the thing wobbled and at the back he saw the edge of what appeared to be a recess chiseled into the rock. Pulling the cupboard aside he found there was indeed a hidden recess. Inside was a small cedar wood casket containing an obviously ancient roll of parchment. Taking it to the worktable and relighting his candles, he carefully unrolled it. It was in old Valerian script but still quite legible. Across the top, in large, bold letters, was the title, "Dimmian of Odo, His Record." Valerius felt his pulse quicken and his fingers tremble. The Scroll of Dimmian! Quickly, he began deciphering the text:

"I, Dimmian of Odo, set down these words of Valerius, King of Valeria, at his request and for the promise of an easy death:

'I, Valerius, High King of Valeria and all the Inland Sea, do bequeath this record to my son and heir, Valerian, who shall hereafter succeed to the name and title Valerius, High King of Valeria and all the Inland Sea, and to his son and heir thereafter who shall also succeed to the name and title. Thus will Valerius become known as Valerius Everreigning. I leave here the record of the red gemstone, the Eye of Valeria, of its finding and its use... '"

His eyes adjusting to the script, Valerius read eagerly how the original Valerius had found the Eye among ancient artifacts in a cave on the mountain at Darlung. There were two of them- Valerius and his cousin, both nobles from the town of Valeria-on the run from Palmerian forces, and hiding out on the mountain after a raid in which their fellows had been killed. A fierce thunderstorm had overtaken them, lightening striking seemingly at their heels. They had taken shelter under what appeared to be an overhang, but behind a boulder, discovered the entrance to a cave.

Inside, lightning flashes revealed mystical runes carved along the walls, and parts of skeletons scattered about. The Eye, with its golden chain, they found resting on an altar. When the storm passed, Valerius' cousin grabbed the stone and went out to look at it in the light. But as he held it up to the sun, it appeared to explode in his hands and both men were knocked to the ground. Valerius was stunned, but when he came to, he found his cousin dead and the stone, whole and unharmed, lying quietly in his outstretched hand.

Valerius was at first loath to touch the thing. He shook his cousin's hand, spilling the gem onto the ground, then dragged his body back into the cave and started to leave. But he could not get past the stone lying before the entrance. He felt drawn to it and stood there for a long time, staring down at it. Finally, he picked it up by the chain and, turning his face away from the sun and shutting his eyes, slipped it over his head.

At once, a feeling of lightheadedness came over him, like he had drunk too much wine. He headed back down the mountain with a jaunty step, not really aware where he was headed or why, but feeling very confident, like things had somehow taken a turn for the better. At the base, he happened onto a patrol of Palmerians, but rather than run, he walked up to them boldly and demanded an audience with their king.

The leader of the patrol scoffed at him and reached to snatch away the gem hanging from his neck. But the stone flashed red, burning his hand and all the Palmerians backed away, terrified...

Suddenly, Valerius' own reading was interrupted by a draft from the door that brought with it a horrid, putrid smell, like rotting flesh, and with it the soft, muffled sound of movement. Taking up his great war falchion, Valerius slipped out into the darkness to investigate.

Chapter 20

Outside it was very dark. The moon was hidden in cloud and a swirling mist dappled his face like rain. The stench was strong in his nostrils, like the field of a week-old battle. But the rocky plateau before the cave was empty of forms of any kind, living or dead. Cautiously, he moved around the shoulder of rock to the carved-out stable: the mules were there, living and seemingly unharmed, but they stood with hackles raised, nostrils flared and their ears laid back. Surely, there was something...

With the stealth of a hunter, Valerius stole along the path towards the great pillar that marked the edge of the cave enclosure, his sword at the ready, his body crouched and tense. But still, when action came, it came with a speed and ferocity that caught him unaware. As he moved under the shadow of the pillar, a large, head-sized rock crashed down from the darkness onto his outstretched right forearm. He felt the bone snap and his sword-his great curved falchion that had long ago earned him the nickname "Balazar the Butcher"-flew from his hand and clanged loudly in the rocky dell. The pain was like a blinding flash and his knees began to buckle. A huge figure leapt in front of him and a great swinging blow swished just over his head. And with it, came the stench of a thousand deaths.

It was Condor. Valerius recognized him as he dove and rolled to the left. But it was not the living, breathing Condor he had done battle with the previous week. This was the corpse of that Condor, a rotting, stinking, oozing corpse of Condor, one with his own dagger still protruding from its chest, but one animated now by a dark, obsidian light that glowed behind its dead, staring eyes.

Valerius sprang to his feet, hugging his flopping forearm to his chest and circled towards his fallen sword as the corpse lurched towards him. The thing was stiff and clumsy but moved incredibly fast. As Valerius reached down for his sword, he was met with a body block that sent him sprawling onto his back-but not before he was able to grab the hilt of Condor's dagger with his good hand and yank it free. Valerius bounded to his feet, and as the corpse came at him again-armed now with Valerius' own sword-he crouched to meet it, the dagger poised in his left hand.

Condor swung the blade and Valerius leapt aside, slashing down onto Condor's wrist. The blade bit, opening a vicious gash, but the corpse paid no heed. It swung again with a backhand that nearly gutted Valerius, who leapt clear just in time. Again the corpse swung and again Valerius dodged and slashed, this time, taking Condor's hand off at the wrist. But the hand did not fall: though a space of an inch opened between it and the wrist, it kept its place and kept its grip on Valerius' huge falchion.

Thus they circled about the rock behind the pillar. Valerius leapt in and slashed at the thing's throat this time, opening a foul, oozing gap in the rotten flesh. But it hindered the corpse not at all and only made the dark obsidian light from its eyes glow with a deeper, more purple rage. As he leapt back, Valerius took a deep biting cut in the thigh, and as he tried to hobble away, caught another thrust in the side. There was no pain from these wounds, but he could feel the blood coursing down his body and knew he had to get away. But as he backed, his heel caught on the rock Condor had first hit him with, and he tumbled, sprawling onto his back.

In an instant, the fetid thing leaped on him, its rotting hands grabbing his wrists and forcing them down. Valerius twisted and struggled, but the thing was too strong and pinned his hands beside his head. 'This is it,' he thought, as the thing opened its slavering jaws and plunged down towards his throat. And as he saw death descend, Valerius was suddenly moved by a deep sadness, not for himself, but for young Valerian, and tiny Alair, for Eomer his Queen and all he had left undone. 'I will not be able to help them now,' he thought.

But instead of tearing out his throat, the greedy corpse latched onto the Eye of Valeria, and rearing back with the Eye stone flashing red in its mouth, snapped the golden chain that held it to Valerius' neck-and in that instant, the stone exploded in a brilliant red fireball. Condor's head was blown to pieces, and as the red glow faded in the night, the body slowly toppled sideways. A shadow shot from its form and with a wailing cry, dissipated into the darkness.

Valerius wriggled free of the body and sat up. He was bleeding profusely and his vision swam, but there, lying on the ground between him and the corpse, he saw the Eye still whole, still glowing softly. Picking it up, he stumbled back towards the cave, but fell after only a few steps. Vainly, he tried to staunch the flow of blood from his wounds but, but his hands only fluttered feebly then fell senseless at his sides.

Dulcai was adorned for a festival of mourning as the trireme, *Valadator*, came to rest at the dock. Looking out over the town, Eomer had no idea there was so much black muslin in all the empire, let alone Dulcai. It was like the entire city had hung out its laundry, all of it black. Walls, windows and building fronts were draped with black, fountains were swaddled in it, and the tall statue of Reuters in the center of the square was totally swathed in deepest mourning. The people, too, were adorned in black. Jammed around the quay, packed in the square and spilling up along the road to the palace, they were all, if not entirely dressed in black, at least wearing some bit of black; a black cape, a scarf, a sash, an armband. Reuters had been a fair and much beloved ruler-the only king most Dulcaians had ever known-and it was clear he was sorely missed. They were also clearly ready to greet their new Queen, and as Eomer stepped to the head of the gangway-her own and her children's mourning reflected in black silk-the populace knelt in silent obeisance.

To Eomer, the scene was at once solemn and surreal. As she made her way through the silent throng to where Rhondo, her acting Regent, awaited her, she could feel the emotions of the crowd wash over her like waves of summer heat. The news of her father's death had been a heavy blow, and while its impact had been intensely painful and personal, it had also been-in far off Valeria and on the long voyage since-somewhat abstract. Now, as Rhondo fawned over her hand amidst a sea of black and bowed heads, the public fact of that loss and the enormity of the change it occasioned threatened to overwhelm her. She had been schooled in maintaining poise and dignity in public from her earliest youth, of course, so as she ignored the waiting palanquin and led a growing procession towards the palace, her facade of equanimity remained unruffled. But behind it, behind her smiles and gracious nods, she felt as if brutal hands were twisting and wrenching her insides. She had trouble breathing and by the time she mounted the palace portico and turned to face the crowd of Dulcaians spread out below her, running tears streaked her cheeks and she feared she might faint.

Still, she knew her duty, knew what it required, and taking a deep breath, addressed them.

"Citizens of Dulcai," she called out in a voice that faltered only briefly before rising rapidly in power and confidence, "My friends. Your welcome has overwhelmed and moved me beyond poor words. Thank you! Since I received the news of the

King, my father's passing, I have felt very much alone. Now you have shown me that I am not alone, that we have all suffered a great loss. I take great comfort from that and I promise you we will move through this together."

The crowd began to cheer then, first a voice here and there, then a sudden tumult of acclamation. "Long live the Queen!" they shouted. "Long live Queen Eomer. Long live Eomer, Queen of Dulcai!"

But when the palace doors closed behind her, the realization hit her that he had not been at the docks to greet her, and she realized anew just how alone she was. Nor was he here at the palace, filling the great halls with his bustle and infectious cheer. The personal apartments, too, seemed especially empty and drear, despite the flurry of servants carrying baggage and seeking to assure her comfort. As soon as she could, she bundled the children off with Nurse Brenda, dismissed the servants from her private chamber, fell across the bed, and wept.

The days that followed were busier than any she had ever known, so busy as to be bewildering. But at least the business kept her mind from her grief and when she fell into bed at night, she was too exhausted to weep.

There was an endless stream of things to attend to. There were the funeral arrangements, of course, along with her own coronation ceremony and the attendant games, but also innumerable matters of state, both great and small. The justice courts had backed up with no royal to preside and cases of all sorts had to be heard and adjudicated. There were petitions to be heard, matters of trade policy to discuss, staff appointments to be made, personnel and administrative issues to deal with, and just plain problems that probably could have been solved by someone else, but which inevitably devolved upon her as the ultimate finality. And too, there were matters of accounting and budget on which she spent many hours closeted with Rhondo- a Rhondo who, while unfailingly polite and correct, seemed to her just a bit too pat in some of his answers and not quite as forthcoming as she would like him to be.

But neither was this all, and certainly not the worst. There were also just people, old friends and acquaintances who wanted to see her, or who besieged her for favors of all sorts; advisors whose best and most considered advice always seemed to also serve them; courtiers and young nobles of the realm whose compliments always carried an edge of insinuation and a look that bespoke favor; even servants who seemed always to want more than to serve. In short, from the moment of her arrival, she was so flattered and feted, so complimented and cajoled, she was at a loss to know what was true and what was not, who was honest and who was not, who had the kingdom's interest at heart, and who had solely his or her own.

It was bitter, this last, and tinged her days with a rancor that threatened to seep inside and sour her very heart. It was during one of these moments that

Grumwald appeared at her apartments, begging for a private audience.

"And what do you want?" she snapped at him, "The eastern half of my kingdom?"

The old admiral was taken aback at the question and stared at her for a moment. "I want no kingdom, Ma'am," he said. "I come on another matter: to ask for the hand of Nurse Brenda."

Eomer looked at his honest sailor's face, at the obvious discomfort her rash words had caused and felt ashamed for lashing out. And she realized that in faces like his-and innumerable others she knew-there was truth, and that she had but to look for it to be made plain. And she also realized, with a sudden gush, how happy his words had just made her.

"Oh, with my blessing, dear Grumwald!" she cried. "With my blessing," and she threw her arms around his rangy old frame.

Valerius lay on the barren rock, his life force slowly draining from the deep gash in his thigh. The blood formed a puddle which expanded until it hit a dip in the rock, then formed a rivulet which flowed quickly for several feet until it hit the Eye Stone which had fallen by his side. At the touch of the blood, the stone began to glow and pulse. A red aura grew and swelled until it enveloped the fallen High King-and as it did, the blood, which had been flowing from his body, began to flow back.

But Valerius was aware of none of this. He found himself marching along a flat, open plain upon which nothing was visible for miles except a faint cart track, which he followed. How long he had been marching, he did not know, but the sun was hot overhead and the sweat trickled down his back and beneath his breastplate. His legs were tired and the buckler on his left arm weighed heavily, yet the track seemed to stretch on forever. But he was surprised to see, on glancing down at himself, that he was young again, his arms and chest full and packed with solid muscle, his thighs bulging with every step. 'How can this be?' he thought, and stopped to take a better look at himself.

"No time to stop now, Your Majesty," said a voice beside him, and there was Volkmir, the Mage, crooked and bent and leaning on a stick for support, but with bright blue eyes and a clear, determined look on his face.

"Where are we going?" Valerius asked, the presence of the dead Mage no stranger than his own rekindled youth. They walked on and Valerius could hear the thump, thump, thump as the old man's stick struck the ground, where before there had been only silence. "I've been wanting to talk to you, Volkmir," he said after a time. "About the Eye."

"We had that conversation, remember? I can tell you no more now than I told you at the cave when I first gave it back to you."

"Yes, but I still haven't figured out how to use it, and I'm at the point where I really need to know."

"I understand. But there's nothing I can tell you. I don't know how to use it: never did."

"But you did use it!"

"No, it used me. There's a difference."

"But what about your archives? The Scroll of Dimmian?"

But the Mage made no answer and when Valerius looked around, he was gone. Gone, too, was the vast emptiness of the plain, the bright heat of the sun. It was dusk now and looming before him was the entrance to a great cave or tunnel. For an instant, he thought it the mouth of the tunnel into the Hidden Valley of Kantar, but as he was walking on solid ground, that couldn't be. And besides, inside this gaping maw was a light, a deep russet red, flickering and shimmering in the darkness, like the reflected light of a distant fire.

He entered and made his way carefully along an uneven floor as the tunnel wove this way and that, the light brightening all the while. Finally, he stepped out into a large chamber, lit by a roaring central fire and lined about with large, polished bronze panels, which reflected the firelight back and forth until the whole chamber was suffused with a bright red glow. At the far end, a group of men sat feasting around a large table. They were big men, all. Each wore a crown, and so resembled the others that they might have been brothers or close cousins. More, there was a familiarity about them, a feeling of kindred. As Valerius approached, the nearest one rose and turned to him. It was his father.

"Your Majesty!" he exclaimed. "Father! I... " but words failed him and he stood stricken dumb and felt again like a frightened boy.

"So, you've come, have you?" said his father, glaring at him with his old anger. "But you're not to stop here, not to sup with us! Oh, no, not you!"

"But father, who are all these men'?"

"Why, your ancestors, boy! Can't you see? They're Valerius Everreigning, everyone. But not all: oh, no, we're not all! We're just the stubborn ones. The ones who denied. We're supped here in royal splendor, day after day, warmed by a royal blaze and entertained by our own glorious reflections, those visages we were never able to look beyond. And I! I, my boy am considered the worst of the lot for not only did I deny the Eye, but in my stubbornness I lost the bloody thing and the Empire with it!" And at this he threw his head back, as if to laugh, but instead, his face contorted in a spasm of pain and a great gap opened at his neck. "If you look just there," he said, resuming as if nothing had happened, "in the center of that panel, you can see my reflection has no head!"

Valerius looked, and there, etched on the panel, as real as life, was his father's headless corpse, lying on battlefield before Valeria, just as he himself had found it all those years before, except that now, the head itself remained animated, lying some few feet away from its body, its eyes flashing about wildly, its mouth working and twisting, screaming out a stream of silent invective.

"Aye," said the father before him, his voice softer now and edged with sadness. "I was not happy to see so suddenly what a fool I had been. But so too with these others, boy. They were all fools in their way, all vain and presumptuous, and left now with only the reflections of their own silly glory. But you are to go on, lad, on up the stairs, just beyond there, though whether you'll return to us one day remains to be seen, eh?" And without another word, his father turned from him and resumed his seat at the feast.

Valerius started up the steps, but as his foot touched the first, the stair disappeared and he found himself on a lofty mountain meadow. Around and below, soft white clouds drifted in a serene blue sky, while beneath his feet, thick turf, deep green and as soft as a carpet, stretched ahead into a shimmering haze of white, effusive light. There was about the whole of his surroundings, a deep feeling of peace, but it was of a peace with power. He was impelled onward, towards the light, but he felt deeply afraid.

Dread filled him and his legs began to tremble. His hands shook, and his heart hammered in his chest. Yet there was no threat facing him, no enemies lurking in the mists, no sense of danger of any kind. Still, he panted with fear and his limbs trembled so badly, he could barely keep to his feet. He staggered on the velvety turf, twice stumbled and fell, but drawn on by he knew not what, rose up again and tottered on.

After a time-and he had no sense of how long-the white, misty light began to resolve itself and he found himself moving towards a center of brightness, so white and searing he could not look directly at it, but approached with his head down and his face averted. He put up his hand to shield his eyes but still the brightness grew until it felt like a physical force, pushing and pulling him at the same time. He felt faint and exhausted and yet, empowered; at once like a tiny mote of dust pinned in a shaft of sun light, and yet like a glint off the tip of a mighty spear.

Finally, his legs would no longer bear him and he toppled onto his face. Still impelled forward, he began to crawl on his belly like a babe making its first moves in the world. But then, even this was too much: the light, the brightness, the awesome might of that which was before him pressed down upon him like a huge weight so that he feared he would be crushed, and he lay with his face pressed into the earth, utterly inert in a screaming, swirling silence of light, waiting for whatever was to come.

But there was nothing else. At least, so it seemed for a while. Valerius lay like a sailor washed up on a sheltered shore by a hurricane. He felt safe, delivered from the immediate peril of the wild sea, and yet was still in the center of a howling, swirling storm, screaming overhead. But it was a storm of silence and light, and its wind-for that was the only word he had for it-swirled so fast it seemed not to move at all. It was a contradiction, an impossibility, as plain as truth before him.

Then he realized that he was not alone, that the light was not empty but full of tiny specks of energy that were-and again, he had no other word-alive, and the roaring silence he heard was their cosmic conversation.

He sensed rather than saw a huge throne room, ringed with golden thrones, upon which sat scores of kings all bearing the Eye. The room seemed to float and spin, fade in and out of the light, the figures of the kings to at once sit stationary on their thrones and yet flit about like tiny sparks. One's face suddenly loomed before his own.

"You would know about the Eye?" it asked, but there were no words.

"Yes, I would, Sire," he said in the same manner. "But who are you?"

"I am Valerius Everreigning, High King of Valeria and all the Inland Sea, the father of your father's great, great grandfather."

Valerius bowed before him. "Can you tell me then, Grandsire, how to use the Eye?"

The image of the ancient Valerius smiled. It was a smile one gives a child, at once wise and indulgent: "How to use the Eye... Always you must be the master, is that not true, my son? It is a common fault among kings, I'm afraid. Well, all I can tell you is what you do not know," it said. "You do not know how to submit. And you can never truly master, until you learn to serve."

Something else approached and the Valerius backed away. Valerius saw, or sensed a number of huge shapes, human shapes, both male and female. A pair of feet in golden sandals stood before him, but when he tried to look up, it was too bright and he lowered his forehead to the ground, trembling with fear and made obeisance. He felt a hand touch his head and in his mind flashed a thousand, a million lights. It was brilliant, but it happened slowly like a cascading mist of light and he saw so many things he could not begin to comprehend, could not begin to catalog them. He was not sure whether his eyes were open or closed-whether or not he even needed them to see. But then the hand was lifted and he saw the feet turn and walk away. With them, the light faded, and suddenly, it was black night and he found himself lying on hard rock.

He tried to sit up but a wave of dizziness took him and he toppled back again, this time into a blackness of oblivion.

Chapter 21

That was how Chad found him, stretched unconscious on the barren rock, still bathed in the red glow of the Eye. The sight did not startle Chad. Rather, he seemed to expect it and went to work with a calm efficiency. He passed his hands over Valerius' wounds, closing them; set his broken arm and bound it; placed the still pulsing stone gently on his chest; then picked up the huge monarch as if he were a child and carried him in to his bed in the cave. He might have been a butler, tidying up after tea.

As Valerius settled into the soft mattress, the still gently pulsing stone on his chest, his body began to relax. His breathing grew deep and regular, his pulse slowed, and he appeared to sleep. But somewhere deep inside he was again conscious and aware, or at least, dreamed that he was conscious and aware.

He found himself in a strange place, a non-place, one with no up or down, no earth or floor, no roof or ceiling, only a red glow that totally enveloped him. He was floating, yet felt no sense of suspension, no wind, no heat or cold, no sense of time. He was just there. But as he looked about, he sensed a barrier, a limit to the encapsulating space, like a wall. It was like he was inside something, but it was not a solid something, and the wall was not solid, but soft and translucent.

Then, quite suddenly, he realized he could see through it. He could see out, could see ...

The room around him, its rough-hewn stone walls at first solid and hard, then fading into a transparent opalescence ... the rest of the cave with Volkmir's study and work table just as he had left it, the Scroll of Dimmian half unrolled on its top ... the barren rock outside where Chad was quietly busy cleaning up the remains of Condor's corpse ... the long trail down the mountain, up the final assent of which now labored a train of mules and men, among them his old friend, Thorngere ... the river with his schooner, *Kantar* snugly moored in mid-stream, and behind her, the late Condor's galley, the *Steiger*, manned now by Thorngere's sturdy Thuringians ... and beyond that, out over Zagorbia and the Inland Sea, out over the straits to the Outer Ocean, around and down southward, zooming along the coast he had sailed so often, past the high cliffs guarding New Kantar to the Bay of Dulcai, and the city itself, and then to ...

Eomer in the royal palace, in the very chamber he and she had shared. She was sitting before a bronze mirror, putting up her hair. He knew now this was not memory, not a dream, though he did not know how he knew. He just knew that it was now and that he was actually there and that she was real and ... not alone. There was another ... presence ... in the room, watching her. A dark shadow that hovered in the corner, just beyond his view ... a shadow with form.

Suddenly, Valerius' eyes jerked open. He was back in Volkmir's cave, and there, bending over him, was Thorngere. He had gained weight and there were gray strands now in his golden mane and beard, but his eyes still twinkled, and despite their obvious concern, still had their old warmth.

"So, you've decided to come back to us, have you?" he said, a wry grin lighting his face. "It's a good thing, too, for I've a bone to pick with you: What did you think you were doing, dragging my wife over half the Southern Mountains, and her with child?"

"I should ask what were you doing letting my sister wander off so in the first place!" Valerius retorted with a grin of his own. He reached up and clasped his old friend's hand.

"But you needn't have worried: Vahla's tougher than you'll ever be. And, it is good to see your face, my friend! Good to see you, for now you must help me up out of this bed and out of this cave. We need to get to Dulcai as fast as we can!"

Despite its tribulations, Eomer found the ascension to power actually easier than she had expected. She had been groomed to it from her earliest youth, of course. Her father, having no expectation of ever having a son-and not being of a chauvinistic nature in any event-had raised and educated her to rule. Plus, her mother had been a very public-and much adored-Queen, an authority figure in her own right, so the public was well disposed to a woman in power. Besides that, Eomer was the wife of the High King-no mean recommendation itself-and the memories of Fantar's recent reign were too fresh for there even to be much complaint over her succession, let alone any serious objection.

So her word was law, her merest wish an absolute command, and that was that. It was more power than she had ever consciously held, but it was what she had been taught to expect, so it did not seem heavy in her hands. There were matters with which she was unfamiliar and had to study, of course, she having been physically out of touch for several years. But there were many other matters whose antecedents were as fresh and familiar to her as the flowers which daily graced her chambers, and whose recent threads she was able to untangle and weave to her liking. So while the hours were grueling and while she fretted at the time away from her children, she quickly grew accustomed to the tasks of power and comfortable wearing its mantle.

Except in one area. And even here it was not so much that she felt uncomfortable as that she sensed something was amiss. She did not feel she was being deliberately thwarted-indeed, she could not point to any deliberate acts at all. Rather, it was a feeling, a suspicion, an instinct, a foreboding. There was a sense of obfuscation, that something was not what it appeared.

The problem had to do with Rhondo, her nominal regent and the erstwhile ambassador, and while she couldn't put her finger on it exactly-he was as correct and formal as any minister of state could possibly be-she felt a deep suspicion and was convinced there were things he was not telling her. Either that, she thought, or her dislike of the man-for some reason, she had never been able to abide him-was clouding her judgment.

He was a thin, hawkish figure with lank, oily hair, black eyes and a beaked nose, and there was a condescension about him, a smugness that irritated her like a canker. He had an attitude that seemed to imply she shouldn't bother herself with petty matters of state, that such things were better left in more capable hands-his own-and that the sooner she returned to the confining care of her husband, the better things would be. Knowing her visceral reaction to his personality and not wanting to be unfair, she was always measured and considered in her response to him. But his continued haughtiness incensed her and she began to suspect there was something more to it than mere arrogance.

Her suspicions were confirmed when she showed him the plans she had commissioned for her father's monument and he objected to the cost.

"Forgive me, Majesty, but I'm afraid I don't know how we would fund such a project as this."

"Fund? How so?"

"I realize Your Majesty is still new to the throne and perhaps does not fully understand these matters," he said with an oily assurance that set her teeth on edge. "But the realm is not so rich as is generally supposed. Surely, something more modest would be in keeping with your father's wishes?"

"I grant you that last, Rhondo," she said her voice level and as pleasant as she could make it. "My father was ever a modest man. But it is not my wish alone to honor the late King thus: a commission of leading citizens drew up these plans. And what do you mean, 'the realm is not as rich as is generally supposed'? We mine gold, do we not?"

"Certainly, Your Majesty. And ore and precious gems as well. But it takes gold to mine gold, as I'm sure you know. The costs of these works are high-as has been the drain on the treasury by your husband the High King. Factor those things together, and I'm afraid there is not that much left."

"Do you mean to say Dulcai is impoverished?"

"Oh, no, my dear girl... Your Majesty. Not even close. We just must be cautious of extravagance is all."

"I was not aware of that," said Eomer, watching his thoroughly composed, thoroughly closed face. "But if that is the case-and please don't think I doubt you for a moment, Lord Rhondo-then I must see for myself. What are the costs of the works? How much, exactly, have we been sending to the High King, my husband? It is my duty to know these things, would you not agree?"

"Certainly, Your Majesty. I will prepare a report at once," said Rhondo, bowing his way from her presence.

But the report, when it came, several days later, was less than satisfactory. A mere single-sided sheet, it listed only summary totals with none of the detail that comprised them. Looking it over quickly, blood began to suffuse Eomer's cheeks, but was quickly checked. "Thank you for taking such trouble, Lord Rhondo," she said with a tight smile. "I'm sure these totals are all correct, but I need to know more. Please assemble all the books, so I can conduct an audit of the palace and the mining operations. "

"As Your Majesty wishes," said Rhondo. And while a casual observer would have seen no discernable change in his expression as he bent his head over Queen Eomer's hand, she-who was watching closely-saw the quick flash of an angry scowl.

Later, she sat nursing Alair in her chambers while her own old nurse and long-time family servant, Lilly, puttered about the room. "Lilly," she said, "you attended my father at the end, did you not?"

"Every minute I could, Ma'am. T'was I who closed his eyes at the last, poor dear. He called out for you often, you know, he missed you so ... Though I beg pardon for adding to your grief."

"That grief is absolute, Lilly, and I know you feel it as much as I. But tell me, was Lord Rhondo much in attendance during the King's last days?"

"On the good days, yes Ma'am. There was much business for the King to attend to, even then. T'was a shame, too. He hadn't the strength to bear such a burden and it always seemed to go worse for him afterwards. But Lord Rhondo said he only brought the most pressing matters, those he could not handle on his own. I know he felt it, though."

'What pressing matters might those have been,' Eomer wondered, 'that he has not since seen fit to bring to me?'

With the heavy door of his basement counting room hideaway securely bolted, Rhondo paced in the guttering light from a pair candle stubs on his ledger-strewn desk and fumed, his anger alternating with fear.

"Pushy bitch!" he spluttered. Why could she not leave things alone as her fool of a father had done? How was he to deal with an audit now? The palace books were fine, he was sure of that: she would find no trace of imbalance there. But the mine ledgers! A simple comparison would reveal the discrepancy between ingots produced and ingots logged at the palace or transferred. Had she the wit to unravel that, he was undone. So, how to avoid her looking? Prepare a false set? There wasn't time. Another summary report? He doubted she would buy it. Destroy the ledgers? Then how to explain their absence?

Panic rising in him like a fever, Rhondo paced, the fury of his passing whipping the candle flames like a lash.

"There is a way," said a voice close beside him. Rhondo jumped, nearly fainting from the shock.

"You!" he gasped, glaring into the darkness. "Again! Who are you to come upon me like that? Come forward and show yourself!"

"You know who I am," said the voice, all reason. "At least, a part of you does. And you know what 'way' I mean, too. Don't try to be coy with me."

"I don't have any idea what you mean."

"Do I underestimate you so? I doubt that. But let me be plain, then: kill the creature. She is all that stands between you and dominion."

"Murder and treason! Is that all you can offer? If so, you're a fool, whoever you are! I'd be hunted down and gutted within an hour."

"There are other means than brute violence... means you may already have some experience with?"

"What are you implying?"

"Oh, come now. Do you expect me to believe poor old Reuters died naturally?"

"I had no hand in that!"

"Entirely beside the point," said the shadow, the nothingness of its voice sharp, nonetheless. "We are speaking of means."

"Poison the Queen?"

"At last the light dawns!"

"No, no, I couldn't. It's impossible. It couldn't be done! Go away from me now. Such things are not even to be spoken of!"

"Ah, but you think them, my friend. You know you think them."

"Get away from me!" Rhondo screamed, and snatching up his stool, he rushed about the darkness of the chamber, swinging it like a cudgel. But the only thing he hit was the stony wall.

Chapter 22

They had to carry Valerius down the mountain on a litter. Made from a blankct lashed to poles, it was slung between two mules on the easier stretches but had to be lowered precariously by hand down the steeper slopes. Either way, it was an ignominious way for the High King of Valeria and all the Inland Sea to travel. But he had no choice. Although there was little visible evidence left of his wounds after Chad's ministrations-just some swelling in his right forearm and a bit of bruising on his side and thigh-they had left him as weak as if all his blood had indeed been drained from his body. He could stand, and with assistance, totter to a chair or back to his bed, but that was about all. Thorngere argued for rest, at least for a few days, but Valerius would not hear it. His mind was in a torrent of anxiety: they must depart for Dulcai and they must do it now.

Had there been more sign of his wounds, or had he any real inkling of what Valerius had been through, Thorngere would no doubt have assumed the doctor's prerogative and refused to move his patient. As it was, he had no idea what had really happened, and as Chad was his usual, uncommunicative self (would he have believed him in any event?), he ascribed the weakness to something akin to a common flu, and could come up with no compelling argument not to go. Leaving the bulk of his rescue party to pack up everything in the cave and transport it to Valeria, they left at first light with Chad, a few pack mules and a half-dozen burly Thuringian warriors to act as honor guard and litter bearers.

It was not a pleasant trip. In addition to the weakness, Valerius quickly discovered his wounds were as sore as if they had not healed, and that the rest of his body was stiff and bruised from the beating he had taken as well. So by the time they had worked their way down the barren and boulder-strewn upper slopes to the tree line, he was already in agony. Then, when they hit the first of the 'scramble points'-those steep, all-fours-and-a-prayer slopes around the several cliffs and scree fields-where he had to hang on to keep from tumbling head first out of the litter, things only got worse. By mid-afternoon, he was exhausted and barely conscious.

But it was a muddy, deceptively shallow slope that put an end to the first day's march and nearly put an end to him. Thorngere had insisted on lashing him to the litter to keep him from falling out, and when the trailing bearer's feet slid out from under him, there was nothing he could do to protect himself. The weight of the man behind knocked down the one in front and all three went skidding and tumbling down the long slope. The two bearers were able to catch hold of bushes near the bottom and break their falls, but bound as he was, Valerius was helpless, and bounced along like a log towards a large boulder that would surely have dashed out his brains had not two luckily placed saplings caught the two ends of the litter, and bending under its weight, suspended him over the rock like a roast on a spit.

"You know," said Valerius as Thorngere and the abashed bearers worked to untangle him, "this reminds me of our first encounter with the Kantarans. Do you remember?"

"When they carried us over the mountains, bound to poles like a pair of stags from the hunt? I think I still have some of the rope marks!"

"Well, this has just refreshed mine. I hope this episode ends as well as that one."

"There's a decent spot to camp not very far along from here. I think Your Majesty has had quite enough for one day."

"You, my friend, are very perceptive," said Valerius and fell asleep before they were halfway to the camp.

He was impatient to push on again in the morning, but while the remaining decent was incident free, it was still a long five and a half days before the troop reached the river where the *Kantar* lay moored snugly fore and aft in mid-stream with Condor's captured galley behind. Valerius was nearly spent from the ordeal and lapsed from delirium to near coma. Word was sent to King Ragnar in Zagorbia, who hurriedly escorted Vahla and Illana through the labyrinthine swamp, along with additional supplies. Meanwhile, Chad worked some minor medicinal miracles with a concoction of herbs he had gathered along the way, so that by the time Ragnar arrived, Valerius was at least able to sit up in *Kantar*'s main saloon to receive them.

Neither Thorngere nor Ragnar had gotten a close look at *Kantar* and while they were waiting for the king to receive them, a much-improved Boltar gave them a quick tour. It was clear neither was impressed.

"Well, she's pretty," said Ragnar to Valerius as he squeezed along the cushioned benches behind the table in the plush cabin, "But if you want to get to Dulcai in a hurry, I've half a dozen or more galleys will get you there quicker than this thing!" A hard fighting, hard drinking renegade who had spent years as a resistance fighter in these very swamps, Ragnar's tenure as King of Zagorbia had softened his burgeoning girth but not his belligerent spirit.

Weak as he was, Valerius could not repress a smile. "Tell you what, Ragnar, if I survive this expedition to Dulcai, I'll put the *Kantar* up against any six galleys you choose for any amount you want to wager."

"What do you mean, 'if you survive?' What in hell-fire is going on here? First you swear me to secrecy about some crazy pirate and go tearing off up into the mountains, and now you come back half dead and say you might not survive a trip to Dulcai. How about you rest a few days and we all go to Dulcai? We owe Reuters that, anyway."

"Yes, what's going on," asked a surprised Vahla. "What happened to you up there and why the sudden hurry? Condor is dead, isn't he?"

At the mention of that name, Illana shrank into a corner and curled herself into a protective ball. Boltar reached out a comforting hand and she grasped it like a lifeline.

"Yes, Condor is dead," said Valerius, "but the evil that empowered him is not, and it's much greater than he ever was. What happened on the mountain is that it nearly killed me-though the wounds don't show, for some reason-and now it threatens Dulcai. It is a thing I shudder to even think about, much less try to name. So, Ragnar, by all means, come as soon as you can to honor Reuters, but I cannot wait another hour."

There was nothing to say to this and the group sat in silence, their eyes searching each other's before turning back to the High King. Overhead, and from the companionway aft, light from the westering sun slanted along the cabin sole and flickered on the polished table as the little ship shifted at her moorings. A lantern swung in an almost imperceptible arc and the mast creaked on its step.

"That's it then," said Valerius. "Thorngere, if you would be so kind as to see our friend here ashore, we'll get underway as soon as all the supplies are on board."

After several days with no report from Rhondo, a very impatient Queen Eomer sent for him. He arrived, appearing nervous and bearing an armload of scrolls, which he spread out on the dining table in Eomer's private quarters. A pair of scribes stood ready to assist, but Rhondo stayed them with a raised palm. "Here are the records, Your Majesty," he said. "Now, as you can see here... "

"That's all right, my Lord," said the Queen, stepping in front of him and scanning the entries herself. "My father made an accountant of me long before the High King made me a Queen."

Rhondo backed away from the table, but only managed a few steps before the Queen rounded on him.

"These are only the palace books," she said, a sharp edge in her voice that cut at his bowels.

"I beg pardon, Majesty," he said, bowing quickly and clasping his hands before him. "I thought you wanted totals of all the gold shipped and stored. These records contain... "

"I know what they contain, Rhondo," she snapped. "And I also know what I asked for!" Eomer caught her rising temper and took a deep breath. "My Lord Rhondo," she continued in a more moderated tone, moving towards him and forcing a smile to her face, "are you aware of how I got this?" She held up her scarred left arm.

"Yes, Majesty. You were bitten by a viper in Palmeria and nearly died. We were all terribly concerned when we heard of it."

"And do you know what they say about people who have recovered from viper bites?"

"No, Your Majesty." Rhondo shook his head and felt his legs begin to tremble.

"They say you become immune to venom," she said. "And that means venom of all kinds, including lies and deceit. Now, I strongly suggest you stop whatever charade you are trying to play here and fetch me those mine records. And I suggest you do it immediately!"

Clearly frightened now, Rhondo's voice squeaked, "Yes, Your Majesty. As you wish," and he fairly scuttled from the room.

Eomer paced angrily about her chamber, mentally gauging the time it would take Rhondo to walk the several blocks to the mining offices, explain his errand to the head clerk there, retrieve the appropriate records and return. It would not take long, should not take long, and when twice the estimated time had elapsed with no Rhondo in sight, she sent several armed guards to retrieve him.

They returned-in very little time-to report that Rhondo had not even appeared at the mining offices, much less retrieved any records. The clerk there had suggested they look at his country estate.

"His what?" asked the Queen.

"Lord Rhondo has taken over several old farms along the bay east of the city, Your Majesty," said the captain of the guard. "He has built a compound there, Ma'am; quite a large compound."

"Has he indeed! A compound! And has he armed guards at this compound, do you know?"

"Yes, he does, Ma'am, a few. They're mostly local lads, though there are a few hard cases from ... from before."

"Fantar's men, you mean."

"Yes, Ma'am."

"Very well, Captain. Take a squad or a platoon-whatever force you're sure will be sufficient-take the entire Royal Guard if you need-and bring Lord Rhondo to me here. Do you understand?"

"Yes Ma'am!" said the Captain, snapping to attention and slapping his chest in salute.

Chapter 23

Rhondo's estate lay about a mile east of the city gate. It consisted of several outbuildings and a mansion-still under construction-that sat on a modest hill and commanded a fine view of the bay and the city. A large portico extended along the western side of the manse where Rhondo could often be found, enjoying the afternoon breeze or watching the evening sun set over the bay, often with a glass of wine, and very often in company with one or another of the city's more attractive young ladies. But he was not in evidence this afternoon as the Captain and his squad entered the gate-the startled guard there offered no objection-and climbed the dusty drive to the compound.

"You've just missed him," a steward said. "He dashed in here, packed up some things and left. I think he was headed down to the dock. He has a sloop there he's been refitting."

The captain double-timed his men down the hill, but by the time they rounded the boathouse at the jetty, Rhondo's ship had already cast off her lines and was moving slowly away under oars, down the river towards the bay. Rhondo was clearly visible on the afterdeck, standing by the tiller, but though the captain shouted long and hard, he did not look back.

"You four men," the captain said, surveying his squad and picking the four who seemed least affected by their run from town to the compound, then down to the river, "a gold coin to the one who first reaches the commander of the duty galley in the city! Tell him to stop that ship and bring Lord Rhondo to the Queen! Tell him it's Her Majesty's personal order!"

Grumwald whistled softly to himself as he made his way from the palace down the busy street towards the dock. He had just concluded a delightful luncheon with Brenda, his-while perhaps no longer blushing, still nonetheless lovely-bride to be, and he was feeling very well with the world. The afternoon breeze had filled in from the distant sea, relieving the mid-day heat and dissipating somewhat the smells of the city, and from his height he could see his majestic charge, *Valadator*, resting quietly at the dock. She was a noble sight and his seaman's eye contemplated her with satisfaction. Every line of her rig was taut and her black hull glistened with fresh paint. Her gangway was bright with varnish and clean white ropes, and side boys manned the entry port. All was exactly as it should be, and with the exception of a working party slushing down the foremast, he thought the ship might have been cut from a painting... a painting by an artist as exacting as an admiral.

Grumwald smiled at his conceit and pressed a coin into a beggar boy's hand as he swept along, in a gesture as regal as it was benign. Things were, he thought, very well with his world indeed. In fact, he could hardly believe his good fortune. He had survived decades of war-including a stint as a galley slave-had risen to a position of eminence and regard beyond his wildest imaginings, and now, as the prospect of long years of peace and prosperity stretched before him, he had found himself blessed with a love and companionship that came close-though of course not quite-to replacing the love he had lost all those long years ago. For a man who never thought he would live to see this day, the prospects of it were wondrous to contemplate.

And the only chores before him for the remainder of the day were to receive routine readiness reports from his officers, closet himself with a bit of paperwork (i.e., have a nap), and then ready himself for dinner at the palace. So he whistled as he walked and so enjoyed the afternoon and the contemplation of his future happiness that he almost didn't notice the four Guardsmen sprinting along the quay towards the guard boat docked in front of *Valadator*.

But the distant shouts and instant commotion aboard that galley left no doubt that something was up and he quickened his pace. Eastward, where the river widened into the bay, a heavily laden trading sloop labored along under oars and it was towards this vessel the guard boat headed as she slipped her lines. Grumwald hurried up the gangway of *Valadator*, yelling orders that would get the huge trireme underway as well, but belayed them when he reached the quarterdeck and saw that the guard boat had the sloop firmly under control-a squad of archers lined its rail, their bows at the ready and the sloop's crew in point blank range-and was shepherding it towards the dock.

"Do you know what's up?" Grumwald asked the Officer of the Deck.

"No, my lord. All we heard was those Guardsmen yelling, 'stop that sloop by order of the Queen!'

"Curious. Well, I suppose we'll find out in a minute. They're bringing her alongside the quay."

"Say, my Lord, isn't that Ambassador Rhondo there by the helm?"

"Your eyes are sharper than mine, lad, but I believe you are correct. Perhaps I should investigate further," he said, while to himself he muttered, "I wonder what that weasel is up to now?"

Rhondo was still protesting the indignity of his capture to the galley captain as the dock lines were secured and Grumwald clambered aboard with a party of *Valadator*'s seamen. On seeing him, Rhondo immediately redirected his protestations. "I must say, Commodore, this is highly irregular and totally uncalled for!" he proclaimed. "For what reason am I being delayed?"

"Orders of the Queen, from what I understand, my Lord. Or perhaps some misunderstanding. No doubt you'll be able to clear things up in no time. But I say, Ambassador, you're rather heavily laden, aren't you? What's your cargo?"

"Ore for Kantar," snapped Rhondo, not in the least mollified.

"Ore?" Grumwald looked about the deck at the polished bronze fittings and gleaming brightwork. The ship did not look like an ore carrier. "My Lord, isn't this your personal vessel?" he asked. "And why, might I ask, would you be delivering a load of ore, sir?"

"A little side business, Commodore. To ease my retirement. And I often take ocean voyages... I find it soothes my nerves."

"No doubt. I've noticed that effect myself. But I must say, Ambassador, that I am concerned for the safety of your little ship, here. I fear she is quite overburdened."

"Oh, you need have no fear, Commodore. She's a stout little ship. We've made the trip a half dozen times with such a load."

"I'm sure you're right, Ambassador. But if something were to happen, the Queen would never forgive me. We'll just have a quick look." And before Rhondo could protest further, Grumwald directed his men to remove the cover from the ship's hold.

As low in the water as the sloop sat, one would have expected to see ore piled up to the hatch coamings, but as the cover was raised, no such ore was to be seen. In fact, the hold at first appeared empty. But then, as the cover was hauled aside, three large objects were revealed in the yawning darkness below. Each about four feet square, and as high, they were wrapped tight in tarpaulins, and securely lashed and braced to the hull. Grumwald climbed down, and with the help of one of his men, unlashed one of the covers and pulled it up to reveal the bright glow from a stack of golden ingots.

"Very refined ore, wouldn't you say?" he asked Rhondo. "Perhaps it was about this that the Queen wanted to speak to you. What do you say we go see her right now?"

"Well!" said Thorngere, "you certainly weren't lying about how this baby runs. This is the sweetest little ship I ever saw!" He was standing on the starboard side deck, his arm lazily draped around a back stay, his long, unbound hair flowing in the westerly breeze. *Kantar* heeled easily on a beam reach-her best point of sail-and surged southward under clear skies and a westering sun. Foam boiled up around her bows as she breasted the soft swell, then streamed aft in a wake as straight as an arrow. Thorngere shaded his eyes with his free hand and traced it to the horizon where Ragnar's galley was quickly fading from sight. "I think the old boy has given up. It looks like they've shipped oars."

"Just like him to come busting out at the merest hint of a challenge," Valerius murmured. He was stretched, half-asleep, on the leeward cockpit bench, propped up on a large pillow against the cabin bulkhead. Boltar sat at the helm while two crewmen squatted forward by the bits of the main mast. Vahla, Illana and Chad were below. From Valerius' position, the distant galley was hull down, only its mast visible, waving in the summer haze. He made a brief effort to sit up for a better view, then sank back against the pillow with a sigh. "I doubt Ragnar even gave his crew time to pack a lunch."

It had taken the *Kantar*'s crew most of the previous night to stow away their provisions and row the ship down the winding river channel, and it

342

was nearly dawn when they were finally able to hoist sail and stand out to sea. And with the dawn came King Ragnar's war galley hurdling down from the north, the long double banks of oars churning up the sea, the bronze-sheathed ram sliding just beneath the surface like a snake. The morning air was light and *Kantar*'s sails flapped lazily as the galley surged by. Ragnar-a huge grin on his face-saluted the king with a sweeping bow as he passed and yelled, "See you in Dulcai!"

But his joy was short-lived. As the warm, on-shore breeze filled in from the southwest, it headed the galley, slowing her. But *Kantar*'s fore and aft sails filled and hardened. Her pace quickened as she leaned to her work and began rapidly closing the distance between them. As she neared, Ragnar ordered the stroke increased. The long oars flailed at the water with increased frenzy, and for a time, the galley held off the surging schooner. But the breeze continued to build and the men at the galley's oars began to tire, and soon-well before the sun reached its zenith-*Kantar* slipped by to windward with a giddy Thorngere returning Ragnar's bow.

He had been all over the ship since, marveling at its design and the rig's efficiency, and even taking a turn at the wheel. He had been a sailor for years before returning to his home in the north and succeeding his father as Atheling of Thule and still relished anything to do with the sea, especially the fresh air and the sun dappled delights of such a beautiful day. During the latter part of the war, he had sailed the Elusive on recruiting missions with Boltar as his mate. And he had sailed in King Koltar's first experiments with a fore and aft rig, an open galley that had nearly drowned them all, and the small, twin-hulled catamaran that tore through the water at upwards of twenty knots but kicked up so much spray it, too, almost drowned its crew.

So he could appreciate what Koltar had achieved and marveled at the tiny king's ingenuity.

For his part, Valerius drowsed on his bench, lolling to the gentle pitch and roll and only half-listened to the constant banter between Thorngere and Boltar. For him, speed was the only concern, speed that would hasten the journey to Dulcai. Whether he would have the energy to confront whatever threatened Eomer when he got there was of secondary concern. To get there was first.

Even at their current speed, that would take several days, and in several days, he hoped to feel much better. He couldn't, he thought wryly, feel much worse. The sharper pains from his freshly knitted bones and bruised flesh had diminished-as had the remaining signs of his injuries-but the deep-seated weakness remained. Even lounging in the sun, stretched at ease along the bench, his head cradled by a soft pillow, he felt the heaviness of exhaustion pulling him down, and when Chad appeared in the companionway holding a cool drink, it seemed to take all his strength just to lift his arm and take the proffered cup.

"Maybe better come below for rest now," said Chad, his hand guiding the cup and preventing Valerius from slopping the contents on his chest.

"That's probably not a bad idea," said Thorngere, suddenly realizing how pale the High King looked even in the bright sun. "Do you need some help getting below?"

"No, I think I can make it," said Valerius, sitting up with effort. But he could not. It took Chad from below and Thorngere from above to get him down the ladder, then Chad and Vahla to get him safely to his cabin and into his bunk. There he sank gratefully into the soft mattress and fell asleep.

But as it hadn't since his vision of Eomer in Volkmir's cave, sleep would not last. He woke again within minutes and lay staring up at the deck beams and listened to the water gurgling and bubbling along *Kantar*'s hull, within a couple feet of his head. His body rocked slightly with the motion of the ship, and inside he felt the sense of dread and foreboding spread from his chest to his bowels like water sloshing about in a leaky boat.

What he should do, he thought, what he needed to do and what might help ease his mind a bit, was get up and finish reading the Scroll of Dimmian which the appearance of Condor's corpse had interrupted. That was what he should do. And he even reached out his arm to haul himself upright. But it was not to be. Not then. Or at least, not yet.

Giving up the effort, he flopped back into the bunk and this time fell into a real sleep.

Chapter 24

Eomer was nursing Alair when news was brought of Rhondo's capture and of the cargo found in the hold of his ship. She sent word that she would appear shortly, and then sat watching the infant suckle and tried to quiet her thoughts and racing pulse. Such stress, she thought, could not be good for the baby. But here, whether she liked it or not, was her first real test as Queen. Her instincts had been correct: Rhondo had been dissembling, hiding what was obviously a major fraud and embezzlement. And she had acted promptly and correctly: the man had been caught, the gold recovered.

But what to do now? And what else might he be guilty of? Had he been complicit in her father's death as well? If so, how to make him admit it? Should she have him tortured? The very thought so churned her stomach that she pulled her nipple from the baby's mouth, lest the revulsion contaminate her. No, she could not have him tortured. But she must get answers. And how she dealt with Rhondo now would set the tone for her entire reign. Being adored was all well and good, but if she was to rule effectively, she must also be feared. And that meant she could not fear being feared.

She kissed the baby's brow as she laid her in her crib, and then hurried off to the throne room, stopping along the way to issue some special instructions to one of the servants. She swept into the audience chamber and mounted the dais to her throne with all the Queenly dignity she could muster, then called for Rhondo to be brought before her.

When he appeared-held firmly by a guard on each side-Rondo was full of bluster and haughty outrage. What was the meaning of this, he demanded? Arresting a citizen in the legitimate course of his private business? Was this the reward her subjects could expect from lifetimes spent in her service?

Eomer sat quietly, letting him rant until he sputtered into silence.

"Well, Rondo," she said quietly, although there was no corresponding softness in her eye or in the commanding set of her face, "for one thing, you have disobeyed a direct order in not bringing me the books from the mines as I had instructed. That in itself is cause for your arrest, as I think you well know. Secondly, there is the matter of your attempted flight with all this gold stored in the hold of your ship. Where were you going with such a horde, Rondo? Do you expect me to believe this was only a pleasure sail? Have you done so well in my father's service that you can afford to ballast your ship with gold?"

"The gold is mine," Rhondo snapped, "saved through my long years of labor for Dulcai and earned through careful investments."

"Yes, well, I'm sure a thorough audit of the mine and palace books will bear that out, Ambassador. But in the meantime, there is another matter I think you have been less than forthcoming about: the death of my father."

"My dear lady," said Rondo with a toss of his head so haughty and infuriating Eomer's eyes blazed and her fingers clutched the arms of her throne, "I have no idea what you're talking about."

"Oh, you don't, don't you!" she snarled and flew down from the dais to glare into his face. "We'll see about that! Lash him to that pillar!"

Rhondo's eyes went wide with surprise and then fear as rough hands hauled him to a pillar and trussed him there, his arms stretched back around its girth.

Eomer watched this operation with cold eyes, her breast heaving as she sought to control her own emotions, then motioned to an attendant who wheeled in a brazier heaped with glowing hot coals. From their center, she drew a long-bladed dagger, already shimmering with heat.

"The properties of fire have always fascinated me," she said, absently stirring the coals with the blade. "We use it to cook our food and to warm us when we're cold. So it's very precious to us, a necessity of life. And yet, when it gets out of control, it can also destroy us. Some say that fire is like a woman. Did you know that, Rhondo?"

Rhondo watched her stirring the coals with rapt attention, his mouth gaping.

"But what I find fascinating about fire is that these two properties can act as one." The blade of the knife had taken on a rosy glow now, and as she spoke, Eomer pulled it from the coals and held it so close to Rhondo's face he felt his eyes cross looking at it.

"Did you ever think about that?" she said, a wicked smile flickering across her face. "They say a wound made with a red hot knife will heal even as it cuts. The blade sears the flesh and cauterizes the wound even as it's made. So there is very little bleeding and no infection afterwards. That's very helpful. But, of course, since it's doing double duty, the pain of such a wound is probably doubled, too. But that's only to be expected, wouldn't you agree?"

Terror now began to flood Rhondo's features and his eyes darted from the blade to the Queen's face, and back. "Was there something else you wanted to tell me?" she asked.

"I swear, your majesty," he began, but she turned away cutting him off.

"There's been entirely too much swearing from you," she spat, "and not near enough truth. Raise his toga!" she ordered the guards. "Remove his linens." The guards did as they were bidden: Rhondo's toga was yanked up and tucked into his belt and his linen undergarment was cut away. He stood now fully exposed from the waist down. His legs began to tremble.

"My lady... Your Majesty! Please!"

"But what I've often wondered," Eomer said, moving close again but with the glowing blade held low now, "is whether a hot knife actually cuts, or whether it burns its way through the flesh. Did you ever wonder that, Rhondo?" and she moved the blade up close to his scrotum so he could feel the searing heat.

"Oh, please, my lady, please, please," he pleaded, his voice breaking into sobs. "Yes, you're right, I stole from the treasury. I confess! But I never harmed his Majesty, I swear! I swear!"

Eomer pushed the blade closer and the smell of singed hair rose up between them. "Ahhhh!" Rhondo screamed. "No! Please! Please, no! I didn't touch him, I swear. Oh, please believe me! I swear, I swear!"

Eomer stepped back quickly as Rhondo lost control of his bladder, his body convulsing. "Cut him down," she ordered, and watched as he collapsed into the puddle of his own urine and lay there, sobbing and gasping.

"You are a vile worm, Rhondo! And a thief. But I believe you are innocent of my father's death, and for that I will spare you. But all your wealth and lands are forfeit. And in accordance with Dulcaian law, your forehead will be branded and you will be turned loose in the city square that all will know and revile you. How you make your way from there, how you live and eat-if you can live and eat-is up to you. Take him away!"

Fiercely, Eomer jammed the dagger back into the bed of coals and stalked from the audience chamber. Only when she was back into her private apartments did her step begin to falter, and when she entered her own chamber, her shoulders and chest sagged. She collapsed onto her bed, buried her face in her pillow and shuddered. But she did not cry.

Despite the severity of his injuries, bright sun and sea air began to do their magic on Valerius, and after three gorgeous days of sailing, he was feeling much better. So much so that by late afternoon of the third day he curled up in the corner of his bunk like a boy with an adventure story and read the Scroll of Dimmian again, reaching the end this time without interruption. But it was a disappointment. Dimmian of Odo had gone on to relate several other incidents in which the Eye stone had manifested its powers-as a result of which the first Valerius became High King-but the incidents were not unlike those Valerius himself had experienced, and Dimmian did not provide any information on how the original Valerius had actually caused the Eye to manifest. Perhaps, Valerius thought, he did not want to commit such potent information to writing. Then again, perhaps he never had it in the first place.

Only at the very end was there an item of significant interest, a single phrase, set off by itself and scripted in a different hand: "Agam lanaba luabanari." But by whose hand, or what it meant, he had no idea. He did not even know what language it was in.

He was also well enough to have a serious conversation after dinner with Vahla and Thorngere about what had happened on the mountain and what he feared would happen in Dulcai. They sat huddled close around the table in the main saloon, both for privacy's sake, and because the wind on deck had risen and turned cool, and dark clouds had begun to pile in from the southwest. A lumpy sea was also building and *Kantar* began to rear and plunge as she drove southward under reduced sail. As they talked, the rising wind began to moan in the rigging and vibrate with a thrum in the hull. Overhead, the lantern swung erratically, casting patterns of light and shadow about like dice.

"I'm really not sure I can tell you what happened," said Valerius, his voice a low rumble. "A lot happened, but I still don't know what was real and what was, well, not un-real or imagined, but at least 'other-real.'

"I know I fought a dead man... in fact, the rotten, stinking corpse of a dead man. And I know- or I'm pretty sure-I was bloodied and thoroughly beaten, and would be dead but for the Eye. We were wrestling on the ground and when Condor grabbed the Eye in his mouth, it did one of its exploding flashes and blew his head apart.

"But what happened to my wounds, I cannot say. I know I was stabbed in the thigh, and I think he broke my sword arm, but both appear to have healed... at least on the outside. Inside, they still ache like bad teeth."

"I also had dreams-or visions-after the battle. But again, which were real and which fantasies or imaginings, I cannot tell. I know that the shadow I saw threatening Eomer in Dulcai was real, I'm sure of that. It was the same shadow we saw on Condor's galley. But the rest is so fantastic I don't quite know what to make of it.

"But the Scroll of Dimmian," says Vahla. "You did find that?"

"Yes, I was reading it when Condor's corpse appeared, and I just managed to finish it this afternoon."

"And? Did it tell you anything about the Eye."

"Some. The legend you learned of the original Valerius was not far from the truth, if the Scroll of Dimmian is the truth. But of how to use it, not much. There is an incantation, but it is in some strange language I've never seen. And if it were in any way useful, I'm sure Volkmir would have mentioned it, since he had the scroll. Curiously, though, my dreams-or visions if you like-did offer some advice..."

"Yes?"

"Yes, I was told that I before I can master the Eye, I must learn how to serve!"

"Well," said Thorngere, "that would seem consistent with what Volkmir told me... and with your history with the thing."

"Yes, but I'm not sure how that helps."

At that moment, a particularly large wave seemed to pick the ship up and hurl it sideways into another wave. *Kantar* heeled violently, throwing the three into a pile against the hull, before she recovered and staggered to her feet.

"I'd better get on deck and see if Boltar needs a hand," said Thorngere. But the appearance of a sodden crewman forestalled him.

"Captain Boltar requests permission to heave to, your Majesty," the man said, clutching at the table to keep his feet as *Kantar* took another leeward lurch. "He says to tell you the wind has headed us and we can't make any southing in this sea anyway."

Chapter 25

The storm that beset *Kantar* had blown into Dulcai earlier in the day, bringing clouds of swirling dust from the surrounding desert and a preternatural darkness that turned noon into night. Residents prayed the storm would also bring rain to their arid fields, but while thunder rumbled overhead, the temperature dropped and the choking dust was like a damp fog, not a drop of actual moisture fell from the streaming sky. Instead, pasty grit caked in people's mouths and stung their eyes and a dusty film smeared the streets and statues. It blew through cracks in closed shutters, coated floors and furniture, even soiled the sheets of the Dulcaian's beds. Those who had to be out covered their heads and faces and hurried bent through the blowing brown darkness like gnomes in search of their burrows.

Most simply stayed home, stuffed rags around their windows, and waited for the storm to pass. But for one Dulcaian, there was no longer any home. Rhondo's resplendent gates had been closed against him, as had the doors to any other inhabited sanctuary in the city. He huddled in an alleyway, without so much as a cloak to cover him, nursing his various wounds and trying to ignore the growing hunger that gnawed at his stomach.

It was just two days since he had been hauled to the public square, and had his forehead branded with a "T" before a jeering crowd. His eyes still blinded from the pain, he had then been shoved into the crowd, which had summarily beaten him to within an inch of his life. And that was only the first of several beatings he had suffered since, some vicious, some simply casual kickings as he sought a drink from the fountain, or dared to beg on the street.

For a normal thief, public retribution was often tinged with pity. In most cases, it took extraordinary circumstances to drive a person to theft in a prosperous, well-ordered town like Dulcai. But for Rhondo, who had lorded over these very people for years and whose perfidy had now been revealed as incredibly vast, his sins were taken very personally by every man, woman and child in the city and he was shown no shred of mercy. Indeed, being beaten to death would have been a mercy-one for which he several times found himself beginning to pray-and in every instance one citizen or another called a halt to his tormentors lest they accidentally render him that service.

As it was, there was not an inch of his flesh that was not bruised and very little of it that had not bled, so that while the branded "T" itself was still scabbed and sore, it was by far the least of his injuries. Nor had he been able to secure any food or drink. He had managed but a single mouthful of water at the fountain late the previous day before a great bull of a man-probably one of the famed hammer-men from the ore mines-had kicked him so hard in the stomach that he not only spewed out the water, but blood as well. Since then, he had not dared approach the fountain, and after receiving similar treatment for begging alms, he had tried to avoid any appearance in public at all.

But perhaps his lowest point-so far-had come when he tried to snatch a meaty scrap of bone from a scavenging dog. Not only had he been foiled in the attempt, but his arm had been bitten bloody in the process.

Now, as the roiling, dusty darkness faded to genuine night, he huddled in his alley and wondered how much more he could endure before merciful death intervened, or whether he had the will-and could devise the means-to hasten the process. The dark of night, he thought, would be a good time to try to reach the harbor. If he could just find a big rock there and somehow secure it to himself...

"Oh, Lo how the mighty have fallen!" snickered a voice from the shadowed darkness by his side. "I've always thought you a pretty poor specimen of a man, my dear Rhondo, but I never thought to see you looking so pitiful." The voice tittered as if Rhondo's plight was the merriest of pranks.

"You!" Rhondo snarled as the shadowy form seemed to solidify in the dark. "Is it not enough I'm being beaten and starved to death? Must you mock me, too?"

"Mock you? Why, Rhondo, do you know me so little after all this time? I have come to save you, my friend!"

"Oh, yes, you'll save me, all right! You'll lead me straight to the grave, you will!"

"And you're headed exactly where now?" the voice asked, its tone reason itself.

Rhondo had no answer for that but glared malevolently at the bit of darker darkness, his thoughts full of bitterness and self-pity.

"Yes," the voice went on as if it could read them, "your precious Royal Queen has overturned all your little plans, hasn't she? Had you branded like a common thief and turned you into the streets to be starved and beaten like a dog. And what do you plan to do about it, oh Rhondo the righteous, Rhondo the brave? You're going to go throw yourself in the river. Drown yourself like a worthless cur!"

"And you've a better idea?"

"Indeed! Though I begin to wonder why I bother wasting my ideas on you. I thought you were a man of vision and courage, but I begin to suspect you are as cowardly as you are dim."

"Dim! I kept this city solvent for years. That fool Reuters would have bankrupted the kingdom in an hour."

"Yes. And now, I see, you have gotten your reward."

Rhondo's eyes blazed with sudden fury and he lurched to his feet, shaking his fists.

"She tried to unman me, the foul bitch! But she didn't have the nerve!"

"Come to me, my friend," whispered the voice, "and we'll fix her instead."

Rhondo took a step forward, and something of the shadow seemed to envelop his frame, then merged with it. It felt like he had stepped into a whirlpool of warm soothing water. His aches and pains disappeared, his cuts and bruises melted away; even the scabbed brand on his forehead peeled off and fell unnoticed to his feet. He was suffused with a surge of health and vigor-a feeling of raw power-such as he had never known. His eyes blazed, his muscles pulsed, his very tendons seemed to vibrate. Curling his fingers like talons, he snarled deep in his throat, then threw back his head and laughed-a laugh that subsided into a snarl.

He loped out of the alley and down the darkened street, running lightly on the balls of his feet. No longer the harried fugitive, he had become a hunter, searching for prey.

At an intersection, illuminated by the flickering light of a torch mounted on the wall, a lone figure stood guard, his back to Rhondo. Beneath his helmet, his face was swaddled against the swirling dust, and his cloak was flattened against his frame, outlining his burly form. He was a large man, and well-armed.

Rhondo, on the other hand, had never been a warrior. Frail and sickly as a child, he had been apprenticed early to a clerk and when other boys his age played at rough sports, he had stuck to his books. All his life, he had avoided physical confrontation, and had even managed to get himself excused from compulsory military training. When needed, he had applied other, more efficient methods.

But now, he did not hesitate. Approaching in a silent run he grabbed the guard's head from behind, and in a single, swift motion, snapped the man's neck with a viscous twist. There was a loud crack and the guard dropped like a sack. Quickly, Rhondo relieved him of his muffler, cloak and sword. Then after starting off, he turned back and took the man's helmet as well.

This proved useful for the next item on his list: food and drink. Swaddled and cloaked under the guard's helm, he pounded on the door of a nearby house with the hilt of his sword. It was opened by a prosperous looking, middle-aged man who politely asked how he could help. Rhondo answered by ramming the sword up into the man's throat. Shoving his body aside, he barged into the house.

As luck would have it, the man had just been sitting down to dinner with his wife and three children. These, and the single servant, fled screaming to the upper rooms on seeing Rhondo enter with a dripping blade. Bolting the door on them, he assumed the late master's seat, poured himself a large goblet of wine, and proceeded to enjoy a leisurely meal.

In fact, he ate just about everything on the table, then leaned back with a satisfied sigh and savored another large goblet of wine. Then he dabbed his lips with a napkin, balled it up and tossed it at the empty carafe: it unfolded in flight and draped over it as neatly as a shroud.

"That," he announced to the empty room at large, "was a very satisfactory dinner. But now, it's time for me to pay a visit to the palace." Plopping the helmet back on his head and re-swaddling his face with the dead guard's muffler, he stalked out the door.

Hove to, *Kantar* rode out the violence of the storm like a duck. Her foresail backed, her main reefed and sheeted tight, and her helm lashed to leeward, the little ship lay balanced against the forces of wind and sea, heeling slightly to port, and slowly drifted downwind. No longer fighting to make headway, she took the huge swells on her starboard bow and rode them like a skiff on a millpond. Except for a single hand on watch, the crew had retreated below and sat in a strange rocking stillness: while the wind still howled above, its noise now seemed distant, no longer as shrill or threatening. And instead of being slammed about this way and that, the crew now rocked gently, as if they were ensconced in a large cradle.

Vahla and Thorngere sat at the table in the saloon across from Boltar and Illana. Thorngere was leaning back, dozing off with his head against the bulkhead while Vahla listened as Boltar explained what heaving to meant and why it made the ship ride so quietly now. Illana had asked the question, which surprised Vahla, as this was the first sign of real interest the girl had shown in anything since her rescue from Condor. Prior to this, she had stayed as close as she could to Boltar, but had said very little. Now, her face showed animation and her eye followed Boltar's hands as he sketched imaginary drawings on the tabletop.

"Look, here we've got the foresail backed, you see? Hauled the sheet right over to starboard and cleated taut so the sail blocks the wind from the front. That pushes the ship astern. But we've also got the helm lashed over so that when she tries to go back, her stern also drives to starboard. That shifts the force of the wind onto the mainsail, which is reefed and sheeted tight like this. That tries to drive the ship forward, but with the helm lashed, moving forward drives the bow to starboard. This puts the wind on the backed foresail again and drives us back. So the result is that we just rock gently back and forth like a teeter-totter and don't go much of anywhere at all.

"It's a pretty neat maneuver that you can't do with a standard square rig like *Valadator* and the old Elusive. King Koltar thought of it, of course."

"Would it work on Elusive or *Valadator* if they were rigged like *Kantar*?" Illana asked.

"Whoa!" said Thorngere opening an appreciative eye. "Looks like you've got yourself a sailor, there, mate! What say you to that?"

Illana blushed at the compliment and tried to hide a smile.

"I'm not sure," said Boltar. "I don't think the underbody structure of a galley would act the same, even with the rig changed. You know yourself, Thorngere, how that worked..."

"Only too well!"

"But with a deep cargo hull like Elusive, it just might. In fact, I've been wondering how a rig like this would perform on a cargo vessel. There's a lot more weight to move, but being able to sail closer to the wind would certainly help trade."

"You might be right," said Thorngere. "Maybe on the way back we can stop in at New Kantar and talk it over with Koltar."

"Let's not get ahead of ourselves," said Vahla. "We still don't know what's happening in Dulcai. Speaking of which, I wonder how he's doing in there," and she nodded her head towards the closed door of Valerius' cabin.

Behind that door Valerius sat at his own small table, trying to keep his mind from the looming sense of fear and foreboding, which gnawed at him, and the frustration of being held up by the storm. He was reading through the Scroll of Dimmian again, and puzzling over the strange phrase or incantation at the end.

"Agam lanaba luabanari, agam lanaba luabanari," he repeated, and thought: 'What can it mean? How am I to understand this lore? I'm no wizard, nor a philosopher. I am a king, sure, but I'm also just a man and this, I fear, is beyond my poor reach. But what will happen if I can't understand? What can it mean? "Agam lanaba luabanari, agam lanaba luabanari..."

As he ship rocked and his candle began to gutter, he repeated the phrase over and over until it began to sound like an incantation, a mantra. His sense of the room about him began to fall away, and the noise of the ship and clutter of his thoughts quieted. All his thought slowly focused on the Eye. It was there on the table before him, glittering gently in the candlelight. What was it? What did it mean? "Agam lanaba luabanari. Agam lanaba luabanari..."

And then, without awareness, he passed that point of consciousness where we no longer know whether we sleep or wake, and saw, or somehow became aware of a crack-a fissure-on the face of the stone. It was like a defect-an opening-he had never noticed before. Had the Eye been damaged during the struggle with Condor? In dream or in spirit, he leaned closer, drawn towards the Eye like the needle of Koltar's compass was drawn towards the locus of the earth.

And as he leaned, the opening grew, no longer a crack, but a fissure, a gap, a portal: a gate. And without realizing how, or when, or, in reality, even if, he found he had passed through it. He had entered the Eye and stood silently wondering within its facets as in a crystal palace, and wherever he looked, his thought followed his eye out through the stone and across the world.

Chapter 26

The storm was still blowing hard as Rhondo made his way towards the palace, but the skies were beginning to clear. The wind had ripped away great ragged chunks of dense black cloud and flung them off to the north and east. In the gaps, a dull, nimbused moon cast a sooty-yellow glow down onto the deserted streets of Dulcai. It was late now and few lights shown around doors or through cracked shutters. If there were more guards, Rhondo did not pass them. Nor did he care. He walked, head bent against the wind, breasting it with his guard's shiny helm. He looked neither right nor left, and if he noticed the increasing flood of moonlight, gave no sign. He had walked the streets of Dulcai for many years and made his way by rote.

At the palace gate, the guard on duty saw the approaching figure, and stepped from his protective alcove to block the way. Then he saw the guard's helm and cloak and relaxed his stance.

"What brings you in?" he asked, not recognizing the man, but also not wishing to admit it. The figure returned a muffled reply in which the word "report" was about the only thing distinguishable, and in a hurried, yet not threatening way, brushed past him.

It was a bit improper, this, not quite regulation. But it was also a wicked, stormy night, not the kind of night to enforce the law to the letter. But this was also the gate to the Queen's palace, and this man was also-apparently-a member of the Queen's Guard. So forms must be preserved, due process observed...

So while the guard hesitated, he did turn to grab the offender... but a little too late. A wicked chop from Rhondo's sword caught the man's throat just above the clavicle, severing both trachea and his carotid artery. A geyser of blood and expelled breath whooshed into the air, and the man collapsed like a deflated balloon.

At the door to the palace itself, the next guard was not so lax and did step forward to bar the way. But he, too, believed he was facing a fellow guard, not an enemy, and grunted in shocked surprise when a sword blade was suddenly rammed up underneath his breastplate and into his vital organs. At least, as he died, he rendered his Queen and his city one last service of a loud, gut-wrenching scream.

Fearful now that the alarm was raised, Rhondo threw off his disguise and ran into the palace and up the broad stairway to royal apartments. Sliding quietly down the marble-tiled hall, he slipped into the Queen's private chamber and bolted the door behind him.

Eomer heard the guard scream and lay wondering at the cause when the dark figure slipped into her room. She had kept a pair of candles lit to help her get to the nursery in the storm-shuttered room, and as he turned towards the bed, the naked sword at the ready, she recognized him.

"Would you treat me so for a stack of gold, Rhondo?" she asked, her voice calmer than she expected. "My father honored you, as did I until your treachery. I've known you for my entire life. Now you would treat me so?"

Rhondo stalked towards the bed, his face a rictus of hate, the wet blade glistening with a dark, russet-red glow.

"Treat you so?" he hissed. "After what you did to me? You're as much of a fool as your father was if you think there's no payment due for that, you royal bitch. Who are you to lord it over me, anyway? What have you ever done to earn your place but suckle a golden teat and warm the bed of that buffoon, Valerius? I have twice the brains of any of you! Without my skill, you would still be pawns to Fantar-or dead. So what gives you the right, oh High Queen! What makes you think you're better than me?"

It was clear to Eomer that calm words would not dissuade him, that he was bent on killing her-or at best, that one or the other of them must very shortly die. And that being the case, she was equally determined not to die trying to coddle him.

"For one thing, my father and I have both followed the law," she said her voice sharper now and determined, "and worked for the betterment of Dulcai and the Empire. You, on the other hand, have only sought to exalt yourself. I know not or care not who is more skilled or whether the order of the world is just ... But I will stand by my actions, Rhondo. We've already seen how you stood by yours-you still reek of that puddle of your own urine I saw you grovel in. So don't come on high and mighty with me, you bastard! If you want to kill me, come try it now!

Rhondo screamed with rage and lunged towards her. Eomer screamed as well and scuttled across the bed, flinging the bed clothes at him and grabbing up the stool from her make-up table, silently praying that the guards would intervene, that her children would not lose their mother this night.

Rhondo circled the bed, his reeking blade poised. As Eomer backed away into the corner of the room, he snatched up the small table that held her make-up, scattering and smashing the various lotions and powders across the floor. Holding it by one leg as a shield, he advanced upon her with a calm, determined air. There were no guards rushing to intervene. Neither had their screams elicited any other response. Outside her room, all was as silent as the grave. This, she thought, shifting her defensive grip on the stool, was surely the face of death itself.

But then a thing happened which was not to be accounted among the things of this world. A small red ball of light suddenly floated out from the wall. Expanding, it enveloped Rhondo in a soft red glow. It was as if he had lit a red-tinted candle, except that it had no bright pointed source; or as if he'd been struck by one of the Vahla's magic light bombs, except that there was no pop as it exploded. Rather, it was as if the light was a thing itself, was its own source and reality.

It seized Rhondo by the shoulders and yanked him back. He staggered, turned and began to struggle with something unseen. Eomer's cries died in her throat as she watched the battle, the red luminescence growing brighter as Rhondo's struggles became more violent. He was fighting for control of the sword and lunging this way and that, yanking it back and forth as if in the grip of some powerful force. Yelling, he raised the blade up high with both hands but stumbled back as if the thing had advanced upon him. He tried to stab with the sword but his arms were caught overhead, the blade point shaking.

The glow was fiercely bright now, lighting the entire room. Rhondo's arms shook as his strength was tested and Eomer could hear him grunt and his teeth grind with effort. Then, slowly, the blade began to turn towards him, and inexorably, descend.

And in that moment of supreme struggle, as Rhondo gasped and groaned and grimaced, she saw the outline of another figure in the glow. It was just the merest shape, outlined in bright red light, but enough for her to recognize, enough to make her heart leap for joy.

But it was also at that moment that Rhondo's strength failed and the blade suddenly flashed down. It plunged into his chest and he collapsed in a heap. The red glow faded instantly from around his body, and though it was suddenly dark again in the room, Eomer was sure she saw a dark, shadowy form rise up from the corpse and flit out through the shuttered window.

By morning the storm had subsided and the *Kantar* billowed along under full sail again, soaring over the still huge swells like a gull. Thorngere was at the helm, grinning with delight. Vahla, noticeably pregnant, stretched out along the cockpit seat in the bright sun, her head pillowed and her face shaded with her arm. Boltar and Illana were forward, sitting on the fore cabin top. She was barefoot with her seaman's trousers rolled to the knee: he held a piece of small line with which he had been showing her knots. But their attention had been caught by the glory of the moment and they sat motionless, their bodies leaning together, watching the great swelling foresail haul them south. Chad squatted by the weather rail, his eyes gazing off towards the distant south, his face, as ever, inscrutable.

To port stretched the long sand spit that guarded the Bay of Dulcai, the lighter waters of the bay visible beyond, and off the bow, still some miles ahead, lay the entrance to the channel that led into the bay and up to the city.

Suddenly, the stillness of the tableau was broken as the companionway hatch slid open with a bang and Valerius virtually bounced onto the deck. He stretched his great frame, thrusting his chin into the breeze, then stood, gazing about at the morning, the sea and the ship, his face wreathed in a broad grin. He stood easy and relaxed, as if the physical pain and mental strain, which had plagued him, had suddenly gone. He even looked smug.

"You look well this morning, Your Majesty," said Thorngere.

"I am well," said Valerius, his face beaming, "very well indeed."

Vahla removed her arm from her face and squinted up at him. "I'd even go so far as to say you look well pleased with yourself, brother."

"You could say that," said Valerius, his smile now growing quite smug. "You could say We are well pleased indeed."

"Ah, formal it is now!" Thorngere quipped. "By your leave, then, Sire, we must ease sheets to make for the entrance of yon bay."

"Ease away then, lad, ease away. You have the helm."

The entrance to the bay was indeed drawing close now, and Valerius took a seat in the cockpit and watched pleasantly as the booms were swung even wider and Thorngere turned the ship to make their approach. The crew eased the foresail until it luffed, then hauled the sheet in a bit and secured it.

"Shall we make ready with the sweeps?" Thorngere asked as the narrow entrance loomed.

"What's the tide, Boltar?" Valerius called forward

"Looks like it's just beginning to flood, Your Majesty," Boltar yelled back.

"Well, Thorngere, make ready if you must, but I'll wager we won't need to row."

"Oh, no, I've seen enough of how this little ship performs not to let you take my gold that easily, even if you are High King!"

"As you wish, my friend. I know how chary you northerners are when it comes to your gold."

"He'd better be careful," Vahla quipped. "He's soon going to have another mouth to feed."

And good it was for Thorngere's gold that he did not take the bet, for running with wind and tide, *Kantar* shot through the narrow gap and sped on like an arrow towards the distant glimmering shape that was the white city of Dulcai. And as they neared the dock, there on the quay to greet them, regally arrayed with her personal guard in all their finery, was Valerius' beloved Eomer, the beautiful golden-haired Queen of Dulcai.

End of Book IV

www.ingramcontent.com/pod-product-compliance
Lightning Source LLC
Chambersburg PA
CBHW010822250626
47172CB00004B/965